"MAYBE OUR TROUBLE
IS THAT WE LIVE IN
THE TWILIGHT OF THE
OLD MORALITY, AND
THERE'S JUST ENOUGH
TO TORMENT US, AND
NOT ENOUGH TO
HOLD US IN."

Fawcett Books
by John Updike:

THE POORHOUSE FAIR, *a novel*
RABBIT, RUN, *a novel*
PIGEON FEATHERS *and other stories*
THE CENTAUR, *a novel*
OF THE FARM, *a novel*
THE MUSIC SCHOOL, *short stories*
COUPLES, *a novel*
BECH: A BOOK
RABBIT REDUX, *a novel*
MUSEUMS AND WOMEN *and other stories*
A MONTH OF SUNDAYS, *a novel*
PICKED-UP PIECES
MARRY ME, *a romance*

John Updike

MARRY ME

A Romance

A FAWCETT CREST BOOK

Fawcett Books   Greenwich, Connecticut

MARRY ME

THIS BOOK CONTAINS THE COMPLETE TEXT OF
THE ORIGINAL HARDCOVER EDITION.

A Fawcett Crest Book reprinted by arrangement with Alfred
A. Knopf, Inc.

Copyright © 1971, 1973, 1976 by John Updike

ISBN: 0–449–23369–3

Selection of the Book-of-the-Month Club
Selection of the Franklin Library, the First Edition Society

*Chapter 1 has been previously published as a booklet by the
Albondocani Press (New York; 1973). Chapter 2 appeared,
in somewhat different form, in* THE NEW YORKER.

*Grateful acknowledgment is made to Peer International Corporation for permission to reprint lyrics on pages 9 and 96
from the song "Born to Lose" by Ted Daffan. Copyright
1943 by Peer International Corporation. Copyright renewed.
All rights reserved.*

Printed in the United States of America

10   9   8   7   6   5   4   3   2   1

Choose me your valentine,
Next, let us marry—
Love to the death will pine
If we long tarry.

—ROBERT HERRICK

Chapters

1. Warm Wine

ALONG this overused coast of Connecticut, the beach was a relatively obscure one, reached by a narrow asphalt road kept in only fair repair and full of unexplained forks and windings and turnings-off. At most of the ambiguous turns, little weathered wooden arrows bearing the long Indian name of the beach indicated the way, but some of these signs had fallen into the grass, and the first time—an idyllic, unseasonably mild day in March—that the couple agreed to meet here, Jerry got lost and was half an hour late.

Today, too, Sally had arrived ahead of him. He had been delayed by the purchase of a bottle of wine and an attempt, unsuccessful, to buy a corkscrew. Her graphite-gray Saab sat in a far corner of the parking lot, by itself. He slithered his own car, an old Mercury convertible, close to it, hoping to see her sitting waiting at the wheel, for "Born to Lose," as sung by Ray Charles, had come onto his car radio.

> Every dream
> Has only brought me pain . . .

She brimmed in this song for him; he had even framed the words he would use to call her into his car to listen with him: "Hey. Hi. Come quick and hear a neat record." He had grown to affect with her an adolescent manner of speech, mixed of hip slang and calf-love monosyllables. Songs on the radio were rich with new meaning for him, as he drove to one of their trysts. He wanted to share them with her, but they were rarely in the same car together, and as week succeeded week that spring the songs like mayflies died from the air.

Her Saab was empty; Sally was not in sight. She must be up in the dunes. The beach was unusually shaped: an arc of flat washed sand perhaps half a mile long was bounded at both ends by congregations of great streaked yellowish rocks, and up from the nearer sets of rocks a high terrain of dunes and beach scruff and wandering paths held like a vast natural hotel hundreds of private patches of sand. This realm of hollows and ridges was deceptively complex. Each time, they were unable to find the exact place, the perfect place, where they had been before.

He climbed the steep dune before him hurriedly, not taking the time to remove his shoes and socks. His panting under the effort of running uphill seemed delicious to him; it was the taste of his renewed youth, his renewed draft on life. Since the start of their affair he was always running, hurrying, creating time where no time had been needed before; he had become an athlete of the clock, bending odd hours into an unprecedented and unsuspected second life. He had given up smoking; he wanted his kisses to taste clean.

Jerry came into the high land of dunes and was frightened, for there was no sign of her. There was no sign of anyone. Besides their two, less than a dozen cars were scattered through the great parking lot. In another month, this lot would be crammed, the boarded-up snack-bar-and-bathhouse building would be alive with brazen bodies and canned music, and the dunes would be too hot to inhabit. Today the dunes still wore the look, inherited from winter, of clean-swept Nature, never tasted. When she called to him the sound came fluted by the cool air like a birdcall. "Jerry?" It was a question, though if she could see him she must know it was he. "Jerry? Hey?"

Turning, he saw her now, on a dune above him, in the two-piece yellow bathing suit; as she descended, her eyes downcast to avoid pricking her bare feet on the beach grass, she seemed, blond and freckled and clean-swept, a shy creature of the sand that had hidden her. Her arms and front felt hot and her curved back cool. She had been sunbathing. Her heart-shaped face was pink. "Hey? I'm glad you're here?" She was slightly panting and her voice excitedly lifted each phrase into a question. "I've been waiting in this dune with a pack of horrible boys without shirts whooping and yelling all around me; I was getting quite frightened?"

As if his manner of speech kept shifting around an unsayable embarrassment, he momentarily lapsed from hipsterism and spoke in a courtly way. "My poor brave lady. The dangers I expose you to. I'm sorry I'm late; listen. I had to buy the wine and then I tried to buy a corkscrew and these absolute idiots, these Norman Rockwell types in some run-down country store, tried to sell me an auger instead."

"An auger?"

"You know. It's like a brace and bit without the brace."

"You feel so cool."

"You've been lying in the sun. Where are you?"

"Up here? Come."

Before he followed her, Jerry kneeled and took off his shoes and socks. He still wore his city coat and tie and carried the wine bottle in its paper bag like a commuter walking home with a present. Sally had spread her red-and-yellow-checkered blanket in a sweeping hollow bare of any footmarks but her own. Jerry looked for the boys, and saw them several dunes away, watching nervously with the sides of their heads, like seagulls. He stared at them boldly and murmured to Sally, "They're young and look harmless. But do you want to go deeper in?"

He felt her nod at his shoulder, her nod like a word only she could pronounce, a uniquely rapid and taut jiggle of her head, *yes yes yes yes*; it was one of her mannerisms he found himself, in situations far removed from her, imitating. He gathered up her blanket and her braided beach bag and her book (by Moravia) and set them in her warm arms. As they walked up the slant of the next dune he placed his hand on her naked waist to steady her, and turned to make sure the boys had witnessed this sign of possession. Embarrassed, they were already whooping off in the other direction.

As usual, Jerry and Sally walked in and out, down ragged paths between scratching bayberry bushes and up slithering slopes, laughing with exertion, looking for the ideal spot, the spot where they had been the last time. As usual, they failed to find it and finally put the blanket down anywhere, in a concavity of clean sand that became, instantly, perfect.

He posed before her and stripped. His coat, his tie, his shirt, his trousers.

"Oh," she said, "you wore a bathing suit."

"All the damn morning," he said, "and every time I felt the drawstring bite into my belly I thought, 'I'm going to see Sally. I'm going to see Sally in my bathing suit.'"

Letting his skin exult in the air, he stood surveying; they were hidden and yet themselves could see the parking lot below, and the tranced arm of sea held fast between here and Long Island, and the little glittering whitecaps hurrying in to break soundlessly on the streaked rocks.

"Hey?" she said from the blanket. "Come see me in your bathing suit?"

Yes yes, the touch, the touch of their skins the length of their bodies in the air, under the sun. The sun made his closed eyes swim in red; her side and upward shoulder warmed and her mouth gradually melted. They felt no hurry; this was perhaps the gravest proof that they were, Jerry and Sally, the original man and woman —that they felt no hurry, that they did not so much excite each other as put the man and woman in each other to rest. Their bodies sought with the gradualness of actual growth to enlarge and refine their fit. Her loose hair drifted strand by strand onto his face. The sense of rest, of having arrived at the long-promised calm center, filled him like a species of sleep even as his insteps tightened upward into the arches of her feet: "It's incredible," he said. He turned his face upwards, to merge her with the sun; red flooded his lids.

She spoke with her lips against his neck, where a shadow was gritty and cool. He felt this, though it was her sensation. "It's worth it," she said, "is what's so surprising. It's worth it, all the waiting, all the obstacles, all the lying and hurrying, and then when you reach it, it's worth it." Her voice grew progressively small pronouncing this.

He experimentally opened his eyes and was blinded by a perfectly hard circle smaller than the moon. "Do you mind," he asked, his lids clamped on a pulsing violet echo, "the pain we're going to cause?"

As if he had dropped a chemical, the stillness of her body against his changed quality. Her curved feet lifted from his. "Hey," she said. "What about the wine? It'll get warm." She rolled out of his arms, sat up, and brushed her hair back from her face, blinking and pushing the sand from her lips with her tongue. "I brought some paper cups because I knew you wouldn't think of it." This tiny possessive insight made her licked lips smile.

"Yeah, I don't have a corkscrew, either. In fact, lady, I don't know what I *do* have."

"You have you. That's more than I have."

"No, no, you have me." He became nervous and active; he walked on his knees to where he had folded his clothes and pulled the bottle from the paper bag. The wine was a rosé. "Now I got to find a place to break it."

"There's a rock over there."

"You think? Suppose the whole thing goes smash in my hand, like?" On the excuse of a sudden shyness, the hipster had taken over.

"Be careful," she said.

He tapped the neck of the bottle on the little ledge of striped tan rock and nothing happened. He tapped again, harder; it clinked solidly and he felt himself blush. "C'mon, man," he pleaded, "break your neck."

He swung firmly; a spatter of splinters glinted in his eyes before he heard the sound of broken glass; he plunged his startled gaze down through a jagged glinting mouth into a small deep cylindrical sea of swaying wine. She had waded on her knees to his side and exclaimed, "Mm," like him subtly shocked to see wine this way, so much of it naked in the violated bottle. She added, "Looks great."

"Where are the cups?"

"Let's forget the cups." She took the bottle from him and expertly fitted the jagged glass to her small face and tipped her head back and drank. His heart tripped as if at some danger but when she lowered the bottle her face was pleased and unharmed. "Yes," she said. "It doesn't taste of paper this way. It just tastes of itself."

"Too bad it's warm," he said.

"No," she said. "Warm wine is good."

"Better than none, I suppose."

"I said it's *good,* Jerry. Why don't you ever believe me?"

"Listen. I believe you all the time." He took the bottle and imitated her; when he tipped his head back, the redness of the sun and of the wine mixed.

She cried, "You'll cut your nose!"

He lowered the bottle and squinted at her. He said of the wine, "It kind of swings."

She smiled and said, "You did." She touched the bridge of his nose and showed him a pink blot of blood on her white fingertip. "Now," she said, "when I see you normally, I'll see the little cut on your nose, and only I will know how you got it."

They moved back to the blanket and drank from the paper cups. Then they drank the wine from each other's mouth; he spilled a little into her navel and lapped it up. In time he shyly asked, "Want me inside you?"

"Yes? So much? All the time?" Her voice was lifting everything into questions again.

"There's nobody around, we're really quite hidden."

"Let's hurry?"

As he kneeled at her feet to pull off the lower of the two pieces of her yellow bathing suit, he was reminded, unexpectedly, of shoe salesmen; as a child he had worried about these men who made a career of kneeling and tugging at other people's feet, and had wondered why they did not appear to feel demeaned by it.

Though Sally had been married ten years, and furthermore had had lovers before Jerry, her lovemaking was wonderfully virginal, simple, and quick. With his own wife he had a corrupt sensation, often, of convolution and inventive effort, but with Sally there was always, for all the times she had endured this before, a priceless sense of her being, yet once again, innocently amazed. Her face, freckled, rapt, the upper lip perspiring in the sun and lifted so her front teeth glinted, seemed a mirror held inches below his own face, a misted mirror more than another person. He asked himself who this was and then remembered, *Why, it's Sally!* He closed his eyes and fitted his breathing into her soft exclamatory sighing. When this had ebbed into regular breathing, he said, "It's better outdoors, isn't it? You get more oxygen."

He felt her rapid little nodding flutter on his shoulder.

"Now leave me?" she said.

Lying beside her as she wriggled back into her bathing-suit pants, he betrayed her by wishing for a cigarette. It would have gone so well with the plenitude, the gratitude, the wide sky, the scent of sea. Ashamed of slipping back into a polluted old self, he poured the last of the wine into their cups, and rooted the empty bottle like a monu-ment, mouth up, in the sand.

She looked down into the empty parking lot and asked, "Jerry, how can I live without you?"

"The same way I live without you. By not living most of the time."

"Let's not talk about it. Let's not spoil our day."

"O.K." He took up the novel she had been reading and asked, "You dig this guy?"

"Yes. You don't."

"Not much. I mean, it's not untrue, but"—he waggled the book and tossed it aside—"is this really what has to be said?"

"I think he's good."

"You think a lot of things are good, don't you? You think Moravia is good, you think warm wine is good, you think lovemaking is good."

She looked at him now, quickly. "Do you mind that?"

"I love that."

"No, you don't believe me sometimes. You don't be-lieve I'm so simple. I am simple. I'm just like"—similes were hard for her, she so instinctively saw things as them-selves—"that broken bottle. I have no secrets."

"It's such a beautiful bottle. Look how the curves of broken glass take the sun. It's like a tiny roller coaster, around and around." He wished again for a cigarette, to gesture with.

Whenever a distance between them seemed about to grow, she would call, "Hey?"

"Hi," he'd answer gravely.

"Hi," she answered back.

"Sweetie, why did you marry him in the first place?"

And she told him, told him at unprecedented length, hugging her knees and sipping wine, told him so charmingly, in her delicate, careless voice, the twentieth-century story of her marriage, that he kept laughing and kissing the small of her naked bent back. "So I kept taking riding lessons and miscarried *that* one, too. So he sends me into analysis and this Goddamn analyst, Jerry—you would have liked him, he was like you in being very ethical—tells me—I don't know what the matter with me is but I always try to do what men tell me to do, it's my terrible weakness—he tells me, 'You're going to have this one.' So O.K., I had it. I was so confused I probably thought it was the analyst's baby I was having. But it wasn't. It was Richard's. And then once I'd had one it seemed I had to have some more to make the first one right. But it doesn't work that way."

"You know why *I've* had all *my* babies?" he said. "I never really understood until the other night, something Ruth said. You know she's this great believer in natural childbirth. Well Joanna was really quite painful for her so now it turns out we had to have two more so she could perfect her technique."

He had hoped Sally would laugh at this, and she did, and in a sudden mutual gush they cashed into the silver of laughter all the sad secrets they could find in their pockets. She had more secrets than he. This inequality of their exchange grieved him, and as the dunes looped longer shadows into their small valley he kissed her

wrists and confessed, in a desperate attempt to balance
their plights. "I did a very bad thing in marrying Ruth.
Much worse, really, than if I'd married for money. I
married her because I knew she'd make a good wife. And
that's what she's done. God, I'm sorry. I'm so sorry,
Sally."

"Don't be sad. I love you."

"I know, I know, and I love you. How can I *not* be
sad? What can we *do*?"

"I don't know," she said. "Go on like this a little
more?"

"It won't stand still." He gestured upwards and stared
as if to blind himself. "The fucking sun won't stand still."

"Don't be melodramatic," she said.

Both on their knees, they began to gather up their
equipment and to revolve in their minds the fragile lies
they must deliver to their homes. She looked so calm
and docile, his Sally, in the sandy light, her pale hair
falling as she bowed into some tiny simplicity of this,
their only housekeeping, that he angrily embraced her,
for the last time this day. All their embraces felt to be
the last. Almost lazily, she kneeled against him and
flattened her body to his and encircled his back with her
arms. Her shoulder tasted warm; his lips moved on her
skin. "Baby, I can't swing it," he said, and the flutter of
her nodding made their bodies vibrate together. *I know.
I know.*

"Hey? Jerry? Over your shoulder I can see the Sound,
and there's a little sailboat, and some town far off, and
the waves are coming in to the rocks, and it's so sunny,
and just so beautiful? No. Don't turn your head. Believe me."

2.   The Wait

"GOOD-BYE?"

"Don't say that word to me, Jerry. Please don't say it." Sally's wrist ached from holding the receiver so long, and now her whole forearm began to tremble. She pinched the receiver between her shoulder and her ear and used her freed hands to button one of Peter's straps; in the last few months he had learned to dress himself, all except for the buttons, and she had hardly found it in her scattered wits to praise him. Poor child, he had been standing there for ten minutes waiting for his mother to get through talking; waiting and listening, waiting and watching with that wary glimmering expression on his face—she began to cry. It came upon her like a gentle fit of retching; with clenched teeth she tried to keep her sobs from carrying into the telephone.

"Hey? Don't." Jerry laughed in embarrassment, faintly and far away. "It's just for two days."

"Don't *say* it, damn you. I don't care what you mean, don't *say* it." I'm crazy, she thought; I'm a crazy woman

19

and he'll start to hate me. At the thought of his hating her after she had given so much of herself to him, she became indignant. "If all you can do is laugh at me maybe we should say good-bye for good."

"Oh, Christ. I'm not laughing at you. I love you. I hate it that I can't be there to comfort you."

Peter nudged closer, to have the other strap buttoned, and she smelled a Life Saver on his breath. "Where did you get that candy?" she asked. "We mustn't eat candy in the morning."

Jerry asked, "Who's there?"

"Nobody. Just Peter."

"Bobby gave me," Peter said, and now his glimmering expression seemed about to resolve into fear.

"You go find Bobby and tell him I want to talk to him. Go, sweetie. Go find Bobby and tell him. Mommy will be off the phone in just a minute."

"Poor Peter," Jerry said in her ear. "Don't send him away."

How could he say this, he who had robbed her of all joy in her children? Yet of course it was just that he *could* say it that enlarged her love so helplessly; he refused to remain fixed in the role of lover as she imagined it should be played. A needless kindness kept shattering his shell. Tears burned her cheeks; she held silent to keep her soaked voice from him. Her abdomen and arms physically ached. God, could he be doing it on purpose?

"Hey? Hi?"

"Hi," she answered.

"You O.K.?"

"Yes."

"You can go to the Garden Club while I'm away, and take the children to the beach, and read Moravia—"

"I'm reading Camus now."

"You're so intelligent."

"Won't you miss your plane?"

"Take Peter to the beach, and play with the baby, and lie in the sun, and be nice to Richard . . ."

"I can't. I can't be nice to Richard. You've ruined him for me."

"I didn't mean to."

"I know, I know." Jerry's fault as a lover, his cruel fault, was that he acted like a husband. She had never had a husband before. It seemed to Sally now in the light of Jerry that she had been married ten years to a man who wanted only to be her lover, keeping between them the distance that lovers must cross. Richard was always criticizing her, analyzing her. When she was young it had been flattering; now it just seemed mean. Out of bed he must always try to strip her down to some twisted core, some mistaken motive. Whereas Jerry kept trying to dress her, flinging at her sad little scarves of comfort and advice. He saw her as pathetically exposed.

"Listen," he said. "I love you. I wish you could come to Washington with me. But it can't be. We were very lucky to get away with it once. Richard knows something. Ruth knows."

"She does?"

"Her glands do."

"Do what?"

"*Know*. Now don't worry about it. It wouldn't have been so lovely the second time anyway. I'll miss you constantly and won't sleep at all in the bed by myself. The air conditioner going *whoosh, whoosh.*"

"You'll miss Ruth too."

"Not so much."

"No? Hey, I love you for saying, 'Not so much.' A real lover would have said, 'Not at all.' "

He laughed. "That's what I am. An unreal lover."

"Then why can't I shut you out? Jerry, I *hurt*, physically *hurt*. Even Richard feels sorry for me and gives me sleeping pills from his own prescription."

"Greater love hath no man than to give sleeping pills from his own prescription."

"I could call Josie this evening and say I'm in the city and the Saab has broken down. It's been acting funny lately, I know they'd believe me."

"Oh, sweetie. You're so gallant. It would never swing. They'd find out and he wouldn't let you have the children."

"I don't want the children, I want you."

"Don't say that. You love your children very much. Just looking at Peter made you cry."

"It was you who made me cry."

"I didn't mean to."

She didn't know how to answer this; she could never tell him that you were responsible for things you didn't mean to do as well as things you did. He believed in God, and that inhibited her from giving him instruction on anything. Through the kitchen window she saw Peter finding Bobby. Peter had forgotten the message she had given him, and his older brother led him out of sight into the woods.

She asked, "Will you be at the State Department all afternoon? Could I call you there if I come?"

"Sally, don't come. You'll just crucify yourself for nothing. We'd only be there one night."

"You'll forget me."

His laugh shocked her, she had meant this so seriously.

"I don't think in two days I'll forget you."

"You think a night with me is nothing."

He paused; she felt in the unreeling seconds that she was being given line. "No," he said. "I think a night with you is almost everything. I'm hoping for a lifetime of them."

"Hoping's a nice safe thing to do."

"I don't want to fight with you. I never fight with women. I don't think we should take any risks until we know what we're going to do."

She sighed. "You're right. I say to myself, 'Jerry's right.' We mustn't be reckless. There are too many other people involved."

"Hordes of them. I wish there weren't. I wish the world was just you and me. Listen. You don't want to come. The airlines are all messed up by this strike at Eastern. Right now I can see six four-star generals and two hundred guys in Dacron suits shoving toward Gate Seventeen. My plane must be about to board." He was in a phone booth at LaGuardia. The flight he had planned to take had been full; he had killed the time of delay by calling her. She thought, If he had gone on the right plane, he wouldn't have called me; and this casualness, the implied smallness of her place in his life, enlarged him, scooped wider with its insult the aching hollow of her love.

He was waiting for her to laugh or agree, she couldn't remember which. "I love you so much," she said limply.

"Hey, how will you explain this on your phone bill? I wouldn't have called collect if I'd known we'd talk so long."

"Oh, I'll just say—I don't know what I'll say. He never listens to what I say anyway." Sally sometimes wondered how many of her accusations of her husband were unfair. Her conversation was like a garden gone wild; surprising weeds sprang up in it every day.

"They *are* boarding. Good-bye?"

"Good-bye, darling."

"I'll call you Wednesday morning."

"Very good."

He heard a rebuke in her tone and asked, "Shall I call you from Washington? Tomorrow morning?"

"No, you'll have things to do. Be busy. Just think of me a little."

He laughed. "How could I help but?" He waited, said, "You're the one," pecked a little flat kiss into the telephone, and hung up. She replaced the receiver quickly, as if stoppering a bottle from which Jerry might escape.

Her hair uncombed, her bathrobe flapping, Sally went outdoors and screeched at the edge of the woods, "Bo-oys! Bee-each!"

The woods screening the houses of the neighborhood from one another smelled profoundly of summer, not the usual delicate Connecticut scent of thinned underwood and grass but a rich warm odor of layered leaf mold and moldering logs—the way vacations had smelled when she was a child from Seattle summering in the Cascades. She went upstairs to change, and this nostalgic ferny fragrance, persisting through the bedroom window, intersected the faintly corrupt tang of salt water on her bathing suit. Sally bundled and pinned her hair. Alone in her bathroom, she conjured up Jerry; she gave the air his eyes. In making love his first motion was always to remove her hairpins and in the daily details of her toilet she seemed to bend close to him, sharing with him his careful love of her body.

She mixed a thermos of lemonade, scolded the boys into their bathing suits, and got into the car. The Saab had lately developed a reluctance to start, so she parked it pointed downhill and used momentum to turn the engine over. Josie was laboriously pushing the baby carriage, with a bag of groceries propped at Theodora's feet, up the driveway as Sally coasted down; she had reached the steep place where Sally let out the clutch. The women could exchange only frightened looks in the precarious moment as the spark ignited and the engine jerked into power. Sally felt that Josie had something to ask her, something about meals or naps, but Josie knew the routine as well as she—better, because she was less distracted, was middle-aged and past love.

Under the tranquillizing June sun the Sound was a

smooth plane reflecting the command, *Don't go.* She led
Peter and Bobby well down the beach. Sally thought she
spotted Ruth in the pack of mothers at the other end,
and Bobby said, "I want to go play with Charlie Conant."

"You can find him after we get settled," Sally said. She
discovered herself crying again; she didn't notice until
her cheeks registered the wetness. *Don't go.* Everything
agreed on this—the grains of sand, the chorus of particles
alive on the water, the wary glances of her sons, the distant splashes and shouts that came to her when she lay
down and closed her eyes, like the smooth clatter of an
ethereal sewing machine. *Don't go, you can't go, you are
here.* The unanimity was wonderful. He didn't want her
to go, he thought a night with her was nothing, he told
her she was crucifying herself, he said it would not be as
good as the first time. She grew furious with him. Her
breathing felt oppressed under the tyranny of the sun; a
rough touch gouged and abraded the skin of her exposed
midriff, and she opened her eyes prepared to scream.
Peter had brought her a crab claw, weathered and fra-
grant. "Don't go, Mommy," he pleaded, holding out close
to her eyes his fragile dead gift. Her ears must be de-
ceiving her.

"It's lovely, sweetie. Don't put it in your mouth. Now
go away and play with Bobby."

"Bobby hates me."

"Don't be silly, darling, he likes you very much, he
just doesn't know how to show it. Now please go away
and let Mommy think."

Of course she shouldn't go. As Jerry said, they had
been lucky the first time. Richard had been on one of his
trips. Jerry had waited for her at National Airport and
they had taken a taxi into Washington. Their taxi driver,
a solemn tea-colored man who drove his cab with a
proprietorial gentleness, had noticed the quality of their
silence and asked if they wanted to go through the park,
around the Tidal Basin, to see the cherry trees. Jerry told

him yes. The trees were in blossom, pink, mauve, salmon, white; tremblingly Jerry's fingers kept revolving Richard's wedding ring on her finger. A black nurse was playing catch with some small boys in a shady clearing and the smallest of them held out his hands and the ball fell untouched at his feet. The hotel lobby was dark-carpeted and rich with Southern accents. With a lowering of his eyelashes the desk clerk accepted her as Mrs. Conant. Perhaps her face had been too radiant. Their room had white walls and framed flower prints, and looked out on an airshaft. Jerry shaved with a brush and soap bowl, which she would not have guessed. She thought all men used electric razors, because Richard did. Nor would she have guessed that the first evening, while she was painting her eyes in the bathroom and he was watching Arnold Palmer sink the winning putt on television, he would fall into a depression, and that for fifteen minutes she would have to hold him on the bed while he stared at the white wall and murmured about pain and sin, before he gathered the courage to button his shirt and put on his coat and take her to a restaurant. In an eye-whipping spring wind they walked block after block on the wide, diagonally intersecting streets, looking for a restaurant. Away from the illuminated monuments and façades, Washington seemed dark and secret, like the rear of a stage set. Limousines swished by with a liquid, lonely sound heard in Manhattan only very late at night. She felt the curse slowly lift from Jerry's mind. He became manicky, and leaped-frogged a parking meter, and in the restaurant, a fancy-priced steakhouse catering to Texans, he impersonated a Congressman escorting the Queen of the Minnesota Dairyland. *Honeh, Ah could take a shaaan to you.* Their waiter, eavesdropping, had expected a huge tip, had been plainly disappointed. Strange, how fondly she remembered the awkwardnesses. In a narrow little gift shop, where Jerry had insisted on buying toys to take home to his children, the saleswoman kept turning to her as if she were their mother, tentatively, puzzled by her silence. On the last morning, by the elevator, on their way to breakfast, she had been asked by the head chambermaid if the room might be cleaned, and she had said yes; this woman was the first person to treat her without a flicker of doubt as Jerry's wife. When they returned at noon, the venetian blinds had been torn away from the window, their bed was stripped and shoved against the bureau, and a slouching Negro was lathering the carpet with a softly screaming machine. Jerry and Sally left the hotel in one taxi and took separate planes home and found that the coincidence of their absences had not been noticed. Their momentary marriage, a wedding ring overboard, sank greener and greener into the past and became irretrievable. No matter what happened, it would never happen again, never happen the same, in all of time. It would be silly—insane—to risk everything and go to him now. For now the venetian blinds of their affair were, if not quite torn off, at least set at a revealing tilt: Josie blushed and stiffly left the kitchen when Jerry's usual ten o'clock call began ringing; Richard sat drinking the evenings away with a thoughtful dent in his upper lip; and the glimmering, watchful expression almost never left Peter's face. Even the baby, who was learning to walk, seemed shy of her and preferred to lean on space. Perhaps this was an hallucination —at times Sally truly feared for her sanity.

She stood up. The seam of water and sky, marked by the thin beige line of the Island, seemed to exclude an immense possibility. Panic struck her. "Bo-oys," she called. "Time to go-o!"

Bobby's body twisted and dropped to the sand in a tantrum. He shouted, "We just came, you nut!"

"Don't ever call people that," she told him. "If you're rude, people won't know what a nice little boy you are."

It was one of Jerry's theories that if you often enough told someone he was nice he would become nice. In a way, it did work. Peter came to her, and Bobby, afraid of being left alone, sulkily followed to the Saab.

Don't go. No. Yet the command had no weight, no weight whatsoever, and though she read it in a dozen obstructive omens that bristled about her as she dressed and lied her way out of the house and drove to the airport and paid her way onto the airplane, it remained a weightless sentence, afloat on the deep certainty that she should go, that going was the only possible thing to do, and absolutely right. A righteous tide lifted her over the snag of Josie's surprise, carried her past the children's upturned faces, pushed her through the choked hurry of dressing and the ominous clogging of the Saab's starter, urged her down the swerving allées on the Merritt Parkway and the metal-strewn boulevards of Queens, and sustained her nerve during the wait at LaGuardia while United found her a seat on a Washington flight. Then Sally flew; she became a bird, a heroine. She took the sky on her back, levelled out on the cloudless prairie above the clouds—boiling, radiant, motionless—and held her breath for twenty pages of Camus while the air-conditioner nozzle whispered into her hair. The plane canted above a continent of loamy farms where dot-like horses galloped. Acres of pastel houses in curved rows swung into view, and then a city composed of diagonal avenues and miniature monuments. Washington's shaft was momentarily aligned down a breadth of Mall with the Capitol dome. The plane skimmed water, thumped, reversed its engines, shuddered, and with a stately swaying waddled to a stop. A departed shower had left the runway damp in patches. The afternoon sun struck from the cement a humid warmth more tropical than the warmth she had left on the beach. It was three o'clock. Within the terminal, people were rapidly threading their way through the interwoven aromas of floor wax and hot dogs. She found an empty phone booth. Her hand fumbled inserting its dime. The quick of her index fingernail hurt as she dialled the necessary numerals.

Jerry was a designer and animator of television commercials, and the State Department had hired his company to create a series of thirty-second spots plugging freedom in underdeveloped countries, and he was the intermediary for the project. From their first trip Sally remembered the section of the State Department that could find him. "He's not a regular employee," she explained. "He's just in town for two days."

"We've found him, Miss. Who shall I say is calling, please?"

"Sally Mathias."

"Miss Sally Mathias, Mr. Conant."

Some electric noises shuffled. His voice laughed harshly. "Hi there, you crazy Miss Mathias."

"Am I crazy? I think I am. Sometimes I look at myself and think, very calmly, *You nut.*"

"Where are you, at home?"

"Sweetie, can't you tell? I'm here. I'm at the airport."

"My God, you really did come, didn't you? This is wild."

"You're mad at me."

He laughed, postponing reassuring her. And when he spoke, it was all in questions. "How can I be mad at you when I love you? What are your plans?"

"Should I have come? I'll do whatever you want me to. Do you want me to go back?"

She felt him calculating. She saw a Puerto Rican child Peter's age standing apparently abandoned on the waxed floor outside the phone booth. The child's dark eyes rolled, his little pointed chin buckled, he began to cry. "Can you kill some time?" Jerry asked at last. "I'll call the hotel and say my wife has decided to come down with me. Take a taxi in, go to the Smithsonian or something for a couple of hours, and I'll meet you along Fourteenth Street, at New York Avenue, around five-thirty." The door of the booth beside Sally's opened, and a brown man in a flowered shirt angrily led the child away.

"Suppose we miss each other?"

"Listen. I'd know you in Hell." It frightened her that when Jerry said "Hell" he meant a real place. "If you feel lost, go into Lafayette Square—you know, the park behind the White House. Stand under the horse's front hoofs."

"Hey? Jerry? Don't hate me."

"Oh, God. Wouldn't it be nice if I could? Just tell me what you're wearing."

"A black linen suit."

"The one you wore at the Collinses' party? Great. There are some terrific old trains on the ground floor. Don't miss Lindbergh's plane. See you five-thirtyish."

"Jerry? I love you."

"Love you."

He thinks it would be nice to hate me, she thought, and went out and caught a taxi. The driver asked her which Smithsonian she wanted, the old or the new, and she said the old. But at the door of the brownstone castle, she turned away. To her the past was a dingy pedestal erected so she could be alive in this moment. She turned away and walked along the Mall in the sunshine. The subsiding afternoon, the pavement dappled with shadows and seeds, the Popsicle hawkers, the tinted-windowed tourist buses stuffed with glaring Americans, the flocks of children, the fairy ring of fluttering red, white, and blue flags planted around the base of the great obelisk, the little Indian women wearing saris and Brahmin dots and nostril pearls and carrying both parasols and briefcases were for Sally all fragments of a fair; in the distance the Capitol dome, cleaner than its gray wings, had the glazed lustre of a piece of marzipan. The sunshine, imprinted everywhere with official images, seemed money to her as she walked past the Natural History Building, up Twelfth Street, through the dank arcades of the Post Office Department, along Pennsylvania Avenue to the fence of the White House. She felt airy, free. The federal buildings, fantastically carved and frosted, floated around her walk; their unreality and grandeur permeated her mood. Through the gaps between guards and greenery, she looked in at the White House; it was made of brilliant fake stuff, like meringue. She thought of the wall-eyed young Irishman who reigned here, wondered if he were good in bed, and didn't see how he could be, he was President. She turned up Fourteenth Street, strolling to her fate.

Sally carried a toothbrush in her pocketbook, and that was her luggage; she had inherited from her father a love of traveling light. Free, cool in her black linen, she felt like an elegant young widow returning from her husband's June funeral; he had been an old man, greedy and unkind. In truth, Richard, heavier than ten years ago, was still handsome enough, though his head seemed to weigh more on his shoulders and his quick gestures had been slowed and blurred by what he called, with a clipped, resentful intonation, his "responsibilities." When their marriage was young, they had lived in Manhattan, and in their poverty had walked miles as amusement. She felt Richard's ghost at her shoulder, remembered the novel rhythm of walking with, of *having,* a man. She had hated schools, prim places of Eastern exile. Richard had rescued her from Barnard and made her a woman. Where had it gone, her gratitude? Was she wicked? She couldn't believe it, feeling still so full of sky from the airplane ride, sidewalk mica glinting under her, her nostrils pricked by the peppery odor of tar. The crosswalk stripes had been tugged and displaced by the melting summer heat. On the wide pavements her stride kept overtaking the saunter of Southerners. Church chimes, the chimes of

lemon-yellow St. John's, sounded the hour. It was five.
She walked west along I Street. Government clerks in
flapping light-weight suits squinted through her, toward
the wife and Martini waiting in Maryland. A multitude
of women had been released. Like a rolling golden orna-
ment the sun rode the glassy buildings on her left, and its
rays warmed her face into self-awareness. She realized
she was pouting as she searched the faces for Jerry's face.

How he would grin! Despite his scruples and premoni-
tions he would grin to see her; he always did, and she
alone could bring out that smile in him. Though only a
few months older than she, and remarkably innocent for
a man of thirty, he made her feel like a daughter whose
every defiance testified to a cherished vitality. Sally felt
carved on her face a deep smile answering his imagined
one.

Danger flicked from the other faces. She seemed to see
a man she knew, about to turn the corner of the BOAC
building, across from Farragut's gesturing statue—a
young Wall Street scion Richard had had to the house.
His name was Wigglesworth, preceded by two initials she
could not remember. His face, expressionless, rounded
the corner and vanished. Surely she was mistaken; there
are millions of men and only a few types, only a few men
who aren't types. But in fear of being recognized she
lowered her gaze, so as Jerry had predicted, it was he
who found her, though this was not Hell.

"Sally!" He was on the sunless side of I Street, hatless,
his arm lifted as if for a taxi. In a business suit, he
looked disconcertingly like everyone else, and as he
waited at the intersection for the electric permission to
walk, her stomach dipped as if she had been snapped
awake two hundred miles from home. She asked herself,
Who is this man? The sign said WALK. At the head of
the pack, he trotted toward her; her heart thrashed. She
hung helplessly on the curb while the distance between
them diminished and her body, her whole hollowed

body, remembered his twitchily posing hands, his hook nose that never took a tan but burned all summer long, his sad eyes of no certain color, his crooked jubilant teeth. He grinned proudly but nervously, stood uncertain a moment, then touched her elbow and kissed her cheek. "God, you looked great," he said, "rolling along with that farm-girl gait, your big feet wobbling away in heels."

Her heart relaxed. No one else saw her this way. She came from Seattle and this made her in Jerry's eyes a farm-girl. It was true, she had always felt uneasy in the East. There was a kind of Eastern woman, Ruth for example, who never bothered with make-up or conspicuously flirted and beside whom Sally felt clumsy. Richard noticed this and tried to analyze her insecurity. Jerry noticed and called her his girl in calico. Not since before her father died, on a trip to San Francisco, had she felt, what she supposed all children are supposed to feel, that it was somehow wonderful of her to be, in every detail, herself.

"How on earth did you get away?"

"I just said good-bye and got in the Saab and drove to the airport."

"You know, it's marvellous to meet a woman who can really *use* the twentieth century." This was another fancy of his, there there was something comic and inappropriate in their living now, in this century. While making love he sometimes called her his squaw. He took pleasure, she felt, in delicately emphasizing, in never letting her forget, the incongruities that hemmed them in. His tenderness itself proclaimed that their love was illicit and doomed.

"Hey," he said, calling to her across the silence. "I don't want you to take risks for me. I want to take them for you."

But you won't, she thought, looping her arm through his arm and bowing her head in concentration on his walking rhythm. "Don't worry about it," she said. "I'm here."

He said nothing.

"You're mad at me. I shouldn't have come."

"I'm never mad with you. But how did you manage?"

"I managed."

His body was mainly big bones and nerves; she felt she was holding on to a corner of a kite that was struggling to get high into the wind.

He tugged her along. He asked, "Is Richard going to be away tonight?"

"No."

He halted.

"Jesus, Sally. What happened? Did you just break out? Can you get back?"

His voice rose sharply, asking this last question. Her answer sounded in her own ears scratchy and faint. "Don't worry about it, darling. I'm here with you, and everything else seems very far away."

"Talk to me. Don't try to shame me. Tell me what happened."

She told him, reliving it all, frightening herself: the beach, her panic, the children, Josie, the airplane, her walk, her plan to call home in an hour saying she was in Manhattan and that the Saab had broken down, refusing to start, and the Fitches had invited her to stay the night, since the art-appreciation course she was taking at the Metropolitan Museum met tomorrow morning.

"Sweetie, it won't swing," he told her. "Let's try to be sane. If I put you on the plane now, you can still get back by eight."

"Is that what you want?"

"No. You know I want you with me always."

And, for all the evidence to the contrary, she felt this as true. She was his wife. This strange fact, unknown to the world but known to them, made whatever looked wrong right, whatever seemed foolish wise. She, Sally, was Jerry's woman, and what had been precious in the first illicit trip was that in those two days she had felt this

truth growing, had felt him relax. The first night, he had
not slept. Several times she had been twitched awake by
his body sliding from the bed, getting a drink of water,
adjusting the air conditioner, rummaging in his suitcase.

"What are you looking for?"

"My pajamas."

"Are you cold?"

"A little. Go to sleep."

"I can't. You're unhappy."

"I'm very happy. I love you."

"But I don't keep you warm."

"You *are* a little cooler than Ruth, somehow."

"Really?"

Her voice must have shown that this unexpected comparison had hurt her, for he tried to retract. "No, I
don't know. Forget it. Please go to sleep."

"I'll go back tomorrow. I won't stay tomorrow night
if I give you insomnia."

"Don't be so touchy. You don't give me insomnia. The
Lord gives me insomnia."

"Because you're sleeping with me."

"Listen. I love insomnia. It's a proof that I'm alive."

"Please come back to bed, Jerry." She had held on to
his body, trying to drag the kite down from the sky, and
herself fell asleep suspended between the earth and the
dawn growing in the brick airshaft beyond their blinds.
The second night, though still twitchy, he slept better,
and on this, the third night, three months later, when
spring had relaxed into summer, his breathing slowed and
became mechanical while her heart was still lightly
racing. She thought herself flattered by his trust. But
early in the morning, having slept on a vague sense of
loss, she awoke to a sharp deserted feeling. The room
was different from the first one. The walls, though it was
the same hotel, were yellow instead of white, and instead
of the flowered prints there were two pallid Holbein
portraits. It was brightening enough beyond the blinds

for her to see the faces, so dim they seemed real pres-
ences—small-mouthed, fastidious. How many adulterous
and drunken couplings had they been compelled to witness? A street-sweeper passed swishing on the avenue
below. Their first room had given on an airshaft; this
one overlooked, from five stories up, a square. Somewhere below them in the maze of the capital a collection
truck whined and a trash can clattered. She thought of
her milkman crossing her porch to set his bottles, clinking,
inside an abandoned house. Jerry lay diagonally, the
sheet bunched around his throat, his feet exposed. She
nudged him awake and made him passionate. In the
heart of intimacy, he drowsily called her "Ruth." It
took him a second to realize his mistake. "Oh, I'm sorry.
I don't seem to know who you are."

"I'm Miss Sally Mathias, a crazy woman."

"Of course you are. And you're very beautiful."

"But a little cool, comparatively."

"You've never forgotten that, have you?"

"No." It fascinated her; at home, stepping into a bath,
she would quickly lay fingers on her skin as if to surprise
there the tepidity he had mentioned, and once, shaking
Ruth's hand good-bye after a dinner party, she had held
on curiously, trying to grasp the subtle caloric advantage
this cool-looking woman had over her. She had noticed
how Jerry's skinny body often seemed feverish. When
they first began to make love, she had felt through his
motions the habitual responses his wife must make; while
locked in this strange man's embrace she struggled jeal-
ously against the outline of the other woman. On her
part she bore the impress of Richard's sexual style, so
that in the beginning four contending persons seemed
involved on the sofa or in the sand, and a confused, half-
Lesbian excitement would enclose her. Now these blurs
were burned away. On the brightening edge of the long
June day that followed the third night they had ever spent
together, Jerry and Sally made love lucidly, like Adam

and Eve when the human world was of two halves purely. She watched his face, and involuntarily cried out, pierced by the discovery, "Jerry, your eyes are so sad!"

The crooked teeth of his grin seemed Satanic. "How can they be sad when I'm so happy?"

"They're *so* sad, Jerry."

"You shouldn't watch people's eyes when they make love."

"I always do."

"Then I'll close mine."

Oh Sally, my lost only Sally, let me say now, now before we both forget, while the spark still glitters on the waterfall, that I loved you, that the sight of you shamed my eyes. You were a territory where I went on tip-toe to steal a magic mirror. You were a princess married to an ogre. I would go to meet you as a knight, to rescue you, and would become instead the dragon, and ravish you. You weighed me out in jewels, though ashes were what I could afford. Do you remember how, in our first room, on the second night, I gave you a bath and scrubbed your face and hands and long arms with the same methodical motions I used on my children? I was trying to tell you then. I was a father. Our love of children implies our loss of them. What a lazy lovely naked child you were, my mistress and momentary wife; your lids were lowered, your cheek rested on the steaming sheet of bathwater. Can I forget, forget though I live forever in Heaven among the chariots whose wheels are all eyes giving God the glory, how I saw you step from a tub, your body abruptly a waterfall? Like a man you tucked a towel about your woman's hips, and had me enter the water your flesh had charmed to a silvery opacity. I became your child. With a drenched blinding cloth that searched out even the hollows of my ears, you, my mother, my slave, dissolved me in tender abrasions. I forgot, sank. And we dried each other's beaded backs, and went to the bed as if to sleep instantly, two obedient children dreaming in a low tent drumming with the excluded rain.

Jerry closed his eyes and it hurt her. She loved to watch love, to witness the nibbling, the mixing of ivory and fur, the solemn softening of the eyes. Was she corrupt? In Paris on her honeymoon with Richard, her shock at the mirrors in their room had subsided to a level interest. This was what people did; this was what they were. She was proud, a little, of having taught Jerry how simple it was. Somehow Ruth had not taught him that. But the sadness of his eyes had penetrated her and for the rest of the day that unfolded Sally was laid open to a vivid and frightening sense of her existence in other people's eyes. The puffy-lidded news vendor in the perfumed lobby saw her as a spoiled young matron. The waitress who served them breakfast at the counter cheerfully took her for a fucked secretary. When Sally relinquished Jerry to a taxi and became alone, she felt herself reflected in every glance and glass entryway. To the Japanese souvenir-store attendants she was big. To the Negro doorman she was white. To everybody she was nobody.

Who was she? What was this burden she carried within her, this ache that like an unborn child was so unquestionably worth bearing? Was she unique? That young black girl like a chocolate swan, that dowager in rouge and wool—was each of these also prey to a clawing love that could literally lift her into the sky? Sally could not believe so; yet she did not like to believe either that she was totally unique, eccentric, mad. She remembered her mother. When her father had died on that last trip, a quiet calm man finally too quiet in a room of the St. Francis (there were no pills, no bottle, all the authorities had agreed), they had moved to Chicago, to be near her mother's people, and her mother though a Catholic had taken not to religion or drink but to gambling. The strangest happiest islands of that time were those days when together they would go by train and bus to Arlington Park, or to the Hawthorne track in Cicero, or to see the trotters at Maywood; at these places everything was thin and nervous and obliquely illuminated by chance— the legs of the horses white with tape, the whips of the jockeys, the slats of the fences, the rods of the turnstiles polished by pushing hands, the sideways glances of the men who might be gangsters, the fluttering scraps of losing tickets torn in half, the oblique rays of the sun like the spokes of a slowly turning wheel. Her mother's fattening hands fiddled again and again at her pocketbook. Horses or men, is the instinct any different? Oh God, when he came he bucked as if he were dying, and now he was gone, lost among these marble buildings. One minute all over her, filling her, whimpering; the next minute keeping an appointment with the Undersecretary of Animation. What sense did it make? Who had made these arrangements? He had gotten her so confused, her husbandly lover, she didn't even know if she believed in God or not. Once she had had a clear opinion, yes or no, she had forgotten which.

As the sun passed noon, her shadow pinched in; her hot feet hurt. Idly Sally wandered north from the hotel, through stagnant blocks of airline offices, past verdant circles where pistachio-colored military men on horses were waving to catch her attention. Jerry was to meet her at the National Gallery at one. The time until then moved forward or backward, depending on the clock she glimpsed; in the haste of her departure she had forgotten her watch. There was a gap in the tan of her arm where the watchband had been.

The iron braziers and stone vases and Asiatic paper knives in the windows of antique shops glinted back at her stupidly as she sought to find herself in them. Once she had cared about these things; once, being in a city

alone had fulfilled her and coveting objects and fabrics
had been a way of possessing them. Now she sought
herself in bronze and silk and porcelain and was not
there. When she walked with Jerry, there was something there, but it was no longer her, it was them: her
explaining to him, him to her, exchanging their lives,
absorbing fractions of the immense lesson that had accumulated in the years before they had loved. She saw
each thing only as something to tell him about, and
without him there was nothing to tell; he had robbed her
of the world. Abruptly, she became angry with him. How
dare he tell her not to come and then make love to her
when she did come! And then with such sad eyes beg
her to feel guilty! How dare he take her free when she
could sell herself for hundreds to any honest man on this
avenue—to that one. A foreign official with snowy cuffs
and an extravagantly controlled haircut preened, gray-
horned on the burning sidewalk beside the Department
of Justice. He was eyeing her. She was beautiful. This
knowledge had been drawing near to her all morning
and now it was hers. She was beautiful. Where she
walked, people glanced. She was tall and blond and big
inside with love given and taken, and when, at last, she
mounted the steps of the museum, the gigantic scale of
the rotunda did not seem inhuman but right: our inner
spaces warrant palaces. She studied Charles V, sculpted
by Leone Leoni, and existed as a queen in his hyper-
thyroid gaze.

"Stop," Jerry said, taking her elbow from behind.
"Stop looking so beautiful and proud. You'll kill me.
I'll drop dead at your feet, and how will you get the body
back to Ruth?"

Ruth, Ruth: she was never out of his mind. "I was
feeling very indignant about you."

"I know. It showed."

"You think you know everything about me, don't you?
You think you own me."

"Not at all. You're very much your own woman."

"No, Jerry. I'm your woman. I'm sorry. I'm a burden to you."

"Don't be sorry," he said. "It's a burden I need." His eyes were watching her face for a warning, a change. "Shall we look," he asked timidly, "or eat?"

"Let's look. My stomach is funny."

And in the galleries, she was conscious of existing among paintings, of shining in portraits' eyes, of glancing, bending closer, backing off, of posing in a rapt and colorful theatre. Jerry was manic in museums; all the old art school came out in him. His enthusiasm tugged her from room to room. His hands demonstrated, slid hungrily through the motions of tranquil masterpieces. People obedient to lecturing boxes plugged into their ears glared. She must seem his dumb student. He had found what he wanted—the wall bearing three Vermeers. "Oh, God," he moaned, "the drawing; people never realize how much *drawing* there is in a Vermeer. The wetness of this woman's lips. These marvellous hats. And this one, the light on her hands and the gold and the pearls. That *touch,* you know; it's a double touch—the exact color, in the exact place." He looked at her and smiled. "Now you and me," he said, "are the exact color, but we seem to be in the wrong place."

"Let's not talk about us," Sally said. "I'm too tired to be depressed. My feet hurt. I must have walked miles this morning. Couldn't we sit down and eat?"

The cafeteria walls were hung with beady-eyed Audubon prints. Sally's stomach sank under the weight of unwelcome food. She had no appetite, which was unlike her; perhaps it was sleeplessness, perhaps the pinch of dwindling time. Whereas Jerry ate briskly, to keep from talking, or in relish that another adulterous escapade was all but safely completed. They were silent together. The immense lesson she thought they had for each other felt to be fully learned.

She sighed. "I don't know. I guess we're just terribly selfish and greedy."

Though she had said it to please him, he disagreed. "Do you think? After all, Richard and Ruth weren't giving us much. Why should we die just to keep their lives smooth? Quench not the spirit, didn't St. Paul say?"

"Maybe it's just the newness that makes it seem so wonderful. We'd get tired. I'm tired now."

"Of me?"

"No. Of it."

"I know, I know. Don't be frightened. We'll get you back safely."

"I'm not worried about that. Richard doesn't really care."

"He must."

"No."

"I don't think Ruth really cares either, if she just knew it."

And though she knew Jerry said this just to match her, she heard herself pressing him with, "Do you want to not go back? Shall we just run off?"

"You'd lose your children."

"I'm willing."

"You say that now, but a week with me and you'd miss them and hate me because they weren't there."

"You're so wise, Jerry."

"But it doesn't help, does it? My poor lady. You need a good man for a husband and a bad man for a lover, and you have just the opposite."

"Richard's not such a bad man."

"O.K. Pardon me. He's a prince."

"I love it when you get mad at me."

"I know you do. But I don't. I won't. I love you. If you want to fight, go home."

She looked around at the tables—the art students, the professors with taped spectacles, the plump women escaping the heat, the ever-so-dead-looking birds on the walls. "That's where I'm going," she said.

"Yes. It's time. We'll have to stop somewhere and buy my damned kids something."

"You *spoil* them, Jerry. You'll have hardly been gone a day."

"They expect it." He stood up and they left, by the ground level exit. His anxious long stride hurried her past the Popsicle vendors and the tourist buses, and she had no breath for words. Pitying, he took her hand, but the contact was damp and made them self-conscious; they were too old to hold hands. At the door of the drugstore displaying the usual cheap souvenirs—piggy-bank monuments, flags, sickly Kennediana—she panicked and refused to go in.

"Why not?" he asked. "Help me choose."

"No. I can't."

"Sally."

"Do it yourself. They're your children—yours and Ruth's."

His face went pale; he had never seen her like this.

She tried to make it better. "I'll walk to the hotel and pack your suitcase. Don't worry. Please don't make me buy the toys with you."

"Listen. I love—" He tried to take her arm.

"Don't embarrass me, Jerry. People are trying to get by."

In walking down Fourteenth Street alone, the pavement pricking her eyes with mica, she began to cry, and realized it didn't matter, for no one was looking at her, no one at all in these multitudes.

Together they left the hotel and caught a taxi. They crossed the Potomac and passed an inexplicable wreck on the Washington Memorial Parkway. An old blue Dodge with red Ohio plates had turned turtle in the middle lane, it was impossible to guess why. No other automobile seemed involved. Laughing policemen were redirecting traffic in the sunshine. Two fat women with dishevelled hair were embracing each other on the median strip, and the road surface glittered with glass powder. Jerry's hand tightened over hers. Then the wreck was behind them, the traffic expanded and speeded, the taxi driver ceased muttering, and they wound their way through a series of loops to the north terminal.

The waiting room was unexpectedly crowded, for a weekday afternoon. In the faces that turned toward them Sally felt them register as a handsome couple, vaguely ordinary and vaguely striking, he in gray and she in black, he with a suitcase, she with a paperback Camus. She pictured them entering a lifetime of airports, depots, piers, and hotel lobbies, and knew that they would always look like this, tallish, young, bumping together a bit too much. She wished Jerry would stop touching her; it damaged the illusion that they were married. The maintenance of this illusion did not seem to concern him here. He put down his bag and walked to a waiting line, leaving her, flustered, blushing, to take a place in the adjacent line. The line was long and sluggish; it slowly dawned on Sally that the air of jocular agitation in the room did not center around her embarrassment. She was startled—as a sleeper is startled to find, upon awakening, a room whose furniture has steadfastly kept its shape throughout her long immersion in dreams—to realize that other people and other problems existed. A plump flushed man in rumpled Dacron joined the line behind her and in sheer force of worry several times nudged her legs with his briefcase. "I'm supposed to be in Newark by seven," he explained. His anxious face had forgotten the attempted suavity of its blurry little moustache. Once, Richard had affected such a moustache, and she wondered if that was why his upper lip seemed now, in profile, so bald and vulnerable.

When the two lines wobbled close enough to touch, Jerry held her arm and said, "Apparently the strike at Eastern has created a jam-up here. We should have thought to make reservations. What time must you be back?"

"I had thought between five and six. Don't look so *worried,* Jerry."

"I'm not worried for myself. She won't meet me until nine. Let me think. It's five after three now. Assuming we miss the three-fifteen, that puts you on the four-fifteen, your car's at LaGuardia—"

"It may not start."

She said it to tease him. But he was not amused. His long face tensed and lost the laughter wrinkles that gave it some look of maturity, of having endured. Richard had more than once remarked of Jerry that he never suffered. She took the remark to mean that Jerry skimmed where Richard burrowed, or that Ruth was easier to live with than she. But it haunted her, and she wondered if that was why Jerry had taken her into his life, to be taught about suffering. He said, "Let's assume it does start. You'll be home a little after six, allowing for the rush. Is that good enough?"

"Whatever is possible will be fine," she said curtly. Their conversation was beginning to distract the man behind her from his own difficulties.

Jerry tugged the money from her hand and irritably motioned her out of the line. "I might as well buy both the damn tickets. I don't know what the hell we're trying to establish." He looked the Newark-bound man full in the face and recited, "Travel by air, and swear." This was like him, this impudence; he was pleased to have people guess he was with a mistress.

All the plastic chairs were occupied. A young Chinese sailor rose to offer her his seat, and she stepped across his duffel bag to take it. Usually she disliked being treated as weak, but now she was willing. She wished herself away. She concentrated into the Camus. The gun in his hand, the blinding light. The Arab in dungarees. The whiplike gunshot. The unreality. Jerry came to her with two yellow tickets and said, "What a mess. Apparently there aren't any reservations to be had on anything to New York tonight; we're all standbys. But they're expecting word on an extra section any minute now. I'm sure you'll get home by six."

"Shhh. You're talking too loud."

"Too loud for what?"

"Oh, never mind."

Chastened, he said, "I got these numbered boarding passes."

"What name did you put on them?"

"Mine. O.K.?"

She had to smile. "It seems illegal," she said, because this was so clearly what he felt.

The loudspeaker left off a Muzak version of "Easter Parade" and burbled unintelligibly. A fresh wave of weary travellers came down the ramp and washed up to the ticket counters. The personnel behind the counters, uniformed in aeronautic blue, seemed very young, and frightened. They stapled tickets with an exaggerated precision and answered questions in an emphatic way that reminded Sally of her own lies to Richard. "You lie like a man," he had once told her. "You pick an incredible story and keep repeating it." So Richard knew something about her that Jerry didn't. She never lied to Jerry. This realization made him seem hopelessly innocent, helpless; she went to the counter herself, bypassing the lines of men. There must be some advantage to being a woman; it can't be all waiting and wanting.

The girl handling tickets was so young she had dared bleach her hair white; Sally felt haughty toward her, a woman above her. This child had no children, no married lover she could not marry. She had frosted her hair in play. "I *must* get home by six o'clock," Sally told her.

But her voice came out fragile and shy, whereas the girl's answering was professionally firm.

"I'm very sorry, Miss," she said. "The next LaGuardia plane departs at four-fifteen. Standbys are advised to be at Gate Twenty-seven with their numbered boarding passes."

"But will we get on?" Sally asked.

"The next scheduled flight to LaGuardia is at four-fifteen," the girl repeated, stapling a ticket smartly.

Jerry had come up behind Sally. "We were told there would be a section."

"We're waiting for word on that, sir," the girl said. Her doll-like eyes, cleverly enlarged by the company's official make-up, took in Jerry and Sally together but did not change expression. Sally wondered if she should say "we" or "I." Other people, overhearing the conversation and scenting preferred treatment, had begun to bunch behind them. "Hold your lines, please," the girl called, her voice rising. "*Please* do not get out of line." Suddenly Sally felt only sympathy for this girl: while she and Jerry had been making love, children had been compelled to assume management of the world. And now the grown-ups, returning from their selfish beds, were angry to find that the world had fallen apart. How greedy we all are, how pushing! Ashamed, Sally closed her eyes and wished she were herself a child. A child before her father failed to return. All trips, she saw, have that possibility, of no return.

"I'm thirsty," she said.

Jerry asked, "What sort of thirsty? For a real drink or just for anything?"

"Just anything. A drink might make me dizzier still." A part of her still dreamed back on the beach with Meursault and the Arab.

The hot-dog counter was too crowded to approach, but a hundred steps down the corridor toward the main terminal they found a bar, wide open on one side like a stage, with an empty table in a far corner. Jerry sat her here and fetched two containers of milk, in the shape of little wax-paper tents, from a dingy oasis marked by bubbling urns of colored water. Coming to her at the table, Jerry set one carton on his head and balanced it. He waved a white-wrapped drinking straw at her like a magic wand. She was Cinderella.

She said, "Don't be an exhibitionist."

"I am," he said. "I'm a terrible person, I've decided. I can't imagine what you see in me."

She pried up the dotted corner and inserted the straw and sipped; she knew by the edge in his face that he was going to talk.

"Let's analyze this," he said. "What do you see in me? It must be that you can have me only for moments, moments you have to fight for, and this makes them seem precious. Now, if we got married, if I destroyed my wife and waded through my children's blood for you—"

"That's a horrible thing to say, Jerry."

"It's the way I see it. If I did this, I'd no longer be the man you think you love. I'd be the kind of man who abandons his wife and three children. I'd despise myself, and quite quickly you'd concur."

"I'm not so sure that's how it works," she said, trying to fit her impression of life into some sort of generalization. He really didn't know. Jerry believed in choices, in mistakes, in damnation, in the avoidance of suffering. She and Richard believed simply that things happened. After everything was said about how unhappy her childhood had been—her father's casual death, her mother's craziness, her sullen older brother, the succession of boarding schools—there remained her sense that she would, now, be less of a person if it had happened any other way. She would be somebody else, somebody she had no desire to be.

"On the other hand," he said, cocking his wrist elegantly—he took more pleasure in his hands than anyone she had ever known—"why do I love you? Well, you're gorgeous, brave, kind—really so kind—alive, female, and all the rest of it that anybody can see. To this extent, anyone who sees you come into a room loves you. The first time I saw you, I loved you, and you were eight months pregnant with Peter."

"You're wrong, though. Very few people like me."

He reflected a moment, as if reviewing the hearts of their common acquaintances, and then said, with his abrasive dispassion, "You may be right."

"You're really the only man who sees me as very special." Her chin trembled; saying it, she felt it clinched her claim on him.

He said, "Other men are stupid. Anyway, in addition to your evident charms, you are unhappy. You need me and I can't give myself to you. I want you and I can't have you. You're like a set of golden stairs I can never finish climbing. I look down, and the earth is a little blue mist. I look up, and there's this radiance I can never reach. It gives you your incredible beauty, and if I marry you I'll destroy it."

"You know, Jerry, a marriage makes something, too. It isn't all destroying illusions."

"I know that. I do know that. It kills me. I want, part of all this is, I want to *shape* you, to make you all over again. I feel I could. I don't feel this with Ruth. Somehow, she's formed, and the best kind of life I can live with her will be lived in"—his finger illustrated the word in the air—"parallel."

"Let's face it, Jerry. You still love her quite a bit."

"I don't dislike her, it's a fact. I wish I did. It might make it easier."

Her straw sucked air from the bottom of the carton. "Shouldn't we be going out to catch this four-fifteen?"

"Don't shut me up quite yet. Please. Listen. I see it so clearly. What we have, sweet Sally, is an ideal love. It's ideal because it can't be realized. As far as the world goes, we don't exist. We've never made love, we haven't been in Washington together; we're nothing. And any attempt to start existing, to move out of this pain, will kill us. Oh, we could make a mess and get married and patch up a life together—it's done in the papers every day—but what we have now we'd lose. Of course, the sad thing is we're going to lose it anyway. This is just too much of a strain for you. You're going to start hating me." He seemed pleased at this perfect conclusion.

"Or you me," she said, rising. She didn't like this place. Some children squabbling at another table made her miss her own. Their mother, though no older than Sally, looked exhausted forever.

As they left the stage-shaped bar, Jerry laughed to himself so theatrically that heads turned around. He seized her arm and said, "You know what we're like? It just came to me. We're like the Lord's Prayer written on the edge of a knife. Remember, as a kid, how in Ripley's 'Believe It or Not!' there were always things like that? Done by an old Cherokee engraver in Stillwater, Oklahoma?"

They walked down the poster-lined corridor, painted blue along one wall and cream along the other, to the departure gates. Sally felt weak under his torrent—disarmed, somehow, and ridiculed. "Jerry, our marriage would be like other marriages, it wouldn't be wonderful every minute, but that doesn't mean it wouldn't be good."

"Oh, don't," he moaned, his eyes colorless, flickering away. "Don't make me grieve. Of course it would be good. My God. Of course you'd be a better wife for me than Ruth. Just on your animal merits alone."

Animal—the word stung, but why? She had looked into the mirrors in Paris and seen the truth of it; people were animals, white animals twisting toward the light. At Gate 27 the animals were wearing suits, but they had packed

themselves like cattle in a chute, and they smelled of
panic. For the first time, Sally felt the blindness of the
situation. Dozens had arrived ahead of them. The illusion
of order maintained by the curt young ticket-sellers in the
ample waiting room disintegrated out here among the
strident posters for Bermuda and for New York musicals
with long fey titles. No airline employee was in sight.
The steel door of Gate 27 was shut tight, like a gas
chamber. The concrete floor tipped, as if to drain blood.
Jerry set down his suitcase near the corrugated wall and
motioned her to sit on it, then left her to go and talk to
the men at the head of the crush. He came back to say,
"Gee, two of those guys have been waiting since noon."

"Do you have those numbered passes?" she asked.

He rummaged, distraught and limp, through all his
pockets twice before finding them; then snapped them
into view like a magician. An invisible loudspeaker
barked. A Negro in big blue sunglasses and a pilot's cap
opened the steel door from the other side. A pale little
narrow-faced purser huddled close to him. The loudspeaker announced the boarding at Gate 27 of the
four-fifteen flight to LaGuardia, and a serene parade, displaying lightweight suitcases, well-dressed children, and
flowered hats, came down the corridor. These were the
people with reservations. The rest of them, the standbys,
were herded to the other side of the pipe railing. One by
one, the reservations were checked through at the desk
and disappeared. A crescendo of complaint from the jam
of standbys threatened the Negro in blue sunglasses; he
looked up from tearing tickets and flashed an exhilarating
grin, a great smile dazzling in the depth of its pleasure,
its vengeance, its comprehension, its angelic scorn. "Keep
cool, men," he said. "Let the wife get him out of the
house."

Disproportionate laughter answered this jest. Jerry
laughed too, and looked down at Sally warily, and she
was disgusted; they were toadying to the Negro with their

laughter. That he had noticed them at all gave them hope of passing through the gate. The gate had become something shameful that they must bribe and beg to enter. When the last of the reservations were checked through, there was a consultation at the desk and two numbers were read off, numbers that had no relation to the numbers Jerry and Sally held. Two men, the mysterious elect, in costume and appearance no different from the others, detached themselves from the pack and passed through. The Negro lifted his blue sunglasses and slowly gazed at the remaining faces. His eyes were bloodshot. They rested a moment on Sally, who had risen from sitting. "That's it, friends," he said.

A guttural moan of protest went up. "What about a section?" a man shouted. The Negro didn't seem to hear. He sidestepped, and the steel door clanged shut behind him. A phalanx of people who had disembarked farther down the corridor marched into them; they were all forced back into the waiting room, which had grown smaller. Sally's heels ached, her throat felt dry again and the man beside her appeared painted and strange, both close and far, like, in a school play, another girl playing the part of her husband. His gathering fright, which she could scent, insulted her. She told him, "Jerry, you're not seeing the humor of it."

He asked, "Shall we try American?"

"I don't have enough money for another ticket."

"Jesus, neither do I. I'll have to get ours endorsed."

He stood in the bunched, protesting line for fifteen minutes, and, their tickets endorsed, they raced down the long rats'-passage of corridors and stairways that connected the north and main terminals. The American Airlines quarters were on the far side. They were larger and more subtly lit, but the slick surfaces had not repelled the plague of confusion. Coming away from the ticket desks were several familiar faces, other veterans of the wait. "No soap, kids," one man called to them cheerfully.

So they were known. They must be conspicuous; did they look so illicit? Did they stink so of love?

The American ticket agent, speaking like a recording, confirmed the bad news; no space north until tomorrow morning. Jerry turned, his mouth puckered distastefully under his peeling nose.

Sally asked, "Can we get our United places back? We still have our passes."

"I doubt it. Oh, I am incompetent. You better get a pilot for a lover."

They raced back, her blistered heels crying out at every step, and Jerry stood in line again, and the girl with the artificially white hair, grimacing, cancelled the endorsements. He returned to Sally and told her, "She says there's no point in trying to board the five-fifteen, but they expect a section to be ready by six. Will Richard be home?"

"I suppose. Jerry, don't look so wild. It can't be helped. Let's just accept these extra hours together."

His hands hung exhausted at his sides. He reached for her arm. "Let's go for a walk."

They walked past machines vending candy bars and Harold Robbins, and pushed through a besmirched double door into the open air. She took off her shoes and he carried them one in each hand. She took his arm and he shifted a shoe to his coat pocket so one of his hands could hold one of hers. They found a long pavement, down in front of some faceless low brick buildings, where apparently no one ever walked, and walked a distance down this pavement. The cement was warm to her stockinged feet. Jerry sighed and sat on a cement step between two patches of weary grass that needed mowing. She sat down beside him. They looked across a no man's land of raw earth where a solitary bulldozer rested tilting, as if abandoned in the middle of a lurch on the stroke ending the work day. An air of peace hung above these scraped acres. Beyond, a filament of highway bridge silently glittered with the passage of cars. There were trees, and some reddish rows of government housing, and a distant plantation manse on a low blue ridge, and an immense soft sky going green above the hushed horizon. It was a landscape of unexpected benevolence. Her toes felt cool out of her shoes, and her man regained his reality in the presence of air and grass.

"I see us," he said stretching his arm toward the distance, "in Wyoming, with your children, and a horse, and a cold little lake we can swim in, and a garden we can make near the house."

She laughed. She had once said, in passing, that she had always wanted to return to the West, but not to the Coast, and he had built their whole future on it. "Wyoming"—the very word, when she wrote it to herself, seemed open and free. "Don't tease me," she said.

"Do I tease you? I don't mean to. I say these things because I feel them, I want them. I'm sorry. I'm afraid I'm not very strong with you; I guess I should pretend I don't think it would be wonderful. But it *would* be wonderful, if I could swallow the guilt. We'd spend the first month making love and looking at things. We'd be very tired when we got there, and we'd have to start looking at the world all over again, and rebuild it from the bottom up, beginning with the pebbles."

She laughed. "Is that what we'd do?"

He seemed hurt. "No? Doesn't that make sense? I always want land after making love to you. This morning, stepping into the street with you on my arm, I saw a little plant in the window of a shop, and it was terribly vivid to me. Every leaf, every vein. It's the way I saw things in art school. In Wyoming, I'd take up painting again, and draw toasters for an ad agency in Casper."

"Tell me about art school, Jerry."

"There's nothing to tell. I went there, and met Ruth, and she painted quite well in a feminine way, and her father was a minister, and I married her. I'm not sorry. We had good years."

"You know, you'd miss her."

"In ways, perhaps. You'd miss Richard, oddly enough."

"Don't say 'oddly enough,' Jerry. Sometimes you make me feel it's all my doing. You and Ruth were happy—"

"No."

"—and along came this miserable woman pretending she wanted a lover when what she really wanted was you for a husband."

"No. Listen. I loved you for years. You know that. It didn't take our sleeping together to tell me that I loved you; it was the way you *looked*. As to marriage, you weren't the one who brought that up. You assumed it was impossible. It was I who thought it might be possible. It was bad of me to mention it before I was sure, but even that, I did out of love for you; I wanted you to know— Oh, I talk too much. The word 'love' is beginning to sound nonsensical."

"You've done one thing wrong, Jerry."

"What's that? I've done everything wrong."

"In making me feel so loved you've convinced me being somebody's mistress is too shabby for me."

"It is. You're too nice, you're too straight, really. You give too completely. I hate myself for accepting."

"Accept, Jerry. If you can't take me as a wife, don't spoil me as a mistress."

"But I don't *want* you as a mistress; our lives just aren't built for it. Mistresses are for European novels. Here, there's no institution except marriage. Marriage and the Friday night basketball game. You can't take this indefinitely; you think you can, but I know you can't."

"I guess I know it too. It's just that I'm so scared of trying for everything and losing what we have."

"What we have is love. But love must become fruitful, or it loses itself. I don't mean having babies—God, we've all had too many of those—I mean just being relaxed, and right, and, you know, with a blessing. Does 'blessing' seem silly to you?"

"Can't we give each other the blessing?"

"No. For some reason it must come from above."

Above them, in a sky still bright though the earth was ripening into shadow, an airplane hung cruciform, silver, soundless. He put his arm lightly around her shoulders and looked at her in a different mood; his face broke into its fatherly smile, forgiving, enveloping. He said, "Hey," and looked at his knees. "You know, I can sit here with you and talk about loss, about my losing you, and us losing our love, but I can do it only because you're with me, so it doesn't seem serious. When I *have* lost you, when you're not there, it's a fantastic ache. Just fantastic. And everything that keeps me from coming to you seems just words."

"But it's not just words."

"No. Not quite, I guess. Maybe our trouble is that we live in the twilight of the old morality, and there's just enough to torment us, and not enough to hold us in."

The timbre of his voice, dipping toward some final shadow, chilled her. She moved forward, out from under his arm, stood up, inhaled, and let her mind expand into the landscape. "What a beautiful day," she said, trying to recapture their pleasure in discovering this place.

"Almost the longest of the year," he said, rising with the pert little dignity he put on when he felt rebuffed. "I can't remember if the days are drawing in now, or still opening up." He looked at her, imagined she didn't understand, and explained, "The solstice." Both laughed, because he had explained the obvious.

They returned to the waiting room and found it still full. The five-fifteen had departed. The aroma of hot dogs had intensified; it was suppertime. The three young people behind the counters had grown bored with the indefatigable emergency. They passed wisecracks back and forth between them, shrugged a great deal, and did not so much answer as indulge the angry press of anxiety before them. The girl with white hair was sipping coffee from a mug displaying the airline insignia. Jerry asked her if the six o'clock section was ready yet.

"We have not received word, sir."

"But you said an hour ago there would be one."

"It will be announced, sir, as soon as definite word is received."

"But we *have* to get home. Our—our baby-sitter has to go to a dance." How like Jerry, Sally thought, to lie, when he did lie, so badly. A dance on Tuesday night? She and the girl looked at each other, and Jerry, exposed between them, nakedly asked the girl, "Is there. any hope?"

"We have requested a section from the head office and are awaiting word," the girl said, and turned away to sip her coffee in privacy.

Jerry looked so grim that Sally told him, "I'm hungry," hoping to elicit one of his rude friendly jokes about her appetite. But he accepted the statement simply, as a responsibility, and, heavily retrieving his suitcase from behind a plastic chair, led her back through the blue and cream corridor to the bar. All the tables were full. He put the suitcase by a metal post and had her sit on it while he went to ask if they had sandwiches. He returned with two thin dry ham-and-cheeses and two paper cups of coffee. Why not a real drink? Perhaps he thought it would be indecent, in their predicament, or that they needed to keep their wits. At home Richard right now would be bringing her a gin and tonic, or a Daiquiri, or even a rum Collins or a gin daisy. She had bought him a cocktail shaker for their first Christmas, and even in their bitterest times he would ceremoniously bring her a sweet drink. She imagined that Richard would have made an occasion, somehow, out of this wait—an occasion at least for bluster and indignation. A burly man with imperfect vision, he loved to come to grips. He loved kitchens, he loved to make the refrigerator tremble. She could taste now the Daiquiri he would bring. So cold.

Jerry ate standing above her, and the pose revived the actor in him. If the area was a stage, they were on the very lip. A constant shuffle of people passed a few feet from them. "I've figured out the bind I'm in," he told her. "It's between death and death. To live without you is death to me. On the other hand, to abandon my family is a sin; to do it I'd have to deny God, and by denying God I'd give up all claim on immortality."

Sally felt weak; what could she say to such an accusation? She tried to fit herself into his frame of mind; she could hardly believe that minds still existed in that frame.

Having gobbled his sandwich, he squatted, and murmured to her. She turned her head aside in embarrassment, and caught a familiar-looking man gazing at them from over by the bar. He averted his gaze; his little moustache, profiled against a neon advertisement, made a dab of green light under his nose. Jerry was murmuring, "I look at your face, and imagine myself lying in bed dying, and ask myself, 'Is this the face I want at my death-bed?' And I don't know. I honestly don't *know*, Sally."

"You're not going to die for a long time, Jerry, and you'll have many women between me and then."

"I will *not*. You are my only woman, you're the only woman I want. You were given to me in Heaven, and Heaven won't let me have you."

She felt he enjoyed making things impossible by carrying them into these absurd absolutes, and furthermore she felt he enjoyed it because it punished her. Punished her for loving him. And she knew that in his mind this punishing was a kindness; his conscience insisted that he keep abrading her on the edges of pain that bounded their love. Yet she knew also that he did it like a child who states the worst, hoping to be contradicted. "You're not a woman, Jerry, so I think you exaggerate what your leaving would do to Ruth."

"Really? What would it do? Tell me." Ruth was the one earthly topic that never failed to interest him.

"We'll she'd be stunned, and very lonely, but she'd have the children, and she'd have—this is hard to say, but I remember it from the times I've been alone—she'd have the satisfaction of getting through every day by herself. It's something marriage doesn't give you. And then, of course, she would remarry."

"Do you think she would? Say yes."

"Of course she would. But—Jerry? Now don't get mad."

"I'm listening."

"You ought to do it if you're going to do it. I don't know how much she guesses, or how much you tell her, but if you torture her the way you torture me—"

"Do I torture you? God. I mean to do just the opposite."

"I know. But it— I . . . I don't want to sell myself. I'll come to you as long as I can, and you don't have to marry me. But you mustn't keep teasing me with the possibility. If it's possible, and you want it, do it, Jerry; leave her, and let her make a new life. She'll live."

"I wish I was sure of that. If only there was some decent man who I know would marry her and take care of her—but every man we know, compared to me, is a clunk. Really. I'm not conceited, but that's a fact."

She wondered if that was why she loved him—that he could say something like that, and still look boyish, and expectant, and willing to be taught. "She won't find another man until you leave her," Sally told him. "You can't pick her new husband for her, Jerry; now that *is* conceited of you."

Whenever she tried to puncture him, he seemed grate-

ful. *Come on*, his grin seemed to say, *hurt me. Help me.*
"Well," he said, and put his coffee cup inside hers. "This
has been very interesting. We're just full of home truths."

"I guess we're talked out," she said, trying to apologize.

"It's nice, isn't it? It would be so nice for us to have
said everything, and just be quiet together. But we'd
better go back. Back to Pandemonium."

Standing up, she said, "Thank you for the sandwich.
It was very good."

He told her, "You're great. You're a great blonde.
When you get up, it's like the flag being raised. I want to
pledge allegiance." And in front of everyone he solemnly
placed his hand over his heart.

The crowd had swelled; around the ticket counters it
was impenetrable. The enormous hopelessness of their
position broke upon her, and for the first time since noon
Sally wanted to cry. Jerry turned to her and said, "Don't
worry. I'll get you home. What about renting a car?"

"And driving all that way? Jerry, how *can* we?"

"Well, don't you feel we've had it, planewise?"

She nodded, and tears burned in her throat like a re-
gurgitation. Jerry virtually ran; the skin of her heels
seemed to be tearing loose as she chased him down the
corridor. The automobile-rental booths were far away,
three lonely islands side by side.

The Hertz girl wore yellow, the Avis girl red, the
National girl green. Jerry had a Hertz credit card, and the
girl in yellow said, "I'm sorry, all our cars have been
taken. Everybody wants to go to New York."

It was their destiny to be late. Everywhere they went,
crowds had been there before them. Jerry protested in-
effectually; indeed, he seemed relieved to have one more
possibility closed, one more excuse for inaction provided.
Richard would somehow have managed; nothing was too

complicated for him to finagle, finagling was a sensuous pleasure for him. Richard's shape, stocky but quick, moved in the corner of her eye; a man came up to them and said, "Did I hear you say New York? I'd be happy to share expenses with you." He was the man who had to be in Newark by seven o'clock. It was twenty of seven now.

The girl at Hertz called across the aisle to the girl at Avis, "Gina, do you have any more cars you can let go to New York?"

"I doubt it but let me call the lot." Gina dialled, bracing the receiver between her shoulder and ear. Sally found herself wondering if Gina had ever been in love. She was a young girl, but with that sluggish facial expression, of satiety and discontent, that Italian girls got, Sally imagined, from being pressed too long against the breast of a sorrowing mother. Sally had run away from her own sorrowing mother as soon as she could, fled into school and then marriage, and maybe that was why every sorrow came to her new, jagged and fresh and undreamed-of; she wondered, if every woman in the world carries this ache, how can it go on? How does anything in the world get done?

The tall green girl at the National desk asked, "Why does everybody want to go to New York? What's in New York?"

"The Liberty Bell," Jerry told her.

"If I were you two," she said to him, "I'd take a cab back into the city and see a movie."

Jerry asked her, "What's good?"

The Hertz girl said, "My boyfriend liked *Last Year at Marienbad* but I thought it was terrible. The bushes didn't have any shadows. 'They call this art,' I said to him, and he said, 'It *is* art.'"

The Avis girl called over, "There's a new Doris Day and Rock Hudson downtown that everybody likes."

Jerry said, "I love Doris Day. Hollywood should let her sing more." It saddened Sally to see how easily he talked with women, any women.

Gina put down the phone and said, "Alice, they have one just came in they'll let go."

And Alice, sweet chinless Alice with her easily pleased boyfriend, smiled bucktoothed and said, "There you are, sir. She'll take care of you."

"Don't forget me," the man who had to go to Newark said.

Jerry turned to the man, blushed, and explained, "My wife and I, I guess, would prefer to drive alone."

The man stepped forward and shook Jerry's hand. "My name's Fancher. I make my home in Elizabeth, New Jersey, and I'm in the chemical additives line. I don't want to pressure you one way or another, but it would be a great kindness to me if I could ride along."

Jerry gracefully clapped his long hand to the top of his head and said, "Well, let's think about it. Let me get the car first."

He dropped his Hertz credit card on Gina's desk and she explained that since this was an Avis car she would need a cash deposit of twenty-five dollars.

"But we don't have twenty-five dollars, do we?" Jerry asked Sally.

"The tickets," she said.

Fancher stepped forward. "You want twenty-five dollars?"

She and Jerry studied each other, and the romance of driving together alone under moonlight, toward midnight and their fate, hung between them like a painted screen. "I'll cash in the tickets," he said. "I'll turn that girl's hair really gray." To Gina he said, "I'll be back in ten minutes." To Sally he said, "You wait here and guard the car." He winced apologetically in Fancher's face and flew away.

Long minutes passed. Mr. Fancher stayed with her

silently, touching his moustache, guarding her while she guarded the phantom automobile. The three girls, in the lull that had settled over their islands, chatted back and forth, about boyfriends and bathing suits. Sally felt dizzy. The acid taste kept rising in her throat; she felt sick of love. Love, love was what had clogged the world, it was love that refused to let the planes leave, love that hid her children from her, love that made her husband look senile in profile. Fancher hovered close to her; he was in the chemical additives line and should be in Newark, yet she had promised to love and obey this man till death did them part. *Dear God, let go.* She held herself very upright and quiet, wondering if she would throw up. The cement floor was littered with cigarette filters and heel marks. The green girl from National was saying that she didn't think she had the right figure for a bikini, being so tall, but her boyfriend bought her one for a joke, and now she wouldn't wear anything else, it felt so free.

Red-faced from running, Jerry came back, Jerry with his sun-burned nose and elusive eyes and his beautiful look of being a kite. "Forget it," he announced, making a triumphant V with his arms, and including all four women in his emblematic embrace. To Fancher he said, "You can have the car. Good luck in Newark." He touched Sally's arm and told her, "The girl at United says there's going to be a section and to see a name she gave me." He showed her a slip of paper on which a hasty female hand had scribbled the one word "Cardomon."

"Have you seen him yet?"

"No, he wasn't there at the moment. Let's go back and find him."

"Jerry, your suitcase."

"Oh. Right. God, you're so competent, Sally."

Fancher said, "You said there's a section? Then I don't want the car either." He knifed past them and, moving with a quickness surprising in a stout man, beat them back to the waiting room.

Here an instinct of movement seemed to have seized the human tides; almost all the people were moving toward the boarding gates. Jerry and Sally, alarmed, followed them out of the doors and down the corridor. A crowd had accumulated. A strange chant was going up; it seemed to Sally to be "The bridesmaid, the bridesmaid." She thought it was another hallucination, but it proved to be exactly what they were shouting. At the center of the crowd the Negro in blue sunglasses was conferring with a sandy-haired man wearing a company coat and carrying a clipboard. Beside them, a shinily dressed arc of the middle-aged was urging forward, with deep Dixie accents, a girl in a flowered hat and a shimmering dress of yellow silk. Sally understood: she was a bridesmaid, and had to be on the plane or miss a wedding; or had she come from a wedding? The chant deepened. Jerry joined in. "The birdesmaid, the bridesmaid!" Indignation bit into Sally's stomach, and the press of tears overwhelmed her eyes. What was so unfair, the girl was not even pretty. She had a strawberry birthmark beside her nose and a tense wrinkled simper. The sandy man nodded to the Negro, who flashed his deep ironic smile and took the bridesmaid's ticket. A cheer went up. The girl passed through the door. The gate clanged shut. The seven-fifteen flight to New York had departed.

Back in the waiting room, Jerry left Sally and went to look for Mr. Cardomon. As she stood alone by the tired blue wall, a tall man came up to her and said gently, "Aren't you Sally Mathias?"

It was Two Initials Wigglesworth. The two initials abruptly came to her: A. D. He asked, "Are you here with Dick?" He spoke with a velvet smoothness; he was well shaped and very combed, and so wealthy that Richard had fairly danced the few times he had come to the house.

"No, I'm here by myself," she said. "I do this every so often. My mother lives in Georgetown. Are you trying to get to New York?"

"No, I'm en route to St. Louis. My flight leaves in half an hour. Could I get you a drink?"

"That would be lovely," Sally said, "but I'm a standby and I think I'd better stay here. We're waiting for a section." She adjusted the pronoun. "I've been here since three o'clock. It's a grotesque mess."

"I do think you could use a drink." He smiled like a great brushed cat purring; he was perfectly handsome and perfectly repulsive, and beneath all his grooming he knew it.

"I think I could too," she said, glancing around for Jerry. He wasn't anywhere.

Wigglesworth interpreted her glancing around as acquiescence, and took her arm. She snapped it away. She hadn't realized how tense she was. "I'm sorry," she said. "I'm honestly on the verge of tears; Richard expected me back by supper."

"It makes one rather miss the dear old trains, doesn't it?" he said soothingly, offended.

"What are you going to do in St. Louis?" she asked. She felt the tight mask of charm fitting across her face; felt herself, unstoppably, beginning to flirt.

"Oh, very dreary. Banking business, a rail merger. A desperation move. I loathe the Midwest."

"Do you?"

"Tell me, how did Dick do with his Canadian oil issue? I was fascinated, but I couldn't interest Father."

"I never heard about it. He never tells me anything. How is Bea?" She had been groping for his wife's name, remembering only the woman's waxen ballerina's face and that her name, too, was some sort of initial.

"*Very* well. We have two children now."

"Do you? That's wonderful. Another girl?"

"Another boy. Are you sure you wouldn't like that drink?"

"It's tempting," Sally said.

"Have you heard about Jamie Babson? He's married

again—a spectacular Indonesian girl. She does simultaneous translation at the U.N."

"Yes. He would like that."

Wigglesworth laughed; his teeth were immaculate, but small for his face. "And Bink Hubbard—I know Richard has met him—has disappeared in Florida; the rumor has it he's shipped out on a Liberian freighter again."

"I don't think I know him."

"No, you wouldn't. He's one of those men other men rather envy."

"Yes, there is that kind of man." Sally sounded mechanical to herself. Push, pull, push, pull: a real whore.

Wigglesworth gazed over her head and asked, "Isn't that Jerry Conant?"

"Where? Do you know Jerry?"

"Of course. Doesn't he live rather near you out there?" He glanced down, his immaculate eyebrows (did he pluck between them?) lifted at the intensity of her concern. "Through Ruth," he explained. "My parents went to her father's church. She was considered quite a beauty."

"She still is."

"Nobody ever understood quite why she married Jerry."

And there he was. She felt him in the side of her vision when he was still far away, coming back from the counters. She felt him hesitate, then decide to approach. His voice, close to her ear, harshly announced, "Anno Domini Wigglesworth, the Rock of Ages himself."

"Jerry. Are you stranded here too?"

"Apparently. I've just been looking for a mythical man called Cardomon who's supposed to unstrand us."

"You and Mrs. Mathias?"

"Yes, Mrs. Mathias and I seem to be caught in the same pickle." He looked down at his hand, which held two tickets. He held them up. "I've taken over negotiations for her. Do you have a reservation?"

"Yes."

"How would you feel about giving it to Sally?"

"Splendid—but I'm going to St. Louis."

Jerry turned to Sally and said, "Maybe we should go to St. Louis. We could get on a raft and float down the Mississippi."

She laughed, shocked. How dare he tease her, right in the teeth of disaster!

Wigglesworth's smile had become fixed, and from the heightened composure of both men's faces she knew she had become an object, a body, between them. "I was just telling Sally," Wigglesworth said, "that Jamie Babson has married an Indonesian."

"Excellent," Jerry said. "Miscegenation is the only permanent solvent for world tensions. Kennedy knows it, too."

"Come, Jerry," the other man said. "When did you get religion? I thought you were stooging for the State Department."

They were fighting over her. Sally's sick dread returned, a desire to sleep; she thought of Richard sitting alone, puzzled, worried for her, sipping his second Martini, and she yearned to faint, to sink down into the trafficked, dirty floor, into the spaces between the cigarette filters, and awake at his feet. The men talked on, bantering angrily through her daze, until Wigglesworth, routed by Jerry's superior rudeness, said, "I believe it's time for me to board. Good luck to both of you." And in his farewell, in the way he bowed from his rigid height, there was something genuinely gracious, almost a blessing. Only a stuffed shirt could have brought it off.

Jerry was sulky and opaque. Had it come, his hating her? She asked him, "You didn't find Cardomon?"

"No. He doesn't exist. Do you think it's a code? Cardomon spelled backwards is Nom-o-drac." The eight o'clock flight to St. Louis was announced and Wigglesworth, staring straight ahead, chin high, was carried out of the waiting room on a river of briefcases. Jerry took Sally's hands. "You're trembling."

"A little. That upset me."

"Does he see Richard often?"

"Almost never. He snubs Richard."

"He won't say anything. There'd be no percentage in it for him. He'll save this on the chance he can use it with you."

"He's right, isn't he? I mean, what he saw me as, I am."

"What did he see you as?"

"Don't make me say it, Jerry."

Jerry mulled this refusal. "Actually," he said, "you'd be much better off with him than with me. He'd get you on a Goddamn plane, I know that."

"Jerry."

"Mm?"

"Don't blame yourself. You told me not to come."

"But I wanted you to come. You knew that. That's why you came."

"I came for myself, too."

He sighed. "Oh, Sally," he said. "You're so kind to me." He looked at the tickets in his hand and put them into his side coat pocket and looked up at her wearily. A little smile of regret brightened his face. "Hey?"

"Hi."

"Let's get married."

"Please, Jerry."

"No, let's. The hell with this. We can't get back. God has spoken."

"I don't think you mean it."

His voice was listless. "No. I do. You act like a wife to me. You look like Mrs. Conant to me."

"But I'm not, Jerry. I'd like to be."

"O.K., then. Proposal accepted. I don't see any other way but to go back to the hotel and call up Ruth and Richard and eventually get married. It's the only thing I can think of. I'm tired right now, but I think I'll be very happy."

"I'll try to make you happy."

"I think we can get your children. The courts don't really care who commits the adultery any more."

"Are you sure it's what you want?"

"Of course. I didn't think it would come quite this way, but I'm glad it's come." Still he didn't move. She waited there beside him, her heart a perfect blank. Joy and sorrow, fear and hope—all the things that had been crowding upon her had dispersed. There was even an empty space of floor around them. People were clamoring and gesturing, but she heard only silence. She became aware that she was thirsty and that the blisters on her heels hurt. She could take off her shoes in the hotel room. Later, they could get a drink in the bar.

The girl with unnaturally white hair advanced into the empty space around them. "Mr. and Mrs. Conant? I've found Mr. Cardomon." She was followed by a sandy man wearing an airlines jacket and carrying a clipboard. Sally had seen him before; when?

Jerry lurched explosively away from her. He pulled out his tickets. They were tattered and looked worthless. He explained, stammering, "We've been trying to get on a New York plane since three this afternoon and turned down a car rental because we were told there was going to be a section."

Mr. Cardomon asked, "Could I have your numbered standby passes?" While he examined them, he rubbed the underside of his nose with a knuckle. Then he examined both their faces, constantly returning his fingers to the itch on his nose. Sally felt that she and the white-haired girl were standing on tip-toe. A tender, very distant scent of sweat came to her from Jerry's neck. Mr. Cardomon wrote on the clipboard, saying to himself, "Conant, two." Then he lifted up his youthful head of sandy curly hair and showed Sally that his eyes were gray, the color of aluminum. He knew. He told Jerry, "Miss March will staple boarding passes to your tickets."

"You mean there *is* a plane?" Jerry asked.

Cardomon looked at his wristwatch. "It should be leaving in thirty minutes, from Gate Twenty-eight."

"And we're *on* it? My God, thank you. *Thank* you. We had just decided to go back to the hotel." And, unable to convey his gratitude sufficiently to Mr. Cardomon, who had turned his back, Jerry turned to the girl and gushed, "You know, I've grown to love your hair. Don't ever dye it back."

He went off with her and came back with two blue squares stapled to the tickets and picked up his suitcase containing toys for his children and walked with Sally down the corridor. She knew all the posters by now. Shows she would not see, islands she would not visit. An apprehensive mob, scenting redemption, had gathered at Gate 28, and in time the Negro appeared, his sunglasses tucked into his shirt pocket, and slowly, enjoying it, read off a list of names. Theirs was the last name on the list. Conant. They passed through the gate, and in glancing behind her Sally thought she saw, amid the press of those who had been left behind, the worried moustached face that should have been in Newark.

The plane was a little DC-3 with a steep tilt to its aisle. Inside, all the men, coats off, briefcases tucked away, were laughing. "I wonder what attic they got this out of," one man called, and Jerry laughed, and tapped her bottom. His delight and relief were so vivid she tried to share them, but she had little capacity for sharing left. She took the inside seat and through the oval window studied the mechanics waving flashlights while Jerry stroked her arms and begged to be praised for having got them a plane. She thought of the Camus in her pocketbook and closed her eyes. Her painful shoes slipped off. Behind her she could hear a stewardess talking, and below her window a machine whined. It was chilly in the plane, as if it had been brought to them from a great cold height. Jerry laid something over her—his suit coat. The collar rubbed her chin. He stroked her arms and the backs of her hands and she felt the metal curving close around her; men were murmuring and she was the only woman in the plane and Jerry's coat smelled faintly of him and she was nearly asleep before the plane moved.

Oh, Sally, it was such a beautiful ride! Do you remember at what a low altitude we flew? How our little plane, like a swan boat mildly bobbing in an occasional current, carried us through the middle air that was spangled with constellations above and cities below? I saw, past the halo of your sleeping hair, the capital's spoked wheel of light expand, tilt, and expand again: Dante could not have dreamed such a rose. Our DC-3, fetched from Heaven knows where to carry us home, was chilly—unheated, unpressurized; it was honest ether we inhaled. We floated, our two engines beating, just high enough to be high, across Baltimore, the Chesapeake Bay, New Jersey dark with farms. Any higher, and we could not have seen each forked car sliding home, each house embedded in its nest of light. Each bridge was a double strand of diamonds, each roadhouse a sunken ruby, each town a scarf of pearls. And the stars level with our windows rode along motionless to keep us company.

And it was you, your beauty. Through the strait gate between your legs I had entered this firmament. You seemed, asleep beside me while the band of men guarding us rustled newspapers and accepted coffee, you seemed —what? You were not my wife, you were not my sister, nor my child. I stroked your forearms to tell you, even in your sleep, that I was there. Your arms seemed wonderfully long, Sally; your physical size as you slept was a great pride to me. How proud I was, for the hour and more that it took our pilot to pedal our quaint craft from star to star, to be your protector. Never before, never since, did I so surely protect you. For if you were to fall, and die, I would come with you, and into that fabulous kingdom we would pass together, my coat laid over you, my sperm still alive in your warm turns. Two struggling horses pulled us, swaying, up the still black hill of air northward. Oblivious, you were mine. I loved the oval of black Heaven beside your face. I loved the chill that brought your head to my shoulder. I loved your rough knuckles, and your downy forearms, and the way you were lost in the shape of my coat.

Then I left you. The engines roared in a graver key, Manhattan bristled, the ocean lifted to swallow us, the wheels smacked the runway, our moment passed, we did not die. I hated our failure to die. I hated my haste in taking my coat from you and pulling my suitcase from under the seat and shoving down the aisle to be the first off. Ruth would be meeting me; it was after ten. I left you half-asleep, pushing the hair back from your lips, abandoned, the prey of feeding eyes. I felt you watching me race, cowardly, across the cement, diminishing, flickering in the whirling lights. Already I had seen Ruth's face lifted in the crowd behind the glass doors. I felt myself disappear in your eyes. I remembered her.

When the telephone rang the next morning at ten, Josie blushed angrily and left the kitchen. Sally answered it in her bathing suit; Peter had been waiting to go to the beach for half an hour. "Hi," she said. If it were someone else calling, her tone of voice would seem a joke.

"Hi," Jerry said. His voice was frightened. "What happened?"

"Nothing," Sally said. "I got home before midnight and he was in bed asleep. This morning, before going off, he asked me how the Fitches were, and I said fine, and that was all we said."

"You're kidding. He must know something."

"I don't think so, Jerry. I just think we've got to such a point he doesn't really care what I do."

"No. He cares."

"How did it go with Ruth?"

"Fine. The plane mix-up gave me something to talk about, leaving you out, of course. I told her about the rent-a-car girls and Fancher and Wigglesworth. It made me sort of sad, how happy she was to see me. She was about to give up hope."

Sunlight lay sharply on the salt and pepper shakers on the windowsill. Sally wondered vaguely if the salt would melt. "I saw her meet you," she said.

"Did you? I wasn't sure how much you could see."

"The way you hustled her out of the waiting room, it looked like she was under arrest."

He laughed. "Yes, she said, 'What's the rush?' She's actually kind of depressed. Geoffrey broke his collarbone while I was away."

"My God, Jerry. His collarbone?"

"Apparently it's not as serious as it sounds. Charlie pushed him down on the grass and he cried all day and held his arm funny, so she took him to the hospital and all they did was wrap an Ace bandage around his shoulders, to hold it back. Now he walks around like a little old man and doesn't want you to touch him."

Peter came into the kitchen and began bumping, infuriatingly, against her bare legs. "I'm sorry," she said.

"Don't be. You didn't do it. Hey?"

"Yes?"

"You were lovely. Just killingly lovely."

"So were you. It was even nicer than the first time."

"I felt rotten about the ordeal in the airport. I'm amazed you survived it."

"I didn't mind it, Jerry. It was fun."

"You're great. You're really so great, Sally. I just don't know what to do with you. You were so beautiful in the plane back, I'm all upset."

"I felt badly about falling asleep. It's such a waste of my time with you."

"No. It's not a waste. It was right."

"I was really feeling quite weak. You make me weak, Jerry."

"Hey. Was it really all right? Are you sorry you came?"

"Of course not."

"It was sort of a sad lunch in the museum, and then the business about the toys was very sad."

"I'm sorry about that. I wish I were a bigger person. I'm just not big enough to be your cheerful broad."

"Listen—"

"And you make me feel terribly guilty about Geoffrey's collarbone."

"Why? Don't. It has nothing to do with you."

"Yes it does. It's the sort of thing I make happen. I'm bad luck. I'm destroying Richard, and my children, and your children, and Ruth—" Her eyes smarted and she wondered again if the salt in the sunstruck salt-cellar were melting.

"No, listen. You're not. It's me. I'm the man, and you're the woman, and it's up to me to control this, and I can't. You're good. You must know you're great; but do you know that you're good?"

"Sometimes when you tell me I feel it."

"Good. Right. Do."

Peter began plucking at her dangling arm, and his voice began to grind. "*Go*, Mom. *Go-o*." His soft plucking body was jogging in exasperation.

She told Jerry, "Peter's being horrible and Josie is throwing one of her fits in the living room so I'd better hang up."

"Sure. In a minute I have to go tell the big cheese what

they told me in Washington about seducing the Third World. I'm sorry about Josie. If we get married, must we keep her?"

"We aren't going to get married, Jerry."

"Don't say that. I live by thinking that somehow we will. Are you sure we won't?"

He wanted to know, he wanted to be told she was sure. "Not always," she said.

He paused and then said, "Good."

"I'll be appreciating all day tomorrow, so don't call me until Friday. I think we should take it easy now for a while, so I don't know when I'll see you again."

"Yeah. I suppose we shouldn't press our luck."

She had hoped he would argue, and set a day soon. *"Peter,"* she snapped. "Shall Mommy have to smack you?"

"Don't be cross with Peter," Jerry's voice said in her ear. "He worries about you."

"I must hang up. Good-bye?"

"Good-bye. I love you. Don't be too lovely for anybody else."

"Have a good day, Jerry." She hung up, quickly, for she knew they could go on and on, and she would never tire of hearing his voice say things she doubted he believed. *Don't be too lovely for anybody else*—this was a favorite concept of his, that she would take on another man. He thought she was a whore; Sally experienced a flash of hating him, and stood there, desperate, beautiful in her bathing suit, her naked feet caught in the warm slant of sun. Was she wicked or crazy? How could she possibly take this man away from his blameless wife and helpless children? Though Peter was frantic, she stood a moment longer, waiting to be told how.

3.   The Reacting of Ruth

*T*WO snapshots, curled together in a box.

One, in color, shows the Conant family back from
church, on a raw clear Palm Sunday, the Palm Sunday of
1961. Geoffrey, a toddler of two, has just been baptized;
there is a slick place in his hair. Ruth is squatting, in a
white coat, on the dead lawn in front of their house, between Charlie and Geoffrey, both of whom, with their
slack expressions and winter pallor, look chunky and un-
comfortable in matching gray shorts, bow ties, and blue
blazers. Joanna, seven years old at the time, stands behind her mother, wearing in the year's young sunlight an
apprehensive squint and a green beret. Ruth's upward
smile is rather mischievous; light shines baldly on her
knees, and her hat is crooked. She had borrowed the hat
from Linda Collins. Beneath the game try at a cheerful
expression, she looks tired and drawn. The Conants had
returned home from a party at the Mathiases' at two
o'clock that same morning. Above her head, beside Joanna's shoulder, like a blurred yellow moth, or an im-
pending star, is the year's first crocus. It had opened early

in the warmth reflected from the white clapboards of the house, and Jerry had posed the picture to include it.

He himself is present only as a purple shadow in the lower left corner of the snapshot. What does not show is how Joanna, when her parents had returned to the pew of the tall white Congregational church, reached over and wonderingly touched the wet spot on her brother's head. Or how Ruth, attempting a nap that afternoon, while Jerry walked the kids on the beach, had cried, thinking she had betrayed her father and emptied herself of all identity.

She was the daughter of a Unitarian minister. When she met and married a Lutheran, Jerry Conant from Ohio, religion didn't matter to either of them. They were students at an art school in Philadelphia, naïvely immersed in the cult of true color, of vital line. They adored the silent gods of the museum-temple that floated above the city. When they first saw each other naked, it was as if a new object of art had been displayed to each, and their marriage carried forward this quirk of detachment, having more in it of mutual admiration than mutual possession. Each admired the other's talent. Ruth, though her perspective was always awry and her formal definition vague, so that even the bottle and bowl of her still lifes had a vegetable softness, showed a rare color touch. Her paintings were remarkably unafraid. Cadmium yellow danced boldly through her pears, her skies were an intense solid blue that yet stayed airborne, and the tint of her shadows bodied forth a color not nameable, simply itself, the shadow, now luminous for having passed through a mind. The tone of truth rang through the shuffle, neither careless nor careful, of her calm, squarish strokes. Her talent struck Jerry as remarkable because his lay the other way. His gift was for line, for outline. Each subject, when he sat down to it, became a kind of overanimated ghost, wherein swerve and energetically "worked" detail replaced the dense and placid life of substance. Though he worked hard at color, trying to learn from Ruth's unstudied candor, his paintings, when seen next to hers, fell, for all the ardor of the drawing, on one side or the other of the fine line that divides the garish from the muddy. Their easels, the last year of art school, were always side by side. Someone viewing their paintings thus might well have concluded, as did they, that between them they had everything.

Their merger was perhaps too easy, too aesthetic. As the art school receded, and Jerry became an unsuccessful cartoonist and then a successful animator of television commercials, and Ruth became a housewife and mother, too harassed to unpack the paintbox and load the palette, unexpected shadows deepened, emphasizing differences overlooked in the ideal overhead light they had once painted by.

The baptism of the children became a sore point. The first, Joanna, was christened by Ruth's father, in their first apartment, on West Twelfth Street. Jerry had been shocked by the ceremony, which seemed to him a parody of the sacrament; his father-in-law, a civic-minded man active in the interracial councils of Poughkeepsie, had joked about "holy water," drawing it from the kitchen tap. So the next child, a boy, was baptized as a Lutheran in the dour country church, smelling of apple blossoms and moldy velvet, where Jerry as a boy had been confirmed. The score thus tied, the third child hung two years above the mouth of Limbo while his parents fought to a standstill on behalf of their heritages. Ruth was surprised by their passion; she had put religion behind her. Having been obliged to attend church automatically as a girl, she felt faint, guilty, and disoriented whenever she entered a church now. Just one stanza of a hymn would make her voice falter, and by the third stanza she was fighting tears, while the organ thundered at her like a pompous, hurt father. Whereas Jerry, defeated in his ambition to become a "name" cartoonist, and immersed, with their move to

Greenwood, in the organic and the mediocre and the familial, suddenly dreaded death. Only religion helped. He read theology, Barth and Marcel and Berdyaev; he taught the children bedtime prayers. Each Sunday he deposited Joanna and Charlie in the Sunday school of the nearby Congregational church, sat through the sermon, and came home cocky, ready to fight. He hated Ruth's pale faith, which receded and evaporated still further under his hatred. There was a goodness, she did feel, a diaphanous truth and excellence floating in the world, like the dust of buds in the elm outside their bedroom windows. Otherwise, we must not hurt others deliberately, and we should take pleasure in each day. That was all. Wasn't it enough? Once, wakened from sleep to hear him protest that some day he would die, Ruth had said, "Dust to dust," and rolled over and gone back to sleep. Jerry never forgave this. She regretted it, that when he lay in bed staring at the ceiling, and when he moved through the midnight house as if his whole body were sore, fighting for breath, she could not enclose his terror, and withdraw it from him as she did his seed. The child's non-baptism tormented him, as a face of his own extinction. Ruth pitied and yielded. Geoffrey was baptized in his father's arms, while she stood beside, in a borrowed hat, vowing never to attend church again, trying not to cry.

The other snapshot, black and white and several years older, taken in '58 or '59, shows Jerry, his skinny chest gleaming like metal in the dying light, submerged up to his waist in water, an incandescent kettle held balanced on his head. He is bringing mussels back to a boat where Sally Mathias had sat, snapping the picture. Ruth had been startled that this woman could operate a camera. They were all new in town, with tiny children and houses that felt like enormous playhouses, and the Mathiases had invited the Conants to go musselling in their boat. An-

other couple invited could not come. The Conants had
shied from accepting; they distrusted the Mathiases, the
little they knew of them. Sally, big blond expensively
dressed Sally, made a show of lugging gallon bottles of
milk home from the supermarket to save the few pennies
delivery would cost, yet they drank wine by the case.
There was something excessive about the Mathiases, something both generous and greedy, violent and self-contra-
dictory. Richard was a big overweight man with dark
wiry hair in need of a haircut, a deep voice that in every
swollen syllable expressed oral conceit, and a blind eye,
the result of a childhood accident. It didn't show, except
in the slightly anxious, over-watchful tilt of his somewhat
leonine head. And if you dared look, you could see that
the pupil, which should have been black, wore a kind of
cap of frost. As if in pain, he drank a lot, smoked a lot,
drove his Mercedes and philosophized a lot; but what did
he *do*? He had money, and took trips about it. His dead
father had owned a liquor store in Cannonport, which
had fostered branches in shopping malls as the little city
metastasized and merged with exurban New York. Unlike
most of Greenwood's young marrieds, Richard was native
to the region. He loved the sea, and seafood. He had gone
to Yale two years, and dropped out, as if half an education were enough for a man with one eye. He had married young; his wife was flashy and overanimated and
highly visible. Both of them seemed determined to enjoy
life; such determined hedonism seemed blasphemous to
Jerry and vulgar to Ruth. Yet the day, which they had
wanted to avoid, proved to be an idyll. The sun sparkled,
the wine and words flowed. Jerry, an inland boy, squeam-
ish and hydrophobic, consented to learn from Richard,
and gathered the courage to press his face into the water
and to tear clusters of mussels, purple and living, loose
from submerged rocks. Proud of his exploit, he waded
back to the whaler with a full kettle.

His face is harshly shadowed and curiously savage. His

eyes are hollow, a shadow dashes from his nose, his lips grin. A skinny slave, preoccupied and cruel. Above his left shoulder Richard's legs, soft and fuzzy and shod in sopping tennis sneakers, grip a shelf of slippery rock. The smudge between his legs must be Grace Island.

In the time that flowed from this frozen moment, they took the boat in to the little sandy cove on Grace Island. The four of them gathered wood and built a fire and boiled the mussels. Richard had packed butter, salt, garlic. They had gathered so many, they took to feeding them to each other as a game. Eyes shut, Jerry could not tell the difference between Ruth's and Sally's fingers in his mouth. As night thickened around them, they played word games, Indian-wrestled, finished the wine, undressed, and went swimming. Their naked shapes made chaste blurs in the whispering wet dark. Jerry was surprised how much warmer and less menacing the water felt when you were naked. When they regathered around the fire, Richard and Jerry put on trousers over their wet legs and the women held towels about their bodies. The drops of water on Ruth's and Sally's shoulders glinted with scarlet centers, reflected from the fire. How gorgeous she is, Ruth thought. But heedless, and vain. Readjusting her towel, Sally had showed her her breasts, and Ruth had envied their smallness, unembarrassed and firm. Since the age of thirteen Ruth had felt her breasts were too big. It was as if, Ruth felt, there had not been enough of her grown inside to carry them off; and this sensation had persisted; her life pushed on ahead of her, betraying an inner woman not quite ready to be unveiled. Across the fire, Jerry looked unfamiliar, happy in his skin, beside the bigger, softer man, who was benignly drunk, as were they all. Yet the idyll was not repeated. The rest of that summer, the Mathiases took other couples musselling, and that winter they separated—another piece of excess, it seemed to the Conants, another showy extravagance—over an affair Richard had evidently been conducting in

Cannonport. By the time they reconciled in the spring, and Richard returned to Greenwood, the boat had been, in one of his mysterious financial maneuvers, sold.

He took satisfaction in being mysterious. He travelled to no apparent purpose, often overnight, and his money-making schemes—a local coffeehouse, a publishing firm specializing in Oriental erotica, a firm that would re-upholster automobiles in the same kind of tapestry-cloth being used in the newly fashionable "carpetbag" suitcases —never came to much. In conversation with women, he would pretend not to understand the simplest statements, and his good eye would water, in sympathy with his bad, in sympathy with the sadness of what was being confessed to him.

It made Ruth blush, as if a secret were being pried from her, and then blush with anger, anger at herself for blushing, and at Richard, for being an intrusive fool. Yet not merely that. Possibly she *was* betraying a secret, the secret of herself that she had kept from Jerry these eight years of being his wife. It was a wordless secret, that is, one that Ruth did not seek words for. She liked Richard's smell, tobacco and liquor and a leathery staleness reminding her of her father's study after one of his weary Saturdays writing a sermon; she liked the protective baffled way he hunched and lurched at parties, and always, sooner or later, came to talk to her. Jerry noticed this, he hated Richard. Richard was one of the few people they had ever met, in their thirty years in materialist America, who professed being an atheist. When she had mentioned to him Jerry's insistence that the children go to Sunday school, Richard's wiry eyebrows arched and the live eye widened and he laughed disbelievingly. "For God's sake, why?"

"Because it matters to him," Ruth said, loyally—

though perhaps such clearly reflexive loyalty was disloyalty.

After this, Richard didn't always pass up a chance to "bug" Jerry, as he put it. Once, on the Mathiases' side lawn in the pride of a summer afternoon, Richard produced a plastic dashboard Christ that had arrived unsolicited in the mails, and proceeded to clean his fingernails with the tip of the hand upraised in blessing. "Look, Sally-O," he had said, "doesn't Christ make a good fingernail-picker?" Sally, who had been raised, Ruth had gathered, as a Catholic, snatched the little doll from Richard's hand and said something to the effect that she didn't know what she believed, but . . . really, Richard. Jerry had turned pale under the sun. He always used the incident afterwards to illustrate how sadistic that bastard Mathias was to his wife.

Whereas in truth Richard was too good to Sally. As her voice rose shrill from a corner of a rumpus room or the patio of a lawn party, he would wince, but clamp his lips shut on the conclusion of a bargain, the price he was paying for her high visibility. He had a family sense that Jerry quite lacked. No matter how late the night's drinking, he rose early, often cooking breakfast for his wife and children, while Jerry didn't get up until the children were fed and out of the house and there were minutes to make the 8:17. Though Jerry mocked Richard's lack of vocation, he *did* do things: build bookcases, refinish furniture, grow tomatoes and lettuce and pumpkins, go musselling. He helped Sally bring their old colonial farmhouse into a state of polished modernity; dozens of touches in the house were his. Often at home all day, he gave Sally, what Ruth envied, an audience for her housework. Though it strained his good eye, he read, and read books women read—novels, biographies, psychology. He saw the raising of children as a kind of problem, where Jerry saw none: he was the original, and in the children God had made some reproductions which in time would be distributed. Jerry loved duplication and its instruments—cameras, printing presses—but did that make Ruth one? Richard, half-blind as he was, saw through her, to a secret no one else had seen since Martha, the fat black woman her mother had hired to cook and clean in the days of the Buffalo parish. In her reign the kitchen had become a haven, a cave of what only had been whispered inside her before. "Ruthie," Martha would sigh, "you're a magical girl but the world's going to do you in. You don't fear the right things." The more dire the pronouncement, the more cherished Ruth had felt. Richard, too, saw through her to some doom. And she saw through him, to the truth that Sally was hard on him, made him pay for her beauty; with her cool painterly vision Ruth watched him clown and drink and be a fool and saw that she could have eased him in a way he was not being eased, though the Mathiases did share a love of parties and the things money bought and a certain callowness that was reflected in the faces of their children, which were lifted toward their parents like bright empty plates. Yet he would talk Piaget and Spock and Anna Freud with Ruth, and Iris Murdoch and Julia Child, and furniture and cooking and style. He noticed her clothes, sometimes with a compliment, sometimes with an insult. He complained when she cut her hair; Jerry had asked her to, and had wanted it even shorter, "to show off her skull."

Why should he want to show off her skull? Dancing with her at a party, Richard stroked, not patted, her buttocks and told her he had always thought she had the sexiest bottom in town. "He talks to me woman to woman," Ruth replied, when Jerry complained of how much time she spent with Richard at parties; she knew as she said it that this was the first deliberate lie of her married life. At another party Richard invited her to have lunch with him, and even named the restaurant, a Chinese one toward Cannonport. She thanked him, and refused.

She wondered afterwards if it had been proper to thank him. To be grateful seemed to be half-willing. Again, she having told him (why?) that she was distressed by Jerry's "religious crisis," Richard offered to make a date with her so they could discuss it fully. "He sounds neurotic as hell, and I've read some books." She was sorry, she thought not. He didn't press her. She liked that. His propositions were like a rather flat joke that, through being repeated, comes to be funny; she came to look forward to the moment at parties when Richard, his slightly pinched and lipless mouth prim with earnestness and his head atilt like a lame god's, would put the jaded question to her.

But away from parties, in hours of sudden privacy, in the weird solitude she would awake to in the middle of the night, as if in answer to a shout, Richard became an incubus upon her. She felt him fumbling and butting his way toward a secret that ached to be discovered. The unpleasant frost in his eye, where other people had a black point feeding on the light, chilled her; defensively a wild towering love for Jerry would rise up. She would give his dead body a hug, and he would stir, rotate, and fall asleep again. They slept differently; Jerry was an insomniac and slept deeply and late, Ruth fell asleep without effort and woke too early.

If there was a supreme Unitarian commandment, it was *Face things.* "Having things out" had been her father's phrase, returning post-midnight from some ecumenical, interracial scrimmage in Poughkeepsie. One empty winter afternoon, two children at school and Geoffrey asleep, the whole house ticking like a clock, the furnace heaving, the floorboards drying, the outdoors brilliant with snow, Richard appeared at the door. Seeing his old tan Mercedes from the living-room windows as she went to answer the ring, she knew who it would be. The door was stuck and the wrench it took to pull it open startled them both. Framed in the doorway, wearing a raincoat and a plaid lumberjack shirt open at the neck, he seemed a huge, woeful apparition. He had brought her a book they had discussed, the new Murdoch, as an excuse. As an excuse, it was cursorily offered; his instinct had told him he would not need much of one.

She grew used to him, as winter yielded to spring.

Under his corpulent weight, his shoulders filling her vision with soft black hairs, Ruth felt herself responding matter-of-factly to the thick, careful pounding of Richard's carnal attack. It was all matter-of-fact, controlled, satisfactory; under this alien man there was time, time in which to make the trip to the edge and fall, fall and arrive where she had begun, pressed to the earth as if safe. The earth was her bed, hers and Jerry's. The light of early afternoon opened around her. Geoffrey was having his nap at the other end of the upstairs. Curiously Ruth touched the little arc of purplish marks in the fat of Richard's shoulder, teethmarks left there, it seemed, by a third person. "I'm sorry," she said.

"Sweet pain, as they say."

He had a phrase for everything. Unwilling to test herself against his eyes, she studied his lips. There was a disturbing elderly jut to the lower one, and lovemaking had left them liquid with saliva. "It's so unlike me," she said.

His lips hardly moved when he talked. "It's part of the act. Mistresses bite. Wives don't."

"Don't." She wriggled to shift his weight, which was beginning to crush. "Don't poke fun."

His breath, sourly crested with whiskey, though he had come in the back door at noon and they had gone straight to bed, was still scattered, panting. "Poke fun, my ass," he said. "I'm drunk. I'm fucked out."

She turned her eyes down, to where the skin of their chests melted together, her breasts half-clothed in the fur that made him feel in her embrace like unevenly woolly bear. Jerry by comparison felt smooth as a snake.

Richard asked, clairvoyant, "Do I seem freaky to you?"

"I seem that way to myself."

"Why have you let me in, Ruthie babes?"

"Because you asked."

"Nobody ever asked before?"

"Not that I noticed."

Richard's heavy breath gathered for an effort; he pushed himself up from her chest; sadly she felt him receding into the perspective of their lives. "I don't know why," he said, "you and Jerry don't work in bed. You throw a great piece."

She lifted her knees and cradled him in her thighs and rocked him back and forth, a touch impatiently, as if he were a baby refusing its nap. He had been naughty to mention Jerry; it threatened to spoil it. The house shuddered, and a moment later a jet breaking the sound barrier boomed above them, in the blue that stood unbroken at the windows. On the other side of the house Geoffrey began to fret in his crib. Richard must go; she must use him while he was with her. She must learn. "Is that really a phrase?" she asked. "Throw a piece?" The words sounded so strange in her voice that she blushed, though naked.

Richard looked down; his rather boneless hand stroked her hair and his good eye tried to feed on her face, which was afraid. She brought her eyes to his; she owed him that much. "No one's ever told you," he said, stroking, "how cunty you are."

He had this conception of himself as a teacher, a teacher of worldliness. In that spring and summer of 1961, they met more often to talk than to make love. Ruth, knowing Jerry's contempt for Richard and his proud passion for himself, felt most faithless when she disclosed, not her body, which seemed hers to share, but the private terror Jerry shared only with her. "He says he sees death everywhere—in the newspapers, in the grass. He looks at the children and says they're sucking the life out of him. He says there're too many."

"Has he ever seen a psychiatrist?" Richard pinched a slice of water chestnut between his chopsticks and carried it to his mouth. They had reached the Chinese restaurant, on a brilliant July day. The curtains of the restaurant were all drawn, making a kind of amber evening out of noon.

"He despises psychiatry. He hates it if I suggest there's anything abnormal about his state. When I say *I'm* not afraid of death, he tells me I'm a spiritual cripple. He says I'm not afraid because I have no imagination. No soul, I think is what he means."

Richard sipped his Martini, his third, and rubbed his mouth with a knuckle. "I'd never appreciated how neurotic this guy is. I would have written him off as a simple manic depressive, but this death-wish sounds pretty psychotic. Has it affected his work?"

"He says he can still do it, though it takes him twice as long. A lot of what he does now is conferences and thinking up ideas for other people to execute. He never draws at home any more; I miss it. Even when everything would come back in the mail it was nice to see him work. He always drew to the radio; he said it helped loosen up the inking in."

"He never was any Al Capp, though."

"He was never trying to be."

"I like your loyalty," Richard said: there was an intense dead selfishness in Richard's tone—the note the Mathiases shared.

She looked at her plate with caught breath, suspended miles above the possibility that she was making a dreadful mistake. "Not loyal enough," she said. "Now I have the feeling that you and I have filtered into his brain and made him worse. He says I'm not there."

"Not where?"

"Not *there*. Anywhere. With him. You know."

"You mean you feel you're my woman now instead of his?"

She wished to shield Richard from how repulsive this idea and this terminology were to her. She said, "I'm not sure I'm anybody's woman. Maybe that's my trouble."

A grain of rice clung to his lower lip like a maggot. "Try to describe," he said, "this business of not being there. You mean in bed?"

"I'm better in bed. Thanks. But it doesn't seem to matter. The other night after we'd done it he woke me around three in the morning and asked me why I didn't love him. Apparently he'd been running around the house reading the Bible and looking at a horror show on television. He has these fits where he can't breathe lying down. You have some rice on your lip."

He brushed it off, with a deliberation that struck her as comic. "How long has he had trouble breathing?" he asked.

"Since before I began with you. But it hasn't gotten better. I guess I thought it would. Don't ask me why."

"So. I've been screwing you just to cure Jerry's asthma." Richard's bitter laugh was one of his less persuasive effects.

"Don't twist what I mean."

"I'm not. It's perfectly clear what you mean. You mean I'm a special type of patsy. Don't apologize. I've been Sally's patsy all these years, I might as well be yours too."

He was begging her to tell him she loved him. She couldn't form the words. She had always known she and Richard had no future; until now she hadn't realized how short their present was. His head in the amber light seemed enormous—a false, defective head put on over a real head, whose words sounded hollow. "I'm sick," she told him suddenly. "I'm not built for affairs. I've had intestinal upsets all summer and I get terribly depressed after I've seen you. He doesn't even listen to my lies. I keep wondering, if he knew, would he divorce me?"

Impatiently Richard set down his chopsticks with a click on his clean plate. "Never," he said. "He'll never divorce you, you're his mother. People don't divorce their mothers, for Chrissake." It sounded so hopeless she wanted to cry; he must have sensed this for his voice softened. "How'd you like the grub? The chow mein tasted like it came from a can."

"I thought it was all good," Ruth said resolutely.

He put his hand on hers. Their hands, it struck her, looked too much alike, his too small for his size and hers too big. "You're very tough," he said. It seemed part compliment, part farewell.

She broke it off finally in September. Jerry had frightened her by overhearing the tag end of a phone conversation with Richard. She had thought he was raking in the back yard. Emerging from the kitchen, he asked her, "Who was that?"

She panicked. "Oh, somebody. Some woman from the Sunday school asking if we were going to enroll Joanna and Charlie."

"They're becoming offensively efficient over there. What did you say?"

"I said of course."

"But I heard you saying No."

Richard had asked if she would have lunch with him next week. "She asked if we were going to send Geoffrey as well."

"Of course not," Jerry said, "he's not even three," and sat down and flipped through the Saturday paper. He always opened it first to the comics page, as if expecting to find himself there. "Somehow," he said, not looking up, "I don't believe you."

"Why not? What did you hear?"

"Nothing. It was your tone of voice."

"Really? How?" She wanted to giggle.

He stared off into space as if at an aesthetic problem. He looked tired and young and thin. His haircut was too short. "It was different," he said. "Warmer. It was a woman's voice."

"I am a woman."

"Your voice with me," he said, "is quite girlish."

She giggled and waited for him to strike deeper. But he had returned his attention to the comics page. She wanted to hug him in his ignorance. "Quite clear and cool and virginal," he added. Her impulse passed.

One day the following week she was shopping in Greenwood's little downtown. The windows were full of back-to-school clothes and Gristede's smelled keenly of apples. The air above the telephone wires seemed to have been laundered and changed. The policemen were back in long sleeves. The drugstore had taken down its awning. As she crossed to her Falcon, her arms hugging two paper bags of groceries, she saw Richard's Mercedes parked in front of the barber shop. She hesitated by the open door, where the odors of hair oil spilled onto the pavement, and saw him, sitting bulky in his lumberjack shirt in the row of waiting chairs. Her heart went out to him; she didn't want him to get a haircut. Richard saw her, put down his *True*, left his place in line, and came out.

"Want to go for a teeny ride?" The "teeny" she heard as a reproach. She had been evading him. He appeared, blinking there in the sunshine, exposed, uncertain of his next move—a phantom left stranded by a dissolved dream. How strange, it seemed to Ruth, that we can sleep with a person, and have him still be a person, no more. She pitied him and consented, settling her shopping bags into his front seat as cumbersome, rustling chaperones. The interior of his car smelled familiarly of German leather and American candy and spilled wine; great gasps of this aroma had once filled her when, making love, the obscene awkwardness and the pain of the door handle on her shoulder blade had tripped her into a climax while he was still drunkenly laboring. Richard drove out of the town's center, past the Connecticut houses tucked into deeper and more concealing blankets of green, to a nature preserve of ragged woods, on the edge of the town away from the water. "I miss you," he said.

Ruth felt forced to say, "I miss you too."

"Then what's up? What's not up, I mean. What have I done wrong?"

Here and there, Ruth noticed as they bumped down the unrepaired road that led to the pond where in winter children ice-skated, a few of the trees, the dry and the dying, were beginning to turn. "Nothing," she answered. "It's nothing I've planned, it's just things are busier, summer is over. All the little animals are going back into their burrows."

Patches of yellow scudded past the shaggy black cloud of his head. "You know," Richard said, "I could make things tough for you."

"How?"

"Tell Jerry."

"Why would you bother?"

"I want your ass."

"I don't think that would get it for you."

"I know you, Ruthie babes. I could hurt you with what I know."

"But you wouldn't. Anyway, isn't it about time you moved on, to another lady?" He had told her about the affair that had precipitated his separation from Sally; and about other affairs. Ruth had been silently offended; they sounded like common women, and Richard spoke of them slightingly.

He turned up the dirt road, two tracks in the grass, that led to the pond. There was a barrier chain; he parked. The bags of groceries on the front seat stood between them. Across the pond a single fisherman communed with his reflection. It was morning; the children who congregated here all summer were in school; she had left Geoffrey in the care of the man scraping the living-room wallpaper, promising to return in half an hour. All this went through her as she waited for Richard to make a move. He asked her, "Is there somebody else?"

"Besides Jerry? Another affair? Don't be repulsive. If you knew me at all you wouldn't even ask."

"Maybe I *don't* know you. You fight being known."

If he thought her a fighter, then she would fight. "Richard," she said, "I must ask you not to call me at the house any more. Jerry overheard a bit of your last phone call and said some very scary things."

His face, turning to favor the good eye, showed alarm; it surprised Ruth, how distinctly this pleased her. "What sort of things?"

"Nothing definite. Nothing about you. But I think he knows."

"Tell me exactly what he said."

"No. It doesn't matter. It's none of your business exactly what he said." It had become none of his business a moment ago, when he had seemed alarmed at Jerry's knowing. Had he loved her, he would have been glad, anxious to come forward and fight.

Richard fingered a cigarette from the pack in his shirt pocket. "Well." He put the cigarette, a bit bent, into his mouth, lit it, and exhaled toward the car roof an extensive upward steam. His lower lip jutted like the lip of a spout. He was hollow. She felt him searching himself for a response that would not embarrass him. "Want to thank me," he asked at last, "for a very nice ride?"

"Don't you think it's best?"

The distant fisherman twitched his pole and birds in the trees around them released a shower of commentary. The grocery bags by her elbow rustled—the ice cream melting, the cans of frozen orange juice thawing. Affairs, Ruth saw, like everything else, ask too much. We all want a fancy price, just for existing. In the corner of her abstracted vision, Richard lunged; she flinched, expecting to be hit. He angrily, mock-decisively stubbed out his cigarette in the dashboard ashtray.

"Come on, Ruth babes," he sighed. "This isn't us. Let's take a walk. Don't look like that, I won't strangle you." He did have a clairvoyant streak; the thought had crossed her mind.

Afterwards she would remember how they walked down a buggy little path through swarms of midges revolving upon themselves in patches of sunlight. Hidden by some swamp maples from the fisherman, they kissed. Her feet grew cold as her tennis sneakers absorbed dampness from the turf. His bulk above her felt like some strange warm tree she was hugging because she was "it" at hide-and-seek. Out of doors, in nature, the queerness of being kissed was clarified; it was something done to her, like the shampoos her mother used to give her at the kitchen sink with its long brass faucet, or like the boy at Gristede's pressing, a half-hour ago, her change into her hand. Richard's hands, rather sadly, stayed on the small of her back, not cupping her bottom as was his habit. "Please forgive me," she said.

"We'll never sleep together again? This is quitsies?"

She had to laugh at his phrasing, before pleading, "Let me go. I'm losing weight."

He squeezed her waist testingly. "Still lots left."

They must have talked more, but what else they said remained hidden from Ruth behind the vibrating veils of midges, the chill in her feet, the image of the fisherman presiding above their parting from the far shore, his pole and its reflection like the two sides of a precarious arch. Though some idle mornings she wished for the phone to ring, she was grateful to Richard for taking her at her word, and for continuing to lurch up to her at parties as if she still had a secret to give him. On the whole she was well satisfied with her affair, and as she zipped up the children's snowsuits, or closed a roast into the oven, thought of this adventure snug in her past with some complacence. She judged herself improved and deepened in about the normal amount—she had dared danger and carried wisdom away, a more complete and tolerant woman. She had had boyfriends, a husband, a lover; it seemed she could rest.

She had not quite intended Jerry never to know. She had done it, her conviction grew in retrospect, less for herself than for him; her surrender to another man came to seem a kind of martyrdom, a martyrdom without an audience. While the affair was on she had pictured Jerry's knowing as a thunderbolt, a burst of noise and revealing light, a cleansing destruction. Instead, her marriage had stood with the stupid solidity of an unattended church, and when she returned to it—guiltily scrubbing the floors, recovering the sofa with blue sailcloth, cooking with a newly bought rack of spices, studying the children's school papers as if each were a fragment of Gospel—Jerry gave no sign of noticing she had been gone. Awareness of Richard, physical memory of him and physical anticipation of their next meeting, had filled every vein; trembling and transparent and brimming she had stood before the mirror of their marriage and was given back—nothing. The sensation was familiar. Her father had been absorbed by love of his fellow-man, and her mother by love for her father, and Ruth had grown up with the suspicion of being overlooked. She was a Unitarian, and what did this mean, except that her soul was one unit removed from not being there at all?

Her invisible restoration to fidelity was achieved in a world of evolving forms. Charlie entered the first grade of the Greenwood elementary school; Joanna became a broad-browed, confident third-grader. This child would never be embarrassed by womanhood; the full brunt of her parents' art-school love had fallen upon her, their first creation in flesh. Gradually Ruth regained the weight she had lost to a nervous stomach during the summer. Winter like a bandage was applied to the flaming fall. That year, the first of Kennedy's presidency, the rivers and ponds froze early and black-smooth for beautiful skating. Skating, Ruth flew and, flying, she was free. She drove cars too fast, and drank too much, and skated upriver away from Jerry and the children—darting, swooping strides, between hushed walls of thin silver trees. This will to fly had come upon her since her failure with Richard—for it was a failure, any romance that does not end in marriage fails.

And Jerry's religious crisis ebbed. By spring his shelf of theology stood neglected, scraps of torn paper marking where he had read enough in each volume. Dread had left him unchastened. He became crazy about the Twist, and at parties his contorted, rapt, perspiring figure seemed that of a mysterious son in whom she could take only an apprehensive pride, his energy so excessive. He gave up smoking, and took to buying popular records, which he would play to himself until he could mouth the words in unison: "Born to lose, I've lived my life in vain . . ." It was grotesque and would have been pitiful, in a man of thirty, if he did not seem, in a frantic way, happy. A quality she remembered from their courtship, a skittering heedless momentum, had returned to him; she could not remember when she had last thought him handsome, but now an edge of good looks cut her when he turned. His color seemed higher, his green eyes foxy. His paralysis and fear had made her feel so helpless and guilty, she rejoiced in this renewal of his liveliness, though it bore toward her a glitter of hostility, of unpredictability. Hanging up his suit pants while he was having an evening game of catch with the children in the yard, she was surprised by the gentle, semi-musical patter of sand on the floor. It had fallen from his cuffs. Oh yes,

he explained after supper, he had stopped off at the
beach, not the Greenwood beach but the one with the
Indian name, the other day when it was so warm, swung
by on the way back from the station, having caught the
earlier train. Why? Why, because it was a lovely May
day—did there have to be another reason? What was she,
a wife or a warden? Feeling the need to taste salt air, he
had walked along the water and sat on a dune for a
minute, there was hardly anybody else there, just a little
sailboat in the Sound. It had been very beautiful.

"The children might have enjoyed going with you."

"You have all afternoon to take them."

As he looked at her, his eyes very green in their bold-
ness and his expression rakishly accented by a tiny cut
on the bridge of his nose, the reason for his insolence
came to her: he knew. He had learned. How? Richard
must have gossipped. Did everybody know? Let them.
Jerry was the one that mattered, and that he knew without releasing a thunderbolt was a relief. All evening, as
the children and the dishes and Jerry's face rotated, she
composed confessions and explanations in her head.
What was the explanation? The best she could say was
she had done it to become a better woman and therefore
a better wife. And the affair had been kept under control.
And had made rather little impression on her. These
truths, and the prospect of speaking them, frightened her,
and she fell asleep to escape the fright, while Jerry rattled
the pages of *Art News* and said nothing. Again, the
mirror had looked through her.

Outside their bedroom windows, beside the road, stood
a giant elm, one of the few surviving in Greenwood.
New leaves were curled in the moment after the bud un-
folds, their color sallow, a dusting, a veil not yet dense
enough to conceal the anatomy of branches. The branches
were sinuous, stately, constant: an inexhaustible comfort

to her eyes. Of all things accessible to Ruth's vision the elm most nearly persuaded her of a cosmic benevolence. If asked to picture God, she would have pictured this tree. On the breadth of the lower crotches pigeons walked like citizens on the floor of a cathedral; in the open air above the road vinelike twigs hung down, languidly greedy, drinking the light, idle as fingers trailed from a canoe. Ruth realized it would not be such a drastic thing, to die. She lay beneath a quilted puff, hoping to have a nap.

Energetic footsteps marched through the downstairs, searching, and came upstairs. Uninvited, Jerry got under her puff. She hoped, guessing it was too much to hope, that he wouldn't try to make love. He laid his arm across her waist and asked, "Are you happy?"

"I don't know."

"Are you tired?"

"Yes."

"Let's go to sleep."

"You didn't come up to pester me?"

"Never. I came up because you're so sad lately."

The wandering curves of the tree, solid as rock and random as wind, seemed far away, like a whispered word. "I'm not sad," she said.

Jerry snuggled deeper under the puff and rested his open mouth on her naked shoulder. When he talked, his tongue fluttered. "Tell me who you like," he said.

"I like you," she said, "and all the pigeons in that tree, and all the dogs in town except the ones that tip over our garbage cans, and all the cats except the one that got Lulu pregnant. And I like the lifeguards at the beach, and the policemen downtown except the one who bawled me out for my U-turn, and I like some of our awful friends, especially when I'm drunk . . ."

"How do you like Dick Mathias?"

"I don't mind him."

"I know you don't. I think that's fascinating of you. He's such a fathead. Literally. His head is literally fat. And that eye. Doesn't it give you the creeps?"

Ruth felt she owed it to her dignity, to the dignity of her secret, not to say anything, to let Jerry name it. Insulated by depression, she waited. He raised himself up on one elbow; she closed her eyes and pictured a knife in his hand. Hot weather brought on pain in her legs since she had carried Geoffrey. Jerry's presence intensified the pain. She took a deep breath.

What he said was nothing like what she expected, though it seemed to be the point of the conversation. "How do you feel about Sally? Tell me about Sally."

Ruth laughed, as if touched in an unguarded place. "Sally?"

"Do you love her?"

She laughed again. "Of course not."

"Do you like her?"

"Not much."

"Baby, you must at least *like* her. She likes you."

"I don't think she likes me especially. I mean, she likes me as one more local female she can outshine—"

"She doesn't outshine you. She doesn't think she does. She thinks you're beautiful."

"Don't be silly. I'm O.K., if the light's right and I'm feeling undepressed. But she's almost great."

"Tell me about the 'almost.' I agree. She's spectacular, but something misses. What is it?"

Ruth found it difficult to focus on Sally, who kept blurring into the conjoined image of Richard. The affair, she realized, had empowered her to dismiss his wife, though when they first came to Greenwood she had been struck by her—her blond hair hanging down her wide back, her mannish walk and startled stare, her eager grin crimped at one corner. "I don't think," Ruth said, "Sally's ever been very happy. She and Dick aren't right for each other, in all ways. They have the public things, but maybe aren't supportive"—she wanted to go on, "like we are," but shyness held her back.

Jerry was off on his favorite tangent. "Well my God, who *would* be right for Richard? He's a monster."

"He's not. And you know it. Lots of women would be right for him. A lazy sexy woman who wasn't ambitious—"

"Sally's ambitious?"

"Very."

"For what?"

"For whatever she can get. For life. Just like you."

"And yet not sexy?"

Ruth remembered Richard on the subject of Sally. In answering Jerry she must not sound like him. "My impression is," she said, "she's not very warm or compassionate. She doesn't let herself feel anything to the point where it would depress her. But I wouldn't know how her sex is. What *is* this burst of interest, anyway?"

"Nothing," he said. "Love of one's neighbor, that's all." He wormed closer to her, snuggling deeper under the puff, so that only the top of his head showed; his hair contained a sudden amount of gray. He began, a trick of his, to purr; a vibration deep in his throat reached her ears. It was a signal for her to turn to him, if she wished; she stayed on her back, though he had chased all sleepiness from her and all sacred magic from the elm. "It seems to me," his voice ventured from beneath the puff, "you and Sally have more in common than you think. Have *you* ever been very happy either?"

"Of course I have. I'm happy most of the time, that's my trouble. Everybody expects me to be calm and contented and, damn it, I am. I don't know what my trouble is today."

"You think you're pregnant?" He accused: "You've been seeing the same tomcat Lulu has."

"I *know* I'm not."

"Then that's it. You have the curse."

"I do feel," she volunteered, "pro*tec*tive of Sally now and then, really quite fond. She *is* shallow and selfish and I know if I ever got in her way she'd walk right over me, but then there's something generous about all her showing-off, something she's trying to give the world. Up at skiing, when she puts on that ridiculous tasselled hat and starts to flirt with the ski instructor, I have moments of just wanting to *hug* her, she's making such a sweet fool of herself. And the time we went musselling, she seemed lovely. But I *don't* feel this fondness when you and she are doing the Twist together, if that's what you're asking."

He had begun to nibble her breast through her slip and after his imitation of a cat it felt uncomfortably close to being eaten. She pushed him off and took the puff away from his face and asked, *"Is* that what you're asking?"

He hid his face against her shoulder, his big nose cold, and shut his eyes. He seemed about to take the nap he had robbed her of. A broadening smile tickled the skin of her arm. "I love you," he sighed. "You see everything so clearly."

Later she wondered how she could have been so blind, and blind so long. The signs were abundant: the sand, his eccentric comings and goings, his giving up smoking, his triumphant exuberance whenever Sally was at the same party, the tender wifely touch (this glimpse had stung at the time, to endure in Ruth's memory) with which Sally on one occasion had picked up Jerry's wrist, inviting him to dance. Jerry's obsession with death the spring before had seemed to her so irrational, so unreachable, that she dismissed as also mysterious his new behavior: his new timbre and strut, his fits of ill temper with the children, his fits of affection with her, the hungry introspective tone he brought to their private conversations, his insomnia, the easing of his physical demands on her, and a new cool authority in bed, so that at moments it seemed she was with Richard again. How could she have been so blind? At first she thought that, having gazed so long at her own guilt, she mistook for an afterimage what was in truth a fresh development. She admitted to herself, then, what she could never admit to Jerry, that she did not think him capable of it.

Jerry asked for a divorce on a Sunday, the Sunday after a week in which he had been two days in Washington, and had returned to her in an atmosphere of hazard, on a late flight. There had been a delay, the airlines were jammed-up, and she met plane after plane at LaGuardia. When at last his familiar silhouette with its short hair and thin shoulders cut through the muddled lights of the landing field and hurried toward her, her heart surprised her with a grovelling gladness. Had she been a dog, she would have jumped and licked his face; being only a wife, she let herself be kissed, led him to the car, and listened as he described his trip—the State Department, a hurried visit to the Vermeers in the National Gallery, his relative lack of insomnia in the hotel, the inadequate gifts for the children he bought at a drugstore, the maddening wait in the airport. As the city confusion diminished behind them, his talking profile, in the warm vault of the car, shed its halo of wonder for her, and by the time they crackled to a stop in their driveway, both felt tired; they had chicken soup and bourbon and fumbled into a cold bed. Yet afterward this homecoming of his was to seem enchanted, a last glimpse of solid headland before, that rainy Sunday afternoon, she embarked on the nightmare sea that became her habitat.

In the morning, she and the children went to the beach. Jerry wanted to go to church. The summer services began at nine-thirty and ended at ten-thirty. She did not think it fair to the children to make them wait that long, especially since the pattern of the summer days was to dawn clear and cloud over by noon. So they dropped him off in his good suit and drove on.

The clouds materialized earlier than usual; little upright puffs at first, like puffs of smoke from a locomotive starting its run around the horizon, then clouds, increasingly structural and opaque, castles, continents that, overhead, grew as they moved, keeping the sun behind them. Waiting for the gaps of sunshine between the clouds was a game for the beach mothers. The clouds blew eastward, so their eyes scouted the west, where a swathe of advancing gold would first ignite the roofs of the cottages on Jacob's Point; then the great green watertower that supplied the cottages would be liberated into light, and like an arrived Martian spaceship the egg of metal on its stilts would glow; then like an onrushing field of unearthly wheat the brightness would roll, in steady jerks like strides, up the mile of sand, and overhead the sun would burn free of the struggling tendrils at the cloud's edge and skyey loops of iridescence would be spun between the eyelashes of the mothers. On this Sunday morning the gaps between the clouds closed more quickly than usual and by eleven-thirty it was clearly going to rain. Ruth and the children went home. They found Jerry sitting in the living room reading the Sunday paper. He had taken off his suit coat and loosened the knot of his tie, but his hair, still combed flat with water, made him look odd to Ruth. He seemed distracted, brittle, hostile; he acted as if they personally had consumed the few hours of beach weather there would be that day. But often he was irritable after attending church.

She took the roast out of the oven and all except Jerry ate Sunday dinner in bathing suits. This was the one meal of the week for which Jerry asked grace. As he began, "Heavenly Father," Geoffrey, who was being taught bedtime prayers, said aloud, "Dear God . . ." Joanna and

Charlie burst into giggling. Jerry hurried his blessing through the interference, and Geoffrey, eyes tight shut, fat hands clasped at his plate, tried to repeat it after him and, unable, whimpered, "I can't *say* it!"

"*Amen,*" Jerry said and, with stiff fingers, slapped Geoffrey on the top of his head. "Shut *up*." Earlier that week the boy had broken his collarbone. His shoulders were pulled back by an Ace bandage; he was tender all over.

Swallowing a sob, Geoffrey protested, "You said it too *fast!*"

Joanna explained to him, "You're stupid. You think you're supposed to say grace after Daddy."

Charlie turned and a gleeful taunting sound, "K-k-k," scraped from the roof of his mouth.

The insults were coming too fast for Geoffrey to absorb; he overflowed. His face blurred and crumpled into tears.

"Jerry, I'm amazed," Ruth said. "That was a sick thing to do."

Jerry picked up his fork and threw it at her—not at her, over her head, through the doorway into the kitchen. Joanna and Charlie peeked at each other and their cheeks puffed out in identical smothered explosions. "Goddamn it all," Jerry said, "I'd rather say grace in a pigpen. You all sitting here stark naked."

"The child was trying to be good," Ruth said. "He doesn't understand the difference between grace and prayers."

"Then why the fuck don't you teach him? If he had any decent even half-ass Christian kind of a mother he'd know enough not to interrupt. *Geoffrey,*" Jerry turned to say, "you *must* stop crying, to make your collarbone stop hurting."

Stunned by his father's unremittingly angry tone, the child tried to enunciate a sentence: "I—I—I—"

"I—I—I—" Joanna mocked.

Geoffrey screamed as if stabbed.

Jerry stood and tried to reach Joanna to slap her. She shied away, upsetting her chair. Something about her expression of terror made Jerry laugh. As if this callous laugh released all the malign spirits at the table, Charlie turned, said "Crybaby," and punched Geoffrey in the arm, jarring his collarbone. Before the child could react, his mother screamed for him; Charlie shouted, "I forgot, I forgot!" Wild to stop this torrent of injury at its source, Ruth, still holding the serving spoon, left her place and moved around the table, so swiftly she felt she was skating. She swung the hand not holding the spoon at Jerry's face. He saw it coming and hid his face between his shoulders and hands, showing her the blank hairy top of his skull, with its helpless amount of gray. His skull was harder than her hand; she jammed her thumb; pain pressed behind her eyes. Blindly she flailed, again and once again, at the obstinate lump of his cowering head, unable with one hand, while the other still clutched the serving spoon, to claw her way into his eyes, his poisonous mouth. The fourth time she swung, he stood up and caught her wrist in mid-air and squeezed it so hard the fine bones ground together.

"You pathetic frigid bitch," he said levelly. "Don't touch me again." He gave each word an equal weight, and his face, uncovered at last, showed a deadly level calm, though flushed—the face of a corpse, rouged. The nightmare had begun.

The two older children had fallen silent. Geoffrey's crying flowed on and on, mercilessly. The double loop of elastic bandage held his naked shoulders back in such a way that his plump arms had an apish defenseless hang. Jerry sat down and took Geoffrey's hand. "You were a good boy," he said, "to want to say grace with me. But only one person at a time can say grace. Maybe this week I'll teach you a grace and you can say it instead of Daddy next Sunday. O.K.?"

"O—O—O—" the child tried to agree, still sobbing.

"O—O—O—" Joanna whispered to Charlie, who sputtered, glanced sideways at Ruth, and sputtered again.

Jerry told Geoffrey, "You're a good boy. Now stop crying, and eat your lima beans. Children, isn't Mommy good to cook us such nice lima beans? Now Daddy will carve the nice roast. Where's the Goddamn carving fork? I apologize to everybody. Geoffrey, do shut up."

But Geoffrey could not quite quit shuddering; the events of the last minutes kept recurring in his head. Ruth discovered she too was trembling, and tongue-tied. Unable to join in as Jerry joked the children into good humor, into loving him, she felt excluded. In the kitchen, washing the dishes, she cried. Through windowpanes beginning to register the first broken dashes of rain, she watched Joanna and Charlie and two neighbor children kick and chase a great green ball under a deep violet sky. She had put Geoffrey down for a nap upstairs. Jerry came into the kitchen, picked up the fork from the floor, and, silent at her side, picked up a towel and began to dry. It had been she didn't know how many months since he had offered to help with the dishes. His offering now, so gravely, felt menacing, and aggravated her tears.

He asked, "What's the matter, exactly?"

Her throat felt too sore to speak.

"I'm sorry," he said, "about that fit. I'm all upset these days."

"What about?"

"Oh—a variety of things. Dying? I've stopped thinking about it and started doing it. Look at my hair."

"It's nice. You're getting handsome."

"At last, huh? And the job. The less I draw, the more they love me. They like me to talk. I've become Al's front man."

"You could quit."

"With all these kids?"

"Don't dry those. Let's let the rest sit in the drainer."

"Should the kids be out in the rain?"

"It's not raining that hard yet."

"I thought I'd take them bowling when it does."

"They'd love that."

"*Get*ting handsome. What made you marry such an ugly duckling?"

"Is it really the job that's bothering you?"

"No."

"What is?"

"Should we really talk about it?"

"Why not?" she asked.

"I'm afraid. Once we start talking, we may never be able to stop."

"Come on. Sock it to me."

Confronted with this command, his face took on a rapture; she had this sense, through the blur of her tears, of his body expanding in release, of gathering mass out of nothing, like the clouds at the beach. "Walk with me," he said, and led her out of the kitchen, into the living room, past the huge old fireplace, to the front windows, which looked up at the elm. On the edge where the sashes met rested a small brown stack of pennies, an orange bead from an Indian necklace Joanna had been making in school, a tarnished brass key to something it would never unlock again—a suitcase, a trunk, a child's bank. Jerry kept toying with these objects during their talk, as if trying to extract from them an inevitable order, a final arrangement. "Does it ever seem possible to you," he asked, in the voice of dogged precision he used for reading aloud to the children, "that we made a mistake?"

"When?"

"When we got married."

"Weren't we in love?"

"Is that what it was?"

"I thought so."

"I thought so too." He waited.

She answered him, "Yes, it has seemed possible to me."

"But doesn't now."

"It didn't, no. I thought we've been getting better."

"In bed?"

"Isn't that what we're talking about?"

"Part of it. Ruth, are you ever tempted to quit while we're ahead?"

"Jerry, what are you saying to me?"

"Baby, I'm just asking you if we aren't making a terrible mistake in staying married forever."

Breath left her; she felt the skin of her face as one wall of a sealed chamber bounded by the brown ledge holding the pennies, the low violet clouds against which the elm's twigs showed pale, the rectangle of glass slashed by raindrops. Jerry's voice called, "Hey?"

"What?"

"Don't be upset," he said. "It's just a suggestion. An idea."

"That you leave me?"

"That we leave each other. You could go back to the city and be an artist again. You haven't painted for years. It's a waste."

"What about the children?"

"I've been thinking, couldn't we divide them up somehow? They could see each other and us all they wanted and it really wouldn't be so bad if we both wanted it."

"What is this we're both supposed to want?"

"What we're talking about. You could paint and go barefoot and be a Bohemian again."

"A middle-aged Bohemian with wrinkles and varicose veins and a belly that sticks out."

"Don't be silly. You're young. You're better-looking now than when I first met you."

"Aren't you nice to say so?"

"You could take Charlie. The boys should be separated, and I'd need Joanna to help me keep house."

"They need each other, and I need them. All of them. And we all need you."

"Don't *say* that. You *don't* need me. *You* don't. I'm not giving you enough of a life, I'm not the *man* for you. I never was. I was just an amusing fellow-student. You need another man. You need to get out of Greenwood." She hated it when his voice got high in pitch.

"So you'd take the town, too. You'd stick me in a loft and keep the house for yourself. No thanks. You work in town, you live in town."

"Don't try to be tough. You're not tough. You're not even listening. Don't you want to be free? Ask yourself honestly. I look at you boring yourself stupid around this house and feel I caught a bird in art school and put her in a cage. All I'm saying is, the door is open."

"You're not saying that. You're saying you want me out."

"I'm *not*. I'm saying I want you to live. It's too easy for both of us. We're protecting each other from living."

"You don't say. What is it, Jerry? What's the *real* reason behind all this? Am I *so* bad suddenly?"

"You're not bad. You're good." He touched her arm. "You're great."

She flinched from his touch; she still wanted to hit him. This time he interposed no obstacle. Her blow, guilty in flight, fell on the side of his head weakly. The tears burned back into her voice. "How *dare* you say that of me! Get *out*! Get out now!"

The rain had intensified and the children, theirs and the two Cantinellis, crowded in from outdoors. "I'll take them bowling," Jerry volunteered. He seemed pleased she had struck him; he became all efficiency, telling her rapidly, "Listen. We won't talk any more. Don't think about any of this. Get a sitter for tonight and I'll take you out to dinner at the seafood place. Please don't cry or worry." He turned to the children and called, "*Whooo* wants to go bowling?"

Their chorus of "me"s battered at her. Behind her, rain tapped sharply at the cold panes. Jerry seemed to exult in her helplessness; "Joanna and Charlie, Rose and Frankie," he shouted, "get into the *car*." He helped young Frankie, who was between Charlie and Geoffrey in age, back into his sneakers. It was as if she were already gone, and Jerry had the children and the house. She felt her head tearing before she connected it with an external sound: Geoffrey had come downstairs, still clutching his blanket, crying. He wanted to go too.

"Sweetie," Ruth said, and her voice hurt her throat, "you can't. You have a broken collarbone and can't throw the ball."

His sob slammed her eyelids shut; the other children, one by one, banged the screen door going out, until she had counted four. "You can't go, you *can't*," Jerry was saying, inside her head; an acoustic strangeness opened her eyes. He had knelt on the floor and was holding the child tight against him. "My angel boy, my poor little angel boy," he was saying. His face above Geoffrey's shoulder was contorted by what seemed to Ruth exaggerated grief. He tried to stand upright, cradling the child like an infant. Insulted, pained, Geoffrey writhed free and clumped to Ruth; the tears on his cheeks wet her thighs. She was wearing the old black one-piece bathing suit from Bloomingdale's; because she thought it had made her breasts too pointy, she had years ago removed the wire from the bra.

Jerry, smiling, brushed the spaces around his eyes. "God, this is awful," he said cheerfully, gave her a peck of a kiss, and left her in the house with the sound of the downpour.

The medium in which Ruth sank seemed to be something other than space, for the furniture continued to float on the wide pine boards, the inverted blur in the side table silently upheld the empty flower vase, and the books in the bookcase maintained against all her doubts

of her own existence the certain fortress of their own, a
compacted solidity more sickening than a city's, for each
book was a city, if opened. Geoffrey, placed on the sailcloth sofa with a slippery stack of children's books,
fretted and puzzled and fumbled himself back to sleep.
Crooked and heavy he lay in his sad little shoulder truss,
one fat square hand twisted so the palm lay up; it looked
all thumbs, like a Picasso hand. She straightened his
body; he winced without waking. Then the rain talked to
her, talked in a metallic tapping voice near the windows,
in a softer voice as she moved to the center of the room,
in no voice at all when she covered her face with her
hands. Each passing car made a comet-shaped swish and
splash on the road. Upstairs in the bathroom, the windows were misted, and the rain-gutter at the eaves,
dammed with maple wings and seedlings, joked at her,
gurgling, burlesquing the fall of her urine into the oval
of water beneath her. As she moved about making beds,
the rain whispered attic secrets—mice, shingles, dry
wrapping paper, Christmas excelsior. She thought of her
parents' house in Vermont, of the pine woods, of the
soft lane that was a double path of dirt between black-
berry bushes, of the blackberries' scratching, of the hidden
pebble that would bite her bare foot, of the baggy pants
her father put on day after day all summer, of the pantry
her mother kept there, so impeccably and thriftily stocked
she and her sister never hungered, and never overate.
Ruth thought of turning to her parents now and they
vanished in her mind. *Face things.* They had overlooked
her, it would take too much explaining, for them to see
her now. She went downstairs, poured a tumbler of
vermouth, and took it to the piano. Lacking time to
paint, she had lately rediscovered satisfaction in her
clumsy access to Bach. The gentle liquor and her spread-
ing hands found a green floor from which music rose in
chords; her heart moved upward in the arabesque cur-
rents, and her ankles ached from pedalling. By the time

Jerry and the children loudly returned from bowling, she had reached, skipping all the pieces with more than four sharps or flats, the middle of her *Well-Tempered Clavier*; when she stood to welcome them, she lurched backwards against the bench, as if the motion of music, continuing, had pushed the room against her halted body. The vermouth bottle was half empty. Jerry stepped forward with an expression of wonder and conceit and touched her cheeks; there was water on them.

"You're still in your bathing suit," he said.

His returning, his opening the door, drained the house of the liquid sounds she had conjured to keep herself company. Geoffrey awoke in pain; the children scraped around her. She made them supper, and called their favorite baby-sitter, Mrs. O, O for O'Brien, a heavyset widow with a bosom like a bolster and the tranquil triangular face of a dutiful child. She lived down the road with her ancient, undying mother. Ruth took a bath and dressed to go out. She rejected the staid colors in her closet and chose a yellow dress she had bought the summer after Geoffrey's birth, to celebrate her return to normal size. The dress afterwards seemed too young for her, too decolleté. Not now, she had nothing to lose. She even dabbed at herself with perfume. Turning from her bureau, she saw Jerry standing before his closet in his underwear, one hand on his hip and the other scratching his head as he too pondered what to put on for this undefined occasion. She saw him, in this rare moment, as beautiful, a statue out of reach, not a furiously beautiful Renaissance David but a medieval Adam, naked on a tympanum, his head bent to fit the triangular space, the bones of his body expressing innocence and alarm. Awkward and transparent—a Christian body, she supposed.

The seafood place Jerry liked was a restaurant in the old heart of town, near some rotting docks, a made-over captain's house whose several little dining rooms had each a fireplace; in this season the ashes had been swept out and sprays of peonies had been arranged between the andirons. The tablecloths were red-checkered and small low candle-lamps illuminated the diners' faces as in a de La Tour. Jerry hedged and gossiped through the gin-and-tonics; she let him. Their clam chowder arrived; his voice changed timbre, going graver, softer. "That's a nice dress," he said. "Why don't you wear it more often?"

"I bought it too soon after Geoffrey. It's too big in the waist."

"Poor Geoffrey."

"He can't understand about his collar-bone."

"Of the three, he seems least like us. Why is that?"

"He's a younger sibling. You were an only child, and I was an older sister. Are you ready to tell me?"

"Are you ready to hear it?"

"Oh, sure."

"Well, I think I'm in love."

"Who's the lucky girl?"

"You must know. You must have guessed."

"Maybe. But tell me."

He wanted to, but couldn't say it; Jerry lowered his eyes, and sipped soup. This couldn't be serious.

Ruth said playfully, "If I guess wrong, you'll think I'm rude."

He said, "It's Sally."

When she failed to respond, he asked urgently, "Who else could it be?"

A fly alighted on her lips and its tingling imposition startled her; she saw herself as she was to the fly—a living mountain, a volcano breathing the stench of shell-fish.

"That's who it would be, isn't it?" she responded, wanting to be delicate, to share with Jerry his justifying faith that Sally was the obvious, the inevitable woman.

"I've always liked Sally," he pleaded.

"And how does she feel toward you?"

"Loves me."

"You're sure of that?"

"I'm afraid I am, Ruth."

"Have you been to bed with her?"

"Well of course."

"Pardon *me*. Often?"

"A couple dozen times."

"A couple dozen! When?"

Her surprise, at last, at something, reassured him. He dared smile at her. "Does it matter?"

"Of course it matters. It's not real to me yet."

"Ruth, I'm in love with her. It's not something to gossip about. We meet here and there. At beaches. Her house. In the city once in a while. This spring she was with me in Washington."

It was becoming real. "Oh God, Jerry. Washington?"

"Don't. Don't make me feel it was wrong to tell you. I couldn't bear to keep on with your not knowing."

"And last week? When you came back late and I met you at LaGuardia, was she with you then? Was she on the plane? She was."

"No. No more. I'm in love with Sally. That's all you need to know. Sally Mathias. Just saying her name makes me happy."

"Was she with you on that airplane I met?"

"Ruth, that's not the point."

"Tell me."

"O.K. Yes. She was. She was."

She smiled now. "All right then. Don't make such a thing of it. When you came up and kissed me and seemed so happy to see me, you had just come from her. You had just kissed her good-bye in the plane."

"I don't think I even kissed her, I was in such a panic. I *was* happy to see you, strange to say."

"Strange to say."

"I hadn't wanted her to come this time, she just came

on her own. I had to call the hotel and lie, I had to leave the State Department in a hurry, it was really quite inconvenient. Then the planes back didn't take off, or rather they kept taking off without us in them. Richard thought she was in town for the night. She had called up and said her Saab had broken down. The lies from her that idiot swallows are fantastic."

"Richard doesn't know?"

"I don't think so." Jerry stared at her, discovering an ally, a consultant. "I'm sure not. Why would he know and not do anything?"

The waitress took away their chowder bowls and gave Ruth her broiled scallops, Jerry his fried sole. Ruth was surprised to discover herself able, even eager, to eat. Perhaps she believed that eating as if things were normal made them normal. Jerry's news felt like an enemy that had broken through the lines but had not had time to occupy more than a small sector of her yet.

"Maybe I should talk to Richard," she offered, "and get his reaction."

"Maybe you shouldn't. If you tell him, and he divorces her because of me, I'd be obliged to marry her, wouldn't you say?"

She looked at him, his features gaunt and glittering in the candlelight, and realized he was enjoying this. Not for a long time had they gone out, just the two of them, to dinner, and in its air of danger, of searching each other out, it was like a tryst, and exciting. Ruth was pleased that she could manage her end of this adventure; the loss of a sector of herself had liberated the rest into a new mobility.

"I wouldn't say," she said. "Maybe he wouldn't divorce her. He's had affairs, and probably she has. Maybe they've agreed to let this be a part of their marriage."

He ignored her certainty that Richard had had affairs. He could talk only of Sally. "She *has* slept with other men before, but she hasn't been in love before."

"Who has she slept with?"

"Guys. During their separation. I've never asked her if she's slept with anybody I know around here. Isn't that odd? I guess I'm afraid to know."

"You should ask her."

"I'll manage my own conversations with Sally, thank you."

Ruth asked, "Do you want a confession from me?"

"Confession of what?"

"Don't look down your nose that way. I'm sure I can't equal your gorgeous romantic affair. But I had one too."

"You did? Ruth, that's wonderful! Who with?"

She had intended to tell him, but knew now he would laugh. His contempt for Richard washed over her, and she blushed. "I won't tell you. It happened a while ago, and I ended it when I realized I loved you and not the man. There was never any question of his loving me."

"You sure?"

"Pretty sure."

"This man wouldn't come for you, if you were divorced?"

"Absolutely not." This may have been the truth, but her blood raced as if it were a lie.

"Why won't you tell me his name?"

"You might use it against me."

"What if I promise I won't?"

"What does a promise to me mean if you're in love with another woman?"

He paused to chew and swallow. "You women certainly see this as war, don't you?"

"How do you see it?"

"I see it as a mess. I love the children, and did love you. I suppose in ways I still do. This man—was the sex good with him?"

"Not bad."

Jerry grunted, comically. "There's a blow Better than with me?"

"It was different. He was my lover, Jerry. to be a husband than a lover."

"He *was* better, then. Shit. People are surprising, aren't they? You're surprising. I wish you weren't. It confuses me."

She measured the space between them, to judge if the time were ripe to touch his hand. She judged not yet. "Don't *let* it confuse you," she said. "It was a silly little affair, and I'm glad it's over. I was unhappy at the time, and I'm still grateful to the man, so don't ask me to betray him. It doesn't affect you and Sally."

"But it does. It makes me jealous. Why won't you tell me the man?"

"If I did, maybe you wouldn't be jealous."

He laughed admiringly. "It was Skip, wasn't it?"

"No."

"Then it must have been David."

"I won't play guessing games."

"It was David. That's why you're so hostile to Harriet. It was."

"I won't tell you now. Maybe later. I need to think about it. I told you I had an affair because I got over it. You *do* get over them, Jerry. It's great, it's exquisite, it's the nicest thing there is, but it doesn't last, and in fairness to Sally—forget about me if it makes it easier—in fairness to Sally and your children and her children and even Richard, you should give it time."

"It's *had* time. It began early this spring, and before that there were years when I loved her. I didn't have to screw her to love her. Though it helped. Ruth, listen. Don't try to shrug this woman off. She's not stupid, and she's not unkind. She's never said anything unkind about you; she's very worried about you. When it showed that we were getting in too deep, she tried to break it off, but wouldn't let her. It's been me, not her, who's insisted. She's mine. She belongs to me in a way you never have. I can hardly describe it, but when I'm with her, I'm on top. When I'm with you, it's side by side." He illustrated "side by side" with two long fingers in the air.

Why must he put her through this? Why didn't he just go? Why must he try to force her to tell him to go? She refused. Her silence refused him. Act like a man, be a man then. Face things.

"Would you folks like some coffee and dessert?"

Ruth wondered how long the waitress had been standing there. A stringy woman leaning as if to minimize pain in her feet, she looked down upon them like a bored mother. Nothing about their conversation had been exceptional, her stance implied.

"Just coffee, please," Jerry said, and took his napkin from his lap and folded it by his glass with a strange affectionate legerity; he was unburdened. In the burden he had shifted to her, certain awkward points protruded.

"She came to Washington the second time without your asking her?"

"Yep." His face betrayed how much he had been flattered. "I begged her not to. For her own safety."

"That bitch."

Now he looked alert, hopeful. "Why say that?"

"She is a bitch. I've always thought so. No other woman would pursue you that way when you have three children."

"It wasn't pursuit, somehow. It was flight. She's not a bitch, sweetie, she's a good woman who doesn't understand why she has to be unhappy. She's like you. In many ways she's very like you."

"Thanks. I suppose in your mind that's a compliment."

"If it is, accept it, is my advice."

"I'm going to talk to her."

"Christ, why?" Jerry shifted his napkin from one side of his plate to the other. "What will you say?"

"No idea. I'll think of something."

"There's nothing you can tell Sally she hasn't told herself already."

"Then it might please her to hear somebody else say it."

"Listen, you. I'll protect that woman. If I have to marry her to do it, I will. Is that what you want to bring about?"

"I don't want you to marry her, no. You're the one who wants that. True?"

He slowly answered, "True."

His hesitation gave her leave to touch his hand. His hand submitted. The two fingers that held a pen had inky calluses. "Let me talk to her," she said. "I won't tell Richard. I won't shout and scream. It's important. Women can says things to each other men can't say for them. I know she's not a bitch. I like her. I respect your loving her. I know you went to her because of—failings in me."

Though his hand withdrew, she had felt him soften; she saw him sit back content with the possibility that she and Sally would settle it all between them and relieve him of a decision. The coffee had come. All around them, they noticed now, conversations were proceeding; the world proceeded through such conversations. Jerry and she, after years of living together like children with invisible parents, had begun to talk to each other like grown people. Before they rose, Jerry asked her with the gentleness of a formality: "Do you want me to leave tonight?"

The answer came to her lips so quickly, so instinctively, she felt no decision in it. "Of course not."

"Are you sure? It might be cleaner. I can't promise you anything."

"Where would you go?"

"That's a point. Into town?"

"You know you can't sleep in hotels. Don't be silly. You don't want to leave me tonight, do you?"

He thought. "No. Apparently not."

"She's probably off at a party with Richard and couldn't come to you anyway."

"I wouldn't ask her to. I have to leave you first."

"Well, *you* must explain it to the children. I don't envy you that."

He studied the checks of the tablecloth as if its threads would spell an answer. He kept tracing one square with the middle finger of his left hand. When they had married, Jerry had refused to wear a wedding ring, because he said he would fiddle with it. "Let's take a walk on the beach."

The Conants paid, smiled at the bored waitress, left, and got into his car, his Mercury convertible. Above the beach the sky was yellow after the rain. The stars showed faint, but a three-quarters moon laid a light on the sand so strong that shadows tagged along behind them. The Sound appeared pinned to the horizon by the lights of Grace Island and, in the opposite direction, of the cottages on Jacob's Point. Ruth could hardly believe that not twelve hours ago she had lain here watching the sun stride toward her; the tide had erased all the day's footprints. Now in the night her bare feet made neat cold prints as the waves slapped and receded, phosphorescent. Jerry halted her and embraced her and kissed her neck, her cheeks, her eyelids. "I don't know what to do," he said. "I can't give either of you up."

"Don't decide now," she said. "I'm not ready."

"You'll *never* be ready!"

"You don't know that. I can get ready. But promise not to do anything until the end of summer."

"All right," he said.

She felt guilty at having won so much so easily. "Can you bear it?" Sally and Jerry: their thinking they were in love appeared pathetic. Ruth held their image in her mind and grew so big above them she wondered if she were going to faint. The polished night about her spun like the atmosphere of a Chagall; she held tight to Jerry, out of pity.

"What's to bear?" he asked.

"Giving up Sally," she said.

"Is that part of the promise?"

"You must try with me," Ruth told him, "to the end of summer. Otherwise, what's the use?"

"The use of what?"

"Of trying."

"And then what?"

"Then decide."

"God," Jerry said, releasing her. "You've been such a lovely wife."

Next day, Monday, she called Mrs. O, then Sally.

"Sally, it's Ruth."

"Hi. How are you?" Sally had once been a secretary, and her voice had a controlled richness over the phone, a professionalism one forgot, seeing her shriek and flirt at parties.

"Not so good."

"Oh. I'm sorry."

"I'm calling to ask, could I come over for a cup of coffee?"

Sally's words spaced themselves carefully. "Su-ure. You wouldn't rather come late this afternoon, for a drink? Aren't you going to the beach? Yesterday was so dismal."

"Yes it was. I won't stay long."

"Would you like to bring your children?"

"Well I've gone"—Ruth startled herself with an apologetic laugh—"and arranged for a sitter."

"Richard's taken Bobbie off somewhere, to look at some land or something, but I have Peter and the baby. Do you want—do you mind their being here?"

"Of course not. I suppose I was silly to get a sitter."

"It depends," Sally ventured. "You could bring Geoffrey to keep mine company."

Ruth felt she was being maneuvered, and the other woman was still in the dark. "I suppose I could do that." Geoffrey hated Peter, who he said pushed him around. "I'll see."

"That'll be nice," Sally said, and sang, "We'll be here," and hung up. Ruth was furious at having to squeeze Geoffrey's feet into sneakers. When Mrs. O arrived, he cried at being taken away, and Joanna and Charlie complained at not being taken along.

On winter weekends when there was snow, people would take their children sledding on the Mathiases' hill; Richard and Sally would serve cookies and hot chocolate to the children and tea and rum to the grown-ups. Their driveway curved upwards and Ruth, though full of irritation and indignation and fear, was reminded, by the familiar swaying of the Falcon now this way and that, of the seasonal hospitalities that had awaited her at the top: winter sledding, summer lawn parties, dinner parties, word games, poster-making, a class in weaving, meetings of little committees to render Greenwood even more of a Paradise.

Sally was waiting at the side door. The sun was in the east and the soft fret of tree-shadow that fell on the red clapboards fell on Sally as well, accenting her animal muteness, mottling her like a deer. She wore white pants, tight-hipped and low-waisted in the St. Tropez style, and a boatneck jersey with broad amber stripes. Her long feet were bare and her toenail polish needed redoing; her ash-blond hair hung down with a witchy severity. Her sharp-chinned face looked pale, as if she had lost a pint of blood, or just had a baby. "Jerry just called," she announced.

"Did he?" Ruth was holding open the car door so Geoffrey, fussing and gingerly, could climb out.

"He wanted to warn me." Sally grinned, and as always Ruth found it impossible not to smile with her. Peter Mathias and the baby, a tiny girl with a ridiculous name, had gathered around their mother's legs. What *was* her name, something barbaric, an empress, not Cleopatra—Theodora. "Go show Geoffrey the swing!" Sally cried, in her voice of violent melody, and though the children hung back timidly, Caesar, the Mathiases' big-headed Golden, bounded through their legs and led the way into the back yard, where the swing set stood in the shadow of the woods.

Sally turned; Ruth followed her into the house, seeing the familiar furnishings afresh, with Jerry's eyes—the square-armed sofas, the nubbly abstract rugs, the glass tables, the Arp-shape lamps, the framed prints by mediocrities like Buffet and Wyeth. He would love it, it would speak money and light to him. Sally did have a gift of light, of inviting, with white paint and potted plants, the sun to enter the windows and stay. The kitchen was the brightest room of all; light splintered on the sills and lay in long shards on every wood surface Sally's energy had polished. Last night, as Ruth and Jerry talked and tossed in bed, sleepless like children under the threat of Christmas, growing actually silly, he had complained what a better housekeeper than she Sally was. Ruth had answered that Sally had Josie, but knew this was a weak truth: she could have a Josie too, if she had cared. She didn't care; she thought housekeeping a second-rate passion.

"I put the coffee on but I don't think it's dripped yet," Sally said.

Ruth sat down at the breakfast table. It was a heavy walnut antique Richard had recently bought in Toronto: she remembered his pride of acquisition. "Where's Josie?" she asked.

"Upstairs. Don't be nervous. She won't bother us."

"I wasn't nervous. I didn't want you to be embarrassed."

"That's very sweet of you." Sally by the stove flicked her hair back with a toss of her head; it was a little head, the head of a mannikin. "I'm sorry Jerry told you. I think it's too soon."

"Too soon for what?" When Sally didn't answer, Ruth told her, "Don't be sorry. It's better for me to know where I am. I've been unhappy all summer without knowing why."

"I wasn't thinking so much," Sally studiously said, setting a cup of coffee before her, "of you."

Ruth shrugged. "It was bound to come out. Jerry's just bursting with pride."

"He told me you promised not to tell Richard."

"He said if I did, he'd run off with you."

"He also said, Ruth, that you'd had an affair."

Sally's back was turned as she poured coffee for herself and Ruth studied her body, looking for traces of Jerry's touch, wondering if he really adored those high broad hips, that curved, fattening back. "He shouldn't have told you that."

Sally turned. Her stare was exquisite, in the shape of the eyes and the arch of the slightly frowning brows. "He tells me everything."

Ruth lowered her own gaze. "I'm sure." She was sliding backwards; she halted herself. "No, I'm not sure. I'm not sure he's been entirely honest with either of us."

"You don't know him. He's painfully honest."

"I don't know my own husband?"

"In ways, no." Sally sounded blithe saying this, but after she set the coffee on the table, with an excessive care, she sat down heavily and her voice continued husky. "Let's not be so cold. He told me so I wouldn't feel like a whore with you. He wouldn't tell me the man."

"He doesn't know the man."

"Was it David Collins?"

"No. It happened long ago, and there was never any idea of my leaving Jerry. I ended it, and the man was very nice. Surprisingly nice. I don't think it had been very deep for him either."

"You're so lucky," Sally said.

"How?"

"You didn't fall in love with your lover."

"I did a little. My stomach was upset for months. I lost ten pounds." She lifted her cup to her lips, found it too hot, replaced it into its saucer, where it looked like a cup in a Bonnard, seen from an upper perspective, blurred by light. Sally moved her hands on the bare table as if shakily smoothing a cloth. Ruth touched her own cup, and, whenever she tried to recall this conversation, the image that first came to her was of their four white hands trembling and fidgeting on the sunstruck, polished walnut.

"You know," Sally said, "you've rejected Jerry."

"I didn't mean to. I didn't want to. Perhaps he's rejected me."

"You and he have a problem."

"Do we?"

"Don't do that, Ruth. Take that tone. For years Richard and I admired you two as an ideally married couple. We've never had an easy time of it, and we envied you, I guess—you seemed so sure of each other, so close. Then, this last year, you and Jerry, something was happening, I could feel him venturing out, toward me, toward other women. I figured it was going to be somebody and it might as well be me." Sally's chin had reddened in this telling and abruptly she grinned to hide the trembling of her lips.

It would be so easy, Ruth thought, to lie down and die, to sacrifice herself to this other woman's vitality. Sally had no doubts of her right to live. Ruth asked her, "Have you had a feeling for Jerry for a long time?"

Sally nodded, *yes yes yes*, and tried to sip her coffee, found it too hot, and untangled her hair from her mouth, her wet cheeks. She said, "Always."

"Really?" Ruth was affronted by what must be an exaggeration. "Would you have, if you hadn't been unhappy with Richard?"

The words felt clumsy; Sally stiffened at the intrusion. "I wasn't *that* unhappy with Richard until Jerry. Now, it's terrible. I hear my voice going on and on at him and I can't stop it. I want to destroy him." Her tears renewed themselves. "I don't give that man shit."

Ruth laughed, hearing Richard in that expression.

Sally, just as Ruth was relaxing, became hard and angry. "You mustn't just sit there and be amused. You must take responsibility for your actions, Ruth. You can't starve a man emotionally and then when he turns to somebody else pull a string and have him back. Jerry needs to be loved; I can do it. I do do it. He's told me himself, I've earned him. I have. I've earned him and he's earned me."

Ruth felt in Sally's speech a disconnection, as if she were linking together things she had prepared to say, that made her answerable only in part. She said, "Listen, Sally. Don't think I relish my role in this. If it wasn't for those three children I wouldn't be here. It's too humiliating."

"You can't build a marriage on children."

"I didn't think we had. You talk," Ruth said, "you talk as if Jerry wants only you. Are you sure? He told me last night he wants us both. I don't doubt he thinks he loves you. But he loves me too."

Sally, gazing down, let fall a sad, off-center, infinitely superior smile. Ruth stubbornly continued: "He's deceived me about you, maybe he's deceived you about me. Last night we made love."

Sally lifted her gaze. "After everything?"

"After talking. Yes. It seemed natural and right."

"You're killing him, Ruth. You're smothering that man to death."

"No. It's not me. Since spring, his asthma has been worse, he wakes up every night. I thought it was the pollen count; but it was you. You're killing him by asking him to rescue you and three children he's not the father of from the bad marriage you made. It's too much for him to do. Find somebody else. Find a tougher man."

"Why must you keep harping on *my* marriage?"

"You are married, aren't you? And rather well, if you ask me. Why *don't* you give Richard shit? If you tried more with *him*, you wouldn't be doing this to *us*."

"I'm not doing anything to you. All I've ever asked from Jerry is that he make up his mind."

"In favor of you. He needs me. He needs his own children. Children are very important to Jerry. He was an unhappy only child and he loves being able to have three of his own and support them and raise them the way he wasn't."

"They'd still be his children."

"They would *not*," Ruth said. Her vehemence embarrassed her. She said, "Let's be rational. Would you be poor with him? I was, and I'd gladly be poor again. I hate our money, the way he has to make it. I'm not afraid of doing without. You are."

"I don't think you can say what I'm afraid of."

The primmer Sally became, the hotter Ruth felt. Her cheeks burned. "You're afraid of everything," she said, "of not *having* everything. It's your charm, this greed. It's why we all love you."

"How can you love me?" Sally asked. As if attacked, she stood; Ruth found herself standing also, and in the mood of a desperate child, of a mother in a dream who is also the child, embraced the other woman at the corner of the table where the coffee cups made circles within circles. Sally's body was strange, hard, broad. They let each other go, having discovered, in their embrace, that they were enemies.

The varnish and white paint and metal and sun of Sally's kitchen surrounded Ruth with uplifted daggers as she tried to explain: "You need more than the rest of us. You need your new furniture, your clothes, your trips to the Caribbean and Mont Tremblant. I don't think you understand how precarious Jerry's living is. He hates what he's doing. I keep telling him to quit. He's not like Richard. No matter how many mistakes Richard makes, money will still be there."

Standing by the table, Sally followed a whorl of walnut grain with her finger, retraced it, and traced it again. She said levelly, "I don't think you know us very well."

"I know you better than you think. I know that Richard isn't going to be generous."

Sally's eyelids were still pink; she seemed a big perfect child about to cry. "I've told Jerry," Sally said, "he'd kill himself, trying to support two women."

"That would just challenge him. Everything you say like that makes him wild to prove himself."

"You know, you're very condescending to Jerry."

"I've known him more than a few months."

"Look, Ruth, there's no point in our quarrelling. What we think about each other doesn't matter. Jerry must decide."

"He won't. As long as he has us both, he won't. *We* must decide."

"How can we?"

And Sally's question seemed so sincere, so helpless and hopeful, that Ruth told her the answer, as smoothly as the end of a sermon. "Give him up for now. Don't see him, for God's sake stop telephoning. What's left of the summer, give him some privacy. In September, if he still wants you, he can have you. The hell with it."

"Are you serious?"

"Why not? None of us is going to live forever; I'm not so pathetic as you and Jerry seem to think. In fact I think getting a divorce is something I'd be rather good at, once I got started." And both women laughed, as if a conspiracy had been disclosed.

But Sally's hands, the sunlight made clear, were trembling again. She smoothed back her hair. "Why should I give you anything? This summer may be all I'll ever have of Jerry, why should I give it away?"

"I'm not asking for me. I'm asking for my children. And yours, for that matter. Richard is their father."

"He doesn't care about them."

"Every man cares."

"You only know Jerry."

"I beg your pardon."

"Excuse me, I forgot. You did have this little lover. That seems so unreal."

"You know, Sally," Ruth said, "you're gorgeous, but you have one fault."

Sally said carelessly, "Only one?"

"You don't listen. You strike a pose and hold it and don't pay any attention to what anybody is saying. I'm trying to be generous. I'm trying to give you Jerry, if that's the way it has to be, and keep some honor for both of us. How much better *you'd* feel, in the end, if you let go now. I came here determined not to be angry, or weepy, or preachy; and you haven't given an inch. You haven't listened at all."

Sally shrugged. "What can I say? That I'll give him up? I've tried. He won't let me. I love him. I wish I didn't. I don't want to hurt you and your children. And Richard and my children."

"You weren't trying very hard when you went to Washington."

"Jerry asked me. He *took* me."

"The second time. The time you forced yourself on him."

Sally's gaze lost focus, remembering. "It didn't seem so wrong. I can't justify myself to you. It's not up to us, Ruth. Jerry's the man. I'm his if he wants me. But he has to be man enough to come for me."

"That's your idea of a man, isn't it? Somebody who leaves his children."

Sally lifted her cup and put it to her lips but set it down

without drinking. It was cold. "I learned very early," she said, "to put a face on things. I may not show it, but I've been in hell over this."

"No doubt," Ruth said. "But it's a hell you made."

"All by myself? You've been talking about faults as if you don't have any. You and Jerry have been living too long up on that little arty cloud of yours. You have so much conceit, behind that gracious-lady manner of yours, you've never learned how to take care of a man. I've had to work at my marriage, you never have. You've turned Jerry loose, and you're too conceited to take the consequences."

"I'll take them when they come. But—"

"I don't think you will at all. I know damn well you can keep him if you pull out all the stops and use the children. But do you want him at such a price? I know I wouldn't want Richard that way."

"I haven't meant to scold and don't expect to be scolded. I'm asking you, I think very nicely, to keep your hands off my husband for a few weeks."

Sally's pale face went pink. "You and Jerry do whatever you Goddamn please. You're both, in my opinion, extremely immature."

"I'll tell him you said that. Thank you for the coffee." In returning through the living room, Ruth saw that the square arms of the white sofa were worn and the Wyeth print was askew. Outdoors, on a lawn that needed mowing, Caesar had just knocked Geoffrey down. The child screamed, less in pain, Ruth judged, than in fear that his collarbone would be reinjured. "*Caesar!*" Sally shouted, and Ruth said to her, "It's all right. Geoffrey's had a hard week."

"I heard," Sally said.

Ruth glanced at Sally for confirmation that the scene in the kitchen had not happened; the other woman grinned back. But when Ruth was in her car, Geoffrey whining behind her, Sally in her white slacks kneeled on the grass, her long hair flowing, and classically put her arms about her children, one on each side, the dog standing as additional guard on Theodora's other side. The Invader Repelled: this was Ruth's impression of their pose as the spark ignited, and a mixture of gasoline and gravity flung her down the drive.

Home, she paid Mrs. O, who had fed Joanna and Charlie and seen them vanish into the neighborhood, then settled herself in the wing chair for a nap. Ruth poured some vermouth into an orange juice glass and called Jerry's office. His line was busy. She tried four more times in twenty minutes, before the busy signal lifted, and she heard his voice.

"Who were you talking to so long?" she asked.

"Sally. She called me."

"Really, I think that's treacherous."

"Why? She was upset. Who else could she call?"

"But I had just got done asking her not to."

"And did she promise not to?"

"Not exactly. She said she thought we were both very immature."

"Yeah, she said you'd tell me she said that."

"What else did she say?"

"She said you said I still loved you."

"What did you say to that?"

"I forget. I said I supposed I did, in a way. I don't know why this should upset her, she more or less assumed it was the case anyway. Obviously."

"Why should it be obvious to her? You've told her you love her, you made love to her, you've led her to think I don't matter to you."

"You think?"

"Of course, baby. Don't be so dumb, or sadistic, or whatever you're being. You've led her to think you love her."

"Well, sure; but clearly it isn't a case of my feelings for her cancelling out my feelings for everybody else."

"Oh, clearly."

"Now *you're* mad. This is hopeless. Why don't you both just shoot me and marry each other?"

"We don't want each other. We tried a sisterly embrace and recoiled like a pair of wet cats."

"She said you told her to stay away from me."

"Till the end of summer. That's what you and I agreed on."

"Did we?"

"Didn't we?"

"Well, I didn't think you'd go over and ram it down her throat."

"I didn't ram anything down her throat. I was so amiable I sickened myself."

"She said you were very cool and arrogant."

"Not true. *Not*. If there was any arrogance it was hers. I thought she acted like a pretty tough cookie."

"She feels betrayed," Jerry pleaded. "She says she's in love with me and I'm just playing with it."

"Well. In a way you did confess to me as an experiment. You wanted to see what would happen. If I blew up, it would relieve you of a decision."

"That's not quite fair. For one thing, you were on the verge of guessing. For another, she's been pushing me to do *some*thing."

"I do think 'betrayed' is an exaggeration. *I'm* the one who should feel betrayed. But nobody seems inclined to let me feel anything. All the time I was talking to her, I had to keep telling myself I wasn't the one in the wrong. You both seem to think it's terribly unkind of me not to drop dead."

"Neither of us thinks that. Now don't start crying. You're heroic. Sally said so."

"What else did she say about me?"

"She said you talked very well."

"She did? How funny. I didn't at all. I talked in tight little spurts that went in all directions."

"Did she talk about Richard?"

"Hardly a word."

"What did she say about the children?"

"She doesn't seem to think the children part of it is very significant. She thinks they're just an excuse we're using."

"She said that?"

"She implied it."

"Anything else?" His hunger for Sally's words seemed something bottomless she must forever feed.

"Let me think," Ruth said. "Yes. She was very interested in my lover and asked if it had been David."

"Sweetie, forgive me for telling her. But I thought it somehow evened things up for her to know."

Ruth had to laugh, through the tears and vermouth, at the image of Jerry the judicious handicapper of this little horse race he had arranged.

"What's so funny?"

"You are."

"I'm *not*," he said. "I'm a perfectly reasonable decent human being trying to do right by everybody and at the same time participate in umpteen dumb conferences on the exact shade of gray to make your average third-worlder in this fucking dumb series of thirty-second spots!" When she failed to respond to this outcry, he asked, "*Was* it David?"

"No it was not David Collins. I have never been attracted to David Collins. I can't even dance with him. I don't like the way my old affair is turning into comic relief for everybody."

"It's *not*, sweetie. Everybody takes it very seriously. Actually, I think your affair is the clue we all need."

"I think it's the clue your little friend needs for some friendly blackmail."

"Why are you so Machiavellian? What else did Sally

say? Did she sign this hands-off contract you offered her?"

"Not at all. She just kept saying, you must decide."

"You meaning you, or me?"

"You. The man. God, the way that woman says 'man,' like it's the holiest word in the language, I wanted to throw up."

"How *can* I decide? I don't know enough. I don't know if you love me or not; you say you do, but I don't feel it. Maybe a divorce from me is what you really want, and you're just too polite to tell me. Maybe it would be the best thing that ever happened to you."

"I doubt it," Ruth said slowly, trying to picture herself divorced, single, barefoot, graying. But Jerry was hurrying on.

"I don't know if the children would have nervous breakdowns or not. I don't know if Sally, once she had me in the bag, wouldn't find me pretty boring. Sometimes I think my charm for her is that I'm *not* in the bag. Maybe she only likes things she can't have. Maybe we're all like that."

"Could be," Ruth said, not following.

"Well, if so," Jerry pointed out, as if she were arguing to the contrary, "it's ridiculous to smash up two households that more or less function and screw up half a dozen children. On the other hand, there *is* something about Sally and me. Something very solid, in a way."

"I don't want to hear about it."

"You don't? O.K. Tell me about you. How do you feel? Happy? Sad? Want a divorce?"

"I'm not happy, and I don't want a divorce."

"You're sad."

"Low. I'm into the vermouth. The talk I had with her is just beginning to hit me."

"Was it so unpleasant? Weren't you amazed, how neat her house is? It's that way no matter when you go there, day or night. And wasn't she more sensitive than you expected?"

"Less."

"Less?"

"Much less. What time are you coming home?"

"I don't know. Normal time. A little later, maybe."

"You're going to go see her."

"That O.K. with you?"

"No."

Jerry seemed surprised. "I think I better. She sounded pretty frantic."

"Seeing you will just make it worse for her."

"Why would it? She likes me. I always cheer her up."

"Richard might be there."

"We could meet at some beach."

"It's clouding over."

"It always does at noon," Jerry told her.

"I suppose you'll make love," she blurted.

Jerry's voice pulled back, became the receiver's components of metal and crystal. "Don't be grotesque," he said. "That's gone. Thanks to you. Congratulations." He hung up.

She felt chastised; she had overstepped. There were rules in this mystery, like stairways in a castle; she had mistakenly knocked on the door of the chamber where the lord and lady lay and made love. Before this door she felt small, appalled and ashamed, rebuked and fascinated: a child. Ruth noticed that while her left hand had been holding the receiver her right had been doodling, on the back of a windowed bill envelope, squares interlocking with squares. Their areas of overlap were shaded; light and dark were balanced, confused though she had been. She studied this abstraction, wondering if, abandoned, she might be revealed to herself as an artist after all.

The day was hot and the children clamored to go to the beach. They did not understand the day she was giving them. Rats of fear seemed to skid through their noise.

Ruth felt she must stay here, to be here when what happened next happened. She did not know what it would be, but imagined that Jerry would need her. This imagined need was a positive pull on her stomach. In time, Geoffrey slept, and the two older children dispersed into the neighborhood. They were happy to leave her. She settled herself at the piano, but the music had no power; Bach's baroque scrolls failed to interconnect. Ruth went to the phone and called Jerry's office and was told he had left for the afternoon. It was after five when he came home; she happened to be upstairs, having come to check on Geoffrey. The length of his nap seemed unnatural; perhaps, she thought, being knocked down by the Mathiases' awful dog, what was its name?—

The front door opened. Jerry's voice called; his steps struck the bottom stairs. She called, "Don't come up!" When she entered the living room, he was circling the furniture as if looking for something, and smoking. The lit cigarette looked dirty in his hand, though it had been only three months since he had quit. "Why are you smoking?" she asked.

"I bought a pack driving home," he said. "I gave it up so I could taste her. Now I'm hungry for cancer."

"What happened?"

He straightened a rug and aligned some books. "Nothing," he said. "Nothing much. She cried. I told her I couldn't come to her again unless I was free, and she said, Yes, that's what she expected. I said it was unfair any other way. She agreed, and thanked me for making her feel loved. I thanked her for making *me* feel loved. It was all very reasonable, until she cried." He took a deep, annoyingly dramatic drag on his cigarette, sucking it down as if never to let it out. "God," he said. "I'm not used to this. It makes me dizzy." He paused by an end table and set a lampshade straight. "She said she hadn't expected me to give in to you so soon."

"And then I suppose you took her into your arms and

told her it would just be a few days before you'd talked that old bag into giving you a divorce."

"No, not really. I didn't say that. I wish you'd been there to think of it for me. I didn't say much of anything. I was really quite stupid." He inhaled again, did a little staggering act, and sat down in the Danish armchair so hard its fragile frame cracked; next, with a surge that seemed to gather behind his head and knock it forward, so that Ruth thought he was about to cough, he started crying. His sobs were tangled with loud sighs like the hissing of truck brakes and with the broken words of his attempt to keep talking.

"She told me—almost the last thing she told me—was to be nice to you—not to torture you with her."

"But that's what you're doing."

"I don't mean to. Listen. I don't want our lousy marriage to get better because she taught me how to make love and taught you—that I was worth loving."

"I've never said you weren't worth loving."

"You've never had to—I've always felt it. You married me because—I could draw. I'd make the outlines—and you'd put in the—colors."

"That's absurd. Look, Jerry, I don't want you if you're going to go on this way in front of me. For that female. I'm sorry, I can't stand it. I can't take it seriously."

"Then tell me—to go. Tell me now."

When Jerry had his asthmatic attacks, he would wake in the night and find his breathing shallow. He would go to the bathroom for a drink of water or the ease of moving about and come back to the bed, where she had usually awakened, with his back bent. He described it as a wall in his lungs, or a floor that kept rising, so that he could not take enough air in; and the harder he tried, the tighter the wall became, so that he would break into a sweat, and cry out this was death, and ask her why she was smothering him, why she had had so many children, why she couldn't keep the house dusted, why she refused to believe in Jesus Christ, the resurrection of Lazarus, the immortality of the soul—there was no limit to the height of his accusations against her, and she submitted to them because she knew as long as he could find breath to voice them he was not asphyxiating. At last, after an hour or more, he would tire of abusing her, and God beyond her, and relax, and fall asleep, snoring trustingly as beside him she stared into the dark. She could not understand how he, knowing that only his fright and panicked constriction separated his lungs from the abundance of oxygen, could not will himself free from his attacks; but now, reaching into herself, Ruth found something akin to his strange inner wall, for her imagination could not quite grasp the need to let him go. She saw that he was determined to punish her if she did not, and that her dignity lay with the immediate sacrifice of their marriage. Such sacrifice would be simple, bold, pure, aesthetic. It would remove her from these demeaning people, these Greenwood adulterers. She even sensed, behind the wall within her, a volume of freedom and dream. But she could not break through to it. In good conscience she could not. An innocent man and a greedy woman had fornicated and Ruth could not endorse the illusions that made it seem more than that. They were exaggerators, both of them, and though she could see that beauty was a province of exaggeration, someone must stand by truth. The truth was that Sally and Jerry were probably better married to Richard and her than they would be to each other.

"I'd do it," she told Jerry, "I'd see the lawyer tomorrow, if it was a woman I respected."

"A woman you respected," Jerry responded quickly, "would be a carbon copy of yourself." He had stopped crying.

"That's not true. I have no great admiration for myself. But Sally—she's *silly*, Jerry."

"So am I."

"Not that silly. You'd hate her within a year."

"You think?" He was interested.

"I'm sure. I've seen the two of you together at parties —you're nervous together."

"We're not."

"You both act frantic."

"I can't tell you what I love about her—"

"Oh, do. She comes when you come."

"How'd you know that?"

"I guessed."

"It's true. She hasn't made a religion out of sex, the way you have. She thinks it's fun."

"How have I made a religion of it?"

"Everything has to be perfect. Once a month you're marvellous, but I don't have that much patience. I'm running out of *time*. I'm dying, Ruth."

"Stop it. Don't you see, it's a problem any woman has, when she's a wife; there are no obstacles. So she has to make them. I've felt that thing, of serving the penis, of existing to serve it, it's wonderful. But only as a mistress. Sally is your mistress—"

"No. She is, but I'm sure she makes love to Richard just the way she does to me. Anyway, it's more than what happens in bed. Whenever I'm with her, no matter where, just standing with her on a street corner waiting for the light to change, I know I'm never going to die. Or if I know it, I don't mind it, somehow."

"And with me?"

"You?" He was speaking to her as if to an audience he had ceased to see. "You're death. Very calm, very pure, very remote. Nothing I can do will really change you. Or even amuse you, much. I'm married to my death."

"Shit." How could he sit there so complacently, so expectantly even, having said she was death? He spoke of her Unitarian smugness but *he* was smug, smug in his grief, in his hopeless love, in all his easy absolutes. "You owe us a lot of hard thought and you're just letting your tongue run on. Suppose you did marry Sally? Would you be faithful to her?"

"Is that your business?"

"Of course it is, I'm being asked to give way to your wonderful love. How wonderful is it? You've discovered a fascinating thing about yourself—women like you."

"They do?"

"Stop it. Be serious. Think. How much are you going to Sally, and how much leaving me? How much are you using her as a way out of marriage? Out of the children, out of the job?"

"Do I want out of all that?"

"I don't know. I just can't feel that Sally is my real rival. I think my rival is some idea of freedom you have. I'll tell you this, as a wife Sally would be damn possessive."

"I know that. She knows that." Jerry lifted his hand, she thought to wipe his eyes; but he scratched his head instead. This conversation was drying him out. "In a way," he said, "it does seem reckless to rush from one monogamy into another."

"Reckless, and expensive."

"I suppose."

"And if you did slip up, how long would it be before she paid you back in kind?"

"Not long."

"That's right. Now you let her alone for a while and think about what you're really after—that one big-bottomed blonde, or—"

"Or?"

"Or many women."

Jerry smiled. "You're offering me many women?"

"Not exactly. Not at all. I'm describing what the realities are."

"One nice thing about being a Unitarian, it doesn't saddle you with too much bourgeois morality."

"Being a Lutheran doesn't seem to either."

"It's not supposed to. We live by faith alone."

"Anyway, I'd expect a few men in return."

This surprised him. "Which ones?"

"I'll let you know." She moved a few steps, unconsciously mocking the beginning of a dance, and the gold-framed mirror between the two windows gave her back an unexpected rectangle of herself—hip outthrust, elbow cocked, lips pursed as if having bitten a fruit too succulent. While she was transfixed by this glimpse, Jerry came up behind her and enclosed her breasts in his hands.

"I suppose you think," he said, "corruption becomes you."

His embrace disgusted her; pity for the abandoned woman made Ruth dislike her own success. She pulled away from him and said, "I must go to the beach. I've been promising the children all afternoon. You want to come along, or're you going to leave us?"

"No. I'll come. I have nowhere to go."

"Your suit is outdoors on the line."

The young marrieds of Greenwood, in what had grown to be, as the women had ceased to bear new babies, a ritual need to keep in touch, had arranged constant excuses for congregating. The beach, dances, tennis, committee meetings—to these had been added a Sunday afternoon volleyball game. In all this mingling it was inevitable that the Conants and the Mathiases should meet. Sally, who wore pale colors all summer, white slacks and ivory armless jerseys and a bathing suit whose yellow had sun-faded to the color of lemonade, seemed to Ruth to have frozen, to have become precariously brittle, and to regard Jerry with an inflexible dread and fascination. Ruth was curious about her husband's potency, that it could produce such an effect. The wind that had broken this woman like a tree in an ice storm passed through her sometimes without stirring a leaf, and Ruth naturally wondered if she were alive at all. From an anxious depth within her there reawakened the suspicion that the people around her—mother, father, sister—were engaged in a conspiracy, a conspiracy called life, from which she had been excluded. In the night, lying beside Jerry, she considered running away, taking another lover, getting a job, winning back Richard, attempting suicide: all were methods of hurling herself against the unseen resistance and demonstrating, by the soft explosion, the flower of pain, that she existed. She found herself in the impossible position of needing to will belief; somehow she could not quite believe in Jerry and he, feeling this inability, nurtured it, widened it, for it was the opening by which he would escape. He encouraged her illusion that there was a world into which she had never been born.

On Sunday evenings, when the game was over, the home the Conants returned to seemed all unravelled, all confusion and unmade beds and broken toys and dirty cushions askew. He would sit in a chair and exude grief. His volleyball style involved flinging himself around and diving and falling, and the Collinses' lawn, as feet wore the grass away, yielded bits of old rubbish, bottle caps, and shards of broken bottles, so he often cut himself; he sat there in his sawed-off khaki shorts with a bloody knee like a boy fallen from a bicycle, and as she watched his downcast face a drop of water appeared on his nose, fell, and was replaced by another. She could not take him seriously.

"For God's sake, Jerry. Shape up."

"I'm trying, I'm trying. I really shouldn't see her at all. I get this hangover."

"Well then let's not go to volleyball."

"We have to, because of the children." The children were asleep, or lost in the rustle of television.

"The children, my foot! My God, how you use them! We have to go so you and she can exchange sweet sad little looks under the net."

"Those aren't sweet sad looks. Her eyes are very cold now."

"They always were."

"She hates me now. I've lost her love, which is fine. It's what we wanted, it takes any decision from me, I don't know why I should mind it. I apologize."

"Don't be silly, you haven't lost her love at all. She's doing what you asked her to do, and I think she's doing it very well."

"She's doing what *you* asked her to do."

"Phooey. She doesn't give a"—the next word surprised her, it was so quaint, a favorite of her father's—"*hoot* about me and you don't either. I'm *nothing* in this, it's between her and the children, so don't try to make me feel guilty. I can't hold you here; get up and go to her. *Go.*"

"I'm sorry," Jerry said, and he seemed so. "It's just that a certain angle of her face this afternoon, when I spiked at her, snagged in my head; it's such a humiliating position I've put her in."

"But she *asked* for it, sweetie. Women gamble; they know they can't always win. I think she's being pretty brave and straight about it, so why don't you stop being a baby? You're not doing her any favors by this performance every Sunday."

He looked up, with wet cheeks, a cut knee, a hopeful smirk. "You really think she still loves me?"

"She'd be a fool to," Ruth told him.

Usually on Sunday nights, stirred up, he would insist on making love, and she would accede, and fail to come because she was not there: it was Sally under his hands. His touch fluttered over her as if conjuring her body to become another's, and that in her which was his, wifely, would try to obey. In the dark twist of this effort of obedience she would lose all orientation. Finally he would force her as one forces a hopeless piece of machinery and, sighing from the effort, would fall away pleased. Her failure satisfied him, he desired her to fail, it confirmed his eventual escape. "You smoke too much," he told her. "It's an anti-aphrodisiac."

"*You're* the anti-aphrodisiac."

"Am I so bad? Take a lover. Or go back to the one you had. I know you could be great for somebody."

"Thanks."

"I mean it. You're a beautiful woman. Even if your mouth does smell like a tobacco shed."

"Now you let up on me! You let up!" Exclaiming this excited rather than relieved her fury; she hit at him and kicked with her knees; he seized her wrists, and pinned her body under his. His face was inches above hers, swollen in the dark, a Goya.

"You dumb cunt," he said, and bounced her into the mattress again and again, "you get a fucking grip on yourself. You got what you wanted, didn't you? This is it. Married bliss."

She spat in his face, *ptuh*, like a cat, a jump ahead of thought; saliva sprayed back down upon her own face and as it were awakened her. She felt his body like iron on her; her eyes, seeing in the thin light, saw him blink and grin. His grip relaxed and his body slid from hers. As it slid, a flutter from between her legs seemed to rise in pursuit of his retreating weight. He turned his back, curling up tightly as if to protect himself against a renewal of fists. "Well, that was a new sensation," he said, of her spitting.

"I did it without thinking. It must be pretty basic."

"It felt pretty basic."

"Well you were holding my arms. I had to express myself somehow."

"Don't apologize. By all means express yourself."

"Did it offend you?"

"No. I kind of liked it. It showed you care."

"Most of it came back into my own face."

"Spitting into the wind, it's called."

"Jerry?" She was reaching out to him, encircling him

with her arm, his potency proved by the languor of her muscles.

"Huh?"

"Are we perverse, do you think?"

"Normally perverse. Human, I'd say."

"You're a nice man." She hugged him, having suppressed a declaration of love.

Wary, he wanted to sleep. "Good night, sweetie."

"Good night."

Their sleep together had a strange sanity, as their waking life together had the drifting unreason of somnolence.

Everyone knew. All their friends, as July slipped by, came to know. Ruth felt it at volleyball, she felt their knowledge touching her; whenever she leaped or laughed or fell she felt the fine net of knowing that enclosed her. Men began to touch her at parties. Through all their previous years in Greenwood only Richard had ever asked her to lunch; now in one week she received two invitations, one at a party and one by phone. She turned them both down, but discovered that the refusal was an effort. Why refuse? Jerry was begging her to help him, to betray him, to desert him. She refused to be panicked into another man. Men, she saw for the first time, would always be there for her. In her very emptiness, her serenity, she had value for them. They could wait.

The women, too, began to touch her; after one especially unhappy Sunday, she had confessed to Linda Collins over Monday coffee that she and Jerry were passing through a "rough time"; after that, there was a fresh vivacity in the greetings from the group of mothers on the beach, and singly they would stand beside her making moments of silence, in case she wished to talk. She had been admitted to a secret sorority of suffering. Ruth wondered for how long this sorority had existed, and what lack or dullness in her had delayed her admission.

Sally, she saw now, had always been a member. But now Sally was rarely on the beach, and when she was, two packs of mothers discreetly formed, one around each, this summer's tragic queens. Imitating Sally in this role new to her, Ruth, after her vague confession to Linda, drew a mantle of reserve about herself, saying little, denying nothing.

Nor did she speak to her parents, though they visited from Poughkeepsie. The sight of her father's bespectacled, benign, pontifical face reminded her of an old anger, at his impervious public goodness, and his absent-minded way, increasing as he aged, of turning his public face to private matters. She would *not* be counselled like a parishioner, like the Cuckolded Wife card from the deck of human troubles. She knew that in his deliberate way he would try to rise to her call and give her advice as good as anyone else's (don't panic, let things run their course, keep your dignity, think of the children); she felt guilty that, by denying him the opportunity to pontificate (outside of his family he was considered a shrewd counsellor, and at the time of Ruth's engagement he had observed of Jerry in mild warning, that "he seems even younger than he is"), she was denying him the one gift, a grown daughter's trust, that was hers still to give. But he had failed her, hurt her, in the dark hallways of their parsonages, by acutely preferring her mother, by leaning on her, which made him forever obtuse toward his daughters. In quaint deference to their femaleness he had changed clothes in closets, he had been a sacred presence, he had hid. He had bred into her the reflexes of failure, the instinctive expectation which, when Jerry swung his leg over her like a little boy mounting his unsteady bicycle, sealed a stubbornness in her blood. She sent the old man back to Poughkeepsie untroubled.

It never occurred to her to tell her mother. Her mother had been born to be a wife. She would have been horrified.

Ruth did think of turning to Richard. He, oddly, in his half-blind bluffing way, had not quite failed her. Or, rather, his deficiencies were in areas, of courage and clarity of vision, where she could easily compensate. But the other woman was his wife. Ruth could see, from the way he blinked and grinned and sweated royally at parties, even when Jerry and Sally were being most flagrant, that in the sea of knowing, Richard was islanded, lost. And there was no predicting how he would react, in his lurching way. The consequences might be dangerous to her too, and this checked her chronic impulse to take his familiar hand, under cover of a party's confusion, and lead him to privacy. Also, she was protecting herself from an intuition that he would make a fool of himself or, worse, of Jerry.

So by default she would talk only to Jerry; her assassin was her only confidant. As she studied him, came to know him as another's lover, possibilities that in the first shocks she had suppressed acquired cool shape in her mind. It was possible that she did not love him, it was possible that she would soon lose him. Their sex together greatly improved.

"Heaven," Jerry said one night, entering her as she crouched above him. Afterwards, he explained, "I had this very clear vision of the Bodily Ascension, of me going up and up into this incredibly soft, warm, boundless sky: you."

"Isn't that blasphemous?" She had acquired the courage to be curious about his ultimate intimacy, so opaque and hostile to her, his religion.

"Because it makes my prick Christ? I wonder. They both have this quality, of being more important than they should be. As Christ relates to the universe, my prick relates to me."

"Then when I'm under you is that the descent into Hell?"

"No. You're Heaven in every direction, except side-ways it sometimes hurts."

"Oh dear."

"It's not so bad. I love you."

Her reaction was fear. He had taken care, recently, not to say this. "You do?"

"It seems so. I said it."

"Then you don't want to leave me?"

"No, I do, I do. In the morning I'll be furious because you're making me betray Sally by being so sweetly whorish."

"Am I more whorish," she asked, "than Sally?"

"Oh, much. She's very demure. With you, it's a roll in the mud. Mother Mud. With her"—she felt his body beneath her gather into itself, thinking—"it's a butterfly alighting on a little flower."

"I can't believe it."

"The stem bends, a single drop of dew falls to the ground. *Blip*."

"I don't believe you at all. I think you say to me just the opposite of what you mean. Why do you insult me just after I've made such good love to you?"

"Clearly, because it's confusing. Anyway, Ruth, why *was* it good? What's the matter with you lately?"

"I don't know; I figure, why not. I have nothing to lose. Each time, I think it may be the last time, and it's my aesthetic duty to really enjoy it."

"That makes me sad. Are you so sure I'm going to leave?"

She felt him wanting to be sure, and thereby to place his decision behind them, in the realm of the inevitable. "No, I'm not sure. I think it would be silly for you to go now that I'm getting better in bed."

"Maybe I feel I shouldn't leave you until you have enough confidence in bed to catch the next man."

"Don't worry, I'll manage."

"But how? I can't picture it. Who could you possibly marry, after me?"

"Oh—some idiot."

"Exactly. He would be an idiot. He wouldn't be good enough for you."

"Then don't leave me."

"But Richard's not good enough for Sally."

"He's ideal. They're made for each other. Let them alone."

"I can't."

"I thought you were."

"In my mind. It's a terrible responsibility, being the only man who's good enough for anybody."

"It must be."

"Hey? Make yourself into Heaven again for me."

"No."

August. The days dwindled minute by minute as each twilight came earlier; the growing chill of the nights deadened the heat of the sun at noon, made it seem bland and stale. Gazing from the kitchen windows onto the lawn where her children's feet had worn wide swathes of grass down to dust, Ruth felt the time in which she was immersed as foreshortened, seen from a vague time when Jerry had long since left. The earth, to the dead, is flat; and the moments of her life even as she lived them felt buried within a crushing retrospect. She was in quicksand. As she proved her point—that in the realm of the real she was better his wife than the other—Jerry's heart streamed away from her, toward the impossible woman. Often, calling him at work, Ruth got a busy signal. The bleating seemed a wall that was moving closer. Once, she dialled Sally's number and got the same signal: the wall was continuous.

That evening she told him, "I called her number too and it was also busy."

He did a little dance step sideways. "Well why not? She has friends. A few. Maybe she's taken another lover."

"Tell me the truth. This is too serious."

Frighteningly, he collapsed, shrugging, "Sure. I talk to her."

"You don't."

"You want the truth or not?"

"Who calls who?"

"It varies."

"How long has this been going on?"

He did the little dance step backwards, as if putting something spilled back into a bottle. "Not long. She looked so miserable a couple Sundays ago I called to find out how she was doing."

"You've betrayed our bargain."

"Your bargain. And not really. I don't hold out any hope to her. Look, she and I were close, she was my *friend*, and I feel some responsibility toward her. If it had gone the other way, I'd wonder how *you* were."

"And I'd take it as a sign you were still interested. Well, how *is* she?"

He seemed pleased to tell her, to pour on more quicksand. "Not so hot. She's talking about running away from all of us."

"Why would she leave Richard?"

"He beats her up now and then. He's angry because she doesn't fuck him enough. She says she can't because she still loves me. She feels very guilty about what she's doing to him, and doesn't want to hurt you any more, so she thinks the best thing would be to dispose of herself. Short of suicide, I mean. She doesn't have your death-wish."

"Don't tell me any more, I don't want to hear it. Don't you see, she's trying to panic you? She could perfectly well make love to Richard if she wanted to, she's been doing it for ten years."

"Oh, it's very subtle and delicate when you do it, but *she* has no problems."

"Oh, go to her, go and carry her off to Arizona or wherever you think you're going—Wyoming. Right? If you could see your face when you talk about her, Jerry, you'd hate yourself. You'd laugh at yourself."

"You were saying something."

"I was saying, go, because I can't take these phone calls. I'm sorry, I can't. When I hear that busy signal, it's like a door shut in my face, I get so low I can't describe it. This morning I went into the kitchen and just said the children's names, Joanna Charlie Geoffrey, Joanna Charlie Geoffrey, over and over to myself. It was the only thing I could think of to keep myself alive."

He hesitantly came forward and lightly embraced her. "Don't say that. You have yourself to live for."

"I have no self. I gave it away eight years ago."

"Nobody asked you to do that."

"Everybody did."

"Then it must have been a shaky self to begin with."

His tone was level, vengeful; how dare he gloat! Outraged, she made a vow. "The next time I come across you two talking like that, I'm going to get into the car and drive to the Mathiases and I don't give a damn if Richard is there or not. Now I mean it."

Jerry stepped back, shrugged, and said, "Of course you mean it," suggesting by his smile that of course she didn't. "But if because of you Sally needs to be rescued, I'll have to do it."

"I think you've used that stick on me often enough; it's worn out. I have nothing to lose; I'm losing my mind this way."

"Don't be silly. We're all depending on your sanity." Jerry was always saying things like that, compliments that cut like insults, thrown to trip her mind, which never failed to stop and puzzle over what was meant. For he

did not invariably mean the opposite of what was said.
In this instance she suspected it was true, they were all
in their craziness and infatuation and self-deception depending on her sad, defeated sanity to hold them back
from disaster. Well, she was tired of it.

The next time she called Jerry and got a busy signal,
and dialled Sally's number and got the same, it was
quarter of eleven on a weekday morning, and the children
were playing in the neighborhood. Ruth called the teen-
aged sitter, and the girl was at the beach. Her next choice,
Mrs. O, was sitting for Linda Collins, who had gone to
the city to shop. And Miss Murdock, homely as she was,
was at the beauty parlor. Then rain fell, and Ruth, watching the drops sift through the elm, cooled. Let it pass, she
decided. Let everything pass.

But the sudden summer storm brought the young sitter
back from the beach, and she returned Ruth's call. Ruth
asked her to come after lunch. Why? The momentum of
her anger had dissipated. If she went to see Sally in her
present mood, she would appear flustered and foolish.
Perhaps she should go talk to Richard instead. She would
be vague, betray no one, yet get a rub of advice, of wisdom. He kept an office in Cannonport, above his father's
first liquor store; Ruth had been there, had made love
there, on a sticky sofa of imitation leather, beneath a
framed print of mallards flying, while the secretary of the
realtor next door pounded her typewriter and the machinery of the dry-cleaning establishment nearby hissed
and clattered. She liked noises that could not touch her;
she liked the sensation of being naked behind a frosted-
glass door locked from the inside. Cannonport was twenty
minutes away—fifteen, with a push. She put on a seersucker skirt and a decent blouse, so she would look re-
spectable for Cannonport, yet not too dressed up in case
she decided to visit Sally after all.

Her Falcon seemed lightheaded under her touch, in the drizzly, wanly sunny atmosphere that had followed the rainstorm. The so-intensely green trees beside the road—she had seen them before, in a Monet, or was it a Pissarro? The bits of salmon pink along the birch trunks were Cézanne's. At the place where she could have slowed to turn up Sally's uphill driveway, Ruth accelerated. The road toward Cannonport licked her tires with an eager noise. Then, one by one, a series of images pulled her back toward Greenwood. Richard's dusty desk, an Army green: he was lazy, it was unlikely she would find him in his office. And suppose—she envisioned their naked bodies on the sofa: impossible, but what else might he think? Her children's round, vulnerable heads: they would wonder why she was gone, leaving them to fret in a rain-bound house. Her father's tired way of shrugging on his overcoat, chin tucked down upon his muffler, to go out at night to a biracial meeting: *Face things.* She turned left on a byway that would take her to Orchard Road, which by a slightly roundabout route would take her back to Greenwood and her children, Jerry, and Sally. She would revert to her first plan and face Sally again; this time of the day, they could have vermouth instead of coffee, and it might help. Her few miles in the direction of Richard had been a sinful waste of time, a mistake that must be quickly erased; she sped as if Sally were waiting for her. Afterwards, she doubted she was going over forty.

Ruth skidded on the S-curve just beyond the Rotary-Lions-Kiwanis sign welcoming all to Greenwood; an average of an accident a month occurred here. Not only did the town road crew patch with an oil that was slippery when wet, but the original roadbed had been banked the wrong way. Straightening the road, often proposed, would have meant cutting off a small corner of the van Huyten estate, which had been intact a century and a half; and the present Mr. van Huyten, a graceful, patriotic, long-divorced gentleman of seventy with coal-black hair and all his front teeth, resisted incursions. Since Ruth had been active in the citizens' group that had helped Mr. van Huyten defeat the power lines two years ago, she could not in principle blame him, even as death leaped up in front of her.

The Falcon, with a little skating skip like a sailboat with its centerboard pulled, slid to the left. Ruth steered to the right and was surprised to feel nothing answer her touch; it was as if she looked into a mirror that then turned transparent. Then, in a later portion of the same distended moment, her attempt at control was gigantically distorted; the car slewed heavily around to the right and she saw, omitting to brake, that she was going to go over the wall. A low fieldstone wall separated the roadway from a sunken stand of trees, elm and red maple and swamp oak. Softly bumping, the car coasted over the wall and travelled through swaying, scratching widths of green accented by upright trunks. For a section of her glide Ruth steered between the trunks; when the number of trees seemed to multiply hopelessly, she lay down on the front seat and shut her eyes. The car nuzzled obliquely to a stop. She searched the floor for the burning cigarette she had been holding. It had disappeared. A bird was chirping near at hand, unusually loud. She opened her door, which wanted to stick, and got out, closing it carefully. The rain had diminished to the daintiest touch of blowing moisture. Bluish-brown smoke poured steadily from the rear of the car, and the front wheel on the driver's side was set in its socket at an unexpected angle; she thought of Geoffrey's collarbone. In the damp green hush the engine ticked, insulted, and she supposed that if the car was going to explode she had better save her pocketbook. It had her driver's license in it.

Opening the car door again and reaching across the front seat for her pocketbook, Ruth noticed for the first time, by the caress of air on her arm and the extreme clarity of the leaves she saw, that the front window on the passenger's side was smashed. Shattered. The edges of it that hung in the frame were crazed fine as lace, and the front seat was strewn with fragments like a pale coarse confetti. Touching her hair, she found such fragments adhering to it. Her pocketbook, sitting on the seat mouth up, was filled with broken glass. She thought of emptying it, but imagined it might be some sort of evidence. She extracted her wallet, brushed glass from its leather, and checked that the ignition key was upright in the lock. She admired her own presence of mind, and moved away from the car. Wet branches brushed her. Each veined leaf and jointed twig seemed brightly poised in a sharp space somewhat artificial, like the depth of a stereoscope, unnaturally fresh and clean; but from the sodden, casual swish of the car that passed, unseen and unseeing, on the road beyond the wall, Ruth deduced that this was not Paradise and she was not dead.

She was trespassing, she perceived; she should get off of van Huyten's precious land. She had hurt his wall and his trees. The woods swerved about her with the unmoving motion of a scene painted on the awning of a carousel. She took a few steps farther, in soaked high-heeled pumps that found the ferny earth strange. From the fact of her walking she deduced that no bone was broken. She looked down, smoothed the front of her seersucker skirt, and saw that both her knees were cut; she could not imagine how. The bleeding was slight but she was grateful she had not worn stockings and ruined them. Her right wrist felt stiff. She studied her hands and the longer she held them under her eyes the worse they trembled. Behind her, the motor's ticking blended with the ticking of water drops and inquisitive, repetitive birdsong. She straightened and inhaled; the fine hair of the drizzle tingled on her face. Ruth attempted a prayer, but in the agitated grip of her mind the ambition was crushed. Grabbing a low branch, she pulled herself up the bank. Packed dead leaves made a slippery mulch and moss spongily trapped her spike heels. Level with the road, she found a place where, using a moldering log and a toppled stone, she could step across the wall. Safe and firm, she looked back and was delighted, delightedly grieved, by the sight of her car— her hundred horses, her freedom—parked so strangely and docilely deep and low in the woods. It seemed a Rousseau: the literal leafage, the air of static benevolence, the peaceful monster browsing, self-forgetful, on ferns and soft weeds. She could hear Jerry laughing, and the shy notion formed that he would be proud of her, for having dared do this, and for having survived, which made her as reckless, and miraculous, as Sally.

As Ruth stood at the side of the road, three cars passed her. The passengers of one of them, a station wagon, frowned at her indignantly as she waved. They thought she was a prostitute. Then a town truck heading into Greenwood stopped, and they understood just by glancing at her cut knees and dishevelled hair and at the damaged wall. They gave her a ride to the police station. She sat up high between the two men, who continued their conversation—some scandal about the town manager, his insistence on sewering his own street in contravention of the master plan—as if she were one of them. The truck muttered and rumbled reminiscently: years ago, the summer before she went to art school, she had had a boyfriend who drove a farm truck. Billy had had cup ears, a beautiful back when he worked bare-chested, and little ambition, which had annoyed her father. He had loved her, in his low-key, comfortable way. Everything had been comfortable about them—their petting, their silences— and he had been amiably hopeless about their futures; she was "going on," beyond him. She had wanted to argue, but it seemed presumptuous, and then it had been too late, that summer was over. Now, swaying back and forth so that her body touched now one and now the other of these middle-aged, solid, oblivious, accepting men, Ruth felt more cheerful than she had for weeks. She must tell Jerry.

At the police station a tall blond cop took her statement. Ruth knew him slightly; he had a Polish name, and looked like an exiled prince in winter, standing at the school intersection in a high fur hat with black earflaps. She had never been this close to him before; she explained, "I was driving along I thought very nicely, when the car took it into its head to leave the road and jump the wall." The windows were open to the sunshine that was returning as the afternoon lengthened and the officer wrote very slowly, his ballpoint denting the paper. She described skidding first this way, then that, bumping over the wall so softly, and seeming to herself to be steering through the interwoven trees until the car, of its own desire, stopped. She had no memory of braking. She supposed she thought it would do no good; isn't that what people say about skids? She got out, glass in her hair. Smoke was pouring from underneath the car, so she made sure the ignition was off. The front wheel looked hopelessly twisted, or she would have tried backing out. The officer asked her how fast she had been going. She guessed about forty, it couldn't have been much faster than that. "Since thirty-five," he said, writing slowly, "is the speed limit at that curve, let's say you were going thirty-five."

The elegance of this flat maneuver dazzled her. All summer she had been struggling with inequalities like the one between the speed limit and her actual speed, and this Polish prince showed her how to abolish them, to make the real ideal. Attempting to express her gratitude, she blushed—she felt not only her face heat, but her throat, breasts, thighs. The policeman said he would call the wrecker while she called her husband.

"But he's at work in New York. I can walk home from here. It's less than a mile."

"No," the young cop said, with no more inflection than a traffic light.

"I'm really perfectly all right," she insisted, knowing he would hold her to the truth, that she was not all right.

"You're in shock," he told her. "Is there anybody in town you could call to come for you? A woman friend?"

I have no woman friends: Ruth felt it would horrify him if she said this aloud. She said, "There is somebody. I'm not sure if I can reach him though."

But Richard did answer the Cannonport number, immediately. He had been sitting there, waiting for her silence to end.

"Dick? Hi. It's me. Ruth. This is pretty embarrassing, but I just ran my car off the road and Jerry's in the city and they won't let me out of the police station unless somebody comes for me. They say I'm in shock."

"In minor shock," the policeman said.

"Ruthie babes," Richard said. "This is fantastic, hearing your voice. I'm all shook up."

"Don't be," she said, "it's purely practical. Are you free, or is my successor on the job?"

She was aware of the policemen listening, yet was careless of what she said, as if, in breaking through van Huyten's wall, she had come into a green freedom.

"No successor, no successor," Richard was saying, in that maddening way of his, of playing at being businesslike. "You're at the Greenwood pokey, right? I'll be there."

"You're sweet to do this. Twenty minutes?"

"Ten."

"Don't speed. Please. One disaster a day is enough."

"Listen, I know that road like I know your ass."

She supposed she had asked for that, Ruth thought, hanging up. What had possessed her, to call him? Anger, she supposed. She regretted that not Jerry nor Sally but Richard must be her victim. But then, we pick victims we can handle, that are our size. And how much victimizing was it, to ask an old lover to drive eight miles to drive her one mile more? The policeman offered her a

Dixie cup of coffee, and told her that the wrecker had called back and wouldn't be able to dig her car out until tomorrow. The police radio crackled on in a corner of the station, the cops revolved with sheaves of paper, she felt herself nudged from the center of their attention. Pleasantly she let herself go blank. Thank God there was a world beyond the walls of her house where there were men paid to care about her, not too intensely. She must remember to tell Jerry, how happy she was in the police station.

When Richard came in, he announced himself at the desk by saying, "I've come to spring the broad."

"Mr. Conant?" the other young cop asked, not smiling.

"Mathias," Richard said. "I'm pinch-hitting. How is she?"

"She's a very lucky young lady," the cop told him. To Ruth he said, "The wrecker looked it over and says you won't be driving that car again. You totalled it."

Richard, trying to fit himself to the cop's solemnity, asked, "Should I take her to a doctor?"

"If it were me, I would."

"Don't be silly," Ruth said resentful, perhaps, at the way the policeman had been taken from her. His princely indifference had become a judicious stupidity; he handed her his report of the accident. *At approximately 1:45 p.m. . . . the dark-blue four-door Ford station wagon driven by Mrs. Gerald Conant, of . . . thirty-five miles per hour . . . suffered apparently superficial injuries . . . the vehicle was demolished.* His handwriting was uncouth. She signed, and left with Richard. She had forgotten how much bulkier than Jerry he was. She surprised herself by taking his arm.

"What's up?" he asked, settling into the driver's side of his dear old Mercedes. She had forgotten also that curious dent in his upper lip, the jut of the lower, the vulnerable size of his cowardly-lion's head.

"What do you mean?" Something strange was happening to Ruth's throat; a silvery web had been engendered in it, and in her sinuses and eye-sockets, and all the hollows of her skull.

Richard's mouth twitched impatiently. "You've got the wind up, Ruthie babes."

"The accident could have happened to anybody. The road—"

"Fuck the accident. You've been hysterical all summer. You've been looking like a wallflower at a witch hunt. Jerry giving you the needle again because you can't keep the boogey-man away?"

"No, Jerry doesn't talk about death much any more."

"Must be pretty quiet around the house then."

"Not really. How is it around yours?"

He quite missed the hint. The arc of frost sat on his cornea in profile like a cap. "O.K.," he said grimly. "You don't want to talk. Screw me."

"I *do* want to talk, Richard. But—"

"But the other fellow's wife might get the word if you spilled the beans to me, right?"

"What other fellow's wife?"

"My successor's bride, dame, snatch, *femme,* what the hell. You're playing games again, kee-recket? Davie Collins the lucky dog? He looks pretty woofy at folly ball. Jesus, Ruthie, when're you going to give yourself a break and trade in that neurotic doodlebug you married for half a man? You're just chewing yourself to pieces this way. You're just giving it the old Count Masoch one-two-three."

"Richard, you do go on. I'm flattered you imagine it, but I'm *not* having an affair. I do *not* think Jerry is half a man. Maybe I'm half a woman."

"A woman and a half, as I remember it. But O.K. I'm soft in the head. Soggy in the nog. Screw me. Screw you, for that matter. What you think I am, a once-a-year taxi service?"

"Where are we going?"

He was driving her out of town, to the woods, the buggy path, the pond where the motionless fisherman caught nothing. The web in her head broke and she began to cry; the tears were rapidly at full flood, she was shaking and trying to scream. She kept seeing the trees as she floated between them. The tears scrambled with words and wouldn't stop. "No, take me home. Take me to my house and drop me. That's what I asked you to do, that's what you promised you'd do, I don't want to neck, I don't want to have a cozy talk, I just want to go home and die, Richard. Please. I'm sorry. I can't take it. You're so right and you're so wrong it kills me. It does. You're the only person I could talk to and you're absolutely the worst person. Forgive me. I've liked this. I really have. It's not you. I like you, Richard. Don't make that silly hurt mouth. It's *not* you. It's—*it!*"

"Easy, easy," he was saying, frightened, trying to back around in a driveway too narrow, where people had painted the stones and planted a family of plaster ducks on the lawn.

"I *can't* do it all over, I *can't* go back into all that, into us; *please*. Do forgive me for calling you; I wasn't thinking. I should have called Linda. It was nice. You're so *damn* nice, somehow. You're lovely."

"Stick to the facts," he said, grimacing as he fought with the wheel. "I get the picture."

"You *don't*, as a matter of fact," Ruth told him. "That's what's so killing."

He let her off under the elm. "Sure you don't want to see a doctor? These concussions can be sneaky."

Out of the car, she leaned back in and kissed him on the mouth. He had been a good kisser, firm but not too hungry like Jerry. Ruth's tears were drying; her head felt scoured. "You *are* nice," she told Richard, adding with her needless love of truth, "funnily enough."

"Jesus," he said. "Thanks. Well, I'm around. Call me when you have your next wreck."

"You'll be the first to know," she told him.

The busy signal had ceased; she reached Jerry at work and told him, making light of the accident. He came home from the city a half-hour earlier than usual and wanted to see the wreck before dinner. As he drove her along Orchard Road, curbstones, porches, lawns, children, and trees melted into blurs beneath his speed, and she pleaded, "Don't go so fast."

"I'm only going thirty."

"It seems faster."

"Do you want to drive?"

"No thanks."

"I meant ever again. Have you lost your nerve, do you think?"

"I don't think so. It does seem wild, to be in a car again."

"How did you get back from the police station?"

"A policeman drove me."

"And what about a doctor? How are your insides? Were you bounced around a lot?"

"It seemed very smooth and easy. The one scary thing, I didn't step on the brake. It never occurred to me."

"Where were you going, anyway?"

She described her confusion and panic, the busy signals and the baby-sitters, her driving past Sally's driveway and her frantic doubling back. She left out Richard. She told again, what was becoming as rigid as a sequence of film, of the skid, the skid the other way, the wall, the calm trees, the Edenlike beauty and intensity of the dripping woods when she got out of the halted, smoldering car. At each rerun the images deepened in color; now they weirdly meshed with present reality, backward, end to end, as she and Jerry entered the accident scene from the opposite direction. He parked the car on the shoulder, got out, and began to cross the road. She said she didn't want to see it, she'd wait in the car. He lifted his eyebrows and she changed her mind. He expected her to be sane. Together they crossed the asphalt. Were these skid marks hers? She couldn't tell, there were so many. But here, where two interrupted ruts gouged the soft shoulder and a half-dozen rocks had been knocked from the top of the wall, was where she had leaped. The bark high on the trunk of a hickory had been skinned off; a little farther on, a maple sapling had been bent and patchily stripped. The car had tried to climb it, and had crushed it to the ground. Ruth could not coördinate her memory of gentle flight with these harsh scars. Deeper in the grove, more trees were skinned, and tire tracks showed like the marks of giant fingers that had torn the soft earth of leaf mold and growing ferns. Jerry was impressed by how far the car had slithered, between the trees that could have stopped it, before its momentum surrendered to the mud and underbrush. "You travelled a hundred feet in there."

"It all seemed rather abstract." She wondered if he were inviting her to be proud.

Jerry climbed down to the car, opened the door, and took the maps and registration from the glove compartment and some towels and beach toys from the back. He walked once around the car, smiling, and laughed at the far side, the side Ruth could not see. Returning to her, hopping the wall, he said, "That whole right side is caved in. It looks like tinfoil."

"Can it be fixed?"

"It's had it. Once the frame is bent, you're better off just collecting the insurance. Things never get right again."

"My poor old car." Metal crumpled within her and she felt a shape of grief. "It seems heartless just to leave it."

"The wrecker will come and tow it away. Come on.

Get in." Into his old Mercury convertible: the car's interior suddenly smelled of Sally. Ruth balked. "Let's *go*," he said. "We have children."

"About time you thought of that," she said, sliding in.

"I never stop thinking about it. How about you? If you were thinking about the children you wouldn't go doing automotive stunts all over the country." He popped the clutch in, "burned rubber" as teenagers say. It was ugly of him.

She said, determined to be calm, "It was an accident."

"It was a *stunt*," Jerry said. "A deliberate stunt. The death-defying housewife, with her great big death-wish. You didn't even *brake*."

"I thought you shouldn't brake in a skid. It seemed more important to steer."

"*Steer*! You couldn't steer, how the hell could you steer?"

"I felt I was steering. Then when I couldn't steer any more, I lay down on the front seat."

"Yes, that's the way you cope, isn't it? You just lie down on the front seat and hope everything goes away. And the damnedest thing is, it *works*. Anybody else would have been *killed* barrelling into that woods."

As she sat numb and frightened beside this angry, speeding man, the truth dilated until she felt all hollow with the simple seeing of it. The clouds of green again parted; she slid smoothly through the shuffle of tree trunks. The car nuzzled to a stop. She emerged and the tingling air touched her, loved her. She had had an accident. Jerry had been expecting this to happen. He had been praying for it. His prayer had been answered mockingly: only the car had been destroyed. She remembered his smile as he studied the wreck. "You're mad," she said, testing the words carefully, like a ladder of rotten rungs, "that I wasn't."

"Killed?"

"Yes."

He considered. "No, not exactly. I've been waiting, I suppose, for God to do something, and this was it. His way of saying that nothing is going to happen. Unless you and I make it happen."

"Do you realize what you're *saying*? You're saying you want me dead."

"Am I?" He smiled calmly. "It's just a fantasy, I'm sure." He stopped smiling and patted her thigh solemnly. "Do *you* want to make something happen?"

"No."

"Well, then, relax. You're indestructible. Nothing will happen."

The day after the accident, on the beach, Sally came up to Ruth with a fixed smile and swarming eyes and said how glad she was that Ruth had not been hurt. Ruth believed her, and regretted being too startled to respond with much more than a nod. She had been baking the accident out of herself, the aches in her knees and shoulders (from gripping the wheel harder than she knew?) and the flickering sense of skidding and flying that came upon her whenever she closed her eyes. Sally's face, tinted by the glare violently as a Bonnard—her lips purple, her hair ashen—seemed a pale, feral apparition striking into the cloudless blue to which Ruth had been yielding herself. "Ruth, I heard about your accident and just wanted to say how glad I am you weren't hurt. Truly." Walking away, Sally looked thin; the backs of her thighs had developed a ripple of slack. When they had all been younger in Greenwood Sally's body had seemed smooth as a model's, as a machine. The two yellow pieces of her bathing suit receded and merged with the Prendergast dabs of the beach crowd. The next day, apparently, she packed her three children into a plane and flew to Florida, where her brother and his second wife had their home, in the orange grove country around Lake Wales. Ruth learned about it from Jerry, who apparently had encouraged her to go.

"Why?"

"The bind was getting to be too much for her."

"What bind? What *is* a bind, exactly?"

"A bind is when all the alternatives are impossible. Life is a bind. It's impossible to live forever, it's impossible to die. It's impossible for me to marry Sally, it's impossible for me to live without her. You don't know what a bind is because what's impossible doesn't interest you. Your eyes just don't see it."

"Well, you're looking pretty impossible to me right now. What right, what possible right, did you have to send her off to Florida on Richard's money?"

Jerry laughed. "It *is* that bastard's money, isn't it?"

"Jerry, you are sick. Why should you hate Richard?"

"Because he's an atheist like everybody else and you're all trying to put me in a coffin." Sally's being far away had loosened his tongue unpleasantly; Ruth felt him hardening himself, for a desperate decision.

"What is this trip to Florida supposed to prove?" she asked. "Are you supposed to go after her?"

"Gee, I never thought of that. I've never been to Florida."

"Don't be funny."

"Is September when the orange blossoms come out?"

"You're not coming back into this house if you go."

"How could I go? Be reasonable. She's there for a rest—from Richard, from me, from you, from the whole thing. She's exhausted. This summer of waiting you asked for was the cruellest thing you could have done. We're killing her, you and me and whatsisname. She's been living on pills and she's desperate."

"Pills, piffle. Any woman can work herself up into that kind of desperation when she wants something. She wants you to run off with her."

He focussed on this possibility, and his face took on

the incisive set and sharpened lines—as if drawn by himself—that she remembered from the days when at their adjacent easels they were concentrating in parallel on the model. "I don't think that's the way to do it," he said now. "I think if it's going to be done it has to be ground out with lawyers and trial separations and heartbroken parents and weeping kids and the works. How would our children feel if I just disappeared with Mrs. Mathias and Bobby and Peter and teeny Theodora? Those awful children—they all look like Richard. They're all ogres."

"Stop it," Ruth told him. "Don't complain to me because Sally had children with her husband instead of with you."

"That's the great thing about you," he said, "everybody else has all the problems. You don't have any, do you? Poor Sally and I spend all our time on the phone wondering what dear old Ruth will do when she's abandoned with all her children and you just fucking well don't have any fucking problems, do you? How do you do it, baby? You smash the car up to brighten a dull day and don't get a scratch. Your world's coming to an end and you lie down on that fucking beach all summer happy as a clam. That old One-in-One God of yours must be a real cucumber up there."

"I'm a Judaeo-Christian, just like you are," Ruth said.

The children, especially Charlie, were growing disturbed. Back from work, Jerry used to play catch with the boys in the back yard, or take all three for an evening at the Hornungs' pool, but now he did nothing at home but sit and stare and drink gin-and-tonics and listen to his Ray Charles records and talk to Ruth, trying, by now wearily, to arrange their words and states of mind in the combination that would unlock his situation and free his heart. At meals his eyes kept going out of focus: he was seeing Sally. Days passed, became a

week, then ten days, and neither Jerry nor Richard knew
when she would return. A gaudy bird, outlandish in her
plumage, she had flown to the tropics; from there,
dwindled but unforgettable, she sang to them, and the
busy signal at Jerry's office was her song. In intermit-
tences of rage and despair Ruth felt sorry for him, he
looked so "torn." His speckled irises looked ragged, and
outdoors he held his head at an odd angle, as if listening
for a signal, or offering himself like Isaac to a blow
from above. "Decide, please," Ruth pleaded. "We'll all
survive, just do what you want and stop caring about us."

"I can't," he said. "What I want is too tied up with
how it affects everybody else. It's like one of those
equations with nothing but variables. I can't solve it. I
can't solve it. She cries over the telephone. She doesn't
mean to cry. She's quite funny and brave about it. She
says it's a hundred and ten and her sister-in-law walks
around stark naked."

"When is she coming back?"

"She's afraid it has to be soon. She and the kids have
filled the house and their welcome is wearing thinner
and thinner."

"Has she told them why she's there?"

"Not really. She's admitted being unhappy with Richard and her brother tells her to stop being silly and
spoiled. Richard takes care of her and anyway her duty
is to her children."

"Which is true."

"Why is it true? How does he take care of her? He
sent her off with hardly enough money for the airplane
tickets."

"Have you sent her money?" It made Ruth weak, the
thought that Jerry was pouring the children's education
away, that this expensive woman was haunting their
bank accounts as well as their bed.

"No, I think I'm supposed to send myself. And I can't.
I keep wanting to, but I never quite can, there's always

something, Joanna's piano recital or having the Collinses to dinner or some damn dental appointment. God, it's awful. It's awful talking to her. I wish you'd talk to her since you're so interested."

"I'd be happy to. Just put me on the line. I have lots to say to that woman suddenly."

"The reason she went to Florida was to stop hurting you. She hated your accident."

"I thought you said she went hoping you'd follow."

"I think both ideas were in her mind. She's mixed up."

"Well she's not the only one."

While her waking life was consciously occupied by concern for her children and home, an unaccustomed ferocity entered Ruth's dreams. Violence, amputation, and mad velocity hurled together scenes and faces from remote corners of her life. In one dream, she was riding along the road in Vermont that led to the summer place they used to rent. It seemed to be the stretch below the abandoned sawmill, where the ruts were deepest because the sun never broke through the overhanging branches to dry the mud. They were in a race. Up ahead, in a spindly black open buggy, her father, David Collins, and the little old lady in the Babar books were sitting in a prim-backed row; her father was driving, which frightened her, because he was so reckless, as ministers tend to be, and, lately, being deafer and deafer, oblivious to cars approaching from the side and behind. She and Geoffrey were following in a strange low cart without any visible means of propulsion. They were smoothly flying and yet their wheels were touching the rutted road. She felt her son's anxiety as hers; his tears burned in her throat. Suddenly the buggy stopped, stopped like a frozen film. David and Daddy held on to the sides, but the old lady, between them, had nothing to hold to, and instantly slipped out of sight. They all gathered around her. She lay on the side of the road, in the scruffy grass, a little withered heap of bones. The impact had foreshortened her body within her black dress, and her legs had been hideously broken, so they radiated from her body like the legs of a spider. Her face, yellow and matted in its flowing hair, was bent backwards, and as she opened her mouth her teeth, elongated dentures, slipped down like a drawgate. She was dying, crushed. She was trying to speak. Ruth bent down to listen, and the dream shifted to a watery realm, a realm of blue-green water tinted alkaline by a white bottom of coral sand, the water of the Carribbean, of St. John's, where she had once gone with Jerry, years ago, when she was pregnant with Geoffrey. Perhaps she had meant to dream of Florida.

Saturday Jerry said he had some errands to run downtown and an hour later called her on the telephone. "Ruth," he said, in a voice two tones lower than normal —she could imagine that open pay phone in the drugstore—"could I come back and talk to you?"

"Sure." Her knees began to tremble.

"How many children are home?"

"Just Charlie. Joanna took Geoffrey to the Cantinellis' garage sale."

She went into the kitchen and filled an orange-juice glass with vermouth and drank it as if it were water, water tasting of fire. She was still in the kitchen when he came in the back door; the cry of cicadas, the dry football smell of summer's end, followed him in.

"I've talked to Sally," he said, "and she must leave Florida. Her children are miserable. School starts in a week."

"Yes. Well?" He hung there, expecting something. She asked, "You said all this over that phone in the drugstore?"

"I used the one at the back of the Texaco place. She wants to know if I'm coming to her now. The summer's over."

"It's not Labor Day yet."

"It's September."

The trembling had spread up her legs into Ruth's belly; the dash of vermouth there felt like a knife plunged in so tightly she could not bleed around it.

Jerry blurted, "Please don't look so pale." His own face was wrapped in the look of abstracted compassion with which he would remove a splinter or a thorn from her hand or one of the children's feet.

She asked, wanting him to approve of her control, "Where would you go to meet her?"

He shrugged and laughed, conspiratorially. "I don't know. Washington? Wyoming? She'd have all the damn children of course. It's awkward, but it could be managed. Other people do it."

"Not many."

He gazed at their worn linoleum floor.

She asked him, "Do you want to go?"

"I'm scared, but yes. I want to go, tell me to *go*."

She shrugged now, leaning against the sink counter, the little glass in her hand, with its tilting remnant of liquor. "Then go."

"Will you be all right? There's over a thousand in the checking account and I think about eighty-five hundred in the savings bank." He made as if to touch her, lifting his hands in unison; his body seemed to her a stiff machine determinedly set in motion while the helpless passenger screamed behind his eyes.

"I'll be fine," she said, drained the glass of its last sip, and in afterthought threw it to the floor. The fragments and drops flew in a stopped star across the marbled pattern of the old green linoleum.

Charlie ran into the kitchen at the noise; Ruth had forgotten he was in the house. Charlie was small for his age, with an eager fine face and Jerry's uncombable cowlick. "Why did you do that?" he asked, smiling in readiness to be told it was a joke. He was the most logical of their children, and without a theory of "jokes" grown-ups would not have fitted into his universe at all. He stood waiting, small and smiling. He was seven. He wore khaki shorts, and his bare chest bore a summer's tan.

Ruth burst: she felt salt water spring from her eyes like spray. She told the child, "Because Daddy wants to leave us and go live with Mrs. Mathias!"

With the silent quickness of a whipped cat Charlie fled the kitchen; Jerry chased him, and Ruth saw them together in the living room, framed by a doorway as in one of the domestic Dutch masters, the boy sitting on the wing chair, his bare feet sticking out straight, his head stubborn and radiant, his father in his Saturday Levi's and sneakers kneeling and trying to embrace him. Charlie was not making himself easy to hold. Ruth's elm added to the scene a window of yellow and green.

"Don't cry," Jerry pleaded. "Why are you crying?"

"Mommy said—Mommy said you want to live"—a suppressed sob made his bony chest heave—"with those children."

"No I don't. I want to live with you."

She couldn't watch. Carefully, for her own feet were bare, Ruth swept up the broken glass. The shards, some of them fine as powder, chimed from the pan into the wastebasket. *Dust to dust*. When she was done, Charlie padded to her across the clean floor and said, "Daddy went out. He said he'd be back." He delivered the message full of dignity, as if he were ambassador to an enemy.

Jerry returned while Ruth was putting the toasted cheese sandwiches for lunch into the oven. He looked breathless, weightless, scarecrowlike, staring. A car squealed out on the road. "I called Sally again."

She closed the oven door, checked the setting, and said, "And?"

"I told her I can't come to her. I described the incident

with Charlie and said I just couldn't do it. She's flying back to Richard tomorrow. She said she wasn't too surprised. She was pretty sore at you for using the children but I told her you hadn't meant to. She got pretty shrill, I thought."

"Well in her circumstances who could blame her?"

"I could," Jerry said. "I loved that woman, and she shouldn't have pushed." His mouth was small and his voice cold, tired of passion as the summer was tired of sun. Ruth wondered if she dared mourn for Sally; together they had inhabited this man, and banishment of this other seemed too arbitrary and too harsh. Ruth wanted to know more, to hear every word Sally said, to hear her shrieks; but Jerry clamped shut his treasure. Joanna brought Geoffrey back from the sale—they had bought an ashtray shaped like a chicken—and there was no more talking.

Sally came to volleyball next day. It was a September Sunday of light gray clouds, not so much cool as drafty, as if a door had been left open somewhere in the weather. Sally, who in July would come wearing her yellow bathing suit under one of Richard's shirts, the tails knotted at her belly, had reverted to the white slacks and boatneck jersey she had worn at summer's outset. The skin of her face appeared stiff; the Florida tan had placed tiny white wrinkles at the corners of her eyes. She was greeted on all sides, as if her return were a spectacular self-rescue. Richard, in tartan Bermudas, looked softer than the day he had breezed into the police station. Ruth wondered what he and Sally had done to each other, to make him so amiably dazed. With no depth perception, he kept playing easy shots into the net and lurching into people. Once he bumped into Ruth and, in the jarring, she smelled gin. Once Jerry shouted, "Sally!", for a save, when a ball he had hit badly sailed in her direction; she stretched, attempting to leap, but the ball fell untouched between her body and the net. His shout, a plea to be rescued, hung in the air a long time, untouched by the silence of the others. What had been between them had vanished beneath the surface of the game, leaving stranded Jerry's disjointed, desperate style of play. Leaping, diving, dropping again into the dirt and broken glass to make impossible saves, he seemed a madman detached from reality, a fish out of water. It was all for Sally's benefit, but the woman's sun-stiffened heart-shaped face was dead toward him. For the last time, Jerry poisoned a Sunday evening with the sorrow that followed a volleyball game; the next day was Labor Day. Volleyball, the summer, the affair were over. The children went back to school; the casual gatherings on the grass or by the water on the excuse of the children ceased. Weeks passed without the Conants and the Mathiases meeting.

Ruth felt cheated. She had waited for defeat behind the weak and random defenses she had thrown up, and been cheated of it by her own tears, and the tears of her son—in what right scale do a child's tears weigh more than a man's? Jerry devalued himself by not acting on the strength of his unhappiness. She found in his car a paperback called *Children of Divorce*. He was trying to estimate the cost of an incalculable action: if Joanna and Charlie and Geoffrey each cried a quart of tears, he would stay; if merely a pint, he would go. If the odds on her remarrying were seven out of ten, he would go; if they were worse than fifty-fifty, he would stay. It was humiliating; a man shouldn't stay with a woman out of pity, or if he did he shouldn't tell her. Jerry neither told her nor told her otherwise, or, rather, he told her both at various times. What he said lost all specific point; she hardly listened, gathering only from the churn of words that things were not yet settled, there had been no climax, he was not resigned, he was still in love, though Sally had been lost she lived within him more than ever, the thing was unfinished, Jerry was unsatisfied, his wife had failed him, in clumsily refusing to die she had failed, it was all her fault, she would get no rest ever.

Each evening, coming home from work, he would hopefully ask, "Did anything happen?"

"No."

"Nobody called or anything?"

"Did you expect somebody to call?"

"No."

"Well, then."

He turned to the day's mail.

She asked, "How do you feel?"

"O.K. Fine."

"No, really."

"Tired."

"Physically tired?"

"That's the final effect, yes."

"Just from living with me?"

"I wouldn't put it that way."

"From living without her?"

"Not really. I was never so sure I would have enjoyed living with her. She could be pretty pushy."

"Then what's eating you? This suffering in silence is worse than anything yet. I think I'm losing my mind."

"Nonsense. You're the sanest person I know."

"I *was* the sanest person you knew. 'Did anything happen?' Every time you ask me that I want to pick up a plate and smash it, I want to put my fist through one of these windowpanes. What do you *expect* to happen?"

"I don't know. Nothing. I suppose I'm expecting *her* to do something. But what can she do?"

Ruth moved across the room and took him by the arms as if to shake him, but instead gripped him weakly; his arms felt so thin. "Don't you understand? You've *had* it with her. You've *had* it."

Jerry gazed over her head, through her hair. "That

can't be." He spoke with the heaviness of a sleepwalker. "You can't go from so much to nothing so quickly."

"Please *focus*," she said, trying to shake him now like a child and discovering him too big, so that in the effort it was she who was shaken. "Women are at the mercy of men. She loved you, but you failed her, and now she must hold on to Richard. She needs Richard. She's had her children by Richard. You mustn't interfere any more."

"She'll try somebody else now, to get her out."

"All right, let her. You have no claim on her, Jerry."

"I had to fail somebody. I had to fail either her or you and the children."

"I know that. Don't rub it in. I know if it had been between her and me alone you wouldn't have hesitated."

"That's not true. I would have hesitated."

"Very funny. Why do you *say* things like that? Why do you *bother*?"

"I pay you the compliment," he said, "of trying to tell you the truth."

"Well *stop* it. It's no longer a compliment. I don't want the truth any more. What are you *doing* to me, Jerry?"

"I'm doing nothing to you. I'm being your husband."

"You've stopped making love to me. You know that, don't you?"

"I thought you'd be pleased."

"Why should I be pleased?"

"I thought you didn't like it."

"Of course I like it."

"You used to turn your back."

"Not always."

"We'll make love tonight."

"No. It'll be her. It'll be her in your mind. It's too degrading."

"What do you want me to do?"

"Stop thinking of her."

"I can't."

"Then don't let me *see* you thinking. Do it in New York. Do it at the beach. When you're in my house, think of me. If you're going to make love to me, make me think it's me. Lie to *me*. Seduce me."

"You're my wife. I shouldn't have to seduce you."

"*Make* me your wife. Hold me. Hold *me*."

She pressed herself against him but his arms remained limp. "Why, Ruth," Jerry said. "Poor Ruth. You have me. I thought that would make you happy. Aren't you happy?"

"No, I'm frightened."

"You're never frightened."

"I'm sick."

"Physically?"

"Not yet."

"How then?"

"Let me confess something. The other Saturday when you went to get a haircut without telling me and it took all afternoon I kept looking out the window—I remember how the elm looked so clearly—and around five-thirty I thought, 'He's gone. He's left me.' And it was a *relief*."

He hugged her at last, and there was warmth in the pressure of their bodies, but she could not yield altogether to it, for she felt in his pull a malevolence like that of gravity; he was pleased because she was falling, her mind was letting go.

She had ceased to understand herself; the distinction between what she saw and what she was had ceased to be clear. As September wore thin, the heating man came and reactivated the furnace, and in the cooling nights it switched itself on and off. Lying awake, Ruth was troubled by the unaccustomed murmur, and uncertain if it were real and, if it were, whether it came from the furnace beneath her, an airplane overhead, or the transformers on the pole outside the bedroom window.

Somewhere in the spaces of her life an engine was running, but where? Jerry and Sally, she was sure, had
wounded each other beyond the possibility of collabora-
tion, but Ruth felt a fate working, a pattern of external
events generated by the dark shapes within her mind.
The world is composed of what we think it is; what we
expect tends to happen; and what we expect is really
what we desire. As a negative wills a print, she had
willed Sally. Why else the impatience with which she
viewed the imperfections in Sally's beauty—the bitter
crimp in one corner of her mouth, the virtual fattiness
of her hips? She wanted her to be perfect, as she wanted
Jerry to be decisive. Ruth disliked, religiously, the satisfaction he took in being divided, confirming thereby the
split between body and soul that alone can save men
from extinction. It was all too religious, phantasmal. The
beast of his love had been too easily led by the motions
of Ruth's mind. It had halted three months at her merely
asking by moonlight, and had altogether vanished in
another weak wave of her hand, at the sparkle of Charlie's
tears. Too easy, too strange. Ruth suspected some residue
of momentum in the summer that, now that the nights
had drawn equal to the days in length, must be discharged
by some last act of her will. She was a prisoner; the
crack between her mind and the world, bridged by a
thousand stitches of perception, had quite closed, leaving
her embedded, as the white unicorn is a prisoner in the
tapestry.

The last Friday of the month, the Collinses persuaded
them to come Greek dancing in Cannonport. Old Cannonport, clinging to the sea with its creaking docks and
weeping gulls. The dance was in the basement of a
V.F.W. Hall, a big clapboard building with a square
belfry, on the side of a hill of shingled four-story tene-
ments. Salt water showed black at the foot of the street.

The frosted basement windows of the hall were aglow with a milky fire, of a tumultuous cavern within; music penetrated the walls. Jerry and Ruth and David and Linda descended the concrete steps of a side entrance; a man so shinily bald the sutures of his skull declared their pattern sold them scarlet tickets. Inside, there was light and heat and noise, and people packed solid, sitting, standing, drinking beer, dancing in crammed sinuous lines, their faces glazed, foolish, devilish. The Mathiases were here. They were with the Hornungs. "I mentioned it to them but didn't think they'd come," Linda said quickly to Ruth, as Richard came forward, Sally following.

Richard looked drunk and sheepish; Ruth saw he was having an affair, or about to have one, with Janet Hornung. Sally was wearing an orange dress, its color both dramatic and flattering. Ruth's temples began to ache. Richard took her hand and they joined the dance line winding past them, dragging her away, merging her into the mass.

The orange of Sally's dress kept cutting into the corners of her vision as she danced. At moments they would be opposite in the spiralling lines, Sally's face downcast, her figure seeming intact with those around her, so that she seemed secure in a section of a frieze; whereas Ruth felt pinned, pulled, contrary, and clumsy. Hands copulated with hers. Richard's boneless fingers kept flipping to renew his grip. An unknown man, a hopping, jerking man with hair bubbling from his sleeves, seized her wrist and flashed a snaggled, meaningful grin. Some hands felt thick as buns, some limp as dough. For some moments Ruth danced beside a squat Greek matron in black, her nose hooked and her eyes hooded, and the woman's hand was a little flat bird, trembling with a terrible, inhumanly rapid pulse. The dance over, Ruth released the hand and stared with wonder at the woman's ordinarily weary and stupid face. With the same wonder she looked at Sally

and imagined that she had often come to meet Jerry in
that dress, that Jerry had often removed it to make love.
The bouzouki and the clarinet slashed into another tune;
Ruth's headache sharpened. Jerry came and took her
hand. His touch was so gentle it kept breaking; she
groped for his hand and her feet groped for the steps.
Kick with the left foot, left behind right, step, reverse,
yes, feet together, rest on the heels one beat. Kick.
Orange flickered at the right edge of her vision and,
moments later, on her left. Jerry's hand slipped from hers,
Richard smirked going by, the percussion increased the
tempo, Jerry took her hand again. The music halted.
The ceiling of the hall was a network of pipes painted a
poisonous green; it was lowering upon her.

Jerry said to her, "Come on, get with it. You dance
like there's a stone in your shoe."

"I have a headache."

"You're thinking too hard. I'll get you a drink."

But the bourbon only made her dizzy, and now,
whether she was dancing or standing, the room spun, and
Sally's bright shape with its mocking shadow of energy
cut at her from one side and then another, whittling her
smaller and smaller; she became a lump, a lump of pain.
The light sickened her. The leader of the band rose up
with an electric guitar and yipped and launched a Twist.
The noise seemed to Ruth something solid the band was
stuffing into the far corners of the hall, into the dusty
mysterious spaces between the pipes and the ceiling.
Jerry was leading Sally into the dance area. Ruth was not
surprised. She noticed how, as they moved to the center
of the floor, Jerry and Sally took everyone's eye; there
was something striking about them as a couple, something
adolescent and tall, vaguely comic and dramatically demanding, as actors are demanding of their audience. Not
touching, they faced each other and dropped their angular
bodies into the dance; a ring of people formed around
them and hid them from Ruth's view. David Collins came

up to her, looked at her face, and moved away; she felt he was frightened. She felt she was contagious, foul, cursed, and about to give birth, through the pain in front of her head, to a monster like herself. When the Twist at last ended, she went up to Jerry and said, "Please take me home. I hate this."

His hectic face made eyes of surprise.

"Please."

Jerry looked over her head toward Sally and asked her, "Can you fit the Collinses into your car? Evidently we have to leave."

"Sure. I'm sorry, Ruth, you don't feel well." It was Sally's voice at its most toney, a delicate drawl beyond reproach.

Ruth turned. "You lied to me," she said, determined to be distinct, though panic and nausea were tumbling inside her.

The muscles in Sally's face stiffened, and her eyes darkened so that their sockets seemed deep. But in reply she repeated, "I'm sorry, Ruth," as if she had heard nothing.

Nothing. The dream was moving on without her now. Jerry drove back to Greenwood furiously fast; both could have been killed, and Ruth dared not lift her voice, lest he veer. Yet the danger bound them together, almost comfortably; Jerry was challenging his death, and their speed served to remove Ruth's headache. She felt pain flying in sparks and clumps from the top of her skull like snow in winter from a car's heaped roof. They didn't speak, but his asthmatic breathing was loud. It was midnight when they got home, and later still when he got back from taking Mrs. O home. Ruth had changed into her nightie and terrycloth robe and restored herself with a glass of milk. He came in the kitchen door gesturing. His wet shoes tracked dead leaves in. "Sweetie," he said, flinging down his hands, palms up, "I must leave you. She's too lovely. I can't let her go."

"Don't use your hands in that affected way and keep your voice down. I can hear you."

He spoke in jerky gusts, striding back and forth on the linoleum. "I saw it tonight, very clearly. A revelation. I've been waiting for one, and there it was. I must go to her. I must go to that orange dress and dive in and disappear. I don't care if it kills me, I don't care if it kills you. Anything that gets in the way—the children, the money, our parents, Richard—none of it matters. It's just stuff, bad stuff. Tough stuff. It needs faith. I've just lacked faith, in a funny way faith in you. I didn't think you were a person, apart from me. But you are. God, Ruth, I'm sorry, I'm so sorry. It'll be more awful than I can imagine, I know. But I *am* sure. Quite sure. It's a relief to be sure. I'm very thankful. I'm numb and scared, but glad. Be glad too. Please? I was just nibbling you to death this other way."

Her fingers felt huge, expanded like the noise of a gong, on the cold glass of milk. "All right," Ruth said. "If you've made up your mind, I promised to help you. How shall we do it? When will you tell the children?"

"Don't make me tell the children yet. Just don't make me sleep here tonight. Don't talk me into it. You probably can, but don't. Let me go somewhere else. To the Collinses. To a motel."

"What will I tell them in the morning? The children?"

"Tell them the truth. Tell them I went somewhere. Tell them I'll be home in the afternoon and give them a bath and put them to bed. I won't leave at night until they're asleep."

"I suppose you'll have her with you."

"No. Absolutely not. I don't want her to know. I don't want her to know anything until it's definite, she'll just get herself stirred up."

"You mean this is not definite?"

He hesitated, wide-eyed. He said, "I have to see how you and the kids take it."

"We'll take whatever we have to. Isn't that the idea?"

"Now don't be bitter. You promised to help. Give me the dignity of trying this."

Ruth shrugged. "Try anything you want." When she lifted the milk to her lips, it smelled sour. She saw little curdled flecks floating on the surface, and was unable to drink. "Suppose somebody invites us somewhere, what do I say?"

"Accept, for now. I'll go with you."

"So the only difference is you won't be sleeping with me?"

"Isn't that the crucial difference? It's a start, anyway. It's right. No matter what happens, it's right."

"Oh. What a curious thing to say."

"Sweetie, the bluebird has flown. We're too young to sit around the rest of our lives waiting for it to fly back in the window. It won't. It can't fly backwards."

He was using his hands again in that disagreeable stagey way, and Ruth was angered by the flicker of conceit in his expression when he struck upon the image of the bluebird flying backwards—a piece of animation on the screen of his face. She rose and went to the sink.

Jerry called plaintively, "Now don't start drinking!"

She poured the milk down the sink, rinsed out the glass, and placed it mouth down in the drainer. She checked if there were any crumbs on the counter to attract ants and, finding a few by the toaster, brushed them with one hand into the other, and down the sink, after the milk. With a wet washcloth she erased a smear of jam she had noticed near the toaster. She switched off the counter lights and said, "I'm not drinking. I'm going to bed."

She had to pass Jerry to reach the stairs. "How's your headache?" he asked.

"Don't touch me," she said. "My headache's better, but if you touch me I'll cry or scream, I don't know which. I'm going to bed, it's late. You going to pack, or what?"

"Isn't there something more we should say? I feel there is."

"We can say it later. There'll be plenty of time. I'm not going to be hurried through this."

She brushed her teeth in the children's bathroom, to keep away from Jerry. She used Charlie's toothbrush, which was stiff and sharp from being rarely used; she must speak to him. She went to bed in her robe. Despairingly, chilled, she bunched the two pillows under her head and made a burrow of the covers, curling up on her side. In the purple void, spangled with odd flashes, beneath her eyelids, the tingle of her own hair on her cheek and lips seemed an alien touch. She listened to the distant clicks and scrapes of Jerry's packing. His footsteps approached, the light of their bedrom door opening bleached the purple beneath her lids a translucent blood-pink, he was rummaging in the drawer beside her head. "I better take my Medihaler," he said.

His voice was reedy and the sound of his breathing shallow and forced. "If it's so right," she asked, "why are you having an attack?"

"My asthma," he said, "is a function of fatigue and dampness and the time of the year. It has nothing to do with you, or Sally, or right or wrong or God." He bent over, brushed back the strand of hair that had been touching her cheek, and kissed her cheek. "Shall I wait till you fall asleep?"

"No. I'll be all right. I'm fine. Go away."

Incredibly, he obeyed. She listened as his footsteps patrolled the house, visiting each child's room, summing up their life together, making the decisive sounds of opening and closing doors; his footsteps diminished down the stairs, limping under the weight of something he was carrying. The front door eased open. There was a careful bump on the porch outside. He seemed to be hesitating here; she waited for the door to open again and admit him, for his footsteps to return up the stairs, with that way of his heels clattering he had. But she had misjudged the silence. He had descended the porch stairs without making a sound. A car door opened, and slammed. The starter churned, the motor roared inside her head, lifting in pitch as it diminished in volume. He was gone.

The breadth of the bed felt huge. Ruth uncurled a little into the white. She was skiing, doing a slow traverse across a broad, rather bare and icy slope, concentrating on keeping her weight well forward and on the downhill ski. A patch of brown grass showed through the snow cover, but she glided over it easily, and planted her pole for the turn. The turn felt right; though her speed was not great she lifted smoothly, perhaps because there was no loose powder to snag the heels of her skis.

She awoke Saturday morning with Geoffrey in bed beside her. In the oblivious egoism of his small body he had taken the center of the bed and pushed her to one edge; with Jerry, he being the heavier, it was she who was pulled into the middle. Geoffrey's face, slack and still, was in texture like some dense pale marble into which light penetrates a millimeter. The solemnity of this face, the utterly humorless perfection with which the eyebrows, the eyelids, the fat whorls of the nostrils and the ears had been worked out frightened her, as if, in the night, a stolen masterpiece had been dumped in her bed. She fought down panic.

Joanna came into the bedroom, grumpy and rub-eyed, and asked where Daddy was. "Daddy got up early because he had some special work." The children accepted her explanation without doubt and without much interest. Ruth rose and the fixtures in the bathroom had the unreal sheen of a Christmas decoration. In the kitchen she checked the calendar again and verified her count; she was three days late. After feeding the children breakfast she carried the vacuum cleaner downstairs. Jerry called around ten.

"Sleep well?"

"Not badly. Geoffrey at some point got into bed with me and I didn't even wake up."

"See? I told you you'd like having the bed to yourself."

But she *hadn't* had it all to herself was what she had just told him. She suppressed the impulse to quarrel and asked him, "How did *you* sleep?"

"Awful. The ice-making machine in the motel kept switching on and off outside my door. The lady at the desk couldn't believe I didn't have a woman with me. I thought for tonight, Ned Hornung's parents have a cottage over on Jacob's Point, they've gone back to the city, maybe I could stay there. I'll call him." He was talking rapidly, harried, amused, having an adventure. She shut her eyes. At last he remembered to ask, "Were the children upset?"

"No, they took it very casually. For now."

"Wonderful. It's really so unreal. I'll come home around four."

"That late? It'd be a lovely day for a walk on the beach."

"Ruth, please don't. I'd love to but let's try to feel a little separated. Maybe Charlie and Joanna would like to walk over to the football game at the high school."

"It's just so awkward to begin on a weekend. Why don't you come home for tonight and Sunday and start this regime on Monday?"

"Goddammit, woman, I can't. I *can't*. I wouldn't have the guts to get out again. It was horrible, going down those stairs with my suitcase. When should we level with the kids?" Without waiting for an answer, Jerry said, "I'll have to say something to the Hornungs, asking about the cottage."

She was silent, amazed at the fissures as they widened in the earth of everyday. And Jerry had sounded happy.

The day was fair and clean, the sky pale, a day to be outdoors, though too early to rake leaves. Ruth mowed the lawn, in dungarees and a gray sweatshirt of Jerry's and without shoes; the earth to her feet felt slightly contracted, commencing to harden, to withdraw. The lawn hardly needed mowing, but Ruth wanted to be working. Exercise might bring on her period. And this was the kind of job she must now learn to do. But it was too sad; in his sweatshirt she reminded herself of Jerry too much, and the grass to be cut, the weary plantain and chicory obedient to the obsolete command to grow, reminded her of herself. Her father was fond of saying from his pulpit that man is as grass, to be thrown into the oven, and it was truer than he knew, he who had so confidently expected to be loved, and who had been.

At the end of the mower handle Ruth felt suspended at a great lost height above the earth, the earth with its tangle of tiny lives and deaths that from a distance appears a lawn but up close is unendurably confused and cruel. Face things. We age and are discarded. We weaken and are eaten. Her children's voices as they scrimmaged with the Cantinellis preyed upon her. Charlie tackled Geoffrey, who was hugging the football as if it were a doll to hug, a prize that was his to keep, not understanding the game; he fell heavily and began to cry. Ruth ran to them. His collarbone was not broken again, but she slapped Charlie square on his uplifted face as it challenged her with a sly half-smile like one of Jerry's. He burst into tears so heartfelt that Geoffrey in surprise stopped his own crying, then began again, in sympathy with his brother. "He didn't mean to!" the child sobbed. Dizzy, dismayed at herself, Ruth fled her children and went into her house. She poured herself some vermouth in the kitchen. She walked through the lower rooms marvelling at the furniture she and Jerry had accumulated, as if these common things were extravagant shapes eroded into semblances in a grotto. The mail had come; it lay where it had flopped in the front hall. Jerry would have scooped it up. If she bent over, would she faint? She listened for a voice, and wondered if she were praying. The telephone rang, enormously.

It was Jerry. "Hi. Good news, I guess." But he sounded distant, frightened, boxed into a phone booth and an escapee's bravado. "The Hornungs are delighted to let me use their parents' cottage. Apparently it was robbed twice last fall and they'd love to have me in it. They gave me the keys along with coffee and condolences about us. I told them it was just an experiment. There's no furnace but there is an electric heater and the phone hasn't been disconnected yet. They say everything about it is tacky except the view. I said I was big on views. You want the phone number?"

Ruth picked up the mail and wrote the number down on the back of a bill envelope. She asked, "Could you come back here for lunch?"

"I said I'd be back at four. Why don't you take anything I say seriously?"

She said, "I want to walk on the beach and the children don't want to go to the football game. We need you."

"We're *sep*arated, damn it!"

"I have something to tell you."

"What?"

"I can't tell you over the phone."

"Why not? Is it bad?"

"It's bad now. It might have been good once. Anyway it's nothing definite. It's more of a warning than anything."

"What can it be?"

"Use your imagination."

"Is it about Sally?"

"*No.* For God's sake. You have a boring one-track mind, Jerry. Think about *us* for a change."

"I'll be over in a while."

She waited at the window. Her elm, her sacred elm, was flooding the road with golden leaves and resuming the nakedness in which its arabesques and tracery were all revealed, leading her eye upward and inward, homeward to some undivided principle of aspiration. Jerry's old maroon Mercury, its tattered top down as if to celebrate his escape, wheeled and crunched into their drive; at the same moment Richard's Mercedes slowly passed, and kept going. Jerry came in grinning: "That son of a bitch would have stopped if I hadn't pulled up. How can he smell a rat so soon?"

Ruth ran to him and made him take her into his arms, in the front hall. She felt flustered, erotic. Though he leaned backwards and touched her guardedly, he seemed pleased. "What, baby? How can you miss me so soon?" He stroked her back, through his own sweatshirt.

"Take me to the beach," she pleaded. "Take us all to the beach."

Long Island Sound was such a blue as could never be painted, a color that would swallow all colors, tube after tube, a blue darker than carbon and brighter than titanium white. The high fall tides had swept wrack up toward the dunes; a massive keel beam had been deposited by a storm and in the shelter of its girth bonfires had been set, leaving black traces. The children raced ahead, and beyond them an unleashed dog ran in wide circles, its barks arriving at their ears tardily. When water seized Ruth's ankles it seemed happiness that made her shiver. She leaned on Jerry and took his arm and told him, as the bobbing heads of their children intersected the circles the dog was tracing, that her period was three or four days late, but that he wasn't to worry.

He asked her why not.

She said she would get an abortion.

He closed his eyes and turned his face to the sun as they walked along, though the sun was too low to tan. He said that seemed ugly.

She agreed, but of the alternatives facing her it seemed least ugly. She did not think it was right to bring a child into the world without a father.

He gestured toward the children, dancing in space like spots of sun-dazzle, and said it would be like killing one of them. Which one would she choose, Joanna or Charlie or Geoffrey?

Ruth said it would not be like that at all, it would be less of a death than the death of a fish. As if participating in their talk, the forces of the sea had washed tiny silver bodies into their path, minnows caught in a tidal pool. She remembered, aloud, her miscarriage of six years ago; told him again how she had held the embryo in her hands above the toilet, and had not been afraid.

But that, he said, had been God's will. This would be their will.

Of course, she said, her father's impatience with superstition quickening her voice, it would be not quite the same. But she knew she could do it, and wanted to. She wanted to, as a present to him. She would fly to Sweden, to Japan, if she had to.

But he felt it was his fault, for continuing to make love after he had ceased, or seemed to cease, to love her.

She told him she thought not; that it would have been unnatural for them to have kept living together and not made love.

He disagreed. But his disagreement, Ruth felt, was fundamentally an effort to extricate himself from any moral involvement with the abortion. His next effort, she sensed, would be an exaggeration, a parody. He stopped and waved his arms and proclaimed, "It would be no present to me to kill my child so when I die I'll have this fish in Limbo staring at me."

"Oh, Jerry," she sighed. "Anyway, it may not have to happen."

"Three days is a long time," he said. "The world was half-made in three days." He gestured at the luminous world around them.

"Not necessarily," Ruth said. "Women aren't consistent. I feel kind of cranky and queer, like I do the day before it starts."

"You feel pregnant," he said, and suddenly stopped and put his arms around her hips and lifted her so her wet feet kicked in air. "Sweetie," he said. "You're going to have a little baby!"

"Put me *down*," she said; but when he did, she had to laugh at him, his peeling nose, his hot grin of fear. Laughing jarred things loose; next she began to cry, and turned to go back home, and he called to the children, and followed.

Jerry finished her lawn-mowing and ate an early supper with them. While Ruth did the dishes, he organized the children's baths and pajamas and read them bedtime stories. By the time Joanna was settled, it was after eight, and he seemed in a hurry to go. Perhaps he had prearranged something with Sally; Ruth doubted that their lack of communication was as total as he claimed. She invited him to stay a while longer with her, but he said no, they must be brave. He gathered together a few odds and ends he had forgotten the night before, and took two blankets because the cottage would be cold, and like an overburdened hobo lurched out the door. No sooner had he left than Ruth wanted to telephone him, to share with him her sense of how absurd it all was. It was like one of those accidents—a stray arrow, a flying shred of steel—by which people lose the sight of an eye: a half-inch difference and no damage would have been done.

She resisted calling him, though his number stared up at her from the back of the unopened bill on the telephone table. She circled the house, picked up toys, threw a half-sipped glass of vermouth into the kitchen sink, took a painfully hot bath, and read erratically in *Children of Divorce*. She shut the book. The elm was a pillow of shadow against her eyes. She shut her eyes. Filaments of nonsense, the photo-stuff of dreams, were gathering in her inner darkness when, again, he called. His voice sounded coarse and drugged. He had prepared what he had to say. "I don't want you to have an abortion. It clearly would be wrong. In this life we must seize on anything that is clearly right or wrong, so much is neither. If you're pregnant, I'll come back and be your husband and Sally and I will forget each other."

"That's not the way it should be decided."

"I know, but please accept it. I've been waiting for an act of God and this is it. Absolutely, put abortion out of your mind."

"That's very good and generous of you, Jerry, but I intend to have an abortion in any case. Even if you get over this woman, we're in no condition to make another child welcome."

"Well, we can argue later. I just wanted to say that. Good night. Sleep tight. You're very brave. You're a beautiful Unitarian."

He had sounded relieved at her firmness. She realized, as the receiver went dead in her hand, that his relief was two-edged. If she were pregnant, he would not leave her; if she were not pregnant, he would.

Sunday morning, at first light, before the children were awake, and the mechanical chimes of the Catholic church across town beckoned to the first Mass, she discovered that she was bleeding. In the bathroom she gazed down at the piece of toilet paper in her hand and experienced a clear perception in which the paper, the blood, the morning light intensified by the bathroom tiles, and her own veined hand were interlocked. A kind of photograph had been developed in the night. Her recent life, all her striving and confusion had come down to this, this spot of red on white, this simple stain. A letter from her body to nobody, a blank announcement of emptiness. In the manner of modern abstraction, what she held was not a hieroglyph or symbol of herself, it was herself, that to which she had been reduced; it was, indelibly, what she was. She flushed it down.

4. The Reacting of Richard

"*H*ELLO?"

It was Richard's voice.

Jerry had been about to go out the door. It was after nine, time for him to return to the cottage for the third night. The telephone had unexpectedly rung; unthinking, he had picked it up. Now he held Richard's deep, hollow, pompous, terrible voice in his hand.

He answered, "Hello."

"Jerry," Richard said, "I think the four of us had better have a little talk."

"Why?"

"I think you know why."

"I do?" The voice was at his ear, there was nowhere to put it, no way to reverse this stream, or shut it off, this stream that seemed to be carrying away, one by one, the slippery elements of his sinking insides. He had lost control.

Richard said, "Is that really how you want to play the game, Jerry?"

"What game?"

"Oh, come on—let's be grown-ups. Sally tells me you and she have been lovers for six months."

Jerry hesitated, and in the vortex of silence kept wondering around and around, if it was correct to call a female a "lover."

"Well?" Richard asked. "Is she lying?"

It was a knight fork. When they had all first moved to town, he and Richard had played chess, until Jerry evaded the invitations. He evaded them not because they were not well-matched players—for they were, oddly—but because he displeased himself with his craven fear of losing. There was for Jerry no satisfaction in losing at chess, no pleasant aftermath of exercise, not even the camaraderie of poker—just a nicotinic staleness, a heavy late hour, and the certainty of having been outsmarted. In a knight fork, one piece must be lost.

Ruth, pale with exhaustion, was making agitated signals by the fireplace and silently mouthing, *Who is it?*

Jerry sighed, relieved that there was nothing to do but let it go, let it all go. "No," he told Richard. "She's not lying."

Now Ruth knew who it must be. Her shape in the side of his vision went still, like a freeze-frame.

"Good," Richard said. "Now we're getting somewhere."

Jerry laughed. "Where?"

"Exactly," Richard said, with the same comical satisfaction, scoring points in a game Jerry could not see. "Where indeed. Wherever you want to take us, Jerry boy. Sally and I are very curious as to where that is."

"It depends," Jerry said, stalling. He felt betrayed. Sally had led him to think that somehow Richard didn't matter. He mattered immensely, his knowing made an immense difference. She had lied.

"Could you both come over here?" Richard was asking. It was as if they had returned to the old days, before the Conants had conditioned themselves to refuse, when

Richard or Sally would suddenly call and invite them to a Friday night movie, or a Sunday drink.

Jerry reverted to those days, replying, "It's too late to get a sitter." Then he remembered, what he desperately wanted to forget, the situation. He asked, "Would you two like to come over here? You have Josie."

"This is Josie's night off. Don't you know our schedule?"

"Not terribly well, really. What about tomorrow night? Could it wait until we've collected our thoughts?"

"I have no thoughts to collect," Richard said smoothly. He seemed to have a script to read, while Jerry was improvising. "I'm just a bystander in this. Nobody's consulted me, nobody's expressed any interest in my opinion."

"How could we? What could we have said?"

Richard's voice continued, insinuating, semi-fluid, as if squeezed from a tube. "I have no idea, no idea whatsoever. I want you to say whatever *you* want to say, Jerry. My impression is, this is not a healthy situation as it stands."

"It sure isn't." Jerry felt himself grappling for a hold on some point on the high side of grovelling; his wish was to grovel, to bleat, plead, take Ruth to bed, pull the covers over their heads, and giggle.

But now impatience and consciousness of power were making lumps in the oily voice; Richard asked him, "Why haven't you asked how Sally is? I understand she tells you that I abuse her. Wouldn't you think, if I were such a person, this might be a time when I was justified?"

It's better outdoors, isn't it? You get more oxygen.
Now leave me?

"How is she?"

Richard said, "Untouched. Are you coming over or not?"

"Hold on. I'll talk to Ruth." To Ruth he said, "We've had it. Richard knows."

"How?"—half-mouthed, half-said.

"Apparently Sally told him. Could we get Mrs. O?"

Ruth said, "I hate to bother her. Let me talk to Richard."

He gave her the receiver and she said, in a shy and strangely comfortable voice, "Hi. It's me. The other woman." Jerry thought that she was trying, as she listened, not to smile. "I'm sorry," she said, "I wanted to, at times I almost did, but I didn't know what you'd do. I was afraid you'd make them run off together . . ." As she listened, her neck, and then her cheeks, grew pink. ". . . I *am* realistic." Ruth laughed, and answered some question with, "Vermouth and bourbon. You too." She hung up smiling.

"What did he say?"

"He said, 'Baby, you should have told me. I'm a big boy.' "

"He really never guessed? It seems fantastic."

"He thought she might have somebody, but he never considered you. Except once at volleyball, he said—some look she and you gave each other that he saw. But, if you must know the unflattering truth, he didn't think you were capable of it."

"That son of a bitch. How could I not be capable?"

"He also said he thought I handled it all wrong. I should have told you to go; he's sure you would have chickened out, as he put it."

"What else did he say?"

"He said she said you and she have been sleeping together all summer, that you didn't stop last May at all. Is that right?"

"Kind of. I guess."

"How often?"

"I don't know. Once a week. Less. I've only seen her twice since she went to Florida." His face felt hot, as if being compressed into a smaller and smaller space.

"Then that bargain," Ruth said, "the bargain we made

on the beach, you never had any intention of keeping?
It was just a trick on me?"

It's wrong, isn't it?

Yes. We're right, but it's wrong.

*Don't agree with me, Jerry. You make me feel like
such a sinner.*

"Of course I had an intention of keeping it. But after
a week it seemed silly. How could I judge between you, if
I never saw her? Don't cry. Richard knows now. You're
not alone any more."

Mrs. O walked the quarter-mile down the road to their
house and arrived slightly breathless, her bosom lifting
and falling beneath her faded cotton dress, pale and innocent in pattern, like a dress she had worn as a child
and that had enlarged and aged with her. She came into
the house releasing the scent of autumn and apples. The
Conants settled her before the television set with the
assurance that all the children were asleep. "You're good
to do this," Ruth told her. "We'll try to be back before
midnight. It's some friends of ours, they're having trouble."

Jerry was startled; he had not known that Ruth could
lie. But then, it wasn't a lie. In the car—they took her
new car, a pumpkin-colored Volvo—he asked her, "Did
he say why Sally had spilled?"

"No. All he said was, once he got her started, she
couldn't stop. They've been talking since suppertime."

"It seems so unlike her, to tell. But maybe in a way
it's good."

"What are you going to do?"

"I don't know. It kind of depends on what Richard
does. Do you think he's going to shoot me?"

"I doubt it. He's had affairs himself, after all."

"What did you say 'bourbon and vermouth' about?"

"He asked me what we wanted to drink."

"You know," Jerry said, "I'm really afraid I'm a coward. Did I sound shaky on the phone with him?"

"No, you sounded rather arrogant, I thought."

"Aren't you nice? I think I sounded shaky. Something about angry people, it reminds me of grade school. I was always being beaten up on the playground."

"You've a much firmer body than Richard."

"How do you know?"

They came to the driveway, and turned in, and up the hill. Their headlights made the Mathiases' bushes leap forward murderously. Jerry, his throat feeling warped, as in the moment before vomiting, turned to the shadow sitting beside him. "I don't agree with Richard," he said, "that you handled it badly. You did the best anybody could have this summer. You mustn't blame yourself, whatever happens."

"You're going to marry her, aren't you?" She had cried out as if he were running off the road, or had struck a rabbit. He stopped the car where the driveway ended at the garage. Caesar came bounding and barking at them from the darkness of the side lawn; the dog went quiet when he smelled Jerry. His tongue licked the familiar hand. The three spaced stars of Orion's belt hung bright and pure above the woods of the hill. The Mathiases had turned the back-door light on but left them to grope their way in alone, over the uneven flagstones, past the entanglements of grapevines and roses that had escaped the trellises. Asters, still blooming, flanked Sally's granite stoop, an old millstone. In a little window high on the moonstruck house, Theodora began to cry, waked by Caesar's barking. Jerry remembered:

Is Theodora's nap usually now?

No, but she loves to sleep. She's like me. Lazy.

You're not lazy. You're lovely.

You just like my costume.

Any kid of mine would be barging in right about now.

You and Ruth don't discipline your children.
Is that what everybody says?
I say it.
You're tough.

"Jerry boy!" Richard came down the hall and Jerry flinched in self-defense; but the bigger man merely squeezed Jerry's shoulders, as if to possess some fact offered for his understanding. His wiry dark hair looked tousled, enlarging his already large head. "Dear Ruth." He kissed her hand, a grave antic in the dim colonial hall.

"Thank you," she said simply. "How are you, Richard?"

"Oh, he's *fine*," Sally called, unseen and shrill from beyond the hall. "He hasn't been so happy in ages. Look at him, *look*!" And it was true, Jerry saw, as they moved to the bright living room, that Richard, glazed with sweat, pranced, or minced, with the unnatural freedom of motion of a bear on roller skates.

But Sally's beauty took Jerry's eyes. In the intervals between seeing her, no matter how brief, he lost full knowledge of how she brimmed for him. At volleyball, amid the dodging and shuffle, each time he glimpsed her face through the net and dust he was freshly filled, a few drops of his knowing having evaporated in the seconds since his last vision of her. She sat primly upright in their wing-backed chair, the one covered with yellow gabardine. Her legs were crossed, so the full length of one shin gleamed in the room, and her long hands lay crossed in her lap. She sat tall in the chair. Jerry always forgot, how tall she was, how wide in the hips, as if he could not believe that his immaterial need to love had been given such body. He called to her softly, "Hi."

She echoed, "Hi," and made the mouth that he loved, the humorous and fearful now-what? mouth that would come after a confession.

But why tell me?
I thought you should know. I want you to know me.

*If we must fall in love, I want you to love me as I am.
As I was.*

How many were there?

*We were separated, Jerry. It didn't seem too many. At
first, I was so proud of myself, I went a whole month
without a man.*

"What would we like to drink?" Richard asked. He
was wearing dirty suntans and a striped button-down
shirt whose sleeves he had rolled up above his elbows,
proletarian-style. The back of his shirt was dark with
sweat, as if he were still living in the summer that was
over. "I've already had a drink," he went on, speaking
mostly to Ruth. "In fact, more than a drink. I feel like
celebrating, it's like becoming a father. I've become the
proud daddy of two fine young horns. True, the little
devils are six months old, but I was away on business
when they were born, and somehow they've been growing
up without me, just jutting and poking along."

"See?" Sally said to Jerry. "It's a joke. He doesn't
care about me, he thinks it's funny."

Jerry shrugged. "It's his night," he told her.

Richard turned with his curious massive ease, a jug of
California sauterne slung across his shoulder in hillbilly
manner, his head tilted as always. "*Thank* you, Jerry,"
he said. "I like that. My night. It *is* my night. You've
had *your* night"—he bowed to Ruth—"and you two
have had your night—nights. And now it's mine. Everybody gets a night. Jerry, look." With the hand not
holding the jug he made horns on his forehead. "My son
the cuckold. Nobody's laughing."

"What did you get us over here for?" Ruth asked.
"It's late."

"Ruth," he said, "you're right. You're always right. I
wish you were my friend."

"I am your friend," she said.

"Would you like to marry me?"

Ruth, blushing, refused the proposal as gently as if it

had been seriously made. "Thank you," she said, flirting her head in a way Jerry didn't recognize, "but I don't think *you* want it, and I don't think *I* want it." Richard stood flatfooted and blinking, the jug wobbling on his shoulder. "But it's a pretty thought," Ruth added.

Richard said, "I'm only trying to find out what I'm supposed to do. I've been let in late; forgive me if I seem stupid."

Jerry, always an eager and rude guest at the Mathiases, gestured toward the jug and asked, "Are we going to drink that?"

Richard looked amazed, and slowly said, "No, Jerry. It's not good enough, is it? It's what college kids drink at beach picnics, and I think we're out of that now. I think we're too mature for that now, some of us more than others. Right?"

He waited, and Jerry had to say, "Right."

"But I *do* see wine, don't you, Jerry boy? For this occasion. White, don't you think? White for innocence? For our two chaste brides here? I have some Chilean, but maybe that's a bit artsy-craftsy. You're the artsy-craftiest person here, I'll let you decide. Not Chilean. Some Bordeaux. No, not after dinner. I assume you've both eaten."

"Sure," Jerry said. Like Ruth before him, he felt genuinely asked. He had expected to be condemned, and instead was being fed. Ruth glared to get his attention and drew an upward arc across her mouth, to indicate that he was smiling and should stop.

Richard was rummaging crashingly through the bottles in his crowded liquor cabinet. It was an entire closet, refurbished with a little sink, built thick with shelves bottle-crammed. His stained back straightened and he dragged forth by its neck a yellow bottle, bigger than a quart, with a yellow label. "Retsina!" he proclaimed. "A good-a Grec-a bev*eree*ga! The Greeks know how to meet their fate." From another shelf he produced four wineglasses, tulip-shaped, and blew out the dust, and set them on the tiled coffee table in a careful rectangle. He considered, switched the glasses into a different rectangle, glanced sideways at Jerry, and made as if to guffaw and slap the other man on the back. But the guffaw was noiseless and his hand halted before it touched Jerry, who had already winced. Richard uncorked the bottle, poured, carried a glass to his wife and another to Ruth, handed one to Jerry, and lifted his own to the level of his eyes, to the eye that saw. He studied the liquor as if for sediment and spoke slowly. "I would like to propose a toast, but since all three of you are not my friends that leaves only me. So I propose a toast to me. To *me*." He drank, and the others might have followed, but he lowered his glass before they could lift theirs. "Nobody's drinking," he said. "How rude. How uncivil. May I try again? Another toast. Let me think. To happiness? Let's not be silly. To the Queen? Whodat? Ah. Our children. To our children. To the cunning little devils, all—how many do you have, Jerry? I've forgotten."

"Three."

"Three. Right. You're a good father, I've always thought that about you, that you're a good father. A swell dad. Here we go. To the half-dozen little devils, the future of America, God bless 'em every one." Sally, obedient, sipped; Ruth and Jerry followed. The retsina smelled like scorched varnish and tasted medicinal. Drinking in unison aligned them in a ceremony, whose central mystery was still to be divulged.

Ruth, entering the room, had taken the first chair inside the doorway, a rush-seated ladder-back that had strayed from the dining room. Jerry had seated himself on the center of the white goosedown sofa, so that the two women—Ruth near the doorway and Sally in the wing chair near the fireplace—were equidistant from him. He crossed his legs and spaciously spread his arms along the sofa back. Now Richard overweighted Ruth's side of the room by sitting heavily near her, in the worn leather armchair that Sally hated, Jerry knew.

Why should you hate it?

It's just like him. Isn't that awful? I mean of me to say.

Creased and flaking, it had been his father's chair. As he sank into the dour mass of old leather, Richard became his father's revenant. He put his hand limply to his forehead and his voice took on a deadly, deceptive weariness.

He said, "Jerry, Sally tells me you're a big ass man. Frankly, I was surprised."

Jerry sipped again, and said, "Are you sure this stuff is safe to drink?"

"It'll grow on you," Richard promised. "It has resin in it. I move a dozen cases of it a month. It's only twenty proof. I mean, Jesus, Jerry boy, you just haven't acted the way human beings are supposed to act."

"How is that? Tell me."

"I don't mean just fucking her, I can't get too sore about your fucking her, I've done it myself, and I'm not the only one. I suppose she told you? That winter I was away. She even fucked the ski instructor."

Jerry nodded.

"But for Chrissakes, Jerry, you should've either broken it off or run off with her. You've put that woman through hell. You've put—my wife—through hell." He slapped the arm of the chair three times for emphasis.

Jerry shrugged. "I have a wife too."

"Well you have to pick. In our society you have to pick."

"Don't make him!" Ruth cried suddenly. "This isn't the time."

Richard turned to her lazily. "Shit, Ruth. Six months. They've tried to break it off. If it's lasted six months, it'll last forever."

It was wonderful to hear. Jerry felt that with Richard they had arrived at firm ground at last. "Longer than that," he said. "I've always loved Sally."

"Fine," Richard said. "Done and done. Sally babes, get me a pencil and paper."

Ruth jumped up. "What are you saying, Jerry? No. *No.* I won't stay." She was quickly through the doorway. Jerry caught her in the hall that ran between the kitchen and the front door.

"Ruth," he said. "You know how it is now. You know we have nothing. Let it go. Please let it go now."

His wife's breath was hot and moist and flickering. "She's a bitch. She'll kill you. She'll kill you like she's half-killed him."

"It's silly of you to hate Sally. She's helpless."

"How can you say she's helpless? Who do you think's got us all here? We're dancing at her wedding."

"Don't go. Don't leave us."

"Why should I stay and see you stripped clean by these two vultures? Of your children, of your talent, of your money—"

"Money?"

"Why do you think Richard wants pencil and paper? He's happy. Can't you see that, Jerry? He's happy because he's getting rid of her."

"He's drunk."

"Let me go. Save your lover routine for others."

"I'm sorry." He had been pressing her against the wall holding her shoulders tightly in a forcible arrest. Yet, released, she did not move toward the door, but stood sullen, softly panting, all her skin breathing the strange familiar warmth of his wife. "Come back and talk to us," he begged.

"I'm going back," she said, "and fight for you. And not because I like you but because I don't like these other people."

"Not Richard either?"

"I hate him."

"Don't hate," he begged. "We're all too close to hate. We must all love each other now." As a boy he had been bored by all of church except communion, the moment when a crowd of them rumbled to the rail and dissolved the wafer in their mouths. Now he felt that in the living room something comparable would occur, or had occurred. His unbelieving wife let herself be led back. He was proud to show the Mathiases that he could still control her—that she was his wife to the end.

Richard had found pencil and paper and had shifted to the edge of the chair, so he could write on the coffee table. Sally had not moved, and the eyes of her heart-shaped, swollen face were shut. Upstairs, the baby their coming had awakened was still crying. "Sally," Richard said, "your child is crying." With a rigid reflex of the defensively flamboyant bearing that had distinguished her from the good women of Connecticut, Sally rose and stroked back her hair and with long strides left the room.

Why are you crying? Sally? Why?

It's too silly. I'm sorry.

Tell me. Please tell me.

You'll laugh.

No I won't.

I'm so sorry, I've ruined it for you.

No you haven't. Listen, you're lovely. Tell me.

I just remembered it's Ash Wednesday.

Oh. My poor love. My lovely lapsed Catholic.

Am I lapsed?

Not if you care about Ash Wednesday. Get up. Get up, put on your clothes and go to church and get your smooch.

It's so hypocritical.

No. I know just how it is.

I must really be crazy if I can lie with a man and start worrying about Ash Wednesday. I've ruined it for you. You're getting sad and soft.

No, I love your remembering. There's such a thing as spiritual satisfaction too. You satisfy me. Go. Leave me. Go to Mass.

I don't want to now.

Wait. I'm trying to reach the ashtray.

Don't be blasphemous, Jerry. I'm frightened.

Who isn't?

Ruth, infected by Sally's show of energy, crossed to the Buffet print above the fireplace and said, "That's a lousy painting. All these are lousy." Her wave took in the Wyeth print, the Käthe Kollwitz lithographs, the anonymous watercolor of a single skier poised with his blue shadow beneath a sky of the same slanting blue. Ruth included the furniture. "Trashy," she said. "She has expensive, trashy taste."

Both Richard and Jerry laughed. Then Richard said mellifluously, "Ruth, you have qualities she doesn't have, and Sally has qualities *you* don't have."

"Oh I *know* that," she said hurriedly, blushing, and Jerry resented it, that Richard had taken it upon himself to rebuke her, when she was so naturally shy.

Richard went on, "But you're both very desirable women, and I'm sorry neither of you wants to be married to *me*."

Jerry resented this, too, the insistent note of self-pity. He told him, "You seem to be taking it philosophically."

"Oh, but I'm boiling inside, Jerry. I'm boiling."

"Why don't you take him outside," Ruth suggested, "and beat him up?"

"I'm sure you'd win," Jerry said. "You weigh twenty pounds more. It'd be like Liston and Patterson."

"I don't operate that way," Richard told them. "What I *may* do, I'll have to think about it, is *hire* somebody to beat you up. One thing about the liquor business, you know where the hoods are. Have some more wine."

"O.K., thanks. You're right, it does grow on you."

"Ruthie babes?"

"Just a splash. One of us *must* go back and take the baby-sitter home."

"You've just arrived," Richard said, filling her glass to the brim. "We really haven't seen very much of the Conants this summer, and I felt very hurt. I felt snubbed."

"I knew you would," Ruth said. "I'm sorry, it was one of the reasons I wanted to tell you. My own life falling apart, and I was worried about your hurt feelings socially. But I just didn't feel up to looking at Sally more than I had to. Volleyball was as much hell as I could take."

"You knew all summer they were fucking?"

"No, I thought they'd *stopped*. I thought Jerry had promised to. So I was even dumber than you were."

"That's pretty dumb," Richard said. "I guess I assumed Jerry was queer, I don't know."

Jerry said, "You're sweet. How did you find out, anyway?"

"Phone bills. I went back over the whole year. There was a collect call from the city this spring whose number hadn't rung a bell, but I'd let it pass. They didn't really get careless until August. A lot of a New York number that I figured out as his office and, the craziest thing, she charged a couple calls from Florida to him on *our* number."

Ruth said, "She must have wanted you to find out then. She was angry with Jerry for not coming to Florida."

Jerry said, "She wasn't. He beat the truth out of her. He's a bully. You heard him. He's a big brave liquor store bully, probably he *hired* somebody to beat her up."

Richard told him, "Watch it, Jerry. There's such a thing as defamation of character. I never beat Sally, that's one of her fantasies. She may believe it herself, Christ, though I didn't think she was that far gone. You've been sold a bill of goods, sonny."

"I've seen the bruises on her."

Ruth said, "Jerry. Must you?"

"Let him talk, Ruth, let him spill it. Let the happy

cock crow. I have seen my true love naked. How does it go? I have looked on beauty bare."

Jerry said, "Once you hit her on the side of the head so hard she was deaf in that ear for a week."

"Eh? What's that you say? You've heard of self-defense? I raised my hand to protect my eyeballs and she ran her head right into it. Want to see *my* bruises?" Sweating and inspired, Richard stood and made as if to undo his belt. Sally, carrying Theodora, reëntered the room; she moved with wooden, disdaining dignity through the party that had been building in her absence. She sat in the wing-backed chair and swayed the bleary child back and forth on her knee. To Jerry they seemed two brilliant dolls.

Richard said, "Sally-O, pal Jerry here is wondering why you squealed on him."

"My sister-in-law told him," Sally told the Conants.

"Horseshit," Richard said. "She told me you had a lover who called you in Florida every day, she didn't know who it was, I knew fucking damn well you had a lover all summer from the crappy way you treated me. You just about drove me back into therapy." He explained to Ruth and Jerry, "She wouldn't screw. And when Sally won't have it sunny-side up, there must be a sunny-side down. I'd touch her and she'd run the other way, except once or twice when I guess Jerry hadn't gotten to her for a while. I hope, dear," he said to Sally, "you haven't deceived your lover into thinking you weren't diddled at all?"

"Weren't what?" Sally asked. She seemed sealed with the child on her knee into a soundproof booth.

"Diddled. Fucked. Carnally embraced," Richard said, not quite drunk enough to be unembarrassed.

"See, she's still deaf in that ear," Jerry said, and Ruth laughed.

Richard was humorlessly intent upon his grievance; his good eye and bad eye together focussed on remembrance of his maddening summer. "I couldn't understand it," he said. "I hadn't done anything. We'd had our troubles, but then we'd come to terms. It was just me, old horse-shit me, everybody's patsy."

"Quit it," Ruth said. Her sisterly directness was a revelation to Jerry; he felt now that all four of them had been pressed into a single family and he, an only child, at last had sisters and a brother. He was happy and excited. He wanted never to leave them.

"That woman"—Richard pointed dramatically to Sally, and a smile dawned on Theodora's puffy puzzled face—"put me through hell."

"You're repeating yourself," Jerry said.

"And then," Richard went on, *"then* to complain to her fucking boyfriend that I beat her when I never lifted my hand against her except to keep myself from being brained—Sally, remember that bookend?"

Sally answered him with a cold stare and a prolonged, almost asthmatic sniffle.

"A *brass* bookend," Richard explained to Jerry and Ruth, *"lead* for Chrissakes it felt like, I caught it on my forearm, just because I asked her why she'd stopped fucking me. Remember, Sally-O?"

Sally stiffened, shivering, and cried, "You talk as if I did everything deliberately. I *hate* being in love; I wish I *didn't* love Jerry. I don't want to hurt you, I don't want to hurt Ruth and the ch-children."

"Don't cry on my account," Ruth said. "It's too late for that."

"I've cried plenty on your account. I feel sorry for anybody who's so selfish, who's so weak she won't let a man go when he wants to go."

"I tried to hold my children's father with them. Was that so contemptible?"

"*Yes!*"

"You can say that because you treat your own children

like, like baggage, like little trinkets to set you off when it suits you."

"I love my children but I have respect for my husband too, enough respect that if he made up his mind I'd let him do what he decided."

"Jerry never decided anything."

"He's too *kind*. You abused that kindness. You used it. You can't give him what I can give him, you don't love him. If you loved him, you wouldn't have had this *affair* we all keep hearing about."

"Girls, girls," Richard said.

"He wanted me to," Ruth cried, leaning from her chair as if refracted in water, "I thought it would make me a better *wife*!" She was pulled by her tears into an abject forward-twisted shape; it seemed to Jerry her grief and humiliation were trying to fly her body away. Exposed, rosily flushed, she bit her knuckle in shame. Jerry spoke to shield her.

He said to Sally carefully, "Haven't you been listening? It's all over, don't keep fighting. I'm asking you to marry me."

Sally turned, constricted in her movements by the wings of the chair and the child in her lap, to face him; anger lingered in her eyebrows and her voice: "It hardly seems to me you're in a position." Her sentence dissolved, unfinished, in a slow wet smile, a deep smile that wryly filled the face beneath the angrily arched eyebrows and reached toward him with recognition of how it was, of how they had been, and of forgiveness, forgiveness for what had been done, what was being done, and even what must happen—requesting, too, in this same regretful smile, a like forgiveness from him.

What time is it?

Eight o'clock. Up, man.

Only eight? You're kidding.

I've been up since seven.

I was up all night. Go away. Come back to bed.

It's your own fault. I kept telling you, go to sleep.

I couldn't. You were too lovely and strange. You breathed so quietly. I was afraid you'd disappear.

I'm hungry.

Hungry? In Heaven?

Listen. You can hear my stomach growl.

How stern you look standing there. How grand. You're dressed.

Of course. Do I look all right for the street? Do I look too loved?

Not loved enough.

No you don't. One thing I must tell you about myself, I'm a real bitch until I've had my coffee.

I can't believe it. Anyway, I like you as a bitch.

I can smell coffee coming in through the air conditioner.

Come to me for one minute and I'll buy you a million cups.

No, Jerry. Come on. Get up.

One half a minute, for half a million cups. No, wait. Stay by the window, I'm having a wonderful sleepy sensation, I'm making love to the sight of you standing there, where I can't touch you; it's very perverse. You look glorious.

Oh, Jerry. Go easy on me. You love me too hard. I keep trying to pull back, but you never do.

I know. It's not fair. I'm afraid of death but not afraid of you, so I want you to kill me.

Isn't it funny, that you're not afraid of me? Everybody else sort of is.

Richard lifted his pencil above his pad of paper—each little blue sheet of which was headed with the name in 3-D lettering of the Cannonport liquor store and a tiny linecut of its façade. "Let's nail down some facts. Which hotel did you take her to in Washington?"

In that hotel Jerry had lain with Sally fearing Richard's knock on the door; now the knock sounded and

Jerry had no wish to admit him into that remembered room. He said, "I don't see that it matters."

"You won't tell me. Very well. Sally, what hotel?"

Yet he hardly gave her time to answer before asking, "Ruth?"

"I have no idea. Why do you need to know?"

"I need to know because I've been a horse's ass laughing-stock all fucking summer. I was sitting here remembering, there was something fishy all summer, everybody was too fucking jolly when I was around. I remember, what hurt at the time, down at the Hornungs', going over to where Janet and Linda were talking about something very hush-hush and they looked at me and turned white. 'What's up?' I said, and from the look on their faces I might've let loose a walloping fart."

"Richard," Jerry interrupted, "I must tell you something. I've never liked you—"

"I've *always* liked *you*, Jerry."

"—but being involved with Sally has involved loving you, if you'll forgive my saying so. And don't drink all that rotgut or whatever it is."

"Retsina. Cheers. *L'Chaim*! *Salute*! *Prosit*!"

Jerry accepted more wine and asked, "Richard, where did you learn all these languages?"

"Ist wunderbar, nichts?"

"You men may be having a good time but this is agony for the rest of us," Sally said. She was still sitting rigid as a madonna; in her lap Theodora, head wobbling gently, seemed hypnotized.

"Take the brat to bed," Richard said.

"No, if I leave the room you'll all talk about me. You'll talk about my soul."

"Tell me the hotel." Richard spoke to no one in particular.

No one answered.

"O.K., then. You want to play rough. Very good. *Very*

good. I can play rough too. My daddy played rough and I can play rough."

Jerry said, "Well, why not? You don't owe me anything."

"Goddammit, Jerry, you talk my language. *Sköl.*"

"Bottoms up. Chinchin."

"You miserable bastard, I can't get mad at you. I keep trying and you won't let me."

"He's awful that way," Ruth said.

"How would you play rough?" Jerry asked.

Richard began to doodle on his pad. "Well, I could refuse to divorce Sally. That means she couldn't remarry."

Sally sat even more upright and her lips drew back along her teeth; Jerry saw that, far from reluctant, she was relieved to fight with Richard. "Yes," she said sharply, "and your children wouldn't have a father. Why would you hurt your own children?"

"What makes you think I'll let you have the children?"

"I know damn well you don't want them. You never did. We had them because our analysts thought it was healthy."

They spoke back and forth so rapidly that Jerry gathered they had been over this ground often before.

Richard smiled and continued his design on the pad. Jerry wondered what it would be like to see with only one eye. He closed one of his and looked at the room— the chairs, the women, the glasses invisibly shed a dimension. Things were just so, flat, with nothing further to be said about them; it was the world, he realized, as seen without the idea of God lending each thing a roundness of significance. It was terrible. He had always hated Richard's looks; the tilted ponderous head, the unctuous uncertain mouth, the crazy lack in one socket. Was this why—because this face presented him with this possibility, of his own lacking one eye? He opened it, and a roundness sprang, vibrating, around things, and Richard was lifting his head and saying to Sally, "You're right.

My lawyer would talk me out of it anyway. Let's try to be rational. Let's try to be rational, folks. Let's all try together to keep those little green-eyed devils down. Jerry, I know you'll be a good father to my children. I've seen you with yours, and you're a good father."

"He's not," Ruth said. "He's sadistic. He teases them."

Richard kept nodding. "He's not perfect, but he's O.K., Ruthie babes. He's immature, but who isn't?"

Ruth went on, "He makes them go to Sunday school when they don't want to."

"Children need," Richard said, droning in a doodling drunken trance, "children need a basis for life, however idiotic. Jerry, I'll pay for their educations and their clothes."

"Well, their educations certainly."

"It's a deal."

Richard was doodling numbers now. In the silence, a great immaterial weight shifted, like a tissue page in a Bible, unmasking the details of an infernal etching.

Jerry cried, "But what about *my* children!"

"That's your problem," Richard said, ceasing to be drunk.

Jerry addressed Ruth. "Give me one. Any one. Charlie or Geoffrey; you know how Charlie bullies him. They should be separated."

Ruth was crying; her words issued trembling. "They need each other. We all need each other."

"Please. Charlie. Let me have Charlie."

Sally jerked into speech. "Why won't you? They're as much his as yours."

Ruth turned in her ladder-back chair. "I might if it were any other woman," she said. "But not you. I wouldn't trust you with my children. I don't think you're a fit mother."

Jerry protested, "How can you say that, Ruth? Look at her!" But even as he said it, he realized that perhaps only to him did she seem inhumanly kind, her face brim-

ming with kindness, this face he had seen submerged—
eyes closed, lips parted—in passion, hovering beneath his
face like a reflection submerged in a pool. Having seen
too much, he was as good as blind, and possibly it was
they, Richard and Ruth, who saw her accurately.

*You don't believe I'm so simple. I am simple. I'm just
like—that broken bottle.*

"Sundays, vacations, sure," Ruth said. "If I crack up
or kill myself, take them. But for now they're staying
with me."

"Yes," Jerry said, unnecessarily. He had reached a
strange state; his momentum, thrust upon him by a need
to keep free of Richard, had outstripped his control; in
this state of severed veering he had to exert his voice,
to take soundings on the depth of his helplessness. The
silence that followed this sounding seemed vast.

Richard abruptly said, "Well, Sally-O, congratulations.
Congratulations, girl, you've done it. You've had your
cap set for Jerry Conant for years."

"She has?" Jerry asked.

"Of course," Ruth told him. "Everybody could see it.
It was embarrassing, even."

Richard said, "Don't knock it, Ruth. This may be the
real thing, a true *amour de coeur*. Let's wish the kids
luck. Jerry, one thing you're not going to be is bored.
Sally is not tranquil. She has many fine qualities; she
cooks well, dresses well, she's good—well, *fairly* good
—in bed. But she is not tranquil."

"Weren't we discussing something else?" Jerry asked.

"The children's educations," Ruth said. She stood up.
"I'm going home. I can't stand this."

"I should tell you," Jerry said, with a flicker of his
old desire to annoy this man, "I'm a believer in public
schools."

"So am I, Jerry boy," Richard said, "so am I. It's
Sally who insists on the kids being hauled in the bus to
that snob school."

Sally said primly, "These are my children and I want them to have the best education they can get." *My*: the word, Jerry saw, had a beauty self-evident to her, her mouth never questioned the worth of this jewel of a word.

Ruth asked, falteringly seating herself again, "Suppose Jerry wants to quit his job? Are you willing to be poor with him?"

Sally considered her answer carefully, and seemed pleased with it. "No, I don't want to be poor, Ruth; who does?"

"*I* do. If we all had to sweat for our food we wouldn't have time for this—this folly. We're all so spoiled we stink."

"Ruthie," Richard said, "you're speaking my heart. Let's get back to nature and simple poverty. I've been a registered Democrat all my life. I voted for Adlai Stevenson twice."

Now that Sally had found her tongue, she seemed determined to express everything that had crossed her mind while the others had talked. "You know, just signing a piece of paper doesn't mean you stop being husband and wife." Jerry had heard her say this before, in murmured exploration of their spiritual plight; in the present context it seemed irrelevant, brittle, not quite sane. Ruth caught his eye, then glanced at Richard. Sally, sensing this current of amusement, grew vehement: "And the person here who is going to lose most hasn't gotten a *damn* bit of sympathy. Ruth will have her children and Jerry and I will have each other but Richard doesn't get a Goddamn thing!" She bowed her head; her hair fell forward to complete the rhetoric.

Richard watched the other two for their reaction, and seemed to teeter between complicity with them and a revived union with Sally. He took her tone, and attacked: "Jerry, let me ask you something. Have you ever been alone? I mean real down-in-the-guts honest-to-Christ fuck-you-Jack *alone*. This big dumb broad here was the only friend I ever had and she wants to leave me for you."

"You *do* love her," Ruth said.

Richard pulled back. "Oh, I love her, of course I love the crazy bitch, but—what the hell. I've had my ups. *Que será, será.*"

"Well I think two perfectly good marriages are being broken up by a hideous mistake—by the most pathetic kind of greed," Ruth said, rising again, "but nobody agrees with me so I really am getting out of here."

"It's settled?" Jerry asked.

"Isn't it?"

"If you say so. How do we do this? We can't go back. Sally, you go with Ruth and spend the night in our house."

"No," was Sally's simple, startled answer.

"She won't hurt you. Trust us. Please, it's the only place I can think of to put you. You go with her and I'll stay with Richard."

"No. I won't leave my children."

"Just for one night? I'll be here, Richard and I can make them breakfast. I don't see the problem."

"He'll take my children and say I deserted them."

"You're not serious, Sally. You know your own husband better than that. Richard, you wouldn't do that."

"Of course not," Richard said, and in his face Jerry read an unexpected expression, of embarrassment, for Sally.

Jerry pleaded with her, "Haven't you been listening to him? He won't kidnap your children. He loves you, he loves them. He's not a monster." He turned to Richard. "We can play chess. Remember the chess games we used to have?"

"I don't think I should leave," Sally said. She tightened her arms around Theodora as around a prize.

"Well I can't ask *Richard* to go home with Ruth." The others laughed, which angered Jerry; this wrangle on the edge of the grave was so unworthy of them all, and his finagling position such a poor reward for the sacrifice and fatal leap he had at last made.

"Sally-O, I promise I won't kidnap the kids," Richard said.

"But if I leave her with you you'll beat her," Jerry said.

"Jesus, Jerry, I'm beginning to hate your guts. She's not your fucking wife yet and I'll beat her if I fucking well please. This is my house and I'm not getting out of it because my wife's turned into a whore."

"Who's ever coming, come," Ruth said. "Jerry, I don't think they want us any more."

Jerry asked Sally, "Will you be all right?"

"Yes. I will."

"You'd really rather have it this way?"

"I think so." For the first time tonight, their eyes met. *Jerry, your eyes are so sad!*
How can they be sad when I'm so happy?
They're so sad, Jerry.
You shouldn't watch people's eyes when they make love.
I always do.
Then I'll close mine.

Jerry sighed. "Well I guess we've all spent enough nights together one more won't kill us. Call me," he told Sally, "if you need me."

"Thank you, Jerry. I won't. Sleep well." She smiled and her eyes went elsewhere. "Ruth—?"

Ruth was already down the hall. "Save it," she called back to Sally. "We're all too tired."

Jerry felt dirty; in the beginning, when they were all new couples in town, being at the Mathiases, amid their expensive things, had made him feel gauche and unclean. Now, he needed to urinate, but Richard's silence loomed at his side as a social impatience, and he did not dare delay in the downstairs lavatory. Outdoors, the three spaced stars of Orion's belt had slipped to a steeper tilt beyond the woods and the moon moved illumining through an ashen mackerel sky. The Conants heard Caesar whine and scratch in the garage, but he did not bark. The noise of their motor polluted the night. As they went down the curving driveway, Ruth lit a cigarette. Jerry twiddled his fingers. She passed it to him for a puff. "The odd thing is," she said, "I feel as though I'm coming back from one more evening at Sally and Richard's. At least I wasn't bored. Richard didn't talk about stocks and bonds."

"Yes, he didn't seem as awful as usual. In fact he had his rather grand moments. I felt just overwhelmed. How did I seem? Outclassed?"

"You were you," Ruth said.

His bladder burned. He asked his wife, "Do you mind if I stop the car a minute?"

"We're almost home," she said. "Can't you wait?"

"No."

He stopped her pumpkin-colored Volvo and opened its door and the colorless dry grass and roadside weeds seemed rendered precious by this halt in his motion. There was a telephone pole. Drawing near to it, he tore at his zipper and yielded his pain to the earth. The moon set a thorn of shadow beside each splinter of the pole; a silver ghost of frost glistened in the tall grass. Everything, Jerry saw, was painted on black, engraved on our dull numb terror. An unseen V of geese honked, a car on another road whispered itself into nothing, a smell of apples haunted the air. Beyond his awareness of the night he tried to make himself conscious, as if of the rotation of the earth, of the huge and mournful turn his life had taken. But there seemed to be only this grass, and Ruth waiting for him in the car, and his diminishing arc of relief.

Past many dark houses, they arrived at their own; all of its lights were on. Mrs. O, though sweet with the children, never cleared a dish or switched off a light. As they paid her, she told them, "A woman from the Congregational church called about some posters."

"Oh my Lord," Ruth said. "I'd forgotten. They were supposed to be ready Saturday."

"Those people are turning into tyrants," Jerry said, and asked Mrs. O, "Didn't you wear a coat?" The babysitter shook her head silently; her face was flushed, and as she stepped onto the porch she dabbed at her eyes. Closing the door, Ruth said, "Poor soul. I wonder how much she knows."

"Why would she know anything?"

"She's of the town, Jerry. The whole town knows we're in trouble. I've seen it all summer on the faces of the boys at Gristede's."

"Huh. It never seemed to me that *we* were in trouble. I was, and you were, but not *us*."

"Let's go to bed. Or are you off to the cottage?"

"I couldn't. Want some milk?"

"Do you?"

"If you'll make toast."

"Oh, sure. What the hell. What time is it anyway?"

"One ten."

"That early? Amazing. It seemed we were there for a lifetime."

"Should I call?" Jerry asked. "Do you think she's all right?"

"She's chosen; let her alone."

"She seemed such a waif."

"That's her pose."

"No, I never saw her like that before. I felt there were three people with sense there, and we were all debating the fate of this beautiful—*child*."

"The toast's popped. Want to butter it? It's your toast."

He needed to talk about Sally, and the night past, with its intricate transactions; he needed to render the details aloud, and to have Ruth's light on them. But she went upstairs, refusing discussion. In their cold room, the unexpressed congested his lungs, and his breathing grew tight. "Son of a bitch," he gasped, "my Medihaler's over at the cottage."

"Just relax," Ruth said, in a far-off, singing voice. "Let yourself go, don't think about anything."

"It's cold—up here," he said. "Why do we live—in such a crummy house?"

"Get under the covers," she said, "get nice and warm, take easy breaths, don't think about your lungs."

"My poor—children," he said. The bed, as he climbed into it, seemed a trap in which he would smother face down. Ruth turned off the light, the last light in the house that was burning. Through the window, through the heavy lace of the elm, pierced apertures that were stars slowly readmitted the possibility of his breathing. Ruth got into the other side of the bed and huddled against him, lying with one arm across his chest. Enclosed in slowly growing warmth, warmth he was tasting for the last time in eternity, Jerry felt his chest expand; his limbs relaxed and flowed outward; the wall within his lungs, nudged by each inhalation, was crumbling. Ruth's body against his felt solid, dense, asleep. "I'm so sorry," he said aloud, "but it must be right." The sentence, wrapped in his voice, seemed to be repeated indefinitely, like images in a doubled mirror, like days, like breathing. He opened his eyes. The crosses of the mullions, rigid benedictions, stood guard against the night; an unbounded kingdom of ease and peace had been established within his lungs. This delicious realm he leisurely began lazily to explore.

The telephone shrilled, and shrilled, in the upstairs hall; it was as if a pipe had burst, filling the dark with a shocking fountain. "Oh my God," Ruth said.

She and Jerry had long ago agreed that if she rose with

the children in the morning, he would tend to disturbances at night. He pulled his body up from the warm hole where it had found escape; from the strength of the effort he estimated he had not been asleep long. First plunge is deepest. His limbs and face felt coated in dust. He reached the phone by its fourth peal, which he broke in the middle. A child's bed creaked somewhere. "Hello?"

"Jerry? It's me." Sally's voice sounded impossibly near —a comet that presses from the sky though millions of miles away.

"Hi."

"Were you asleep?"

"Kind of. What time is it?"

"I'm sorry. I didn't know you'd be able to go to sleep."

"I didn't either."

"I called you at the cottage, but you didn't answer. I was terribly hurt."

"You were? It never occurred to me to go there. There's no point now, it's all settled."

"It is? How is Ruth?"

"She's asleep."

"I am not!" Ruth called from the bed. "Tell her to get off my telephone!"

"How are *you*?" Jerry asked Sally.

"Not so good."

"Not? Where's Richard?"

"He's left. I guess that's what I called to tell you. Richard's left the house. He told me he couldn't stand me another minute and walked out the door. He didn't even pack a suitcase. He called me a whore." Her voice broke, and the receiver rustled with tears. Another bed creaked. Were the children all awake?

"Did he hit you?"

"No. I wouldn't have cared if he had."

"Well, that's good, isn't it? Isn't it better to have him out of the house? Can you get to sleep?"

"I should roast in Hell for what I've done to that man."

Jerry shifted his weight to the other leg and tried to speak so Ruth wouldn't hear every word; these words were ridiculous. "Nobody should roast in Hell," he whispered to Sally. "Least of all you. You didn't create this, you tried to turn me away. Didn't you?"

"K-kind of. But I could have worked at it more. I didn't want to turn you away, and I didn't want to push you. Will you tell me something?"

"Sure."

"Tell me honestly?"

"Yes."

"Do you feel pushed?"

"Of course not."

"I didn't want to tell him everything, but once I started I couldn't stop. He made me tell him; he's more clever than you think."

"I think he's very clever. I quite liked him tonight."

"You did?" Her voice lifted so hopefully he dreaded her next words; she might say too much. She said, "I was awful."

"No you weren't. You looked lovely."

"I couldn't say anything and when I tried it came out all angry and wrong."

"That was all right."

"I was so confused, I was so ashamed. I'd betrayed Richard and then I'd betrayed you to him. And you both expected so much from me."

"Too much."

Her silence rustled again and he felt he was pouring his words into a chasm, a void.

"Sally. Listen. I'm glad he knows. I'm glad you told him. Now it's over, and it's all right. But we must be better now than other people, you and I. We've asked a big thing of Richard and Ruth and the children and the only way we can pay it back is by being better than other people for the rest of our lives. Do you understand?"

"Yes." She sniffed.

"Do you believe me?"

"I guess so. I don't know what I'm doing. I just ate a whole bowl of salad I had made for dinner tonight. We forgot to eat, and now my husband's gone off hungry."

"Can you go to sleep? Do you have a pill?"

"Yes. I have a pill. I'll be fine."

Her voice hinted at anger. He asked, "Do you want me to come over?"

"No. It would upset the children. Theodora is still up."

"Poor kid. When is Josie coming back?"

"Tomorrow morning. What can I tell her?"

"I don't know. Nothing? The truth? That seems to me the least of your worries."

"You're right, Jerry. You're always right. You take care of Ruth, and I'll take a pill."

"It's the best I can think of for now."

"Go back to sleep. Sorry to have bothered you."

He had been waiting for her apology. He said, "Don't be funny. I'm glad you did. Of course I'm glad."

"Good night, Jerry."

"Good night. You're great." He could not quite bring himself to say, with Ruth listening, *I love you*.

When he got back into bed, Ruth asked, "What did she want?"

"Comfort. Richard's left."

"In the middle of the night?"

"Apparently."

"Well—good for him."

"What's good about it? Leaving a woman at her wits' end? What a bastard."

"What else did she say?"

"She was sore I was here instead of at the cottage. She evidently expected me to dump you off here and go down there." Ruth's "good for him," with its implied

criticism of his own passivity, rankled. "Should I?" he
asked. "Is that the way to win your respect, get up and
dress and walk off like Richard?"

"Suit yourself. How did she sound?"

"Miserable, thanks."

"Why should she? She has what she wants."

"You think? I think now she wonders what she wants,
now that she has it."

"Say that again."

"No. I'm going to sleep. I have the strangest sensation,"
he said, indulging the streak of fantasy that made him
valuable to the commercials studio, "of being North
Africa, with my feet in Egypt and my head in Morocco.
I'm all sand."

When the telephone awoke him again, he felt guilty
that he had dreamed, not of the "situation," not of Sally
or Richard or Ruth, but of remote corners of his boy-
hood, of a playground slide you had to rub wax paper on
to get a fast slide, of the two battered box-hockey boxes,
of the space of trod grass behind the pavilion shed where
the older kids exchanged unimaginable secrets and left Old
Gold butts, of the past, that Paradise where choice is no
longer possible. He staggered up to stifle the ringing of
the telephone knowing that he was repeating himself,
that he had condemned himself to an eternity of repeti-
tion through the sin that sat leadenly in his stomach.
Again it was Sally, Sally: her voice was centrifugal, its
utterances fleeing outward in all directions from the
humiliating fact of having called him again, her enuncia-
tion breathless and scattered. "Hey? Jerry? If I ask you
something will you tell me honestly?"

"Sure. Did you take your pill?"

"I just did and I wanted to call you before it got to me.
I wanted to hear your voice before I went under. Don't
be mad at me?"

"Why should I be mad at you? You make me feel

rotten that I'm not there with you. Richard's not come back?"

"No, and he won't *be* back." There was something old-fashioned in how Sally pronounced this, too firm in the consonants, like the neighborhood women who used to scold him for walking on their front grass.

"Ask me your question," he said.

"Are you mad at me for telling?"

"Is that your real question?"

"Kind of."

"No, I'm not mad, of course not. *I* told months ago, so you're way ahead of me."

"You *are* mad," she said. "I thought, from when I called before, you were."

"I'm a little dead," he admitted. "I'll be all right tomorrow. I think you're very brave, and held it long enough, and I'm very grateful. You've given me lots of time. After all, he found those phone bills."

"Yes, but I've bluffed worse things than that through. I just had gotten so tired. And Jerry? You know what else? This is really awful."

"What else, sweet?"

"You'll hate me."

He was tired of saying "No" and said nothing.

She went on, "I lied to him. I told him we never—"

"Yes?"

"I said we never made love in this house. I thought it would be too terrible for his ego. Isn't that ridiculous?"

"No, it's not ridiculous."

"Am I insane?"

"No."

"Please don't tell him. If we all go to court I'll admit it but please don't you tell him. It's not your *place*, Jerry." The pill was making her strange.

"Why should I want to?" he said. "The less I have to talk to him, the better."

"His ego has been *so* hurt."

"Well, that's the impression he'll try to give you. Clearly his game now is to make everybody feel as guilty as possible."

"Promise you won't tell him?"

"I promise."

"There are lots of things I would never tell Ruth. Intimate things."

"I said, I promise. Can you go to sleep, do you think? What the hell time is it?"

"Hey?"

"Yes?"

"Remember, in Washington, it was you who had the insomnia? I couldn't see what you were so worried about. Now I know."

"Life is worrisome," he conceded.

She laughed. "I could see your mouth go all prim, saying that. Jerry? I can feel the pill in me now. I feel all heavy."

"Just relax," he told her. "You'll wake up, and it'll be morning, and the world will still be here."

"It's pulling at me. I'm scared. I'm afraid something will happen to the children."

"Nothing will happen to the children."

"I'm afraid I won't wake up. I'll never see you again, and you'll make love to somebody else. You'll fall in love with Ruth again. You *do* love her, I could see that tonight."

"You'll wake up, I promise. You're very strong, you're very healthy, you don't smoke cigarettes." He shielded his mouth and whispered so that Ruth could not hear. "You're the sun."

"I must hang up now, my arm is so heavy. Will I really be safe?"

"Yes. You've been in the house alone before."

"Not like this."

"You'll be safe."

"Good night, love."

"Good night, Sally."

This time, as he crawled back into bed, Ruth only asked, "Why does your voice sound so phony when you talk to her?"

Ruth was up early and in the so strangely inflected sunlight of this Monday Jerry did not feel sanctioned to turn into the center of the bed and sleep another minute before, as usual, she called him to make the 8:17. He remembered a snatch of a dream. There seemed to be the aftermath of a party, in a kind of huge high-ceilinged hotel room. Sally had fallen asleep on the sofa and, as when this happened with Ruth, Jerry searched for something to cover her with. He found draped on the back of an ornate chair a man's dirty raincoat with a plaid lining. He tucked it around Sally's shoulders but her long legs stuck way out; the raincoat was too small. It was a child's raincoat, tiny. That was all of the dream he remembered. He rose and shaved and went downstairs. The children in pajamas seemed soft moths bumbling at candles of milk. Joanna greeted him with a sly broad smile that spread her freckles. "Daddy slept at home last night," she said.

"Daddy always sleeps at home," Geoffrey said.

Charlie reached across a corner of the breakfast table and with a practiced hand slapped his brother on the head. "He does not. He and Mom fight too much."

Geoffrey's face, caught in a pleased expression, slowly reversed its flow of happiness and was tugged into sobs.

"Charlie, that was *not* helpful," Jerry said. "Or especially true."

"He's stupid," Charlie pleaded.

Joanna giggled. "Charlie always says Geoffrey's stupid," she said. "He thinks he's a big shot."

"I do *not*," Charlie told his father, his little features

edged with a fanatic light. He turned to Joanna and said, "*You're* the big shot. Joanna thinks she's a big shot because she has a boyfriend."

"I do *not*. Mommy, he's always saying I have a boyfriend when I don't. He's always telling lies. *Liar*. Big shot. Liar."

"Jerry, *talk* to them," Ruth said, carrying a plateful of buttered toast to the table. "Don't just stand there."

"He—he—he," Geoffrey gasped to his father, "hurt my *feel*ings."

"He was stupid," Charlie explained matter-of-factly, the evidence incontrovertible, his lips shiny with butter.

"You know what I think this conversation is?" Jerry asked them all, and answered himself: "Acky." The children, even Geoffrey, laughed to hear him use a word they had invented. Their faces lifted toward him brightly, ready to be amused further. "You know what I've decided you all are?" he asked. "I've decided you're all a bunch of—poopheads."

They tittered and fluttered. "And wee-wee bottoms," Charlie added, glancing around quickly to see if he had caught the style, and reassured by the ripple of corrupt mirth that came from the other children.

Geoffrey, dimpling deeply, brought out, "And diarrhea."

"And throw-up," Joanna chanted, as if inventing a skip-rope song.

"And diddlespit," Charlie contributed, producing so much evil glee that Jerry stopped laughing with them, not knowing what diddlespit was and unable to believe his guess.

"Say, I don't think this is a very nice conversation for breakfast," Ruth announced. "Joanna and Charlie, you have seven minutes to get dressed for school. Charlie, you'll have to wear the checked shirt again, I haven't had time to iron the white one, I'm *sorry*." Her emphasis forestalled his whine of complaint. "Geoffrey, take your toast into the TV room. Sit on the floor, I don't want crumbs between the sofa cushions." Ruth and Jerry were then alone in the kitchen. "What gets you up so early?" she asked. It was seven thirty-five; he was wearing an undershirt and the pants of a gray business suit.

"Guilt," he answered. "Dread. You think I should go to work today?"

"Anything urgent on?" Ruth asked. She poured the children's leftover orange juice into a clean glass and gave it to him to drink.

"Not really. Those third-world commercials are winding down, the USIS has been cut back on funds." The juice hurt, hitting his stomach together with the realization that today was a different kind of day, that every day henceforth would be different. "I guess I better stay here, to field the flak."

"That would be gracious," Ruth said to him. Her face was cautious and stony. She too was just waking up to where they were. "There's a thing I wish you'd do for me."

"What?" His heart, behind the times, leaped in gratitude, to hear that he could still serve her.

"Those damn posters I said I'd do for the rummage sale. Before you go off anywhere, could you possibly letter them for me? I told her I'd do five. It would take you ten minutes, and they'd be so much better than any I could make, even if I could get enough of a grip on myself."

"You seem to have a grip on yourself," he accused her.

"I've taken a tranquillizer. I figured I couldn't afford to get drunk, so I found these old pills from when I had the post-partum thing after Geoffrey. I don't know what it's doing to me; I feel very detached, and slightly sick."

"Throw-up, diarrhea, or wee-wee?"

"That was wild. They smell trouble, don't they? They could have smashed every dish on the table and I wouldn't have turned a hair. But please, *could* you do

the posters? I can't stand thinking about them, it's just
one thing too many."

"Sure."

"I'll look for the information. I think it's upstairs with
the cardboard I bought. I'll *never* agree to do another
thing for those Congregational women. Why are they so
pushy?"

"Zeal," he said. "I'm sorry I got you into it."

Upstairs, Charlie began to yell for his mother, and
Ruth, moving through the kitchen with the serenity of
the moon navigating clouds, went to his rescue. Jerry
crushed some Shredded Wheat into a bowl, poured the
milk, and remembered the newspaper; it would still be
on the front porch. As he arrived at the front door, the
doorbell rang; he opened the door, and there was a man
picking up the folded newspaper, the top of his head
showing through a tangle of wiry black the approach of
baldness. Richard straightened and, his drawn face reddened by the exertion, handed the paper to Jerry.
"Thanks," Jerry said. "Come on in. You're up early."

"I haven't been to bed. Is Ruth here? I expected Ruth
to be here."

Jerry called, "Ru-uth," but she was already coming
down the stairs. Joanna and Charlie, dressed for school,
clattered behind her, in a hurry. "Good morning," she
said tranquilly. "Richard, I'll be right with you, as soon
as I find their lunch money. Jerry, do you have two dollar
bills and two quarters?"

"My wallet's upstairs on the bureau," he said, offering
to push past.

"Never mind," she said, "mine's in the kitchen. Charlie,
go get the two dollars. It's the quarters that are the
problem, everybody keeps stealing them."

"Here are two," Richard said, having fished.

"Great," Jerry said. "We'll owe you." The silver felt
chill, accepted from Richard's hand. He had been out all
night.

"Mom, there is no *wallet*," Charlie was calling.

Geoffrey, overhearing the commotion, came into the busy hall and, surprisingly, butted his head between Richard's knees. Months ago at the beach, when the surface of their lives was calm, Richard, who floated with an unmuscular ease in the water, had allowed the two little boys, Geoffrey and his own son Peter, to push him this way and that in the shallows, as if he were a large limp boat; recalling his good time, Geoffrey bumptiously offered to play again, and Richard had to unbend or be knocked down.

"Easy, skipper," he said, ruffling with a strained expression the woolly round head pushing at his thighs. Embarrassed, Jerry glanced at the headlines of the newspaper in his hand. *Negro Admitted to Mississippi U.; 3 Dead in Campus Riot. Khrushchev Invites Kennedy to Moscow. Chou Is Adamant in Soviet Dispute. Giants and Dodgers Tie for Pennant.*

"Is Daddy going to play golf?" Charlie asked, returning with Ruth's green wallet after all. He could imagine no other reason why a man would come to the house so early in the morning, though Richard, in his gangsterish checked sports coat and pink button-down shirt and tightly knotted striped tie, was not dressed for golf.

"Stupid," Joanna said. "Mr. Mathias doesn't play golf, only Mr. Collins."

"Mr. Mathias is here on business," Ruth said, exchanging money for kisses and reaching past Richard's shoulder to open the door. Joanna and Charlie without looking back pattered down the steps and crossed the road. How serious they looked, Jerry thought, lifting his eyes from the paper to watch them through the window take their place, beneath the elm, in wait for the school bus. Unconscious of the dwarfing size of the tree above them, they kicked at the dead leaves. Around each fallen leaf on the asphalt of the road there was a damp spot, a kiss.

Ruth asked Richard, "Would you like some coffee?"

"If I may," he said. The suffering sweating clown of last night had evaporated, leaving a husky, rigid presence who menaced their house. "I have something to say to Jerry, since he appears to be here, and some things to say to you, Ruth. What I have to say to you is very short," he told Jerry. "Where can we talk?" Geoffrey was still clinging to Richard's legs.

"The back yard might be best," Jerry said. The words he spoke seemed to hang outside him; he felt like a scared actor reciting lines he had barely learned.

Ruth said, "I'll make some fresh coffee. Geoff, go watch TV. Bozo's on."

Jerry led Richard through the kitchen into the air. They stood beneath a maple; from one of the branches Jerry had strung a monkey swing. The ground all around the swing was packed and scuffed bare; elsewhere, the lawn needed cutting, in the lank neglected way of autumn grass, that dies in August but revives in the September rains. Jerry asked, "Have you really been up all night? What did you do?"

Richard was not to be softened. He stood so the inch of height he enjoyed over Jerry was emphasized by the slope of the yard. "I drove into Cannonport and walked the streets. I had a drink here and there and watched the sun come up from the docks. I've been taking it cold turkey, boy."

Jerry shrugged. "Join the club."

"I had breakfast with my lawyer," Richard went on. "Out of our discussions there emerged two—no, three— statements I must make to you."

Jerry shrugged again; he felt there was a line here for him to say, but he had forgotten it.

"Firstly," Richard stated, "I've just come from my home, my ex-home, where I left Sally in excellent physical health."

"Good."

"I in no way molested her. I showered, shaved, and described to her my decisions as they pertained to her."

"Had she gotten to sleep finally?"

Richard squinted, a little puzzled here, by the implication that Jerry knew more than he did. "She was sleeping like a baby. I could hardly wake her up. She's a late riser, better get used to it. My intention is, in regard to the house, to live in it. I assume you and she will locate a new place for her as soon as possible; until such time, she and I will continue to live together, but not, so to speak, as man and wife."

"So to speak. Are these the lawyer's phrases?"

"This is serious business, Jerry."

"Sure is." He looked up, scanning; the sky was the blue of faded velvet and was being invaded by serious gray clouds from the west.

"Secondly, I will divorce Sally if you agree to marry her."

"If? I thought I had agreed." His voice scratched, to hold fast against the sliding sensation that came with these words.

"The divorce will be out-of-state and on grounds agreed upon by her lawyer and mine. I will not press any claim to the children, though naturally I expect adequate visiting privileges and a continued voice in their upbringing."

"Of course. I can't take your place with them. We're all going to need each other's help to get the kids through this."

"Just so," Richard said, pinching his lips together in a toothless bite. "Thirdly, if you do *not* marry Sally, I intend to sue you for alienation of affections."

It felt like a pillow blow, something more to hide behind than be hurt by; Jerry was distracted, intensely conscious of the yard, the unmowed growth, the paper scraps of toys that needed picking up, the little bumps and granular accumulations at their feet that proved the existence of insect-cities that had their own hierarchies and daily routines and trade routes and queens and five-year plans. Jerry said, "I don't know exactly what aliena-tion of affections means. I suppose I can get a lawyer to tell me. But I think it's a mistake for you to imagine the attraction wasn't mutual."

Richard said, suddenly cozy, "You know and *I* know, Jerry, that Sally was just as aggressive as you were in this affair and probably more so. But in the eyes of the law, she's not a free agent. She's a chattel. In the eyes of the law, by turning my wife against me, you've caused me a great deal of mental suffering, mental and some physical, for which I have a right to be reimbursed. She threw a brass bookend at my head and could have killed me; that's damages. For a while now I may have to hire prostitutes to satisfy my manly needs; that's more dam-ages. These lawyers are wicked people, Jerry boy."

"Shit," Jerry said. "She wouldn't have come to me if she hadn't turned against you in the first place. She was your wife, it was your job to keep her. Because of you, my children are going to grow up crippled. Because you're a shit, my wife wants to die."

"I think that's enough. Don't flatter yourself about Ruth, she can take care of herself. Watch where you throw that word 'shit.' Don't get me mad, Jerry boy. You're playing with grown-ups now."

"I have a question."

"I'm listening."

"About these affections of Sally's you say I've alienated. If I were out of the picture, do you think you could get them back?"

Richard's face appeared to jerk, as when a few frames of a film strip have been lost; or perhaps it was that Jerry blinked, having touched the nerve of the matter. Richard said slowly, "If you desert Sally, I will dispose of her in my own way. I am proceeding on the assump-tion that you *will* marry her. Am I wrong?"

It's wrong, isn't it?

"Am I wrong? Yes or no, Jerry."

"I'll send Ruth out to you. I think you've said your piece to me."

"For now, yes."

Inside the house, Ruth asked him, "What did he say?"

"Nothing. Stuff. If I don't marry Sally he'll sue me."

"For what? Sleeping with her?"

"Alienation of affections, it's called."

"But it was her idea."

"It's a bluff, Ruth. The silly bastard won't talk straight, he has to bluff."

"Well, he's been hurt. He's a weak man."

"Who isn't?"

"We can't leave him standing in the yard. Turn off the coffee water when it sings."

Through the kitchen window Jerry watched Ruth and Richard talk. Relaxed by her company, Richard did a strange tame thing; he sat on the monkey swing and let himself drift back and forth, exhausted. After a while, at some gestures from Ruth, he got up, took off his checked coat, and spread it on the grass, over near the shed where the bicycles and ladder and garden tools were kept, so they could sit down. Side by side, they shared a cigarette. When Richard inhaled, an elderly jut deformed his lower lip; Ruth, nodding as words and smoke came together out of his mouth, seemed pink in the face, her attention heightened almost sexually, as it used to be in art school, when the teacher paused by her easel. The clouds advancing from the west brought wind with them; leaves scuttled and swirled about the absorbed couple, and Jerry wished they would remain like this forever, in his back yard, garden statues, guardian demigods. The coffee water sang; he turned off the burner. Behind him in the house, Geoffrey was squawking; he had attempted to dress himself, and couldn't do up the buttons. Jerry buttoned his corduroy coveralls and phoned the office,

telling them he had wakened with a terrible cold. It was
true, his throat was hoarse and his nose watery, for lack
of sleep. He found the cardboard behind Ruth's bureau
and some dried bottles of Sho-card color in the playroom, and a hardened brush that he washed in the kitchen
sink. When Ruth and Richard finally came back into the
house, they found him settled on the living-room floor
doing the Congregational posters. "Good for you," Ruth
said, and served coffee. Richard sat on the sofa and
stared incredulously as Jerry with fluid confident strokes
lettered R U M M A G E   S A L E in jiggling Disney-
esque capitals and the date and place and drew a cartoon
lamp, battered, and an empty picture frame, and a pair of
comically patched socks. Ruth went to the telephone.

Jerry asked, "Who are you calling?" He had expected
her to sit still, admiring his creative labor.

"Mrs. O again," she said. "Richard thinks I should go
to Cannonport and talk to his lawyer."

"Why talk to Richard's lawyer?"

"He'll get me a lawyer of my own."

Richard said, "I certainly think Ruth should have a
lawyer."

"I guess," Jerry said, dipping his brush in water and
then in purple.

"If she had had a lawyer six months ago, a great deal
of pain could have been avoided, and we'd all be advanced on the healing process."

Unctuous, the purple seemed as it went on.

The men held silent as Ruth arranged with Mrs. O
to come in half an hour. When she hung up, Richard
told her, "He's expecting you. I guessed you'd be in
before noon, can you make it?"

"Sure. I have to be back by three to see that Joanna
gets off to her piano lesson."

"I'll call and confirm. You have his address."

"Yes, Richard, yes. I'm not an idiot. You just gave
it to me."

"I'm tired. Christ, I need to hit the hay. Let's keep in touch." Richard heaved himself up from the sofa and the effort of standing appeared to impose upon him an obligation to make a statement. "It's a dark day," he said, "but perhaps there's a brighter ahead."

Jerry looked up, and obscurely felt his low position on the floor as an advantage. Without rising, he said, "Richard, I'd like to thank you for being such a help to Ruth, and for reacting to all this in such a manly and practical way."

"Thank you very much," Richard said grimly. Jerry saw, what the familial intimacy of last night's revelations had concealed, that Richard had emerged from that soft tunnel with a wound he was determined to turn, in the hard days ahead, to a profit.

When his footsteps had died from the porch steps, Jerry asked Ruth, "What the hell was he saying to you for so long?"

"Oh—you know. Stuff. He told me I was young and good-looking and had a lot to live for. That you weren't the only man in the world and that you had legal obligations to me and the children."

"I've never denied that."

"He said I'd been begging you all summer to stay with me and now I should try something else. I should give you the divorce. He told me to stop thinking about you and to start thinking about what *I* was, and what *I* wanted."

"He sounds like a Chamber of Commerce."

"He made sense."

"What did he say about the children?"

"He said children were important but they shouldn't be the basis of a decision. I mean, he didn't really say anything we don't know already, but it cleared the air to hear somebody else say it."

"The gay divorcée. I'll be damned. O.K., when do you start doing your own fucking Rummage Sale posters?"

"Don't be mean to me about them, I can't possibly do them now. Mrs. O is coming in fifteen minutes. You've already done one and it's beautiful; do four more just like it. Don't try to be original, it'll take you five minutes. What else are you going to do today? Are you going to go over to her?"

"I suppose I should."

"Just do the posters, I'll never ask you to do another thing."

" 'Keep in touch'—that unctuous son of a bitch telling my wife to keep in touch."

"Jerry, I *must* get dressed."

As if he was detaining her. Was he? Though his hand was trembling and the floor under the cardboard rolled like the deck of a ship, he could not help trying to make each poster better than the one before—funnier, vivider, more invitingly rummagy. It took him longer than five minutes; Ruth showered and dressed and came down to find him still working. She was wearing the plain black dress he had always liked; its knit hugged her hips and its blackness dramatized the something pliant about her pale flesh. She kissed him good-bye. Because of the Sho-card color on his fingers he could not touch her with his hands. He asked, "Is this what Richard told you ladies should wear to see their lawyers in?"

"Does it seem right? I suppose I should wear a hat with a veil like for church but I don't have any. I could borrow Linda's again. Do you think he'll want to talk money already?"

"Probably. What does Richard think you should ask?"

"He mentioned fifteen. That seems like a lot. I don't think my father ever made that much in all his life."

"Well, get what you can. I'm sure Richard's lawyer will have lots of good ideas."

"Are you mad? Isn't this right? I mean, I have no choice any more, do I?"

"Of course I'm not mad. I'm sad. I think you're very

spunky and look great. Give me another kiss." He leaned
forward, handless. Her nose was cool and her tongue
warm. The porch steps thumped. Mrs. O had arrived. As
Ruth left, she was searching her pocketbook and Jerry
heard her saying, "Car keys, car keys," to herself.

He finished the posters while Mrs. O fed Geoffrey a
second breakfast. Alone at last with a person perfectly
kind, Geoffrey prattled. Jerry heard the murmur and
realized there was a tone, a muffling amplification, that
altered the voices of his children when he listened to
them through the thought that he was going to leave them
—as the eye would be disturbed by a drawing, meticu-
lously carried out, where perspective nevertheless lapses
on one semi-distant building, whose roof is impossibly
awry, giving to the surface of the whole a vague churning,
an unwanted resonance. All summer, from other rooms,
across widths of asphalt and grass, Jerry had heard that
sound, and it had joined as a species of discomfort the
curious flatted impression made upon him when, awaking
each morning from a sleep permeated with schemes and
desires centered upon Sally, he would see, first thing, the
lightly smiling self-portrait, executed with exquisitely
true touches of color but in line and drawing not really
resembling her at all, given to him by Ruth, blushing, on
his thirtieth birthday last winter. In this way, the way in
which she could, she had given herself to him.

Only when the posters were finished, laid in a row on
the sofa to dry, and brush washed and the paints put
away in the playroom, did Jerry feel obliged to call Sally.
Mrs. O had taken Geoffrey for a walk to the candy store
in the leaves; Jerry was alone in the house. It felt strange,
dialling her number from his house. He misdialled a six
for a seven, replaced the receiver as if hushing a mouth
about to scream, and dialled again. "Hello": her voice no
longer lifted syllables upward into questions.

"Hi there, you crazy Miss Mathias. It's me. How are
you?"

"Fa-air." Her voice dragged the word into two syllables.

"Richard there sleeping?"

"No, he went out again, he's terribly excited. Having anything to do with lawyers always makes him excited. How are you?"

"Alone. Ruth's gone to see your husband's lawyer and the baby-sitter has taken Geoffrey for a walk."

"Have you told your children yet?"

"Oh God, no. Everything's been too confused. Richard's been here, issuing ultimatums and giving advice all around."

"He said you seemed frightened."

"How funny. He was doing his bully-boy act."

"He's been *so* hurt, Jerry."

"Hey. Do you want me to come over?"

"If you want to, I'd like it."

"Of course I want to. Why wouldn't I?" When she didn't supply the answer, he added, "You sound bruised."

"Yes, I guess that's what it is. Bruised."

"Well don't bump into anything more, just stand in the middle of the room. I'll be right there."

"I love you."

He had to do things quickly, or he would sink. Jerry put on sneakers but neglected to tie them and rushed into his back yard with the laces bouncing and flipping. He mistakenly pulled out the choke of the Mercury as if it were winter, and, half-flooded, it was reluctant to start. He made the engine roar and drove past mailboxes, garages with gaping doors, heaps of leaves smoldering untended, empty yards. The entire town felt vacated; he imagined that atomic war had been declared, and glanced at the sky for a telltale change of appearance. But the clouds there only mirrored the desolation of the uneventful. The Mathiases' house silhouetted on its hill seemed a ruin, a stark unturning windmill. Caesar lumbered from the woods and barked, but without heart; by the kitchen doorway the asters swallowed by darkness last night showed russet shades. Inside the door, Sally came shyly into his arms. She was his. Her body startled him by being so real, so solid, so big and stiff; she rested her forehead woodenly on the side of his neck and the heat of her face felt dry. He held her tightly to him; it was expected. Theodora toddled into the hall and stared at them. Her eyebrows, like Sally's, were shaped—high-arched, and darkening toward the bridge of the nose—so that their natural expression was, if not anger, the alertness of a wild and perpetually threatened animal. The lower half of the child's face held Richard's thin, birdy mouth. Her gaze, great-eyed and steady, reflected the vivid transparence all around them; they were exposed, he and Sally, in this high house. He asked, "Hey?"

For answer she tightened her arms at his back and involved him deeper in her stricken rigidity. She wore her amber-striped jersey and white St. Tropez pants, her playful sailor costume.

He asked her, "Don't you feel like we're two children caught with our hands in the cookie jar?"

She pulled back and looked at him humorlessly. "No. Is that what you feel like?"

He shrugged. "Sort of. A little. I'm sure it will pass."

She returned the weight of her face to his neck and asked, "Would you like anything?"

Was she offering, incredibly, to make love, here, with all the world watching? Over her shoulder, he asked the child, to remind Sally that she was there, "No nap, Theodora?"

"She won't take her morning nap any more," Sally said. Trying, what had never before been an effort, to find the stance that fit his body, she backed off slightly, letting a little air between them, but keeping her head bowed, as if frightened to show him her face. Looking down, she laughed. "You forgot to tie your sneakers."

"Yeah, and I forgot my cigarettes."

She decided to back off from him completely. "I think Richard left some in the living room. Where do you want to sit?"

"Anywhere."

Where?

We could meet for coffee sometime, if you'd like. Somewhere outside of Greenwood. Would that be wrong?

No. Well, yes. Wrong but right. When? When, dear Sally? Don't tease me.

It's you who tease me, Jerry.

"How many cups of coffee have you had this morning?" Sally smiled in complicity.

"Not so many. Two," he said, irritated to think that he had betrayed her by not having more. She had not slept, she had drowned in coffee while he had been swimming in his wife's warmth and coloring on the floor like a child.

He sat in her bright kitchen, the glitter of its knives and counter edges and pâté molds at intervals dulled as clouds swallowed the sun, and talked of Richard and Ruth; they found it difficult to talk of themselves. Their love, their affair, had become a great awkward shape, jagged, fallen between them. Jerry was ashamed of his desire not to touch her; he wanted to explain that it was not a change in her, but a change in the world. Richard's knowing had swept through things and left them bare; the trees were stripped, the house was polished and sterile like a shop-window, the hills dangled as skeletons of stones, so that lying embraced even in the earth Jerry and Sally would be seen. His modesty made her repulsive, nothing else; but to plead this, as excuse for not touching her, that same modesty forbade. He was bewildered to be locked with her in a relation demanding tact. She stood; he stood; they seemed, the two of them, bombarded by light perilously. He wanted to hush her brilliance, for it cried out, declared, through the miraculous transparence around them, their position, when they most needed to hide.

They did not hear Richard's car come up the drive. He

found them standing in the kitchen, as if they had just touched. His lips were pinched in like the lips of the elderly. "Here, here," he said. "This is too much."

Jerry, to make himself smaller, sat down on a hard kitchen chair. Sally remained standing and said, "We have to talk. Where can we go?"

Richard still wore his coat and tight tie, as if he had become, through intense consultation, himself a lawyer. "Of course, of course," he conceded. His saying things twice had taken on an air of legal force. "You have to talk, to hash things over. Forgive me, we may not always be rational, but we shall try, we shall try. I came back to get some papers—bankbooks and insurance policies; Sally, you know the folder. Do I have your permission to go upstairs to what used to be our bedroom?"

"We were talking very sadly," Sally offered him, "about *you.*"

"That's very kind of you both, I'm sure. You are both, I am sure, very concerned about my welfare."

"Oh Richard, relax," Sally said. "We're all still people."

"I appreciate that. I appreciate that. I have never denied, so far as I know, that the parties involved in this negotiation are people. Jerry, are those your cigarettes you're smoking, or mine?"

"Yours."

"So I thought."

"Here, I'll give you twenty-eight cents."

"Keep your money, you'll need it. Make yourself at home, Jerry boy. Sally-O, see that Jerry here gets a good lunch, will you? I'm sorry, but I won't be able to join you, though I know you're begging me to."

Jerry stood, saying, "I'll leave."

"Don't," Sally commanded.

"It's not my house," Jerry told her. "It's his. He's right. I shouldn't be here."

Richard stepped over to him and put his arm around him bearishly and hugged; his breath, close, smelled of whiskey, a heavy, helpless, sepia smell. "Of course you should, Jerry. Jesus Christ, of course you should. Forgive me, huh? I had an irrational moment when I walked in, but I'm O.K. now. What's mine is yours, eh? You really put it into her, didn't you?" His hug tightened, and Jerry fought a vivid delusion of himself as infantile, small enough to be crushed, lifted, and tossed. His palms began to tingle, his mouth felt dry. Richard was urging him, "Enjoy your meal. That's one thing about Sally, I can't take it from her, she's a good cook. She's given me one hell of a time, boy, but she's kept those meals coming, three times a day, boy, bang bang bang. She's a good kid, Jerry, you lucky son of a bitch; you really had it into her, didn't you? I can't get over it, I know it's irrational as hell, I know it's a defense mechanism of some kind, but I can't get it into my thick head."

Jerry said, "She never stopped being fond of you." Jerry's heart was pounding, he was trying to make an ascent, up into Richard's approval, his forgiveness. "I didn't realize," he went on, "until last night, how fond of you she is."

"Horseshit," Richard said. *"Merde. Caca.* Take her out of my sight, the sight of her makes me sick, frankly. Good luck, buddy. I give you two butchers three years at the outside."

"Leave him alone," Sally told Richard. "Can't you see he's in hell over his children?"

"I feel sorry for his kids myself," Richard said. "I feel sorry for mine, too. I feel sorry for everybody except you, Sally-O. You've got it made."

"Jerry can go any time," Sally said, her chin proudly tilted. "I have no claims on him. I want a man to *want* me."

But Richard had turned and gone upstairs, three steps at a time. He shouted down, "Where's my fucking bathrobe?"

Sally went to the foot of the stairs and screamed as fiercely, "Stay out of my closet!"

Richard's heavy steps dragged this way and that above them and soon he came down carrying a suitcase; he barged into the open air without a sideways glance in their direction, though they had gone into the hall like servants to receive his orders.

Sally smoothed her long hair back from her ears and sighed. "Everybody's getting so melodramatic."

"You shouldn't stay here," Jerry said. "I can't visit you, Richard will keep coming in and out. He told me he's going to live here."

"It's as much my house as his," Sally said.

"Not really, since it's you and not Richard who wants the divorce."

She stared; her eyes went wide in mock innocence. "Just me! I thought we *all* wanted it."

"Well, some more than others."

"Perhaps I misunderstood last night," Sally persisted. "I thought I heard you say you wanted to marry me."

"I did. And I don't like you here. I feel you're in danger."

"Oh, Richard," she said, mildly, brushing back her hair again. "I can manage *him*." And in the emphasis of *him* strange territories unfolded for Jerry. There was something he could almost glimpse, if Sally would cease setting herself and her solid concerns, her desperate practicality, in the path of his vision. She said, "Want to go look at the painter's house? Remember, I mentioned him?"

He's beautiful, Jerry, you'd love him, he's a beautiful old guy. I don't know how old he is, he's so young at heart.

He sounds pretty sexy.

He likes me. He calls me his daughter.

How nice. For him. And you.

Jerry had hated her flirtation, this summer of their

affair, with the old painter, who taught winters in the city and who was what Jerry might have been: an artist, a free spirit. "How could I forget?"

"It's probably much too expensive for us. He fixed it up himself, did all the carpentry." She lowered her voice, which had lifted in admiration. "It could be a place to put me until we're ready to live together. He wouldn't charge us much. The children wouldn't have to change schools."

"How far is it from here?"

"Only a mile."

Jerry laughed. "Not very far on the way to Wyoming."

Because Jerry's Mercury had a noisy, noxious broken muffler, they went in Sally's gray Saab, whose starter had been fixed. Sally drove; Theodora sat uneasily in Jerry's lap. The painter had built this high little house, a pagoda without dragons, on a slope of pines on the first of the hills behind Greenwood; rocks kicked loose from the road under the Saab's wheels as it climbed. It was a cocky wood structure, three stories each smaller than the one beneath, as if a giant child had arranged them there. Jerry held Theodora uncomfortably in his arms; she was younger and lighter than Geoffrey, but holding her reminded Jerry of his own infant, and then he remembered how years before, in irrecoverable innocent days, Sally and Ruth swapped maternity clothes, their pregnancies tending to alternate, and he would come home to find Ruth in a russet wool dress, with pimento flecks, or a forest-green expandable skirt in which his eye expected Sally, whom he already, in an uncondensed undeclared way, did love.

The key was kept in a house a hundred yards down the road. As he and Theodora waited for Sally to return, the child leaned so far out from this strange man holding her that his shoulders began to ache with the pull, and he set her down on her own feet. She toddled onto the new lawn and made little footprints, at first accidentally, then purposely. He thought of scolding her, but this seemed a betrayal of the children that were his to shape, and the rebuke stayed in his brain. Sally, walking with her wide farm-girl gait uphill, arrived breathless, and let them in. The house was cold, colder than the outdoors.

"He has electric heat," she said.

"It's not turned on."

"It's turned low."

Redwood beams and pine boards shellacked to an orange lustre clashed with elements of glass and flagstone; the space had the mystery of space enclosed within a tent. Between big windows set askew, rectilinear furniture hid its angles under Oriental pillows. Wool throw-rugs tried to soften the flagstone floor. Pine branches just outside, shadows and reflections, entered the room like the spirits of animals, so the slats of the lean Danish furniture had the look of perches and ladders.

"It's a lovely house," he said, meaning it could not be lived in by him. It was the house of a man who had stripped his mind clean of everything but himself, his needs, his body, his pride.

"The kitchen," Sally said, continuing the tour without inflection, a house agent persisting in a hopeless duty. "It's small," she said, "but terribly workable. A typical man's kitchen."

"He lives alone?"

"With guests sometimes."

"Is he queer?"

"Sometimes. He's old, Jerry; he's a philosopher. See all the bookshelves? There would be plenty of room for our books."

"I wouldn't live with you here, would I?"

"You could visit me. I think you *should* visit me, so the children would get used to you. Does that offend your scruples?"

"Scruples? Do I have any?"

"Please try not to be sad. Come. This is what I really want to show you." She led him up stairs that were

polished boards hung in a spiral; she led him down a
hall. Through doorways of untreated pine he saw beds of
teak and airfoam, unmade. "The boys would have to
double up," Sally explained. The hall ended at a bathroom
whose fixtures were on a Roman scale. Beside the door a
ladder had been fitted; Sally climbed it. Her bottom in its
white pants sailed away above him like a balloon. "Come
look," she called down.

She was standing in an octagonal room, the southern
sides windowless, but the other sides open, to the tops of
the pines and the sky, whose northern light was gathered
by a tilted array of leaded panes that suggested, to Jerry,
a man tipping a bowl to drain it, while others stood by
thirsty. Clouds moved rapidly across these fixed panes. A
large easel stood beneath them, vacant and new; only one
season's worth of palette scrapings smeared the sill. The
absent painter was a tidy man, fond of good equipment—
glass shelves, a drawing board of frosted Plexiglas, swivel-
ling drafting lamps of German or Swedish manufacture.
Jerry imagined the man's paintings as abstract, lavish of
canvas, hard-edged in the newest mode. He thought of a
drawing board from his childhood; the pencil kept poking
through the paper because he and a playmate had used
it as a dartboard and as a workbench, and the hammered
nails had left holes.

"You hate it, don't you?" Sally asked.

"No, of course I don't. I admire it. When I was a kid I
dreamed of having a place like this."

Sally waited for him to go on, then said, "Well, it's
much too expensive for us. He wants two-twenty a month,
and the heating bill would be awful."

"I don't know," he confessed. "It—it almost seems too
nice for us. Right now."

He watched her anxiously, to see if she understood. She
nodded rapidly, *yes yes,* like an absent-minded machine.
Sally said, "We must go back. Peter will be home from

kindergarten and I must make lunch. Do you want to have lunch with us?"

"Sure," Jerry said. "We—I have a baby-sitter."

Peter was not yet back. Ruth drove this same car pool Thursdays. It seemed another belt of time altogether in which Jerry had seen Ruth, in her soft black dress, smile and disappear, saying "Car keys, car keys" comically to herself. Sally was saying, as she set four plates at the heavy walnut kitchen table, "I asked the boys this morning if they would like to have Mr. Conant come live with them, and they thought for a while and then Bobby said, 'Charlie Conant.' They love Charlie, everybody does."

"Except poor Geoffrey."

"It's because you don't *discipline* them, Jerry. Bobby tries to pick on Peter but I just won't have it. I will not stand for it, and I tell him why. I think it's very important, that children be told the *why* of everything."

"How shall I tell mine why I'm leaving them?"

She took it as a serious question. "Just tell them, you and Mommy like each other very much but think you'd be happier living apart. That you love them very much and will see them often and give them all the security you can."

"Security. That's sort of your operational word, isn't it?"

She looked up with darkened eyes. "Is it?"

"I don't mean it unkindly. Everybody has to have a word. Mine is faith. Or is it fear? Ruth's, in a funny way, is freedom. Going off this morning, she seemed happy. She was getting a divorce from everything."

"You've given her a pretty bad time," Sally said.

"I did it for you."

"No. I don't think so. You did it because you liked doing it. You've given me a pretty bad time, too."

"I didn't mean to."

She smiled, wryly, then widely. "Don't look so sad, man. We expect it." She was tearing leaves of lettuce from the head for sandwiches. He found himself irritated by her wasteful way of cutting out the heart first. She was full of faintly ruthless kitchen tricks like that. Everything in her kitchen glittered, glinted; whereas his kitchen at home was dim and cool even in summer.

Sally handed Theodora a slice of buttered bread and asked, "What's Richard's word?"

Jerry felt relieved, to have Richard named, to have him brought back into the house this way. "Richard? Does he have a word? I was struck last night by how responsible he is. I mean, he saw everything instantly in its social context—lawyers, schools for the children."

"I don't think you know him very well," Sally said.

"What would he do—never mind."

"Ask it."

"What would he do to you if I backed out?"

"Nothing."

"Nothing?"

"No, he wouldn't do anything, Jerry. Maybe he'd sulk and make me crawl for a few weeks, but he wouldn't do anything, and it's not because of any love of family either. It's just a divorce would cost him money and he doesn't like to spend money. So don't let that stop you."

"Stop me? Am I going somewhere?"

"I feel so, yes," Sally said, turning off the soup, which had begun to boil.

Peter came home; Janet Hornung was driving the car pool, and Jerry, though exposed by the presence of his car in the driveway, hid in the kitchen while Sally called brightly to Janet by the door where asters were still in bloom. Peter raced into the kitchen, stopped, and stared at Jerry solemnly. Of Sally's three children he had least of Richard in him. Jerry found this the opposite of reassuring; for Peter might be the child he and Sally would have created, obliterating the others and demanding for himself the total sum of love now scattered and diffuse. Peter's fine little features—covered, even the ears and nose, with a translucent fuzz visible in the sunlight— brought Sally's tensely spun beauty into a male face, where it posed too sharp a question. Jerry missed that hint of weight, of obtuse toughness, that Richard's other children had inherited. "Hello, Peter," Jerry said. "It's just me. How was school?"

The child smiled. "O.K."

"What did you learn?"

"Nothing."

"Your mommy says you can button your own buttons now."

Peter nodded, strangely made sad and apprehensive again. "I can't tie my shoes." He spoke quite distinctly, with an artificial poise, like Sally when, in Washington, she had spoken to hotel staff and the people at the airport.

"It's hard," Jerry said. "It's hard to tie your shoes. And after you learn that, you have to learn how to tie a necktie and how to shave."

The child nodded, fascinated and wary, perhaps sensing that here, in this not unknown talking man puzzlingly present in broad daylight without his own children, he was meeting the source of the unhappiness that had come from somewhere and filled his house. To show he meant no harm, Jerry sat down on a kitchen chair. Theodora arrived from the hall and with her mouth shiny from the buttered bread tried to climb into Jerry's lap. Not attuned to her movements and expectations, he was slow to help her up; she felt awkward and hurtful in his lap, bonier than Geoffrey. Sally came in from having seen her fellow-mother safely down the drive, and her first thought was to separate him from the children. She settled Theodora and Peter around the table (a deep shadow swept across its grained surface) with milk and chicken soup, and served Jerry a sandwich and wine in the living room

(where the sun came out again, making the tile surface of
the coffee table too bright to look at). The wine was not
last night's wine, but a dry Bordeaux, so pale it glimmered
green, as if with the ghost of the grape leaf, in the two
frail-stemmed glasses. The sandwich, salami and lettuce,
filled his mouth like a plea, a leafy, peppery blend of
apology and promise. He had little appetite but tried to
chew.

You're so big for me, Jerry. Too big.

Not really. Am I?

Oh, yes. Yes. You fill me all up. It's alarming.

It is? How nice of you to say so.

I mean it. Ow.

Sally. Bless you.

He sat in Richard's dirty old leather chair, leaving her
all of the white sofa. She did not sit, or eat, but prowled
along the windows, holding her glass by its stem, her
white pants taking long soundless strides, her hair almost
floating behind her.

"How nice all this is," he said.

"Why are you frightening me?" she asked. "Why don't
you come out and say it?"

"Say what?"

"Ask me why I told him so much. Tell me that I pushed
you."

"You had a right to push me, a little. You'd earned the
right. It was I who had no right, no right to want you—it
was all right to love you, but I shouldn't have wanted you.
It's wrong to want somebody in the same way you'd want
a—lovely thing. Or an expensive house, or a high piece
of land."

"I suppose," she said carelessly, as if her thoughts were
with her children in the kitchen, or with the airplane
rumbling distantly overhead.

"There's this odd blackness within me," he felt he must
explain, "that keeps bubbling up and taking the taste out
of the wine."

She quickly came close to him, potentially wild; in a rough gesture she gathered all her loose hair from the sides of her face and pulled it back in a fist and held it at the nape of her neck. She looked down at him and asked in urgent accusation, "Can't you stop being so depressed?"

He looked up at her and imagined himself on his death-bed and asked himself, *Is this the face I want to see?*

Asking it was the answer: her face pressed upon his eyes like a shield, he saw no depth of sympathy in Sally's face, no help in making this passage, only an egoistic fear, fear so intense her few faint freckles looked pricked, in her skin pulled taut by the hand clamped at the back of her head.

He embraced her upwards clumsily, her body resisting bending, her arm refusing to let go of her hair. As he closed his eyes, the darkness between them reddened and warmed, and continued to widen, beyond them both, so in his mind's eye he saw them from a great height, clasped on a raft in the midst of an unbounded blood-red ocean. The airplane rattled the sky, receding.

The children came in, fed: Jerry quickly whispered, "I've lost my nerve."

Sally stood erect, glanced down, and released her hair from her fist so it fell, relaxing slowly, like a parted rope, down her back. "Let's go for a ride," she said. "It's too nice a day to waste."

He rose stiffly, with the aimless thankfulness of an invalid. "Yes," he agreed, "let's. Maybe if I could get out of this house, I'd get some perspective."

I love this house.

Love my house, love me.

You are the house, sort of. You care, is what your house says. You care about many little things.

I've a trivial mind.

No; you're like a plant with a short growing season that has to put out a lot of tiny roots.

That sounds tragic, Jerry.

I didn't mean it tragically. We all have a season of some kind.

The clouds that Jerry had thought would bring a storm had instead thinned, were dispersing; it was one o'clock, and could have been late afternoon of a midsummer day. They drove, the four of them, not to the Greenwood beach, where Jerry and Sally might have been recognized, but to another, some miles away—an arc of sand between two congregations of great streaked rocks. A few sail-boats, like clinging leaves, dotted the Sound. At one point, while they walked the half-mile to the far rocks and back, he exclaimed, "God. This is the most beautiful place I've ever seen!" The waves, the whitecaps, the yellowish streaked rocks wore for him a religious brilliance; for as they walked they were deciding not to marry. Or, rather, Jerry was revealing that they would not.

Abruptly, after a flick of her head and some rapid word-less nodding, Sally laughed and offered, "Well I must say, Jerry, you let things go right down to the last flag!" Being out of doors had put color into her face.

"I didn't know before, I honestly didn't," he said, and, "I was afraid of losing the only thing that ever made sense."

"Where did it all go, Jerry?"

"Oh, it's still there. Hiding. But there." Resenting her silence, he added, "Why don't you fight?"

She shook her head, gazing down to where her bare feet were treading ribs of rippled sand on the water side of a wavering line of sun-dried wrack, and told him, "No, Jerry, I won't fight. It's not my position to fight. It's your position."

Theodora was falling farther and farther behind and now sat down in the wet sand in despair. Having reached the rocks, the adults turned, and Jerry carried the child all the way back to the car. Terribly, their bodies were beginning to fit, and she gave her weight to his arms with growing trust. The parking lot was as empty as in May, and the high territory of dunes had regained its untenanted innocence. As they got into the car, Sally said, "Thank the nice man, children, for the ride to the beach."

"We didn't stay," Peter complained.

"I'll bring you tomorrow," she told him.

Jerry drove them home and waited in the downstairs hall while Sally went upstairs and brought from her closet, from a hatbox far back on the shelf, the manila envelope containing the letters, the affectionate funny drawings, the bad little poems that had accumulated, like wrack, through the months of their affair and that she had carefully saved. "I think everything's here," she said. "I've always been so scared Richard would find them."

"If he does decide to go through with the divorce—"

"No. Don't even say it. He won't."

"Hey—"

"Don't cry. We knew it would end. I knew it would."

"I'm sorry, I can't quite leave you, I can't quite come to the last moment. Now that you're no longer mine, all my old love has come pouring back. You look glorious."

"Please go. I think you've decided. Be good to Ruth, don't punish her for your decision."

"Will there be somebody else for you now?"

"No." She gave him that rapidly. She touched his cheek with the backs of her fingers. "Nobody else could make me so"—she hesitated, searching for the word, and smiled, finding it—"pleased."

"I never have felt right," Jerry told her, "in my life, I can't express it, except with you. I never was home except when I was with you."

Her face took on the beginnings of the expression she assumed when she thought people were being what she called "melodramatic." She said with a shrug, "I'm glad it was you."

"Could you call me, if you need me? To talk?"

"I don't think so, no. This must be the very very end. Otherwise people will think we're too crazy. Thank you, Jerry."

He offered to kiss her, but she refused him.

Sally had turned in the hall before he had closed the door.

On the path outside, he met Richard. Richard glanced at his face, at the envelope in his hand, and said, "No guts, huh Jerry?"

Jerry imagined they would have to talk a long time, and he tightened his grip on the fat manila envelope. "It's one thing," he said, "to have guts for yourself, and another to have guts for your children."

"Yeah, sure, Jerry boy—you should have thought of that a little earlier. I'm going to make you pay, friend. I've been taking it cold turkey, and in our society people must pay for the pain they inflict."

"What are you going to do to *her*?"

Richard lit a cigarette, and studied the invisible chess-board whereupon his opponent, daringly, had castled. "I don't know, Jerry," he said, exhaling from the side of his mouth, one eye—the good or the bad—closed against the sting of smoke. "I haven't slept, I'm not thinking clearly."

"She's your wife," Jerry said to him. "I've been with her these hours and she's felt like your wife. They're your children, it's your house."

"Thank you very much," Richard said. *"Mucho gracias, señor."* He threw down his cigarette, scarcely smoked, and ground it into the grass, and went into his house, the door banging. Jerry listened, standing there motionless like a burglar. The house was silent, their reunion was silent, there was no sound but that of Caesar's claws rasping the driveway stones as the dog returned from some idle hunt in the woods to his accustomed lair inside the garage.

In his Mercury convertible, top down, Jerry drove home, free. The leaves in the trees above his speed were red and gold leaping out of green and rolling backwards against the sky. The ominous Nature his childhood had known seemed reborn; the air had the aftertaste of humiliation and disgrace, which is also, strangely, the taste of eternal life. He found Geoffrey and the little Cantinelli boy in the back yard trying to play baseball with a bent plastic bat and a whiffle ball, and he threw his son a few pitches before going into the house; these little boys, versions of a discarded self of his own, were his bodyguards. He wished never to move from this safe moment, on this firm autumnal lawn, among small dirty faces clean of accusation, his son's face charged with love and dependence, the neighbor boy's with, more confirming still, simple respect for his superior age and size. But he could not stay; he must flee, he must hide; he had work to do. He told Mrs. O. She nodded and produced out of her bosom a cooing that signified resignation, and hope of Ruth's eventual return, and assurance of the children's continued well-being. Jerry went upstairs and put on the suit whose pants he had put on this morning. In the kitchen he wrote, in crayon, on the back of a milk bill, ALL IS OFF. BE MINE. He signed himself X X. He drove to New York City, quickly, against the tide of afternoon traffic.

Oh Jerry, there's no rush, take all the time you need, because I know, I know every time I see you, that it's you, it has to be you, and it will be. It doesn't matter so much what you decide, or if you decide at all, we're not that important, I mean us as people, it's our love that's important, what we feel for each other, that's what we must protect, what we must never let the world take from us.

I want to climb to you.

Come if you can. I'm here. Just loving you makes me happy, even when you don't come to me.

You say that, but it won't always be true.
Why do you never believe me?

In his office he was told that, without him, his ideas and the animation roughs he had promised, the dog food conference had bombed. He sat down at his desk as the secretaries filled the hall with the chatter and shuffle of their departures, and tried to sketch dogs that walked upright and talked. The telephone on his steel desk rang.

"Darley, what happened?"

"I don't know," he told Ruth. "Not enough happened. Do you want me back? Or would you rather not? I can stay in the cottage a while."

"Of course I want you. Do you want me?"

"Apparently. I could hardly focus on poor Sally, I was so obsessed by the way you put on your cocktail party dress and walked out of my life."

"Was she upset?"

"No, she was terribly calm and resigned. I felt it was what she wanted too. She was obsessed with Richard. All of a sudden the two of us had nothing."

"Was Richard there?"

"In and out. I saw him at the end and he told me I had no guts."

There was a pause, then Ruth said, "How mean."

He asked, "How was the lawyer?"

"Oh, he was charming. Jewish, about my father's age, very courtly and charming. We just talked in general terms; he doesn't think Alabama is the place to go, but he didn't think from what Richard told him it would come to that."

"He didn't." It was frightening, degrading, to think that his move had been foreseen.

His wife offered to distract him. "You should have seen me driving to Cannonport, I was so slow it was agony. People kept honking and passing, and I kept thinking, *Those children have only me now,* and driving slower than ever. It's a wonder I wasn't creamed from behind."

"You can write a booklet, 'How I Became a Safe Driver,' by Ruth Conant."

"Why are you in New York?"

"Beats me. I can't afford to lose my job on top of everything else. I feel safe here."

"Are you waiting for her to call?"

"No, God, that's just what I'm *not* waiting for. Can you manage for a couple hours?"

"Oh, sure."

"Feed the kids, I'll be home for supper around eight. I love you."

"Well, gee. This is all so sudden. I feel swept off my feet."

He laughed, and asked, "Why are women so funny? She kept making jokes too."

"Jerry?"

"Yes?"

"Don't do anything drastic."

He laughed again. "Like slit my wrists? You should all be so lucky."

"Don't talk nonsense."

"You were nice," Jerry told her, "to hang on this summer."

"I can't believe it's over," Ruth said. "I've thought it was over so many times, and it never was."

"It's over. Please relax and be yourself again."

"How? Who am I?"

"You know."

She hung up, but he found he couldn't draw. His hand shook; the lights outside his window were multiplying, as the city sank into night like a vast, twinkling, gently foundering ship. It was after six; he had no business being here. He took the sketchpad and walked to the parking lot, beside a giant excavation; as he drove to Greenwood, through the perilous patchwork of headlights and signals, the terrible conversation on the beach seeped back to him. Her chin and cheeks and eyelids rosy from the salt breeze, Sally had asked, not quite believing his drift, *Can't we make it right?*

Never.

Do you know what you're saying to me?

I'm saying we will never be right. But then none of us will ever be right after this, not me and Ruth, not you and Richard.

Is it my children? Is it my children you can't stand?

I like them. The only thing I have against them is that they remind me of mine.

You should have let me go when I wanted to, and when I had the strength.

I loved you. Still do. If you want me, you can have me. Here I am, tied and delivered, courtesy of Richard Mathias.

I don't want you if you're going to be like this. You're no use to me unhappy.

Oh, I'll become happy again. Once I get in the painter's little fairy house.

No. It's gone. I can feel it.

Can you? I can't feel anything.

Peter, stop pestering Mr. Conant. He doesn't want to play.

He's trying to show me a shell. It's neat, Peter. Do you have a safe pocket?

Should we wait for Theodora?

She walks like you, don't you think?

I never noticed.

Want to go past the rocks, see what's there?

You'd like to get back.

I can wait.

Jerry—

Say it.

I'm sorry I've been stupid, I'm sorry I couldn't talk last night and can't seem to do the right thing today—

You've been fine. You're you.

No, I know I've felt wrong to you today; but I wouldn't always. I know we're all right together.

I know it too. It's not you, Sally. It's things. We can't lift them. You can't lift them for me. I can't lift them for you. I'd love to, but I can't.

O.K., man. If you can't, you can't.

Are you sure I can't?

It's you who are sure.

God. This is the most beautiful place I've ever seen!

His headlights gathered in the Greenwood exit sign. He remembered that he was carrying, on the back seat, the bulky envelope Sally had given him, the corpse of their affair. He stopped the Mercury at the side of the turnoff road and opened the trunk with the key; deep inside, with the greasy lug wrench and a flap of plastic lining that had come unglued and some bailing rope left over from a Cub Scout paper drive Charlie had been active in, there was a cave that would do for now. The envelope was so bulky with tokens of romantic love that as he handled it the little clasp let go and the contents spilled, exposing like edges of broken glass glimpses of his agitated handwriting, on pieces of paper already beginning to yellow. A few fell to the road; the rest slid loose upon the rubber floor of the trunk. Headlights swept over him, again and again; he was afraid someone he knew would stop, seeing him on his knees in the road, pulling a love letter from beneath a tire. With jerking, slippery hands he stuffed the letters back into the envelope; they had expanded; they would not go in, without crumpling. Between two letters in his handwriting were some strands of hair. He tried to examine them in the red glow of his taillights, and couldn't be certain of the color. But they were too short to be hers. And he remembered that sometimes in her house she would comb his hair afterwards. She had saved the combings.

Your hair is so soft, Jerry.

I washed it last night. For you.

For me?

It was full of sand from the beach, and I thought to myself, tomorrow I might see Sally, and make love, and when I'm above her I don't want sand to fall in her eyes.

You know, this is funny, but I knew that's just what you'd say, I knew it just by watching your mouth before it opened.

As he tried to replace the hair, it slipped from his fingers, and joined the detritus at the side of the road. He slammed shut the trunk lid. He was late, late for somewhere, he didn't know where. He was hunted. The road, seized again, wound down through Greenwood, its streets and trees, a maze that he knew better than his hunter. His house, his windows, his front steps, the voices of his children arose as a kind of dream out of the sleep of God.

Apparently in his absence a drama had occurred. Ruth met him with, "Where have you been? We've all been frantically trying to find you."

"All?"

"Yes. They were both here. With the little girl, what's-her-name. They all finally left a little while ago and I just got the food on the table for the children. Come in here and let's talk." He accepted the order without questioning. Ruth led him into the library and shut the door after her. "She came first. She said she came to tell me the kind of man I'm married to, but it was clear to me she was looking for you. She kept looking around and listening for noises upstairs. I said I hadn't seen you at all, just got your note and talked to you at your office. She couldn't believe you'd gone to New York. She said you and she slept together, when would it have been, Saturday night, the night before the blow-up. Is that right?"

"Yes."

"Well that's the last straw."

"Sweetie, it's too late for the last straw. What else unpleasant did she say?"

"Oh I don't know. On and on. She was wild. She was like an actress who'd suddenly realized she was no longer the star of the show. She said you'd treated us both terribly and that if I had any pride I wouldn't take you back. She said you were the devil and she would roast in Hell for what she'd done to Richard. She actually did say that. And she wouldn't let go of Theodora, that's her name, just kept holding on to this poor miserable confused child, and making me *feed* her. 'Ruthie, your husband's a real bastard, do you think you might have a cookie for Theo, he fucked me twice Saturday night, and could we have a little glass of milk?' "

Jerry laughed, relieved to learn that Sally was a fool. And relieved, too, that she still lived; her life was his, always. "And when did Richard come into all this?"

"She was here about a half hour, it seemed longer, when he came to take her away. 'Take her away' exactly describes it. He had the boys in the car. He looked exhausted."

"How was he with her?"

"Tender, really. Gentle. Calm. He told her she was hysterical. When he came in the door she gave out this great whoop and tried to go down on her knees to him. I think she told him to beat her. It was wild."

"My poor doe."

"Listen. If I'm going to live with you, let's have none of that stuff. You had your poor doe."

"Agreed. What else? Did he want to find me?"

"He says he doesn't want to see you, he can't stand the sight of you right now, but there's something he wants to say to you over the phone."

"How furious is he?"

"He's not furious. He's very philosophical. He said he expected you to back out but thought you'd go to bed with her a few more times."

"He didn't realize what an idealist I am."

"He talked about the philosophy of affairs. He said the

woman's responsibility was not to get pregnant and the man's was to stop it when the woman began to get emotionally dependent, which I though was a little odd coming from him."

"Why odd? It sounds like his kind of crap."

"I don't know, forget I said it. When I said what agony the summer had been for *you,* he said, 'Don't be silly. He had a ball!' "

"And then he took her home."

"Eventually. He had a drink. She was furious at his talking to me at all. She even made some crack about how I had to have all the men. Really, she was *crazy.*"

"Well, maybe only crazy women know how to make love."

"You can cut out that kind of remark too. I felt sorry for her. I may love you, Jerry, I don't know, but I have very little respect for you right now."

"Would you have more if I'd gone ahead and left you and the children?"

"In a way, yes. It wasn't the children themselves that worried you."

"It was."

"It was your immortal soul or some inane thing like that."

"I don't say it's immortal, I just say it should be."

"At any rate, I'm sure of one thing."

"What's that?"

"You've had it with her. She said some things so cruel that even Richard defended you."

She watched, to see how he took it. He said, "Good."

Jerry put the children to sleep. With Geoffrey, he always said the same prayer, as the child mumbled with him: "Dear God, thank you for this day—for the food we ate, the clothes we wore, the fun we had. Bless Mommy and Daddy, Joanna and Charlie—"

"And Geoffrey," the child usually inserted, seeing himself from outside, as one of a family.

"—and Geoffrey, and our grandparents, and our teach-
ers, and all our friends, Amen."

"Amen."

Charlie, the most active of the children, slept deepest,
and put himself to bed so quickly Jerry could only rub
the child's head and kiss his ear. There was no question
of prayers. When had they ceased? Perhaps the boy's
rapid sleeping had developed as a way of avoiding them.
Jerry was just as glad. He loved the child's pride, this
child the one of his three who saw most, and therefore
must be bravest. "Good night," he said in the darkened
room, and went unanswered.

Joanna, who no longer allowed her father to see her
undressed, had settled herself in bed with *Mr. Popper's
Penguins*. "Daddy?" she asked as he paused in her doorway.

"Yes, Jojo?"

"Are Mr. and Mrs. Mathias going to get a divorce?"

"Where did you learn the word 'divorce'?"

"Mrs. O said. Her daughter divorced a man in the Army
because he played cards too much."

"What makes you think the Mathiases want a divorce?"

"She was here and she was awful mad."

"I don't think she was mad at Mr. Mathias."

"Who was she mad at? That bratty baby?"

"No. Herself, maybe. Do you like Mrs. Mathias?"

"Kind of."

"Why only 'kind of'?"

Joanna thought. "She never pays attention to anybody
else."

Jerry laughed, perhaps too warmly, for Joanna asked:
"Is she your girlfriend?"

"What a funny question. Grown-ups don't have girl-
friends. They have wives and husbands and little children."

"Mommy has a boyfriend."

"Who?"

"Mr. Mathias."

Jerry laughed at the absurdity. "They like to talk sometimes," he told her, "but she thinks he's a jerk."

She looked at him respectfully. "O.K."

"Aren't you sleepy?"

"Kind of. This book has too many words in it I don't know. I mean, I *almost* know them, but then they don't make sense."

"That's like a lot of books. Don't tire your eyes. Dr. Albany says you shouldn't read in bed at all."

"He's a jerk."

"Your eyes are very precious. Sleep tight, sweetie. Here's a kiss." And in clasping her he discovered that her head was the size of an adult's nearly, and the curves of her cheek and bare shoulder as she turned her face into the pillow were those of a woman. She had grown, since he had last looked at her.

The rooms downstairs, empty of children, streaked with silence and headlights passing, were vast. On the kitchen table Ruth had set two places. He entered the kitchen timidly; when a child, and his mother was sick, he would enter the bedroom this timidly, fearful that she had been turned, as in a fairy tale, into a bear, or a witch, or a corpse. Ruth handed him a glass of vermouth. Her air was of waiting, while he tried, pacing, sipping, eating the lamb chop and salad she served him, to populate the silence, the theatre of loss, with explanations of himself. He said:

"I don't understand what quite happened. As an actual wife or whatever, she stopped being an *idea,* and for the first time, I *saw* her." He said:

"I wanted her to give me no choice. Sally shouldn't have kept giving me a choice; I went over there this morning convinced this is what had to be, and then talking to her I discovered that it *didn't* have to be. It was all still terribly open. She didn't want me enough, she didn't want me as much as *you* did."

Or:

"It's really Richard. Sitting there last night, looking at him, I said to myself, *He's not so bad*. Everything I had felt about him through her descriptions and complaints was wrong; he was human; he was trying. I said to myself, *My God, if he can't make her happy, I can't either.*"

Or:

"She presumed."

Between these attempts of his, embarrassed and strenuous, awkward and vague, to explain, there were intervals of Ruth's voice, gentle yet with something sharp, something Unitarian and confident and even destructive, about its search for truth:

"I didn't like the way they ganged up on you." And:

"If she loved you so much, why wasn't she willing to just have an affair?" And:

"They're both presumptuous people."

And intervals of twinned silence, which did not pain them, for they had begun in silence, side by side, contemplating, by fits and starts, an object posed before them, a collection of objects, a mystery assembled of light and color and shadow. In their willingness to live parallel lay their weakness and their strength.

During coffee, with the night outside as dark as coffee, the telephone rang. By his frightened immobility Jerry made Ruth answer it; in the living room she picked up the receiver, listened, and said, "He's here." She called softly into the kitchen, "Jerry, it's Richard."

He heaved up from the table and walked through streaks of shadow to the phone. Ruth, listening, circled the living room turning on lights. "Yes, Richard": ironically, wearily, conciliatingly.

Richard's voice was narrowed, its expansiveness gone. "Jerry, we didn't talk for very long this afternoon and I may not have understood something. Do I understand you correctly in that if I divorce Sally you will *not* stand by her? Repeat, will *not*?"

The old knight fork.

Jerry could have put out the weak whine of reasonableness he had always found useless against bullies, and argued that life unlike a chessboard was never black or white. Instead he said, "That is correct. I will not stand by her."

Richard waited for him to qualify, then, since he did not, said, "That's what I thought the situation was, but, frankly, Jerry, I couldn't believe it. I couldn't believe you had so little compassion, though Sally assures me you're right in character. You will not stand by her, no matter what?"

From the stagey clarity of Richard's diction, Jerry guessed Sally was on the upstairs extension listening. He sighed. "You stand by her. She's your wife. I have a wife."

"I don't know, Jerry boy, I just don't know. After the way she's treated me, I don't know if she should be my wife or not."

"That's your decision. As you would say."

Richard said, "I'm going to make you pay for this, Jerry boy. I'm going to make you suffer like you've made us suffer. You're an amazing guy. Amazingly cruel."

Jerry cast his mind back, to the beach, the dunes, the yellow bathing-suit bottom, the warm wine, the smell of their skins, and asked, honestly curious, "Am I?"

Richard hung up.

Ruth asked, "What was that about?"

"I think he just wanted to put me on show as rat in front of Sally. She was on the extension."

"Did she speak? Did you hear her breathing?"

"No."

"How do you know she was there?"

Jerry turned and shouted, "Because she's everywhere!"

Ruth gazed at him frightened. Though she had turned

on lights on the tables along the walls, there was left in the center of the large room a core of darkness and it was here that she stood.

Jerry explained, "Richard was sore because now he has to make a decision and he doesn't like it any better than I did; men don't like to make decisions, they want God or women to make them."

"Some men," Ruth said.

She went into the kitchen and Jerry went to the window. The darkness outside the cool glass held Richard; the arms of the elm crawled and rotted in a godless element that was his enemy's essence. Richard was the world. *I'm going to make you pay for this, Jerry boy.* An automobile that had been parked up the road roared by; Jerry flinched, conscious of himself as silhouetted. Its tires screeching, the car went by, kids, nobody; there was no gunshot. Jerry smiled. *You're an amazing guy. Amazingly cruel.* He had never been hated before. He had been disliked and dismissed but he had never been hated; it was a way, he saw, of being alive. *Look, Sally-O, doesn't Christ make a good fingernail-picker?* Gazing through the half-mirroring black glass, glass that seemed the cold skin of his mind, Jerry rejoiced that he had given his enemy the darkness an eternal wound. With the sword of his flesh he had put the mockers to rout. Christ was revenged.

5. *Wyoming*

JERRY and Sally disembarked from the plane at Cheyenne.

As they descended, a bit stiffly, the resounding steel steps, he inhaled and knew that he was home; the mythical western air released his lungs he felt forever from the threat of suffocation. Grateful, anxious to know if she too scented the blessing, he turned to look back at Sally; she was above him, leading the boys, one on each hand, while he carried Theodora and their plastic flight bag bulky with stuffed toys and small books. Again, and still, the sight of her gladdened him. She was wearing a pencil-striped linen suit; its sleeves came halfway down her long downy forearms and the horizontal wrinkles across the front of her skirt, left by long sitting, made vivid the beautiful breadth of her hips. She grinned and said, "It's great, isn't it?"

"The sky," he said. "Fantastic sky." All around them the palest of blues, powdery and demure, was boiling, boiling with thunderheads whose roots were translucent and whose crowns were a white so raw and pure their mass seemed emphasized by a fine black outline, etched by the eye. Though there was superabundant shape in these clouds there was no weight or burden of rain in them; Jerry felt that the slightest change in the air, the smallest alteration in its taste, would evaporate them utterly.

The west was rimmed with mountains, violet and brushed with chalk or, most likely, snow; the clarity of the air brought these distant peaks near yet rendered them unreal, uninhabitable, like the jumpy visions, with compressed perspective, obtained from a telescope. In the tawny middle distance a single horse, apparently riderless, was running, and a line of trees, perhaps cottonwoods, declared the presence of water. The plain was overspread with a youthful, silvery, aristocratic green—sage, Jerry imagined. A constellation of far rocks became a herd of sheep. In the foreground, there were lakes, a golf course, a red fort. Immediately under them like a glaring black page lay the macadam of the airfield, printed with stripes and oil-splotches, numerals and arrows and multicolored lids of buried tanks, symbols in a cumbersome language employed by a worldwide race of myopic giants. His feet on firm ground, Jerry lifted his eyes and said, "Hi?"

"Hi," Sally said, behind him, beside him. "You feel free?"

"Are we free?"

"Of some things." Saying this, she flipped back her hair and took a long step. She was tired. Bobby and Theodora had both been airsick above the checkerboard of the heartland states. Because Bobby was most like his father, Jerry found himself playing to him, whether attempting to overcome an instinctive dislike, or appealing to that odious authority he had felt in Richard, he couldn't decide. Now he asked the boy, "How goes it, skipper?"

"My throat's sore," Bobby said, hiding his face against his mother's thigh.

"You're thirsty," Jerry told him. "We'll get you a Coke in the airport."

"I want a grape soda," Bobby said.

"Where's a cowboy?" Peter asked. Already he seemed to have taken upon himself, young as he was, the task of interceding between his brother and stepfather, distracting them from the deadly business never to be settled between them.

"I've seen *twenty* cowboys," Bobby said contemptuously, and it was true, even the mechanics on the field had been wearing ten-gallon hats. Inside the terminal building, there were so many cowboys that it seemed a troupe of dancers, in theatrically taut Levi's, creased boots, open vests, and string ties, were waiting for a flight back to New York. But, no, these were real men, cured and warped to fit their costumes, which in turn fitted the land. With eyes whittled by weather to a kind of cruel ennui, with uncanny irises from which the sky had scooped all color, the cowboys studied Sally, her calico beauty. Jerry touched her waist, to show possession and deny impotence—for he felt it was evident that the three children were not his. Sally started at his touch, and with a blankness of fright in her eyes turned and said sharply, "I'll take Theodora while you get the bags."

"You can get Bobby a Coke over at that machine. Maybe it has grape soda."

"If I get him one I'll have to get three. He can drink water at the fountain. He's been throwing up, is why his throat hurts."

"I promised the kid a Coke."

"You'll *spoil* him, Jerry."

He wondered if he was not, for some dark reason, trying to win this child away from his mother, who seemed harsh. He felt in his situation patterns he had scarcely begun to explore; abruptly, managing all this, even claiming the luggage, which was undeniably theirs, seemed claustrophobically complex and, worse, improper, impious. He

ad presumed. To steer this ramifying mass of misplace-
ments through the exits into the open appeared impossible.

Sally, sensing some of this, asked, "Glad you're here?"

"With you, yes."

"I'll teach you to ride. You'll look great on a horse."

"I'll break my neck."

"Look, there are our bags. Theodora, don't." The child,
et down on her own legs on the floor, amid the hubbub
of the loudspeaking system and the hurrying of the other
passengers, had begun to cry. "Your new daddy will think
you're not a happy girl."

"Want Coke too," she said.

"Here," Jerry told Sally. "Three dimes."

Once the baggage had been collected, and the porter
bribed, and a taxi secured, the spirit of adventure—the
command to gamble that the parables enjoin upon us—
united them again. Bobby sat up with the driver, Jerry
and Sally had the two younger children occupied the rear.
The taxi was a deep old Pontiac driven by an Indian. His
voice, when he inquired after their destination, was deep
and careful, as if each word were unearthed, or mentally
translated from a language older than English. Bobby
stared, frankly fascinated, at the greasy black hair and
leathery cheek and the beadwork fetishes hanging from
the rearview mirror, and Jerry relaxed, having for the
moment appeased this intimidating child, his new conscience. The road, which upon leaving the airport had
moved through treeless suburbs with slow-down bumps
at the intersections, headed into the plain, and Jerry's first
impression, of benevolent spaciousness, was restored to
him. He guessed, from the guidebooks he had read, at
buffalo grass, at shooting stars and bluebells; there were
peaceful spaces between the clumps of sagebrush where
nothing offered to grow. Rather than greet so much joy
alone he eased an arm behind the children's backs and
interlaced his fingers with Sally's. She had been staring,
dazed, at the monotonous land. Her touch was bony and

tense, with that texture of having done work that he loved. Though she returned his timid pressure, which offered to shelter her, the corner of her mouth crimped with a fractional regret, as if acknowledging that she could no longer give freely what, through earning it, he had imposed on her as a duty. It was as if a chemical had been dropped. The air changed, slightly, but enough to tip the precarious balance of their mutual illusion. The smell of sage intensified; their speed had increased; pale green growths scudded by so quickly their tint became blue. The Indian's head jutted impassively against the light. The children's heads, finely outlined in black, appeared frozen; Jerry called "Hey?" and Sally didn't answer; the desert around them, and they with it, evaporated, vanished, never had been.

Jerry and Ruth descended at Nice. As the plane banked, the glittering Mediterranean leaped upward at them; the pilot had made a fatal mistake. At the last moment, like a card dealt from the bottom of the deck, land was flipped under them; the wheels touched down with a strut-cracking shudder; everything swayed, the engines reversed furiously; and they were down. Charlie laughed. The little tile-roofed houses of the Côte d'Azur were pulled slowly past like a string of boxcars as they taxied to a stop. The ATTACHEZ VOS CEINTURES sign flicked off, then the DÉFENSE DE FUMER. They grappled with their coats and stood, and in the murmur of voices around them Jerry heard that the interior of the plane, so plasticized and powder-blue and American at Idlewild, had been annexed to France. Everyone was speaking French, which he could not understand. *"Au revoir,"* the stewardess said, and they went down the metal steps. The air was soft, clear, and somehow fractionated, Cubistically portioned and dislocated by the diagonal rays of a tepid sun. There were worlds to see here, but Jerry's eyes were mute; loss had dulled them; his children and his wife carried his senses tottering across a width of coded concrete, through a series of broken impressions. In the patter surrounding the relinquishment of their passports he heard, because it was repeated, with an irritated note of surprise from the blue-uniformed official, *"Trois enfants."* Jerry heard his wife talking French to this man and wondered what strange woman this was by his side, who could keep an entire language locked within her. And within the terminal there stood, amid this dreamlike shuffle alien to him, Marlene Dietrich, wearing chamois slacks and high-heeled boots and smoking a cigarette in a long pearl holder. His children, ecstatic at being safe and free, rushed under her gaze, and this ghost, this construct of light and shadow from his own childhood, contemplated them with a frank interest and benevolence unexpected from an apparition.

Marlene Dietrich looked young, behind her battlement of luggage. Jerry saw in her proof of the faith that travel is a forestallment, a method of buying life with miles. He was travelling because Richard's lawyer had suggested he go away for a while. He had taken a leave from the agency and was going to paint. He and Ruth were going to paint side by side again. He passed through glass into the open, where a rank of taxis, incongruously labelled TAXIS, waited.

"A Nice?" a driver asked, dressed in a coat of a blue Jerry had only seen in paintings.

"Oui, à Nice, s'il vous plaît," Ruth said, blushing as she named the hotel, as if their travel agent might have betrayed them. *"Votre voiture, est-ce que c'est assez grand pour trois enfants?"*

"Oui, oui, ça va, madame, les enfants sont petits."

Charlie got in the front with the driver; the four others got into the rear. Geoffrey whimpered that they were squishing him. "We're *all* being squished," Jerry told him, fighting to fend the congregation in his lungs, which had become morbidly responsive to his nerves.

Ruth said, "Everybody look out my window, it's just like a painting." On the side of the road away from the sea, a young terrain supported an ancient agriculture; miserly care had partitioned into fields and terraces steep green mountains that, compared to the worn knolls of Connecticut, had just sprung into shape; towns climbed these hills in medieval perspective. Europe was pellucid in color and in drawing crowded. The tint of gray-green on the near hills, like the nearly colorless shimmer that whips through a woman's hair as she combs it, must be olive trees. On the other side, the scurvy width of drab sand, scarcely wider than the highway, ribbed with sea-wrack and studded with concrete obstructions, was nothing like what Jerry called a beach, and needed another name. A green sign gave it: PLAGE.

Joanna, squeezed between him and the window, said in a voice of stately detachment, "All the road signs have little pictures on." He felt she was addressing less her own parents than the ideal parents in grade-school readers—raceless and happy and mechanically fascinated by the workings of reality.

Wanting to be what she wanted, Jerry told her, "That's so dummies like us won't get lost." Everywhere, when you travel, there are clues, signs, instructions. Only at home are there none.

Joanna asked, "Why are there so many of those glass places?"

"Greenhouses?"

"I guess so."

"They're growing flowers for the perfume industry."

"Really?"

"I'm just guessing."

A blond woman, her hair loose to the wind, passed them on a motorscooter. She wore white St. Tropez pants and a striped jersey of some sort; Jerry pressed his foot to the floor, to accelerate and overtake her and see her face. His heart raced but the taxi's speed remained the same. Ruth had turned to watch his face, and what she saw there, rebounding to her own and rebounding back, like the multiplication between two mirrors, filled the small space of the car with a sickening hush and tension. He offered to her weakly, "Uncanny."

Ruth said, "You didn't see her as soon as I did. There was very little resemblance."

"Too bad," he said. She turned her face away; he felt her spirits sink, and a proportionate exultation lifted his. He took Geoffrey onto his lap, squeezed him, and asked, "How goes it, skipper?"

"Fine." The child always said it sadly, with a dragged diphthong, "oi."

"Still feel squished?"

"Not so much."

Charlie, who had been staring fascinated at the taxi driver, turned, his freckled face bright with mischief, and said, "He always complains because he's a baby."

Geoffrey's lower lip trembled and his belly billowed beneath his father's fingers as he took in a breath to cry. Jerry said quickly, "Look! We're coming into a city that says it's *nice!*"

They entered Nice; it was like entering a prism. High white hotels basked their façades in a sun that from cornices and canopies struck blue shadows at a precise angle of forty-five degrees. Underneath palm trees, ladies and gentlemen sat in overcoats at round glass tables. Along La Promenade des Anglais strollers were divided exactly into halves of shadow and light, like calendar moons. Jerry glimpsed, actually, a monocle. He saw a woman in a chinchilla jacket buying a dense bouquet of mountain violets in a cone of newspaper as a pair of gray poodles symmetrically entwined her legs in their leashes. Beyond the green railing of the promenade a beach curved into a distance where what appeared to be a fort of a fragile pink overhung the glistening steel of the sea; the beach was entirely of pebbles, loose washed pebbles in whose minuscule caves and crevices the ocean musically sighed as through the gills of an organ. On the shore of this music hovered sun, sparkle, colors, umbrellas. He told Ruth, to tell someone, "I love it. I might like it here."

She took the remark as an aesthetic appraisal and checked it by gazing through her window. "Isn't this where all the kings in exile come?" she asked.

The taxi turned off this, the Quai des États-Unis, and up a side street past the rusted shed of a flower market and a MAGASIN with filigreed iron balconies. *"Nous sommes arrivés, mes enfants,"* the driver announced, and turned to include all in the gappy, tobaccoish teeth of a joke. "Ve—is—'ere!" From the hotel the concierge and two assistants emerged to greet them, greedily, gaily, for at this time of year guests were scarce. It was early November. They followed their baggage in, Ruth leading; they climbed, endlessly, toward a wedding-cake façade, cool stairs of grayish-green marble.

Jerry got off at St. Croix. The tropical air, vivid and soft as a gust from an atomizer, that had greeted his face that dawn in San Juan, was drier here. His body felt light and his sensations were pleasantly scattered; he had slept two hours, in a night flight from Idlewild, taken impulsively, to escape constriction. The weight from his lungs had lifted. The terminal was newly built, without doors, so that shade alone marked the difference between within and without. A breeze flowed through, smelling of earth and flowers. Beyond the edge of shade, through the haze of a rhythmic sprinkler and the mesh of an airfield fence, the backwash from the props of the Caribair plane that had brought him raised a torrent of dust in which the black baggage-handlers hung legless. A low green hill, dull as if its color had sunk into an unprimed canvas, supported a conical mass Jerry guessed was a ruined sugar mill. The land looked both exhausted and innocent. It seemed the right place for him to have come to.

At the taxi rank, a Negro with a cigarette behind each ear asked him where he wanted to go, Christiansted or Fredericksted. He had not expected there to be a choice. "Which do you recommend?"

The Negro shrugged delicately. "Your deci*shun,* man. One's that way and one's"—he rolled his eyes to indicate—"the other."

"So I can't go to both?" Jerry said, offering to joke.

Tranquil silence met his self-answering question; he breathed easy, sensing, and beginning to love, the tropical manner of outwaiting everything. He said, "All I want is a room and a beach." It was March, he had been told the hotels would be growing empty.

The Negro gazed over Jerry's shoulder, then turned and tenderly opened the door of his taxi. "We'll fix you up fine," he said. Jerry got in, and as he waited for the car to move, other Negroes, two and then one more, wandered from the shade of the airport terminal and climbed in with him—one in front with the driver, two in back with him. He was crowded into a corner of the seat. The Negroes, all adult men, giggled and chattered incomprehensibly; they talked among themselves a family language of stabbing murmurs and incompleted allusions that was unintelligible, though English. The driver steered the taxi at high speed down the left side of a straight road walled on both sides by sugar cane; another taxi shot toward them also on the wrong side and passed safely, like a miracle worked with mirrors. They passed stone shells showing slots for the axles of vanished millstones, and shacks of overlapping tin, and newer, somehow American houses of white stucco, with louvered windows, bougainvillea, and gutter-fed cisterns. At an intersection, a sign pointed to Upper Love; the taxi stopped, and one Negro got out. The driver asked aloud, in a different voice, meant for Jerry to understand, "Would you love to go by de moun*tens*?"

"Sure," he said. Submit. Forget.

They climbed into a region of rough pastures and vast trees with bleached pods hanging stiffly down like the leaves of trees killed in midsummer. Higher and higher views of the turquoise ocean, mottled with lavender, opened and closed. Now a forest closed around them, where hairy vines dipped through clouds of hibiscus and mahogany roots twisting from the earth formed shrine-sized caves by the side of the road. A quicksilver shape darted under the wheel of the taxi, there was conversational excitement within it, and the driver said, in the voice intended for Jerry, "Mon*goose*." Rattling around a bend in the wretched, pitted road, they emerged from the forest into the sky and stopped. The pair of Negroes walked away from the car without looking back, toward a home unseen. Jerry realized that he would never see their homes. Moving to the other side of the empty back seat, he saw a ribbon of beach, a thread of highways, a scattering of red roofs from the altitude at which, a month before, he had seen the gray roofs of Queens, packed one against the other like cartons in a storage room.

The engines had roared in a graver key, black water lifted toward them, the children fell silent. Ruth squeezed his hand. The wheels smacked the runway, the great powder-blue body swayed and complained, the moment passed. They were home.

From the bedroom window of the house they had rented in Haut-de-Cagnes, Jerry, gasping from his bed as Ruth lay sleeping the sleep of the just, could see, across the sharp small valley where Modigliani had once lived with his mistress, the constellation Orion. The constellation seemed to be the companion of the sea, and its form, so long-limbed and masculine, constituted a sort of pledge the sight of which comforted him beyond reason, and eased his lungs. Restored to America, he found the constellation hard to find, obscured by the ubiquitous trees, overpowered by artificial lights, and subtly re-oriented in the stellar hemisphere. And when, from some open field, he did sight the solace of his exile, Orion had lost the friendly aura gathered perhaps from the proximate moon-clad body of his watery mistress the Mediterranean, above whose rustling sleep the slain hunter had seemed to watch, awake, propped on one elbow.

Back in Greenwood there was no glimpse of Sally, though Richard, driving a new car, a white Porsche convertible, could be seen around town weekends; once indeed, in the dusk of an unseasonably mild day in March, on a relatively little-travelled road, Jerry saw Richard and Janet Hornung riding together with the top down, looking like children surprised in the bathtub.

The driver took a cigarette from behind his ear and lit it; they were descending toward the beach and the town. A congregation of rocks on a hillside became sheep. There were houses, but no people.

Hey, Sally?

Yes, Jerry?

How was it? Was it so bad?

At times. But you were right, I knew that. You were very clever that day to know what I really wanted, I thought I wanted the opposite.

I wish I hadn't been so clever. I wish you had really wanted me.

I did, I do. I do have you, like the sea has Orion.

But they're gods, and we were very simple, as you once said. We were caught at being human. It was a matter of children, mostly.

No, I'd like to think that, it's kind of you to lie to me. But if it hadn't been the children it would have been something else. It would have been Ruth. And if Ruth hadn't reacted like she did you would have found another way. You wanted to keep me pure.

That's it, isn't it? You'll always be pure for me now.

Not always, darling—you don't like me to call you "darling," do you? You never did, you thought it was phony. I never knew what to call you, and when you used to fill me I wanted so much to have the right name for you that I said nothing.

You should have said something. Anything.

I felt shy.

You?

Yes.

And now, how do you feel? I feel dead.

I'm still very shaken, but it's less bad. I'm not yours any more. You should know that. After a while I'll probably get bitter about you and hate you because you humiliated me, and then that will go too, and I won't care either way very much. You'll be my ex-lover and we might even be friends.

Sounds awful. Awful.

Women try to be like men, Jerry, and imagine things, but in the end we're all practical, we have to be. You must go on alone.

No. I don't believe you. I loved you because you believed what I believed. There was a place I went to with you.

Any woman in bed will take you there. There's no place, darling, but right here, here and now, with Richard and Ruth. Love Ruth, Jerry. Now I must stop talking to you, because people will say I'm a whore.

His imagined conversation, between himself and the Sally he carried inside him, ended with words she really had said. It had been at the Collinses' party before the Heart Fund dance, in February. Entering the crowded room, he had seen her, and had the sensation of clasping her to his eyes, of fitting her to the matrix his entire life, including the months in France, had prepared. They had returned from France because the children were homesick and needed school. Linda Collins had written that

Richard wouldn't care, Sally had pacified him. The painting had not gone well; the weather had been slightly too
cold for an easel outdoors, and once it had even snowed,
trimming the cacti in their yard with snow. So though
his leave from the commercials firm had been for six
months, they stayed in France less than three. He drew
cartoons at home, and enjoyed it, though the cartoons all
came back. As he had come back. But after a brief exchange, through the smoke of his cigarette, about health,
and skiing, and children, Sally had said, "Now I must
stop talking to you, because people will say I'm a whore,"
and had turned away. In the hotel in Washington, she
had turned her back and slept, while he had insomnia.
While he roamed the party grieving, she stayed close by
Richard's side. Richard had grown fatter, puffed up with
maturity, and his hair had gone so long uncut it was
curling on his neck, and perhaps to make an impression
at the party he was wearing a black patch over the blind
eye. He looked heroic and huge. From the safety of his
side Sally's voice rang shrilly into every corner of the
party. Ruth came to Jerry's side and whispered that Sally
seemed her old self. He agreed, yes, and wondered if he
had attempted, wrongly, to tear her from her true self.

"Is you comin' to St. Croix for a rest?"

"For a change."

They were coming into a town. Sun-bleached wooden
houses, lacy with old jigsawing, were surrealistically
spaced along a straight blank street. A Negro without a
shadow lopsidedly loped across their path. On the right
the milky green sea quivered and sparkled, and a smoke-
gray freighter rode at anchor. At the end of the street
stood a fort with sloping walls painted red as a valentine.
"Where am I?" Jerry asked.

"Frederick*sted*," the driver answered.

"Am I east or west?"

"West, mon. The end of the islond. Did you want
east?"

"No, this is good. This is great. Can we find a place for me?"

"We're almost there this minute now. Don't lose your pay*shunce.*"

Jerry had rolled down his window, in his impatience to be free, to mix himself up with the spaced houses, the drab and patient shops, the Lutheran church left by the Danes, the fort—all of it lying in the tranquil pink shadow cast by the high green sea. He inhaled the air. This was the place, it tasted right. He had always told her there was a place, and now he had found it, made good his promise, and brought them here. He was intensely, passingly happy. The existence of this place satisfied him that there was a dimension in which he did go, as was right, at that party, or the next, and stand, timid and exultant, above the downcast eyes of her gracious, sorrowing face, and say to Sally, *Marry me.*

A Note About the Author

JOHN UPDIKE was born in 1932 in Shillington, Pennsylvania. He graduated *summa cum laude* from Harvard in 1954, and spent a year in England on the Knox Fellowship, at the Ruskin School of Drawing and Fine Art in Oxford. From 1955 to 1957 he was a member of the staff of *The New Yorker,* to which he has contributed short stories, poems, parodies, and criticism. His own books include eight novels, five short-story collections, three volumes of poetry, and a play, *Buchanan Dying,* produced in Lancaster, Pennsylvania, in the spring of 1976.